THE SYMBOL

Peter Fratesi

THE SYMBOL

DOUBLE DRAGON

Prologue

Alex Falding had an interesting viewpoint on loss. "Loss is a part of life, and we are urged by others to get over it," he would say. "But do we really get over losing someone or simply get older with it?" He had a good reason to ask the question. His friend had been gone for many years now, yet the memories of him and his tragic situation were still fresh and vivid, as if they happened just yesterday.

His friendship with John Polidori began when they worked together as physicians in London in the early 1800s. Later, as profound disturbances unfolded in Polidori's life, Falding became his psychiatrist, as well. He didn't know if this was the most professional thing to have done, but he did know it was the right thing to have done.

He was now long retired from full-time practice, but his son, Jonathon, carried on the good work through his own practice as a psychiatrist in London. The two had become quite close since the death of Jonathon's mother years ago.

Falding observed each anniversary of the loss of his friend by proposing a solitary toast to him in his library and offering a few thoughtful words. However, it was now the twentieth anniversary, and he had thought it fitting to hold a special ceremony. He had invited two of Polidori's closest friends from the distant past to have a dinner together. The two had gratefully accepted the invitation for that evening.

Falding went into his library that afternoon and unlocked a hidden drawer in his time-worn oak desk. He carefully removed a book wrapped in a yellowed, tattered newspaper. It was his old friend's journal. He had acquired the journal many years ago, hoping to preserve some part of his friend in his life. He had read and reread his writings over the years, trying to understand this complex man and what had happened to him. Falding never ceased reflecting upon his memories and poring over the case notes of his treatment. His efforts to uncover the truth also drew upon others, particularly now retired Inspector James McLaughlin of Scotland Yard.

Falding unfolded the old newspaper. It was dated October 18, 1816. The front page screamed out:

BRUTAL MURDER IN EAST END OVER NIGHT!
Body mutilated. Police mystified. East Londoners afraid to leave home after dark.

Falding nodded knowingly as he read the headline. He had hoped that at tonight's dinner he would finally be able to reveal the full story of John Polidori. Yet he had his doubts about that. There was much the others did not know about their friend's strange and bizarre experiences. How could he explain that Polidori's life had become intertwined with a series of mysterious and horrific crimes in London, over twenty years before? How could he convey that the crimes were of such magnitude that they had prompted one of the most desperate and intriguing investigations in the history of Scotland Yard? How could he possibly explain Polidori's curious beliefs that there were ominous, supernatural influences in his life and in the London crimes? He bowed his head and lapsed into a stream of disturbing memories. Faces, voices, and shifting feelings swirled up within him from those long-gone days.

Part 1

"We know what we are, but know not what we may be."

—Shakespeare, *Hamlet*

Chapter 1

Giovanni (John) Polidori was born in his family's grand villa on a sprawling country estate just outside of Florence. It was June of 1789, and the forces of revolution were spreading through Italy and France. As it turned out, that summer of turmoil was a fitting time for his birth.

His parents, the Duke and Duchess of Florence, came from a long line of Italian aristocrats. By the time of his only child's birth, the duke had ruled Florence and Tuscany with an iron fist for some decades, always alert for any democratic stirrings among his subjects.

The marriage of Alessandro and Maria Theresa Polidori had been arranged, in the custom of the day for the upper classes. They had struggled to find love in their relationship, but love eluded them. Maria was no typical aristocratic wife, and that became a source of strife between them. For a long time, they managed to avoid serious arguments, but their antagonism finally broke out into the open in the winter of Giovanni's second year.

Earlier that winter, a caravan of Roma people had arrived in Florence from Serbia. This nomadic band had been driven westward by the unusually harsh winter that year. In the beginning, Florentines tolerated the people in the tents and wagons on the outskirts of their city. However, that changed after a series of mysterious disturbances and disappearances in and around Florence.

The authorities had been investigating for some time. Crisis finally struck on the night of January 30, 1791. Maria was awakened that night by the clattering of a coach in the cobblestone courtyard of the villa. She looked out her window to see the horses glistening with sweat and the Florentine captain of the guards disembarking hurriedly. She heard the door knocker thud and her husband being roused by the servant. She followed Alessandro down the stairs and listened at the gilded door of the drawing room as the two men talked.

Maria heard the annoyance in the duke's voice. "This intrusion had better be warranted, Captain."

"There has been another disappearance, sir..."

"Go on."

"It's the bishop, this time! His eminence was out for a stroll alone just before sunset. His aides became concerned when he did not return after dark. They went to search for him and were shocked to discover his cape on the riverbank. We sent out a party to search by torch light but found nothing of him, I regret to say."

The duke exploded. "It's the damn Roma again. Since they've come here, there has been nothing but trouble!"

"Indeed, sir, the people have been very frightened. The strange lights and sounds at night in the Roman graveyards have been unnerving enough, but the tomb break-ins and the disappearances of townsfolk have pushed them near the edge. They

10

believe the Roma have brought with them a ghoul or vampyre that's been preying on the people and is up to unholy things in the cemeteries. Now that a man of the cloth may have been taken, I fear their terror may soon transform to riot."

"Ghouls. Vampyres! Superstitious nonsense," the duke scoffed. "The Roma are behind this all right, but as thieves and murderers. They vandalize the old tombs for relics to sell on the black market. They murder citizens for their valuables and then get rid of the bodies."

Still listening at the door, Maria knew the duke's hatred of crime was second only to his loathing of democracy. At times, she had thought this was a reaction to the skeletons in his family's closet, the Borgias, who had robbed and murdered for wealth and power centuries before.

"Captain, I have orders for you and the guards. Move on the Roma at first light. Arrest their leaders and drive out the rest of the rabble."

"And if they resist, sir? They *are* accustomed to defending themselves."

The duke showed no hesitation. "Use whatever means are necessary to rid me of the problem."

After the captain had gone, Maria joined Alessandro in the drawing room. He stood facing the low embers in the fireplace, his back to his wife. "I suppose you heard it all at the door."

"I did," said Maria, the faint, reddish light of the embers accentuating her frown.

The duke sighed and turned to face his wife. "I expect you disapprove."

"I certainly do," Maria retorted, her voice thick with anger. "I've been following this matter since the beginning. There is no proof that the Roma are behind these crimes. You know that, Alessandro. You are looking for a convenient scapegoat. Someone to charge before the people's unrest turns to anarchy."

The duke shot an exasperated look in her direction. "Do you think it is a coincidence that all this mayhem began just after these wretches arrived? They have no visible means of support. Clearly, they're in the foul business of robbery and murder."

"Alessandro, I know you take no interest in my efforts to help the poor. This is why you don't know I have been doling out my own monies to help them. They also make jewelry and sell it at the market."

"And no doubt the relics they're thieving from the tombs."

"Alessandro, grave robberies have happened a long time before the Roma came. You know there may be a gang of such thieves in Florence."

"But capable of a dozen suspected murders like this? It is unprecedented. And *now* it's the bishop, for God's sake."

Maria looked down, her lips trembling slightly. "We have all lost a great spiritual leader and a good man who cared about the people."

"And don't forget, I've lost my political connection with the church."

Maria looked him directly in the eye. "You must cancel your orders to the captain. These poor people have had enough suffering this winter, and you would send them to God knows where? And because of false charges?"

The duke pulled himself up to his full height and stepped toward her. "You know I cannot rescind the commands. The social order rests upon them."

"Exactly. This is not about justice," Maria snapped. She began to stomp out of the room and then stopped and turned to her husband. She pointed an accusing finger. "You know how you hate to admit that the Borgias were your ancestors. *Well*, you are acting no better."

After the flare-up, the couple's disagreements quickly worsened. The duchess, like her family before her, was a patron of the arts, and she was a writer of some note herself. She had a rebellious streak in her. She would write poems and short stories satirizing the aristocracy, fortunately published under an assumed name. A confrontation arose when Alessandro discovered that he was one of the buffoon characters in her stories. However, the greatest disagreement arose in the fall of 1795, as the duke prepared to raise taxes on the people—again.

The duke sat in the villa's library at his ornate rosewood desk, signing the decrees to be given to the tax collectors. He squinted as its polished marble top reflected the early morning sunlight, and he rose to close the curtains.

The library's doors suddenly flew open. In marched Maria. "Alessandro, you can't do it," she protested. "They carry too much burden already."

"The city's coffers run low, Maria. What would you have me do?"

13

"I would have you spend less on your standing army, opulent city buildings, and luxuries for us, while the people suffer and have nothing."

"Maria, there are two classes in society: the rulers and the ruled. That's the reality."

She set her jaw. "Does that give you an excuse to exploit the people? You have the power and they don't!"

"I wield that power for the good of the state and, ultimately, for them too."

"You use that power to inflate your own importance and because you blindly carry out the traditions of the nobles. There is much more to nobility than power and wealth, Alessandro. It is also being an honorable and just person."

The duke massaged a furrow in his forehead. "Honor and justice!" he mocked. "These are the cries of those who do not have to stand at the castle walls. Do you think if I had no army to meet the Austrians, they would give us justice? And if the people had power, would they use it justly, even for a moment? Look at what happened in France when the mob seized power. They beheaded Louis and his gentle queen. You don't live in reality, Maria."

Maria remembered how her husband often woke up tormented by nightmares of the beheadings. He would see the bloody executions over and over again. He would find himself in the shadows of the guillotine, beaten, bound, and spat upon by the rabble, waiting his turn. She knew these dark images only fueled his paranoia toward the people.

She snapped back to the present. "But the people were oppressed and starving for years in France. Had they been given democracy and bread, they would have exalted the king, not executed him."

"Democracy! Empowering the people! These are more of your fantasies, Maria. They come from the liberal philosophers you read, not from practical experience of the world. Look at some of the causes your family has undertaken. Enabling Galileo's argument with the church that the sun and not the earth is the center of the universe? Helping artists to decorate the markets with their flowery paintings? Now these are practical matters!"

"I do not call support for Michelangelo's religious frescos unimportant."

Alessandro smiled wryly. "Well, I may concede that point. But, if these frescos are important, it's only because they strengthen the church's hold on the minds of the people. The church and the nobility stand as one. The power of the ruling class is what has made the world work. Government by the masses would be a political tower of Babel, an exercise in chaos."

His wife shook her head in protest. "The true meaning of the church does not lie in power but in its spiritual message. It lies in the teachings of love and compassion toward our fellow man, no matter what his situation."

"Love and compassion will not persuade the people to pay their taxes any more readily."

Her lips became a thin line as she changed her tack. "Think of Giovanni and what you teach him." She pointed to the old, elaborately covered books on hunting and war on a shelf behind the duke. "These are not about manliness and the nobles' honor—

only the exercise of power without conscience and compassion! What will he grow up to be?"

The duke's eyes flashed with anger. "He'll grow up to be a proper ruler, if you let him! You can't teach him how to deal with the world with books on fairy tales, Maria, or by teaching him how to write poetry and draw. Poets and artists do not rule the world."

"No, but they inspire it, Alessandro. They are its heart and soul!" And round and round went the arguments between the two, with no resolution, no reconciliation in sight.

Chapter 2

And so, little Giovanni grew up in this family and society of contrasts and disparities. He was confused and anxious as he listened to his parents argue over how he should view himself and the world; he felt guilty because he thought *he* was the cause of his parents' arguments. The child in him was also frightened when, inevitably, he heard the rumors of the murderous Borgias in his family's past. His fear and his resentment grew as he realized his parents had tried to keep the Borgias a dark secret, especially from him.

Even more frightening were the tales he'd heard of the ghouls and vampyres coming to Florence in the time of the Roma. The servants who told him the stories knew that the disappearances and other strange disturbances had not entirely stopped after the Roma were driven out. They thought that the ghouls or vampyres still stalked the land, perhaps out of revenge for the cruel treatment of the Roma.

As a young child, he often awoke terrified after nightmares about these dark stories. He had been particularly frightened one night when a summer storm blew open the windows of his bedroom. The curtains had billowed into his room with the violent winds.

Maria heard his screams and rushed into his room. She found Giovanni curled up in a corner, terrified. She hurried over to close the window and cradled her son in her arms. "Shh," she said. "It's all right. It's only a dream."

17

"No," he said, "there were monsters in the garden. I saw them out the window. Then they tried to get in!"

"What did these monsters look like?"

"They were big and dark and had long fingers reaching out for me," he cried.

"Where did you hear of such things?"

"Giuseppe told me. They came with the people in the wagons."

Maria reminded herself to speak to the servant about the matter. "No, there's no such thing as monsters, Giovanni. It's just silly stories the servants tell."

She took his hand and walked to the window. "See, it's only the wind blowing the trees and bushes to make shadows."

Giovanni peered, uncertainly, out the window, into the dark.

Despite his mother's reassurances, his childhood fears only grew. He began to believe that something strange had invaded his room, lurking in the dark corners and under his bed.

Matters came to a head one night when he was seven years old. Maria had gone to look in on Giovanni in his sleep, about ten o'clock in the evening, as was her custom. The sun had already set, and she took a candle into his room. She found his bed empty, the bedclothes strewn to one side, mostly lying on the floor. At first, Maria was not alarmed, knowing how restless he was with his nightmares. She thought he'd probably fallen off the bed on the other side. "Giovanni?" she asked as she unfurled the sheets, expecting to find him within them. She was shocked to find them empty. Frantically, Maria searched the room, but found no trace of him. She panicked when she saw the door from his room to the garden was ajar. "Help me! Help!" she screamed.

The household was alerted, and her husband soon appeared at the doorway, his face almost as white as the bedsheets on the floor. "What is it, Maria?" he asked, his voice trembling.

"Giovanni's gone!"

Alessandro looked dumbfounded. "Gone! What do you mean?"

"He's not in his bed, and the door to the garden is ajar. He's gotten out, or someone has taken him."

Alessandro leapt into action. He shouted orders at the head servant, Giuseppe. "Get the servants together in a search party, and call the guards to join us."

The tracking dogs were released, and the searchers headed out on horseback, torches held high. Alarmingly, the dogs lost the scent, and the search went on agonizingly slowly. Maria was gripped by a numbing chill as she remembered that wild dogs had been prowling on the estate since the spring, and some of their deer kills had been found.

She strained to see any sign of a white contrast to the shadowed, rolling hills and thick, black clusters of bushes. "Nothing!" she wailed. "He couldn't have gotten any farther by foot by this time. In the name of God, where is he?"

After several miles of ground had been covered, the party was faced with the heartbreaking prospect of searching the marshlands. Maria had already caught the smell of the stagnant ponds.

19

Suddenly, Giuseppe cried, "Look, there he is!" He pointed to a small figure only a few dozen yards away... There was little Giovanni, standing on a small rise in the faint torchlight. His nightclothes were flapping like white sails in the wind.

The searchers encircled him. "Mother of God! Look at his eyes!" Maria cried. The others were startled to see only the whites of the child's eyes showing. His eyes had rolled up into their sockets.

"It must be some kind of seizure," shouted her husband. "Wrap him up, and let's get him home."

The boy was soon lying on the soft settee in the drawing room, before the fire. He was surrounded by adults who were desperately trying to revive him. "Giuseppe, Augusta, rub his hands and feet!" Maria said. She tapped his pale, cold cheeks vigorously and loudly called out his name.

Alessandro declared, "Look! His pupils have returned." Consciousness had lit up his son's eyes once again.

"Are you all right, Giovanni?" his mother asked anxiously.

There was relief as the child spoke. "I'm cold and have a sore head," he complained, placing a hand to his forehead.

"Get him up and give him some hot wine," ordered Alessandro. The child sat up on the edge of the settee.

Maria bent over him. "Do you remember anything tonight?"

"Yes, when I was sleeping I heard voices from far away calling to me."

"Who were the voices?" his father asked.

"The Roma."

20

The parents looked at one another, puzzled, but said nothing. No one wanted to add to his fears by questioning him further.

The doctor was summoned from the city and examined him that night. He had many questions, and he conveyed his conclusions the next morning to the anxious parents. "I do not believe it was a seizure," he said, relieving them greatly. "Given what you say about his night fears, I suspect the child was sleepwalking. The condition can occur after a bad fright. It may be his way of protecting himself from imaginary creatures in his room by escaping to the outdoors at night."

The parents were only too happy to have an explanation and the good doctor's recommendations. They were to give Giovanni a light sleeping potion for a while. It was advised they take all measures to help him feel safe in his bed, until his fears eventually passed.

Chapter 3

Polidori's night wanderings were not the only peculiarities that he had shown from his early childhood on. It was said there was an even stranger side to him. To the bewilderment and amusement of his family and friends, rather odd coincidences seemed to happen to him that were difficult to explain.

A perfect example was reported to Falding in a letter from Maria, many years after its occurrence. She and Giovanni, then four years old, were sitting in the villa's garden on a warm, sunny Tuscan morning. She was reading to him from a book about birds. This was a fitting topic, for the garden was full of birds going about their business. Maria noticed that her son was intently watching a flock of hummingbirds near a bed of succulent flowers. Suddenly, one of the usually skittish birds hovered over him and landed on his outstretched finger. Mother and son burst into laughter.

Maria asked him, "What did you think of that, Giovanni?"

He giggled and replied, "I made the bird come to me, Momma."

Maria laughed and asked, "Little Polidori, why do you say that?"

"Because I wished it to come to me. What I think in my mind happens."

Maria smiled indulgently and said no more, putting this down to her child's delightful imagination. As he grew up, he would learn the difference between himself and the world, and between his mind and reality, she knew. It was all a matter of maturation.

Maria liked to relate another unusual story about what happened when her son was nine years old. He had made a poem and a drawing for his favorite great-aunt, Sophia, on her eightieth birthday. She lived within easy riding distance of the family's estate, and the young man had ridden his pony to the aunt's villa to deliver her gifts. Unfortunately, she was not at home. Carelessly, he left his poem and drawing for her on a table in her garden.

Six months later, the aunt became very ill one evening, and the family expected her death at any moment. Polidori was caught between sadness and hope, desperately wanting to do something for his beloved aunt.

As it happened, she took a good turn over night, and the family went to visit her the next day. They found her in fine spirits, sitting up in her old, canopied bed.

She smiled at her nephew through the warm autumn morning sunshine pouring into the room. "Giovanni, I received your poem and drawing last night. The gardener brought them to me, and they cheered me up so much. Thank you." Her forehead wrinkled. "But why would you send me a birthday poem when it wasn't my birthday?"

"But I brought the gifts months ago, Auntie. You weren't at home, so I left them on the garden table."

The gardener was called in to clear up the mystery. Aunt Sophia voiced the question that was on everybody's mind. "Pietro, how did you find the gifts?"

"Madam, I was pruning the bush yesterday, and there they were, well preserved, tucked into the bush."

The aunt's eyes widened. "They must have been blown into the bush and were protected all that time from the weather. Imagine that!"

Everyone looked at the boy, amazed, but he seemed to take it all in stride. "My wish for Auntie to get better came true," he said. "My presents came to her when she needed them," he added matter-of-factly.

Chapter 4

As Polidori grew up, his rational mind came to reject the notion that his thoughts could become real. This was merely childhood fantasy, he concluded. It was in the same category as the creatures his child's eyes had seen in the garden or the shadowy figures he had imagined lurking in his closet. However, a residue of this belief remained underneath the surface. It would be at the center of a struggle between himself and his psychiatrist, Alex Falding, in the future.

By adulthood, he was rarely, if ever, disturbed by the painful feelings and memories of childhood. They were not gone, but merely banished to that deep reservoir of unwanted and forgotten things, the unconscious mind. There, like roots cut off from the plant above ground, they had the possibility of growing upward again.

The nightmares, too, had passed as he grew older, and he'd almost forgotten them. However, his sleepwalking happened occasionally, even as an adult, in times of distress. His night wanderings were the only visible sign of the troubled, murky underworld of his mind.

Outwardly, he grew up to be a fine example of a young man, intelligent, even-tempered, and courteous. Physically, he was quite handsome, with dark hair curled at the forehead, deep, dark eyes, and refined features.

In many respects, he was more like his mother than his father. Like her, his compassion and love of knowledge took him on a very different path from other aristocrats. To the consternation of his father, he had enrolled to study medicine in Rome at the age of eighteen and graduated with high honors a few years later.

Maria and the duke had argued two weeks before their son's graduation about his plan to begin practice with the poor of Florence. Maria had confronted her husband in the drawing room over his refusal to attend the graduation in Rome.

Alessandro defended himself. "It's bad enough that an aristocrat's heir has undertaken professional training," he complained. "But to serve the common people? Unheard of!"

"You are acting as if your son's only pursuit in life should be to take your place someday, to carry on the blood lines," Maria chastised.

"Well, what else?" Alessandro shot back.

His wife was dismayed. "Look at his accomplishments. You know his tutors have said he is brilliant in science and languages. He speaks Italian, English, and French fluently and knows some German. Giovanni writes so eloquently and puts such care and passion into crafting his poems and stories. He also graduated as the youngest physician in his class. You would have him waste his talents on inheriting your station?"

Alessandro was undeterred. "Isn't it wasting talent to minister to the poor? At the very least, why not to people of standing?"

"There are only too many of his classmates who will cater to the rich and powerful," she replied. "Who will care for the poor? You should be proud that he is a person of generosity and kindness, who has earned the love of all the people of Florence.

Should he not bring these wonderful qualities into his calling?"

Her husband shook his head disapprovingly. "I've heard how he endears himself to Florentines. Helping the sick and old in the stinking streets," he sneered. "Giving to the schools so that the poor may be educated and still make nothing of themselves. He has lowered himself and our family name through these acts."

"These are terrible words, Alessandro. The true measure of a man is how he treats the poorest and most unfortunate around him."

Polidori's relationship with his father grew even more distant as the months passed by. It had become clear to the duke that his son was never going to follow in his aristocratic footsteps.

Tension between the two eventually reached a breaking point. Polidori and his mother discussed the troubling matter one morning in the garden.

"Father is deeply disappointed and angry with me that I cannot be what he wants me to be. He hardly speaks to me anymore. It's too much to bear!"

Maria's eyes filled with pain and sadness. "I know how hard it is for you to be yourself against his powerful will, Giovanni. I see he how he withdraws from you if you do not bend to his wishes. I understand what it is like to face his coldness and disdain, day after day. But yet you must be yourself, as difficult as that is. To be otherwise is death of the soul."

"Yet I feel so guilty that I can't meet his expectations. If only I could face him on the matter and voice my feelings." Polidori became tearful. "I

27

can only pull back from him, sullen and disappointed in myself."

Maria waited in sympathetic silence.

Her son gathered his strength. "But I must do something. I can no longer stand about helplessly." He gave his mother a telling look. "I have to leave," he said quietly.

"Leave?" Maria asked, half expecting his reaction. "But surely there is some other way."

"You yourself said it. I have to be myself, and I cannot be that in his shadow."

Maria's look turned to resignation and then to worry. "It's going to be far off, isn't it? To England."

Polidori smiled at how well his mother really did know him. "To England, it is. I know I needn't explain why England to you, Mother."

The fateful decision was made. As the weeks went by, his mother's attitude grew from resignation to loving acceptance of his choice. Of course, she was still saddened by the prospect of her only child leaving for such a distant land. His father, perhaps predictably, refused to hear his explanations. This convinced Polidori even further that he had made the right decision.

28

Chapter 5

After saying goodbye to his tearful mother, the young man, barely in his twenties, left for England in the summer of 1814. He took with him his family inheritance, which was more than a small fortune in those days. England had always called to him. The rational, scientific side of him was attracted to the land of Newton and the passionate side to the home of some of the greatest Romantic poets of the time, Byron and Shelley. England's democratic leanings were not the least of its attractions, either.

It was a matter of course to move to London, the intellectual center of the nation, but also its heart. He had always secretly harbored a powerful dream of becoming a great writer. The Romantic poetry movement flourished there. What more inspiration could he ask for?

He found a comfortable old brick-and-stone home for sale in middle-class London. It was more spacious than he needed, but not ostentatious. As an additional benefit, it came with its own small band of servants that had well served the previous owner for many years.

The gentleman acting for the owner had been late the day of the showing. Polidori had met the servants who had turned out to greet him in the foyer in their freshly cleaned uniforms: two servant girls, the head maid, Mrs. Wembley, and the butler, Harris.

Harris conducted a tour of the premises, at Polidori's request. Polidori knew immediately what his favorite room would be.

"This is the library, sir. Very comfortable, especially for men of learning."

Polidori smiled. "I see you have heard about me."

"A little, sir."

Polidori was attracted to the oaken bookshelves, which almost completely lined the walls from floor to ceiling. An ornate moveable staircase stood in front of one section of the shelves. He anticipated filling them up with his precious books, giving a special place to the great English authors he so admired. He knew precisely where to place his writing table and his great globe of the world, mounted on its pedestal.

"There is a beautiful view, sir."

He saw the library had a large casement window looking out upon the garden. He opened one side of the window to let in the fragrance of luxuriant flowers in full bloom. Agreeably, the window faced the east to catch the morning sun. This was a perfect place to reflect on his books and write.

"It's cooled off nicely in the summer afternoons by the oak trees, which are rather grand," added Harris.

Polidori saw the rusty iron fence around the garden, with a lush old vine weaving through it. With its sharp iron tips and occasional gargoyles poking out from its top, the fence looked to him like an overgrown medieval battlement. It was all quite quaint, he thought.

Harris brought him next to the spacious drawing room. "There's plenty of room for guests and family in here," he offered.

Polidori liked the feel of history in the room. He was drawn first to the large stonework fireplace guarded by great brass andirons. Sooty, black, rather warlike poking irons hung from hooks in the old stones. A faded, ancient family crest from the original owner was etched into the stones. The seasoned hardwood floors were covered here and there by islands of old India rugs that came with the place.

It would have to be warmed up, though, he felt. He would hang up some brilliantly colored paintings of Florence and other Mediterranean scenes. Of course, portraits of his mother and aunt would find their rightful place over the mantle.

He took a closer look at Harris. He was a fit, middle-aged man dressed very correctly. He seemed friendly enough, though a bit stiff. "How would you describe your duties, Harris?"

"The first, of course, is attending to the master's needs and wants, sir."

"And the second?"

"I would say it's keeping the staff in order."

"I see. And with three women under you, I'd imagine you have your work cut out for you, Harris."

Harris nodded gravely, apparently missing the humor.

The maid appeared at the doorway. The tardy gentleman had finally arrived. He apologized and completed Polidori's tour. The rest of the house did not disappoint, and the young doctor made a generous offer. He had found his home in England.

31

Soon after moving in, he wrote a letter and had it posted to Florence.

August 14, 1814

Dearest Mother,

I'm letting you know I have arrived in London safely and have established myself in a fine residence. The butler, Harris, is a bit of a stern fellow, but I feel his heart is in the right place. He is trying out a gentler approach to the servants, under my encouragement.

I've begun work in a tiny office at the Old London Infirmary in Whitechapel. You know me; I'm a creature of habit. Each morning at eight o'clock, my coach takes me to the office. The days are full of the sick and injured, mostly the poor. Conditions at the infirmary are woefully inadequate. There is a lack of sufficient staff and medicines. Sadly, many have to be turned away to look after themselves as best they can.

I never miss the opportunity to solicit the local officials and well-to-do for money for the infirmary. Some are generous, but many seem indifferent or outright hostile. The wealthy have their personal physicians, as in Italy. I suppose it's difficult for them to understand the plight of those who have to rely on the meager public services. It is also easy for the rich and powerful to excuse their indifference by blaming the poor for their own poverty.

But I am well and trying to do my part. I seem to be fitting in with the other physicians here, particularly with a fellow named Alex Falding. He is a friendly sort and very bright. He is quite a distinguished-looking fellow, tall, fit and slightly graying on the sides. In many ways, he is the picture of an English gentleman but with an added measure of kindness and thoughtfulness toward others. He and his beautiful wife have invited me for dinner tonight, and I am looking forward to their good company and to meeting their twelve-year-old son.

I hope all is well with you and Father. Now that you know where I am, I await your letters eagerly.

With love and affection,

Giovanni

Polidori and his servants soon settled into the comfortable predictability of their routines. However, a few weeks after moving in, he began to notice the staff sometimes huddling in the shadows of doorways, whispering as he passed. He had an idea of what was going on, but thought it prudent to confirm his suspicions as soon as possible. His butler was taken away by family matters, so he called in the head maid.

The middle-aged maid stood nervously in the drawing room, her hands clasped tightly before her. Polidori smiled benevolently from his chair near the fireplace. "Please be seated, Mrs. Wembley," he said, hoping to put her more at ease. He paused to consider his words and decided to come directly to the point. "I've noticed the staff behaving in a peculiar manner lately, standing and whispering in little groups where they think they won't be seen or heard as I pass by. Will you tell me what is going on?"

Mrs. Wembley's face took on a sickly white shade. "It's all right to be frank," reassured Polidori.

The maid hesitated but finally found words. "Yes, sir. The staff has noticed some strange goings-on lately. On some mornings, things are found out of place or disturbed in some way…"

"Such as?"

"Well, sir, the other morning a book from the library was open on the kitchen table. A candle still burned next to it."

"Do you remember the name of the book?"

"No, sir. It was in strange letters and very old."

"Will you show me the book?"

The two walked to the library, and Mrs. Wembley handed him a thick book bound in leather. "Hmm, I'd forgotten I had this. A book on alchemy in Latin. Curious text… Anything else, Mrs. Wembley?"

"Sometimes things are missing altogether, and some have never been found, like pieces of the kitchen cutlery. And then…"

"Yes?"

"Well, sir, there's the drawings."

"Drawings?"

"Yes. Sometimes we find strange pictures in colored chalk on the kitchen floor…dots, squares, circles, and such. No rhyme or reason to it all, sir. Of course, none of us would do this, so." She looked down.

"So, the staff assumed I've been doing these things?"

The maid looked as if she was about to faint. "Yes, sir. I — I'm afraid so. Some anyways."

Polidori softened his tone. "And are these the only things they've noticed, Mrs. Wembley?"

"No, sir. On some mornings, the main door has been found unlocked, though it had been bolted the night before. Sometimes, too, the staff would notice the master's boots sitting muddied in the foyer or wet footprints on the hallway rugs, though the master had retired early the night before."

"And how are the staff feeling about all of this?"

"I don't think they know what to make of it, sir. They're feeling the house is unsafe at night, with the door unlocked and all. They're wondering what's going to happen next. Some of the superstitious ones believe that a haunting is happening at night."

Polidori smiled. "I see." He decided the best course of action was to be very frank about the happenings and asked Mrs. Wembley to call in the rest of the staff. All the help was soon assembled, looking puzzled and anxious.

The master spoke in his kindliest voice. "I'm sure you are all wondering why I have asked you to gather here today. I've learned that you've noticed some strange disturbances in the household. I want to clear this matter up. I think the best way is to be absolutely honest with you. I want to assure some of you that a ghost is not wandering through the house at night." He smiled again, and some of the staff looked down, trying to stifle their giggles.

"The cause is from *this* world, not the next. Since childhood, I have been affected by a medical condition commonly known as sleepwalking. There is no convincing explanation or cure for it, but for many, it shows itself especially after extreme fatigue or being troubled by the events of the day. Whatever is going on, these night time wanderings are usually

35

harmless. It is advised that if a sleepwalker is encountered it is best not to try to speak to him or waken him, but just allow the wandering to take its course."

Seeing his servants looking rather amazed at his account, Polidori tried to lighten the matter. "For myself, I think there is a bright side to this business: I am fortunate to have a more exciting nightlife than most."

He thought the meeting had its intended effect for, in the days to come, the servants seemed to be much relieved and in better humor. He guessed, though, they were still wondering where their master went outside in his sleep and what he was doing. Such questions were understandable. He, too, would naturally be concerned for the safety of someone who traveled about unconsciously in the night ... or perhaps for the safety of others?

Chapter 6

Polidori would distract himself from his heavy burdens by rummaging through the dusty corners and laden shelves of the delightful London bookshops or taking in the pleasures of the local playhouses. Above all, he enjoyed the Saturday evening meetings of the London Literary Society.

The society met in central London in the vast drawing room of a very old mansion owned by a well-known patron of the arts. The building reflected the wealth of its owner. Lofty windows provided ample light until sunset. After that, gleaming chandeliers poured their candlelight into the great room. The interior walls were dressed in panels of rich oak from Nottinghamshire, punctuated by long, mauve curtains dropping from the ceiling to the floors of bluish white Italian marble.

A platform arose at one end of the room, with a lectern for the guest speaker. Behind him, in a row, sat the society's most honored members. The general assembly sat in comfortable stuffed chairs in a semi-circle around the platform, in small groups centered about smoking tables.

When Polidori arrived excitedly for his first meeting, he encountered a fashionably dressed, rather refined group, heavily weighted on the male side. The paucity of female members disappointed him. He was always interested in meeting eligible women. However, the atmosphere soon caught his attention. The room vibrated with myriad eloquent conversations on the literary works of the day.

He had the good fortune to be introduced to a veteran member, a middle-aged lawyer named

William Lyons. In some ways, Lyons cut a rather unimpressive figure. Short in stature, he was rather portly, his jowls puffing out his already bristling sideburns. He was a personable fellow, though, his eyes sparkling with wit and good humor. Polidori was fascinated to learn that he took an interest in Romantic poetry, especially in Byron's works.

"So, what do I need to know about the society, Mr. Lyons?" Polidori asked.

Lyons smiled and leaned toward him. "Well, you've got to remember there are several cliques here." He gestured to the row of older gentlemen behind the lectern. "They are the patrons of the society. The fellow in the middle is Lord Penfield. He owns the place and is in charge of the proceedings. If you are in his good graces, you can get up and recite your works— providing you've got the nerve to test the critical waters around here."

"Oh? And is that risky business? No torrents of rotten vegetables, I hope, or danger of being tossed out?"

"Ah, it's the cutting words that hurt, I'm afraid, mostly from the literati. They are the academics from the universities. This is the group you don't want to know. They view themselves as the judges of literary excellence and spend their time criticizing everyone else's work. They produce nothing worthwhile themselves. There's an old expression: 'Those who can't write teach literature at university.' Right?"

Polidori laughed. "It's really that bad, is it?"

"It's beyond dismal," verified Lyons. "Many of them are still stuck in the old traditions before Romanticism."

"So, who else do I need to know about, sir?"

"These are the people like you and me. They're amateur writers here to learn the art of poetry, aspiring to be Romantic poets, especially."

"Yes, that would be me."

Lyons nodded. "Be assured that your fellow poets know what you are experiencing and have the same creative angst as you. They're quite supportive chaps, I'd say. But there's more for the novice member to know."

"I pray good fellow, tell me. My curiosity is unbearable."

"The group you'll want to meet for sure is the publishers. You've got to remember that these fellows are first and foremost businessmen. They're fishing the waters around here for new talent, to see what will sell on the market. They're shrewd but don't necessarily know what's good or even necessarily care. But they know what's going to be popular and what's going to be profitable." He looked intently at Polidori. "So, don't take rejection from them too seriously — or acceptance, for that matter. It's just business."

"I'm holding my breath wondering about who's next."

Lyons face brightened. "These people are the really famous writers, like Byron."

"Byron comes here?" Polidori asked in awe.

"Yes, indeed. Once in a while he sweeps in to dazzle the crowd with his latest poem or perhaps a few tantalizing stanzas added to an older one. Byron is the most famous and notorious of the Romantics — nothing short of a literary hero."

"He must cause a quite a stir of excitement when he recites."

"It's unbelievable, really, especially among the women poets. They become captivated by the passion and seductiveness of the great poet's words, literally swaying to the cadence of his verse. I've even seen a few faint dead away. Had to be revived with smelling salts."

"Ah, to be that eloquent!" Polidori laughed. "Do other noted poets grace the podium, too?"

"Indeed. If we are really fortunate, another noted Romantic, like Percy Shelley, might turn up and poetically duel with Byron for the admiration and verdict of the crowd."

"Who usually wins?"

"It's usually Byron who carries the day, so great is the power of his words and his physical presence. He's not been in the public eye long, either. His fame came suddenly a few years back. He wrote a great, passionate poem about his travels and meditations in exotic places in Europe and Asia. His poem preceded him home, and, returning from his travels, he found himself a celebrated author and the toast of London and England."

"Fame achieved so quickly and in such abundance, can go to one's head," Polidori observed.

"Yes, it may have fostered a certain arrogance in him. He quickly became the rage of London's high society, and everybody who was somebody vied to make him the premier guest at their balls and soirees. He is even more popular than some of the royalty. Indeed, he is his *own* royalty as the literary

40

prince of passion. To have *him* grace your ballroom will move you to the top of fashionable society."

"You appear to know much about Byron."

"Yes, I've studied him deeply. I hope to write a book someday on how his character and life have influenced his poetry," Lyons confided.

"Well, I'm speaking with the right gentleman then. So, what can you tell me about the man behind the pen?"

"A great deal, if you swear to complete secrecy."

"I give you my word."

"Very well, then, sir. I'll tell you his story. Have a seat. You're about to go on a fascinating journey." Lyons settled into the comfortable stuffing of an old wingback chair and clasped his hands together around his considerable waist. "Byron was not always so favored, to say the least," he began. "His beginnings were tragic and chaotic. He was born with a deformity, a club-foot, about which he was quite self-conscious as he grew up. His father, Captain 'Mad Jack' Byron, apparently did not even attend his birth and abandoned Byron and his mother after a few years. He had squandered his wife's family inheritance and fled from his creditors to France for good."

Lyons went on with his unhappy tale. "Byron's mother was said to be mercurial, swinging wildly from excessive affection to rejection and black rages. His self-worth was apparently damaged even further by his being abused as a child by a nurse."

"Such incredibly sad beginnings," Polidori remarked. "Deserted by his father, unsure of his mother's love, abused — a terribly weak foundation

41

to build a life upon... How did he *ever* become a great poet?"

"How, indeed," said Lyons. "His luck changed when he inherited his family's centuries-old title of baron from his rather eccentric and violent uncle. This gave him title to the Byron family's ancestral country home and estate, Newstead Abbey in Nottinghamshire. But this was a mixed blessing, for much of the abbey was in deplorable condition, and Byron and his mother were too poor to restore it for many years. Byron was nevertheless very proud of his estate and of being a landed nobleman."

"This must have bolstered his self-esteem."

"I believe so. His outward confidence, at least, seemed to grow with each coming year. He presented a bold, devil-may-care, freedom loving, and irreverent image, much of which found its way into his poetry. He gave the impression that he cared not a fig about moral reaction or others' judgments of him and that he was unafraid to break the rules, even outrageously."

"Could this not be a façade, a mask, to protect him from the hurts of the world?" Polidori asked, fascinated. "To keep his sanity in the midst of chaos?"

Lyons was impressed. "That's quite insightful. To answer your question, I think that he tries to protect his fragile sense of worth by seeking admiration in ways that would guarantee it, like taking on causes of freedom in other countries. He has become a hero in these oppressed lands and that has brought his popularity back in England to a fever pitch."

42

"How ironic," Polidori observed. "He gives the impression he does not care about what others think about him, yet he desperately wants their love. He must be a man in deep emotional turmoil."

"I agree wholeheartedly. I believe this turmoil shows itself in his excessive pleasure seeking and undisciplined conduct. His extravagant tastes and interests — in drink, partying, gambling, and pleasures of the flesh — led him, like his father, into crushing debt, which has plagued him for much of his life."

Lyons drew into his listener. "His sexual appetites are voracious and virtually without bounds. He is a debaucher of women, but it is often difficult to tell who is the seducer and who is the seduced, as women find his attractiveness irresistible. It is not uncommon for women to unabashedly throw themselves at him." Lyons lowered his voice to a whisper. "There are rumors that his sexual tastes extend to men, as well."

Polidori pulled back, but recovered his poise quickly. "Might his throwing himself into sexuality be a distraction from his emotional pain? Perhaps, too, he is a man who is also afraid of deep love and uses carnal pleasures as a safe and pale substitute... There is nothing sadder than those who cannot truly give love, for they cannot accept love, either. They walk through their lives in perpetual loneliness."

Lyons nodded. "I think that these are true insights into the man. It has been said that there is little difference between Byron and the characters in his poems. Nowhere is this clearer than in his famous poem, 'Don Juan.' This tale of his amorous encounters with women shows the extremes of his sexual appetites and adventurism." Lyons glanced over his shoulder. "But it is rumored that there is even a darker side to Byron and his family."

"Oh? What might that be?"

"Well, there are a couple of old villages not far from Newstead Abbey. They are but tiny places, no more than hamlets, really. The people are simple farmers, and one would expect nothing much to be happening there, just a quiet rural life. But I was poking around up there last year about Byron. They say there have been many disappearances in the area since the Byrons came to own the abbey a few centuries ago. It's been mostly young women and girls, but some boys, too, who have disappeared — several since Byron inherited the place."

Lyons went on with his dark account. "The local people admit that some of the disappearances could have been elopers or young people running away from home for other reasons. But search parties have found a few bodies of those missing — interestingly, on the outskirts of the abbey. The bodies were too decomposed for the village doctor to do a thorough medical examination. However, the local constable said they were probably not suicides but victims of foul play."

"There is nothing more tragic than young lives lost," sympathized Polidori.

"Yes, and the villagers suspected Byron because of his eccentric reputation and the history of madness and violence rumored to be in his family. Their suspicions grew as strange disturbances happened periodically at the abbey. Every few months, a caravan of carriages bearing royal or noble crests would clatter through the villages. They

44

were on their way to the abbey for some mysterious gatherings. So many strangers passing through were unnerving enough to the villagers, but then eerie bursts of green light would be seen coming from the great hall of the abbey over the next few nights. Also, some say they have heard unearthly noises, like moans or screams, in the old building after sunset. The more superstitious villagers believe that the abbey is haunted and won't go near the place."

Lyons shifted uncomfortably in his chair. "The apparent murders were never solved and remain a mystery to this day. Byron himself was never questioned by the authorities out of fear of offending one so high in society. This, of course, has caused much resentment among the villagers."

"Sounds eerie enough," remarked Polidori, "but it's hardly damning of Byron. All we have here is suspiciousness of strangers or of Byron's peculiarities, not to mention weird lights and sounds. But it all makes for juicy gossip."

Lyons laughed heartily. "You have to admit, though, that the rumors would be priceless in spicing up my book!"

His new acquaintance grew serious. "So, if you had to sum up Byron, what would you say?"

Lyons thought for a few moments. "I would say that he defies summing up. If I had to take a stab at it, I would say that he is a complex man — a man of great contradictions. He shamelessly seduces women but also portrays them in his poems virtually as celestial beings. He is a man of chaotic passions but miraculously disciplines their expression through his poetry. He is rumored to have a dark, sinister side, but his pen creates beauty and enlightenment."

Polidori sat in silence, taken with his acquaintance's powerful words.

Lyons put the finishing touches to his summary. "He is also a man who likely feels a deep sense of inner worthlessness but holds himself out as a hero to England and the Western world. Even physically, he is a contradiction: he has a clubfoot but nevertheless is the most physically attractive man to women and possibly to some men, as well."

"Utterly fascinating," Polidori said. "And if he gives me the opportunity, I would very much like to get to know him."

Lyons raised his rather bushy eyebrows and looked him straight in the eye. "But at what peril to yourself?" he cautioned. "Can you or anyone else actually survive a relationship with him?"

Chapter 7

It was a watershed moment — one of those dividing lines in people's lives between what they are and what they will be. Polidori had been working for some weeks polishing his first poem to present to the society. He was very nervous as he recited it on February 10, 1815, especially since he knew Byron was in the audience. Sometimes, the noted poet would deign to stay after his own recitals. He would listen to the presenters and, of course, further relish the love and admiration of the crowd.

Polidori was exhilarated and relieved when his poem was warmly received by his fellow poets. Byron flamboyantly approached him. Polidori would never forget the first words from those eloquent lips. "My dear young man," Byron said, with a gracious flourish and bow, "I salute your verse."

With this compliment began the unlikely relationship between the great poet and Polidori. For Byron, it was a simple matter of what Polidori could do for him. He'd found out that the "boy physician," as he called him, was brilliant at his profession. He needed medical attention to keep himself together. He was being worn down by his reckless lifestyle and required a good doctor's help to tone down his emotional storms. Moreover, he knew he would travel again someday to the Continent for more material for his poems. He would need a physician to deal with the rigors of travel.

He also liked to have an intimate circle of admirers when away from the adoring crowds. He had sensed Polidori's blind admiration for him straight away. The doctor's interests in writing made him an even better candidate for his inner circle. Byron's work would appear all that much more brilliant when compared with Polidori's novice attempts. The poet would have his personal Shakespearean foil. There it was! He would have him for his physician!

For Polidori, the relationship was much more complicated. Falding knew his friend had been struggling to make a decision about accepting the position of personal physician Lord Byron had offered to him. Several weeks after meeting Byron, Polidori confided to Falding his mixed feelings about the poet in general. They were sharing a bottle of wine in Polidori's library. It was a rainy, cold day in early spring.

"You know," he began, "Lord Penfield had asked Byron to recite one of his most famous poems at the last meeting of the society. I had read it before, but I was again captivated by 'She Walks in Beauty.' Listen to the introductory lines:

'She walks in beauty, like the night
Of cloudless climes and starry skies;'"

Polidori's eyes glistened. "Alex, he has a profound sense of beauty, and he captured the essence of it in this person. It is enthralling … yet this same man showed an ugly side of himself, that very night."

Falding looked at him curiously.

"Byron and I were boarding our coaches when we encountered a man in ragged clothes lying half-conscious in the courtyard, bleeding from the head. Byron sneered, 'No doubt a drunkard' and deftly stepped around the man without a further look. I was appalled and stopped to attend the fellow. He didn't appear intoxicated but seemed to be an emaciated street beggar. He had likely fainted and struck his head cruelly on the cobblestones. I had the poor man looked after at the infirmary and made arrangements with the charity to care for him afterward."

Falding propped his chin on his fist, his interest piqued by his friend's account. "How are you feeling about all of this, John?"

Polidori's jaws tightened visibly. "I was deeply offended by Bryon's coldness and indifference. I think selfishness is deeply rooted in him."

Falding nodded. "Is this surprising to you, John?" he asked. He was aware of some of the rumors swirling around the poet in the newspapers.

A crimson streak crept up Polidori's neck. "But I'm still shocked when I see a living example of his degeneracy. Why, in the meeting before last, he even made sacrilegious comments: 'God is simply a wishful idea to seek refuge behind when we cannot bear to face the prospects of our own deaths. Atheists are the true realists of the world.' How can I become the physician to such a man?" He shook his head slowly in silent anger. All that could be heard in the library was the rain drumming relentlessly on the window-panes.

Falding took a sip of the rich red wine and fell into his thoughts. It was not hard to see that Byron, the pleasure-seeking, exploitive egotist, collided with what mattered most to his friend. Falding knew that Polidori was profoundly guilty over being near such a man, especially about his wealthy extravagance in the midst of all the suffering and poverty around them.

49

He threw a worried glance toward his glum companion. Surely another layer of guilt would be added if he became Bryon's physician. It would even be hypocritical, given that Polidori had criticized his colleagues for catering to the rich.

Falding looked out the front gates swung open to the street beyond. A young, poorly clad woman, clutching her child closely to protect it from the rain, hurried by. Her face was pinched with the miserable cold.

Suddenly, he vividly remembered himself as a nine-year-old standing on a London street while being escorted to school by the family maid. A train of wagons with little wooden boxes upon them made its way slowly along the street. Adults stood silently on the sides of the street, the men with hats in hand. He asked about the boxes — what they were. The maid told him they were the coffins of poor children who had died from smallpox.

He knew most of his family had been sickened, and his dear little sister had almost died from the disease. But why did all these children die? Was it because they had no doctors to look after them? The adult Falding smiled grimly. It would have made no difference anyway, he thought. But he remembered making a vow to become a doctor, like his father, to help the poor get better.

His thoughts returned to his friend. Why was he still attracted to Byron? What would draw him to someone who, in his roots, stood in such stark contrast to him? He understood Polidori was entranced by Byron's powerful words and perhaps even wanted to become a kind of poet's apprentice to him. But was he also secretly hoping for a share of his fame if he became "court" physician in Byron's entourage? Was he beyond that? Was there some other reason not yet fathomed?

Falding drew closer to the comforting warmth of the fireplace. He was troubled that Polidori did not seem to see he was using Byron for his own ends, just as Byron was using him. Being young and naïve, he might not ask himself the important questions: *When do the ends stop justifying the means? At what point, will I lose my soul in this unsavory relationship?*

He kept his thoughts to himself for the time being. He hoped his friend would eventually come to his senses and refuse a bargain with the devil.

Chapter 8

Falding wasn't entirely surprised when Polidori swallowed his reservations and accepted the position as Byron's personal physician. The young doctor was eager to play the role, and the day of Byron's first medical appointment finally came.

Byron preferred to be seen at Polidori's home. He felt that Whitechapel was beneath him, and he did not want to be harassed by beggars and street people. His physician didn't care for his views about the poor, but he had his duties to do.

He inquired about his patient's symptoms using the medical history method of the great eighteenth century French physician, Dr. Pierre Louis. Byron complained of fatigue, erratic moods, sleeplessness, and stomach/genital pain. It did not take long to connect these symptoms to his undisciplined conduct, including the possible use of the China herb (opium).

To confirm his diagnosis, he performed the premier test of the day. He extracted blood from Byron, letting it sit in a clear glass vial for an hour. The blood separated itself into four distinctly colored layers from black on the bottom up through red, yellow, and pale white at the top of the vial.

Polidori explained the results to his curious patient, who peered into the vial. "You see there. There are different colored layers. Well, these layers correspond to the four basic humors or fluids in the human body. These must be in a certain balance for you to be healthy. If the humors are imbalanced, you are diseased or ill in body and mind, as you have been experiencing."

"Oh?" asked Byron skeptically.

Polidori ignored his doubting tone and went on with his diagnosis. "Yes. Look at the bottom black layer. The black bile humor is very prominent. The yellow bile layer second from the top is the most prominent. Your fluids are out of balance with this excess, and that will produce your symptoms — even your emotional ones. The black bile will produce a melancholy temperament and sleeplessness. The yellow bile produces irritability and bad temper. Your unsavory habits are producing these imbalances."

"Well, I could have told you that," snapped Byron, annoyed that his conduct was being pointed out and questioned.

The physician would not be baited. "Perhaps," he said, "but the tests never lie. This is the latest in the science of medical diagnosis. Medicine has come a long way since it was believed that astrology and the occult were the causes of illness."

"I would hope my diagnosis is not in the stars," sniffed Byron, looking around for any sign of an astrological chart. He did not impress Polidori as a believer in the supernatural. A hint of the occult in his examination — on top of his doctor's impudence in questioning his habits — would have certainly ended the budding doctor-patient relationship.

"So, what are your recommendations?" queried Byron, tapping his finger impatiently on the examining table.

Polidori felt Byron was preparing to sacrifice him on the altar of his personal freedom. "I would not in good conscience tell you what you already know," he responded diplomatically.

Byron brightened considerably and visibly relaxed. "Do you have some cures, then, Doctor?"

"Not cures, but aids to the body to heal itself. I have some medicines, some potions, for you to take daily, which will help purge the excess bile. I also have a tonic to strengthen the body and mind and a hypnotic herb to calm the nerves. Will you take these, Lord Byron?"

"Yes, of course. Whatever will take away my malaise."

"And one more thing. There is so much bad bile that we will need to do some bloodletting to diminish it enough. You need to visit me once per week. Now, with modern medicine you have a choice of using the brass box with cutting blades to open a small wound or the traditional leeches."

"The brass box will do, doctor."

And so ended Byron's first visit with his personal physician. It appeared to be a resounding success.

Chapter 9

Byron disciplined himself enough to visit once a week, as the doctor had ordered. A routine developed. Polidori would inquire if Byron was taking his medicines, and he apparently was. Each week, blood would be let with the brass box to relieve the objectionable humors. The two would then peer hopefully into the vial to see if there were any changes in the colored layers, but to their consternation, the black and yellow were still predominant. Not wanting to offend the great man, Polidori didn't dare bring up the topic of his patient's vices.

The visits went on like this for quite some time. However, there was pleasant news one day when Byron announced that he would be putting on a grand ball at Newstead Abbey in early summer. He asked a flattered Polidori if he would come.

Polidori knew it was the custom of the English gentry to move out to their country estates in the summer, when the heat would create the worst stench of the year in the cities. This was the natural time for the gentry to visit and impress one another through their country balls. They would vie to see who could put on the grandest ball of all.

This would be the first informal social visit with Byron, and Polidori quickly and gratefully accepted the invitation. This would afford him an opportunity to meet potential wealthy donors to the poor. Besides, he thought, there would be many unattached women at the ball flirting with single young men, and that could prove interesting.

He reminded himself to write to his mother about this latest development in his relationship with the famous poet. He had been feeling a little guilty over the fact that her letters to him outnumbered his replies.

Polidori had been looking forward to the grand ball for weeks, and at last, the day of the extravagant affair arrived. The aristocratic guests traveled to Newstead Abbey from many parts of England and even from abroad. Their ornate, luxurious coaches were works of art unto themselves. They boasted carved wooden frames and elegant curved doors, emblazoned with multicolored ancestral crests of the noble families. The coaches were pulled by teams of four horses in festive harnesses and headdresses. The nobles' teams were all pure white or black; no spotted or off-color horses would have done.

The coaches rode on long, bar-like springs to cushion the passengers from the rocks and ruts of the treacherous dirt roads winding through rural England. But the roads were not the only hazard, for there was always the risk of being held up by highwaymen. Many a well-to-do traveler had lost his coin and jewels on these remote back roads.

Before embarking for the Abbey, Polidori had asked his driver their route.

"It's through Nottinghamshire, sir, by Sherwood Forest."

"Sherwood Forest? Of Robin Hood fame?"

"That's it, sir."

"Isn't that a perfect place for a robbery?"

"There's always the chance, sir. And the highwaymen are no Robin Hoods, either. They steal to eat and can be nasty if you cross them."

His master looked appalled. "Is there no other route, driver?"

"Nothing we can get through. Unless we go out of our way, sir, and then we might not make it in time... Besides, I'll be on the lookout. And we're likely to join up with the other coaches before Sherwood Forest. Safety in numbers and all that, sir."

As the driver had predicted, they joined a caravan rolling toward the abbey in the early evening. But the young master was hardly reassured. The coaches had just passed a village when they lurched to a sudden halt. Polidori heard shouting from up ahead and called up to his driver. "What's going on?" he asked apprehensively.

The driver took off his hat and wiped his brow with his sleeve. "I don't know, sir. There's some kind of commotion ahead."

"I hope not a robbery!"

"I don't think so, sir," said the driver, but Polidori heard the trigger of the driver's gun cock. He craned his neck out the side window to have a look. He was shocked to see the driver from the lead coach spring down from his seat and push a frail, white-haired man to the roadside. The man yelped as the driver began thrashing him with his whip.

Appalled, Polidori bolted out of his coach and soon came up on the pair. He stepped between the driver and his victim. "What manner of cruelty is

57

this?" he shouted. "Be on your way fellow, and return to your duties."

The driver made no excuses and sullenly climbed back onto his coach, urging his horses forward.

Polidori extended his hand to help up the old man. He saw that he was almost blind from cataracts. "Are you all right?" he asked as the man unsteadily regained his feet.

"Aye," the fellow replied. "I got the wind knocked out o' me, is all."

"Do you have a home I can take you to?"

The man hesitated to board the luxurious coach but gave in to his pain. Overcome with gratitude, he gave directions to a humble corner of the square in the nearby village.

Polidori helped him into the coach and told the driver to turn back to the village. "What were you doing out there, my good man?" he asked. "You can barely see and might have been run over."

The frail passenger said, "I'm 'ere to give warning."

"Whatever about?"

The old man looked terrified. "The devil's there, he is, and those who go to the abbey, they'll rue the day."

Polidori recalled the dark stories Lyons had told him about the place. "But surely this is all mere rumor, superstition at best."

The man shook his head vigorously. "No! 'Tis God's truth ... I'd a grandson once. Only a tiny lad, playing he was, near the village edge with some tykes after supper. A coach with a noble crest pulled up and took 'im. It drove off t'wards the abbey."

58

The man lowered his head. "We never saw 'im again. We looked and looked. Even ran up to the abbey and pounded on its doors. Big oak doors with iron studs. The devil's doors. Cold to touch they were and in 'em was the pain o' all the children took to the Abbey. The doors ne'er opened, and the constable, he took us away."

The coach suddenly stopped as it reached the square. As the grieving grandfather got out, Polidori pressed several gold coins into his hands. "Godspeed," he said.

The old man looked up and pushed forward a small wooden cross hanging from his neck for his rescuer to touch. Polidori obliged him, and the man limped away.

The road leading into the cobblestone courtyard of the abbey was lined with fire pots lighting the way for the travelers as sunset approached. Newstead Abbey, perhaps like the man who owned it, was a contradiction. The old, unrenovated part of the abbey lay dark, gloomy, and disordered. The great hall and living quarters, though, presented a brilliant, attractive, and festive face toward the world. It was reminiscent of the twin masks of tragedy and comedy in the London playhouses.

The stately coaches pulled up into the courtyard with the worthies of English society. Some of the notables were the more liberal royals, Whig politicians, lords, and the new aristocrats: the wealthy factory owners. Noted artists and writers were also guests, including the poet Percy Shelley and his fiancée, Mary Godwin.

As Polidori's coach approached, he watched the colorful scene unfold in the courtyard. The men stepped first out of the coaches, many dressed casually in open-necked jackets. Some were close-shaven and had short-cropped hair with forehead curls. Polidori smiled to himself. He knew they were imitating Byron's style of fashion and grooming that was so popular among the young blades. They were his true devotees, and Byron was their high priest.

The pomp and prancing then began. The men helped the ladies descend in their long ball gowns, shawls, and bonnets, wearing their expensive jewels. The guests then promenaded up the red carpet to the grand entrance, where they would be escorted to the Great Hall to be greeted by their host.

Polidori was soon waiting in the greeting line. The doors to the Great Hall were all open, and from this vantage point he had a good view of it. The hall was grand even by Florentine standards. It was brilliantly lit by great silver chandeliers suspended from the lofty, vaulted ceilings and by candelabras around the walls. The rugs had been cleared, presenting a vast oak floor waxed for dancing. Arranged along the walls were ornate French provincial chairs and settees. The finest furniture, near the towering windows overlooking the darkening courtyard, was reserved for the more prominent guests.

The centerpiece of the hall was a massive fireplace. Its stones were seared by ancient fires and decorated with the Byron family coat of arms and an assortment of old swords, shields, and pikes. Polidori mused that it looked even more warlike than his own hearth had at home before he'd given it some Mediterranean warmth.

He saw that his host had gone to great lengths to provide an evening of high musical entertainment. Around the fireplace was an ensemble of musicians grouped in their small sections, strings, brass, and woodwinds, with a dash of percussion and piano. They sat behind their ornate wood and brass music stands, presenting a cacophony of sounds as they warmed up and tuned their instruments; their conductor shuffled through reams of musical scores.

Polidori pleasantly imagined dancing the night away with some of the attractive, unattached women. The ladies would soon perch themselves on the stuffed chairs, smiling invitingly as they silkily fanned themselves.

It was Polidori's turn to be greeted, and he was immediately collected by Lord Byron. Byron's strange appearance startled him. He was dressed entirely in black, his face powdered completely white to a deathly pallor.

"Polidori!" exclaimed Byron. "Welcome! Your journey from London was uneventful, I hope?"

His guest smiled, evading the question. "I am honored to be here, Lord Byron."

"Splendid! Splendid!" There was a lull in the influx of guests, and Byron decided to show off his personal physician. He soon found the most notable of his guests to introduce him to first.

"Count and Countess!" he chimed. "Please meet my *personal* physician, Dr. John Polidori. Polidori, the count and countess of Versailles."

"A pleasure sir," said the count. The countess smiled and nodded.

"The count and countess have come all the way from France to join our party." Byron beamed, pausing to see if his doctor was suitably impressed. Before anyone could respond, he added, "Did you know, Count, that Dr. Polidori was first in his medical class?"

"Really! Fascinating!" intoned the count. "And where do you practice, Doctor?"

"Why, East London, sir. I work mostly with the poor."

The count stepped back a bit, staring at him as if he was a curious bug under his magnifying glass. Diplomatically, he changed the topic. "Polidori, Polidori," he mused out loud. "Italian. Tuscan, I believe, yes?"

"Why, yes, I am from Florence, sir," Polidori replied, pleasantly surprised.

"Polidori! I thought I recognized the name. Is this the family of the Duke and Duchess of Florence?"

"Yes, they are my parents, sir."

"Excellent! Excellent!" the count gushed, reaching for the young man's hand. "I have attended some of the duke's soirées and have found him and the duchess to be gracious hosts, most gracious... I hear he has been marshaling his forces against the Carbonari."

"The Carbonari?" queried another guest who was eavesdropping on the conversation.

"Why yes, my good man," replied the count tolerantly. "Those scoundrels, the Italian revolutionaries, trying to oust the aristocracy in Italy."

62

Polidori looked at Byron, expecting him to defend the revolutionary movement. However, he just smiled, hesitant to offend such an honored guest as the count. Polidori had no such reservations. "There *are* different points of view on the revolution, sir," he said curtly, but then he caught himself. A heated political argument could well insult his host. "What about you, Count," he asked. "How have you been managing with the revolution? The aristocracy was supposed to have been virtually destroyed in France."

"Only in the cities," informed the count. "We country noblemen have arrived at, shall I say, an accommodation."

"Accommodation, sir?

"Yes. The peasants are no longer serfs and have been granted their own lands to work, for an annual tax to us, of course. These scraps seem to have pacified them for the moment."

Polidori winced. "And the revolutionary councils?"

The count waved his hand dismissively. "We have come to an accommodation with them too. We pay them an annual fee if they leave us alone."

"A bribe?"

"Heavens, no," said the count, feigning shock. "A fee for services is all. The revolutionary councils need to make a living too." He smiled smugly. "I hope your father is nipping the Carbonari in the bud. I hear they're turning out political pamphlets and marching in the streets. This is how it all begins, and it's downhill to anarchy from there. Our King Louis was weak and indecisive with the people in '89."

"What should he have done, Count?" Polidori asked, not sure if he wanted to hear the answer.

"He should have set the guard upon them right away. A few volleys upon the mob at the right time and place would have aborted the whole sordid matter. But Louis didn't have the stomach for it, nor, ultimately, did he have the head for it either. Pity."

This was too much for Polidori. He was about to confront the count when he noticed the countess giving her husband a subtle, reproving glance. She had sensed the tension building in the air and knew full well where potential disagreements between the men could lead. "Come, Jean," she interjected, taking her husband's arm. "It's soon time to dine, and I need you to escort me to the powder room." And off she went, leading her husband out of harm's way.

Soon the crowd adjourned to the great dining room, which was almost as magnificent as the ballroom. The guests were seated at one enormously long table, made up of many tables placed end to end, covered with silk tablecloths. The table was laden with an assortment of carved meats and fowl, delectable vegetable dishes, and many tasty desserts. The guests dined with fine china and sterling silverware, all engraved with the Byron family crest. They savored French wines served in crystal goblets. It was luxury at its best or worst. Byron spared no expense, although he really couldn't cover the costs. Polidori imagined he'd try to recoup his losses through some heavy gambling tonight with a few of his wealthy guests.

Byron and his inner circle sat at the head of the table, with the rest of the guests placed along the table in descending order of importance. To his surprise and pleasure, Polidori found himself next to his fellow aspiring poet, William Lyons.

"Fancy seeing you here." Lyons smiled. "Moving up the social ladder, I see."

"It's just a ball."

"Ah, but you've almost made it to the head of the table, John. You're practically in the charmed circle."

"Well, you're near the inner sanctum yourself, William."

"The lord has gotten wind that I have a book in the offing about him. He's trying to ensure it flatters him."

Polidori laughed. "I guess that would explain your invitation, then!"

"Right. Remember, everything Byron does is for Byron. Take a look down the row, toward the middle. Who do you see?"

Polidori peered in that direction. "Shelley?"

"None other. And his fiancée, Mary."

A puzzled look crossed Polidori's face. "Why would he invite a rival to his ball?"

"Simple. Shelley is a brilliant presence in the Romantic poetry movement. His accepting the invitation is another jewel in Byron's crown. He's hedging his bets for the future, too. Mary Godwin comes from a family of famous writers, and it's said she's got the gift."

"Talking about the fair sex, I see no Mrs. Lyons on your right. Single like me, are you?"

"I'm afraid so," Lyons sighed. "You know the old saying 'all is fair in love and war'? Well, love hasn't been exactly very fair to me so far. All the ladies are pursuing Byron, I fear."

Polidori broke into laughter. "That would account for our bachelorhood!"

At that moment, Byron stood to give an eloquent, rousing welcoming speech, as only a Romantic poet could give. All began well, according to the best etiquette, until he proposed a toast and the multitude stood up. It was at that point that Byron gave his first outrageous performance of the evening. After he had proposed the toast, he drank from what appeared to be a large, off-white cup.

His physician looked more closely at it. "Good Lord! It's a human skull!"

Lyons took a look. "My word. It is!"

The news of the skull spread quickly on a wave of whispering from one end of the table to the other. But the social waters soon calmed. His guests were accustomed to his antics and his mocking etiquette, sacred customs, and even religion when it suited him.

Lyons, too, soon recovered from the shock. "I don't know why I was surprised." He chuckled. "It's the typically scandalous thing Byron would do. I expect he'll have more in store for us tonight."

But Polidori still lingered in shock. The cup was a sacrilege, he thought, but the stunt also offended the physician in him. Byron's drinking with *that* could undo their efforts to restore his four humors. He was put off on his dinner and spent the rest of the time toying with his fork in his vegetables.

However, Lyons and the other guests seemed to eat heartily enough. When they were finished, Byron stood up to deliver his latest poem to entertain the throng. He called it "The Monk in the Garden." It was about his gardener finding the old skull in a lost graveyard on the grounds and something about the moral implications of this for the "vanity of man."

Frankly, Polidori didn't understand it, and from the blank looks around him, he thought many of the others didn't either. "Did you get the point of that?" he asked.

"I haven't the faintest," confessed Lyons. "For once, the great poet's words fall short!"

With Byron's vague moral ringing in their ears and fine wine going to their heads, the guests dispersed to the ballroom, pausing to bow to the conductor upon entering. The conductor tapped his music stand, and the musicians warmed up the crowd with a few waltzes — outrageous to many of the time but not to the liberal crowd that attended Byron's balls. From there, the evening went pleasantly enough. The ensemble played country jigs and folk songs; then the dancers were swept along with lively adaptations of the classics. Polidori had great success on the ballroom floor, charming more than one of his attractive partners.

He noticed there was a mixture of strict etiquette in the ballroom between men and women *and* flagrant disregard for it. The ladies dutifully kept to their dance cards, listing the names of the gentlemen they were to dance with at certain times. A few blank spots for impromptu selections were available. Other gentlemen, after presenting

67

themselves appropriately, could ask to read the ladies' cards and to place their names upon them. All well and good, he thought.

On the other hand, he was mortified to see some abominable behavior out there as well. "Did you see that?" he asked Lyons. "A single lady just gave the slip to her escort! Another one did it, half an hour ago! Unheard of!"

Lyons laughed. "That's one of the unmentionables at Byron's balls. Everyone knows what's happening but politely pretends otherwise. Now that you mention it, though, have you noticed an occasional young man goes missing, too?"

"No," Polidori replied, taken aback. "But I have noticed that Byron disappears once in a while."

"Right." Lyons smiled. "And he's not powdering his nose, either."

Byron's doctor slowly shook his head. No doubt, he would be treating his patient for groin pain next week.

The ensemble would periodically take a break, leaving a couple of the junior violinists to play a bit of background chamber music. But this time, mysteriously, the drummer also remained. Everyone soon found out why. Byron suddenly announced to the crowd, "Your attention, ladies and gentlemen. Two young men have decided to settle a point of honor with pistols. Please step out of the field of fire." The crowd drew back, startled. The two, with their jackets removed and pistols cocked, then joined back-to-back and took their twenty paces away from each other. The violins had stopped, but the drums slowly rolled.

Polidori blurted out, "My God! The two are about to take aim at one another!" He glanced over at Lyons, puzzled to see him grinning from ear to ear.

The two duellers turned and fired, their pistols deafening the guests. The crowd shrieked and gasped, and gun smoke filled the air. The two, still standing, smiled broadly and took deep bows to the onlookers. It had been a mock duel arranged by Byron, with powder only, for effect. Relieved laughter swept through the hall.

Lyons laughed uproariously. "It just gets better!" he remarked. "He's a born entertainer."

Polidori was not so amused. He had taken the duel seriously and found himself badly shaken.

Byron then played the game of having the guests decide upon who had won and lost the duel. He made a pretense of democratically counting their yeas and nays. He then announced his verdict, which he had already decided on anyway, to the cheers of most present.

"It's incredible how he can play the crowd," remarked Polidori. "He dupes them and then they cheer him for it."

"He'd make a good politician," Lyons observed wryly.

Byron had one more spectacle for his guests. About halfway through the evening, his servants opened the door to the old part of the abbey. To everyone's amazement, in slithered Byron's pet snake, Alexander, a fourteen-foot bull anaconda. Normally, the snake would be allowed to roam freely in the ruinous halls of the old abbey. Tonight, he allowed it to wander the ballroom floor, both fascinating and alarming his guests. The host announced that it was a pet and wouldn't harm anyone. The snake simply slithered about its own business and did not bother people, the real reason being it was well fed with the rats it caught in the abbey's ruins.

Polidori was shaken again. "I can't believe he's got a big bloody snake in the hall!"

"It seems to take a special interest in the musicians," Lyons observed. The snake coiled before the ensemble, swaying its great head to and fro to the music.

"It must be attracted to the sound vibrations, like an Indian cobra to the charmer's pipe," the young physician surmised. "The whole thing is like a mad circus, and Byron is the circus master."

"Yes," Lyons agreed, "he's got everything here but the dancing bears, the jugglers, and the bearded woman!"

The musicians were unnerved by the beast. Periodically, some bad notes would be heard from a distracted violinist here or trumpeter there in this otherwise impeccable ensemble. Polidori, though, thought there was more to be concerned about than bad notes. He imagined that by morning one of the drunken, unconscious guests would find himself the unwitting breakfast for Alexander.

However, his thoughts grew darker. He mused how the great snake, in a way, symbolized Byron. A vivid image of the biblical Garden of Eden flashed in his mind's eye, and he beheld the coiled serpent — the corrupter of Eve and humankind. Overwhelmed and lightheaded from strong emotions

70

and an empty stomach, he bolted for the doorway for some fresh air. As far as Polidori was concerned, the grand ball was mercifully over.

Chapter 10

In the months after the ball, Byron dutifully presented himself for weekly treatments, despite no signs of improvement. The four humors stubbornly resisted change, although Byron was apparently taking the medicines. Both doctor and patient knew why but avoided the taboo topic.

Polidori, disturbed at the lack of progress, decided to consult Falding. The two quietly discussed the matter over a drink one evening in a private room of a gentlemen's pub.

"I'm convinced that his disordered humors reflect a disordered life," Polidori said. "His problems with women, for example, have escalated to alarming proportions this winter."

"He's confided these matters to you?"

"No, but the rumors about him abound in the newspapers — too many to be entirely untrue. London is gossiping about his separation from his wife, whom he is said to have married for her money. She has publicly accused him of some unforgiveable crime. She's coy about what he has supposedly done, and speculation over it is rampant."

"Such uproar," remarked Falding. "And to have it aired so publicly must be troubling, even to Byron."

"I honestly don't know if he cares, Alex. And there's more. Rumor has it that angry women throughout London are accusing him of jilting them.

Falding sighed. "There's nothing worse than the scorn of a jilted woman. But in Byron's case it may well be justified."

"Well, that's not all of it. He's even said to have fathered a child by his half-sister."

Falding looked dismayed. "He seems a menace to womankind ... and how could all of this not influence the balance of his humors? Have you discussed this with him, John?"

Polidori shifted uncomfortably in his chair. "I know perfectly well he would explode if I did. It would be the end of him as my patient."

"But surely, John, you must discuss his reckless habits, even if he stops seeing you. As his doctor, you need to have him face the fact that he is destroying his own health, not to mention that of others... And what of it if he decides to end treatment? Does that have to be calamitous to you?"

Polidori took a drink of his beer and looked away.

"John, I'm your good friend. What is it you're not telling me? What are you afraid of losing? Perhaps the opportunity to bask in his fame as his personal physician? The hope of meeting beautiful women at the soirees you accompany him to? Do you fear losing patrons for the poor? What is it?"

"I need to do some soul-searching about this, Alex," Polidori said. "And then, when I'm clear on my feelings, we'll talk again. I promise."

The two turned back to their beers in uneasy silence, the unanswered questions weighing heavily on their minds.

Polidori's relationship with his controversial patient would become even more complicated. One day, during treatment, Byron made a surprise announcement. "I intend to travel to the Continent soon, for a holiday and to write. I hope you will accompany me as my personal physician."

Polidori was flattered by his proposal, but anxious too. He wondered if this was a prelude to Byron fleeing from his notoriety to the Continent. Perhaps this was for good, just like his father many years ago, he thought. He played for time. "I'm honored by your offer, Lord Bryon. However, it's a large undertaking. Let me consider this further."

Byron seemed satisfied with this answer for the time being, but Polidori knew he couldn't procrastinate too long. He determined to consult with Falding once again.

The two soon met in Falding's drawing room on a snowy, winter morning. Falding saw his friend was vibrating like an over-plucked violin string.

"Byron wants me to travel with him to Europe on a holiday. I'm really worried about it."

"If many of the rumors about him are true, I can understand that, John," he said. "But what exactly is troubling you about it?"

"For one thing, I'll be away from my practice for months. What's to become of my patients? It's not as if they can afford their own physicians, can they?"

"Well, I can see some of your patients, John, but that's not going to solve the problem."

"I know, but thanks anyway, Alex."

"There's something more, John. It's the man himself, isn't it?"

Polidori nodded. "The man is going to inflict his immorality like a plague all over Europe, for months on end. I wouldn't have the nerve to confront him about it, yet I think that if I'm silent about things that matter like this, I lose part of my soul."

"Do you fear he'll mistreat you, also?"

"I'm afraid of his critical words about my poems, Alex, and I can't stop looking for the man's approval over my writing. I feel like a dog waiting for a pat on the head that never comes from his master. I have always wanted to become a great writer, and his help would mean so much to me. But he gives so little."

"But you keep on hoping it will be different?"

"Yes. I can't bring myself to give up on him.'

"John, are you giving too much power to this man, as famous as he is? Surely, you must look within to find yourself as a writer."

Polidori slowly let his breath out, mulling over his friend's words.

The psychiatrist hoped that he was reaching him. "And if you go to Europe with Byron, you know he will have you ministering to him day and night. You'll be troubled even more by the futility of your treatments."

A worried look crossed Polidori's face.

Falding was concerned about his emotional fragility. "John, I have strong doubts about your undertaking this journey. Being around Byron so much could emotionally destroy you, or at least corrupt you, as he has done to so many others."

Polidori thanked him for listening but did not give his decision. This was an ominous sign to Falding.

A few days later, Falding was surprised to receive a letter from his friend.

75

Dear Alex,

I know this is very impersonal, and I apologize for conveying my feelings in this way.

You have asked me to consider what attracts me to Byron at such personal cost to myself. I revealed something important to you in our last meeting, but there is more.

I confess I secretly admire him, and not only for his poetry. Beneath all of his abominable conduct, I see in him powerful strivings for personal freedom and independence. I think the passion for freedom is part of the human soul, the self we are born into this world with. So many lose touch with it, so young. We become victims, prisoners of the rules and expectations of the world around us. I believe that the freedom- seeking part of me was suppressed by the strictness of my father and the Italian aristocracy. If not for my dear mother, I would have lost it entirely.

I know you must be wondering what I am going on about — that my very presence here in England alone is an unmistakable example of an act of freedom on my part.

But yet I feel that I have been unable to express fully who I am or even know myself completely. I am yet unable to explain fully what I mean by this and need to reflect further on the matter.

Though Byron often exercises freedom in the most exaggerated and objectionable ways, I believe there is still much I can learn from him on the topic.

I have finally decided to go to Europe with him in April. I couldn't bring myself to say this to you in person, knowing how you oppose it. I hope you will understand.

Your friend,
John

Falding put down the letter with a deep, reflective sigh. Surely, there were safer ways Polidori could learn about freedom. His attraction to Byron was becoming an obsession, outweighing caution and good sense. Falding wanted desperately to talk to him further but was torn. He decided that the letter spoke for itself. He knew Polidori would not be dissuaded from going to Europe with Byron on his quest for personal liberation, and damn the consequences. However, as worrisome as the choice was, he had the right to make his own decisions.

April came too soon. On the second, Falding went with a heavy heart to say good-bye. His friend was waiting to be picked up at his residence by Byron's coach. Spring was late, and the morning so cold one could see the white jets steaming from the horses' nostrils as they approached. After the driver had loaded the considerable luggage, the two men embraced. Falding quietly cautioned him, "John, take care. Remember, the most important person to look after is yourself."

The coach soon lumbered off in the general direction of Dover. As Falding watched it disappear down the cobblestone road, he feared for the welfare of his friend and wondered if he would see him again … and if he did return, would he be the same man who left that cold spring morning?

Chapter 11

As Polidori began his holiday with Byron, little did he realize that his future would be profoundly affected by happenings a full year before on an obscure island on the other side of the world. Sumbawa was one of the Spice Islands near Java, embedded in the warm, azure seas of the South Pacific.

Europeans had seized power from the ancient rulers of the islands and then competed with one another for control of the lucrative spice trade. By the time Byron and his physician were taking their holiday thousands of miles away, the islands were settling in under their most recent colonial rulers, the British.

The tranquility of the islands was suddenly shattered by powerful explosions in early April 1815. The British in Java worried that the explosions were sounds of cannon fire from pirates attacking off the coast. Heavily armed warships, the British East India Company cruiser Benares and the HMS Dispatch, sailed from Java to investigate.

It was midafternoon, April 6, 1815, the first day of the Benares's search for the source of the mysterious explosions. Fifty-nine-year-old Captain Williams had been standing on the hardwood deck of the bridge since sunrise, scanning the horizon through the ship's telescope. He was tired and exasperated from peering at the near empty seas.

He winced with a sudden but familiar jab of pain. He grabbed onto a guide rope to steady himself. A vivid memory came of the fight in the Bay of Biscayne and the hot slice of the French

78

sailor's musket ball through his shoulder. That battle certainly changed everything: giving up his command and retirement into poverty on a pitiful navy pension. Eventually, it became a matter of his debts outweighing his disabilities. So, when the offer had come of full captain's wages with the company, he had taken it.

But he thought he was getting too old now to be chasing about after absent pirates on the high seas. The voice of Commander Donaldson brought him fully back to the bridge. "Spot anything, sir?"

"Nothing. No signs of the brigands. Just a few of our merchants."

"Well," replied the younger man, "they've been awfully quiet since we sank the *Orient* off Java Point."

"Yes, losing their flagship, with all hands to boot, certainly took the wind out of their sails. Could be the slave trade to Fiji is drying up for them, too… I think we're on a wild goose chase here, Mr. Donaldson." He squinted up toward the ship's crow's nest. "Anything to report?" he yelled.

"Nothing, sir," came the distant reply from the lone lookout perched at a dizzying height up the main mast.

Donaldson was feisty. "If they do show, the men are ready for another scrap, and we'll give them hell, Captain."

"Right. The men are growing bored from too much shore leave, anyways. Battle will sharpen them up... Yet these explosions are puzzling. They were powerful enough to rattle the islands. There's got to be something natural going on."

After several days of fruitless searching, they made for port on Java to visit the governor for any news on the situation. They arrived on the evening of April 10 and anchored in the bay. As the captain walked up the palm tree studded hill to the governor's, he turned to look at his ship. Uneasily, he noticed a band of dark clouds approaching from the southwest horizon.

The governor, in his white, wide-brimmed hat, greeted him on the terrace of the mansion overlooking the beach and deep blue harbor. He put down his well-smoked pipe and rose from his wicker chair to take the captain's hand. There was gratitude in his grip. After all, the *Benares* had saved his life more than once, fighting off pirate attacks on the island. "So, what goes, Robert?" he asked with a note of anxiety in his voice.

"We've scoured the seas for days, Sir John. All we've got for our troubles is sunburn and sore eyes, I'm afraid. There's no sign of pirates whatsoever or any indications of the source of the explosions."

A look of disappointment crossed the governor's face. "Well, whatever it was, it shook the mansion and town violently, with some damage to older stone buildings. Caused quite a fright to the natives... The chiefs thought at first that war had broken out among some of the villages, but their messengers reported that all was peaceful among the tribes."

"I don't think it was manmade."

The governor smiled. "The natives think the thunderous sounds came from a battle between the Jin — the devil — and the souls of their ancestors. They think their dead ancestors go through a

80

probationary period after death inside the mountain and that the Jin then tries to stop them from going up to paradise."

"When I said, 'not manmade,' I didn't exactly have that in mind."

Sir John chuckled heartily. "It gets better. Some chiefs believe that the sounds came from a goddess's marrying off one of her daughters, and she fired off supernatural cannons to celebrate the occasion."

The captain couldn't help but laugh. "Well, that must have been quite a wedding."

He stayed overnight as the governor's guest. Low, ominous rumbling from over the distant sea disturbed his sleep that night. Toward sunrise, he was practically shaken out of bed by the trembling of the mansion. Running to the open window, he looked out at the rapidly darkening sky and the faintly reddish sun struggling to rise on the horizon.

He heard the shouts of panic in the streets as the natives cried and screamed, "The Jin has escaped the mountain! He is coming for us!" Their frightened features were exaggerated hideously by the flickering yellow and red glow from fires that had broken out in the buildings. Piles of rubble from collapsed buildings filled the streets. He was afraid to imagine what might lie beneath them.

The governor rushed into his room with his night clothes on, disheveled. He looked terrified and astonished at the same time as he saw the chaos outside. "My God, Robert! What is it?" he yelled.

"It must be some kind of natural cataclysm," the captain ventured, starting to feel unnerved. He was hardened to the dangers of the sea and of war but

81

was not prepared for the nightmarish scene before him.

Sir John regained some of his wits. "I must call out the guard! A riot's afoot!" he shouted as he rushed out the door.

The cause of the explosions was soon obvious. Captain of the Benares's log, April 11, 1815, 08:00 hrs:

... It was now evident that an eruption had taken place from some volcano, and that the air was filled with ashes or volcanic dust, which already began to fall on the decks. By eleven, the whole of the heavens was obscured, except a small space near the horizon to the eastward; the wind being from that quarter, prevented for a short time the approach of the ashes; it appeared like a streak of light at daybreak, the mountains in Celebes being clearly visible, while every other part of the horizon was enveloped in darkness. The ashes now began to fall in showers, and the appearance altogether was truly awful and alarming. By noon, the light that had remained in the eastern part of the horizon disappeared, and complete darkness had covered the face of the day...

The volcano itself was witnessed by Lieutenant Commander Phillips of the Dispatch on April 10. He described in his ship's journal the awesome scene on Sumbawa at Tambora Mountain, the highest peak in the Spice Islands:

At 7:00 p.m., three distant columns of flame burst forth near the Tambora Mountain, and after ascending separately to a very great height, their tops united in the air in a troubled and confused manner.

Over the next several months, strange and disturbing conditions in the sky and weather were reported in far-flung parts of the world. Catherine Wolsey and her husband, Silas, were a farming couple near Boston, two of the many people who endured the terrible weather in parts of the northern hemisphere. She recounted this trying time in the New England Journal, June 21, 1817.

The weather was unusually cold, rainy, and stormy for months on end — the worst in living memory. Our Professor Matthews, a retired science teacher from Harvard, informed us that it was the coldest spring and summer since records had been kept in the New England states. Later, people called 1816 "the year without a summer."

There were real fears about crop failure and famine over the winter. But the most frightening thing was the persistent dry fog high in the sky and the eerie appearance of the sun. It hung in the sky like a hazy red ball, with its sunspots visible to the naked eye.

I could not remember having been so frightened since the Indians attacked the village when I was five years old and my mother hid my little sister and me in the root cellar. I had the same feelings of helplessness and terror throughout the spring and summer of 1816. Our fear of the unknown eventually turned into panic. We thought that the sun was dying and that it was the end of the world.

One day, many of us flocked into the streets, believing that the seventh sign had come. We fell on our knees and prayed for salvation. I remember the village clergyman feverishly ministering to the crowds, trying to reassure everyone that their souls were safe. Following in his footsteps, the old professor did his best to appeal to the people's reason. "Nature has been at work," he said. "The fog has been caused by some natural happening, I can assure you. The fog has filtered out the sun, bringing on its reddish hue and the cold. Don't despair. It will pass, as all-weather passes." But his scientific explanations largely fell on ears deafened by fear.

No one knew at the time exactly what had caused these severe conditions. However, it became obvious, as reports trickled in from the east, that the Tambora disaster was behind it all. The greatest volcanic eruption in two thousand years of recorded history had occurred. Far greater even than Pompeii, the volcano had blown sulphurous fumes and dust high into the atmosphere. A veil spread over the earth, blotting out the life-giving warmth and light of the sun itself. Old Professor Mathews had been right, after all.

The dark and disturbing aftermath of the volcano was just beginning to be felt in springtime Europe, as Byron and his entourage left for the Continent.

Chapter 12

On the evening of April 8, Byron and Polidori sailed for Belgium on the schooner Sea Sprite. The ship had seen better days. Its sails had patches upon their patches. Its deck was warped by the alternations of sea wash and hot sun.

As Polidori watched the barren cliffs of Dover fading ghost-like into their mists, he felt a brooding anxiety well up within him. Was it about leaving his adoptive home of England, he wondered, or was it his apprehension about leaving with Byron, or both? His mood was not helped by the heavy seas they encountered. Many of the passengers, including himself, were seasick, retching over the side.

The Sea Sprite was far from spritely. It struggled against the wind and waves for sixteen hours before reaching Ostend, its old timbers groaning with the strain.

In between his bouts of sickness, Polidori noticed a sailor expertly coiling a bit of rope near the rails. An old salt by the look of him, he seemed unbothered by the squall. Rather, the commotion among the passengers seemed to be a source of vast entertainment to him. Byron's spirits also remained high. After finally arriving at a well-kept inn at Ostend, he soon found and fell upon the first chambermaid within range.

The next morning, they set off in a gaudy, rented coach made in Paris, copied from the celebrated coach of Napoleon himself. The coach was enormous, containing a small library, dining paraphernalia, and a bed, no less. It was just as well it was huge, for along with them came three of Byron's pets: a peacock, dog, and a monkey, all but his pet snake, Alexander.

As the party lumbered down the road in this monstrosity, Polidori looked upon the menagerie. He suddenly recalled the image of the grand ball as a circus with Byron as the circus master. *Now I'm in a traveling circus*, he thought, rolling his eyes up to the Napoleonic ceiling.

They traveled in Belgium and later into Prussia, stopping at luxurious inns for the well-heeled. The nights were filled with further debauching of chambermaids on Byron's part. The days were busy with visits to famous cathedrals, old battle sites, and art museums, which would serve as further inspiration for Byron's epic poems.

They took the tourist routes, but Polidori still noticed the sad juxtaposition of poverty and misery with wealth and contentment. Beside the grand inns and soaring cathedrals were hovels and unemployed men from the war, injured in body or mind, sitting about aimlessly. Dirty, begging children held their hands out to the coaches clattering indifferently by.

Byron seemed oblivious to the hardships around him, petting his animals and working on his poems. However, Polidori was greatly troubled by it all, tossing coins and fruit, at times, to the street urchins.

Byron finally looked up from his work, noticing his travel mate's downcast mood. "Whatever vexes you so, my dear boy?" he asked, more out of curiosity than compassion.

Polidori gestured out the window toward the suffering crowds.

Byron sighed. "Oh, *that*. They are but the latest casualties of war, just as there will always be casualties of war. War making is deep within the human soul. We can do nothing about it. Why trouble ourselves over it?"

Polidori flinched at his words. "Surely there is more to the soul than darkness," he protested. Was that his mother's voice or his own that just said that? he wondered. "There is kindness and responsibility in the human heart."

"Well, my good fellow," retorted Byron, "when you find them please let me know."

Polidori felt his anger rise as an acid taste in his throat and swallowed it. *The man is too blind to see that compassion is sitting right here beside him*, he thought. He turned away, looking out on the passing streets.

The travelers stopped to water the horses in a small Prussian town. Polidori got out to stretch his legs and spied a group of men sitting disconsolately on a wooden bench along the stonewall of a small roadside church. He went over to inquire about them. He asked if any spoke English and noticed one cringing from his words. Polidori looked closely at him. He appeared quite dried up from the cares of life. His eyes seemed to be held up by the large, puffy, dark bags under them. Patches of his white hair were missing, like bare spots in a garden where the vegetables had been pulled out right to the roots. Beside him was a homemade crutch.

Polidori approached this wreck of a man and was appalled to see him tremble with fright. He placed a gentle hand on the man's shoulder which seemed to calm him. "Tell me, sir, what has brought you and the others to sit out here so gloomily on this hard bench?" The man started to tremble again and Polidori wondered if the fellow thought he would report him to the authorities for loitering or some such thing. He backed up a step. "I only want to know about your plight, sir."

The fellow finally spoke up in a croaky voice, but in good English. "I — all of us here — fought against Napoleon. I was their officer..."

"You were wounded?"

"In the very last battle, wouldn't you know it. I was shot through the leg by a sniper at Waterloo."

Polidori looked down in a doctorly fashion at the leg near the man's crutch. "The leg is lame?"

"They were able to save it, but it was so damaged I can't walk without a crutch. It pains me at night, too. What I wouldn't give for a good night's sleep."

Polidori listened sympathetically.

"But that isn't the worst of it. It's the dreams ... my friends dying next to me in a volley of musket balls, trampled into the earth by their fellows bearing down behind them. Their faces and screams rush up at me. I cannot shake them off."

Polidori sat down beside the man in the small space still left on the bench. "And have you received any treatment since the war?"

"No. No one can afford it. The small pension we had from the government dwindled away and then dried up altogether. We have nothing — nothing but our beggar's bowls." He handed one out to Polidori, who placed several gold crowns in it. Suddenly, five more bowls appeared, and Polidori

88

got up and walked along the line of bowls, donating carefully to each.

"Wait," Polidori said. He walked back to the coach and brought back his doctor's bag. He reached in for two vials of medicines, which he pressed into the man's hand. He heard the restlessness of the horses behind him, now watered and straining to get going. He quickly gave his unexpected patient instructions and wished him godspeed.

As he made his way back to the coach, he noticed Byron watching him with a thin, mocking smile. Polidori burned slowly with unspoken resentment. The two sat in silence for the rest of the day's journey.

Their travels took them to Berlin, where the hotel staff lived up to the stereotypical Prussian reputation for being prim and proper, stiff and efficient. The head clerk at the front desk was an insufferable fellow, without doubt the most condescending and authoritarian they had yet met in Europe. Consequently, not even Byron dared pursue any of the hotel's chambermaids that night.

A visit the next day to the superb Berlin Museum of European History made up for some of this unpleasantness. The pair examined the exhibits, especially in the section for Romanian history and relics. Here they viewed some of the old books, armor, and artworks regarding Prince Vlad Dracula of medieval times.

After carefully studying some of the pieces, Byron remarked, "Fascinating, isn't he? Have you heard of the prince before?"

"Just rumors, no more."

89

"He was a man of such power and fame, a leader of great armies, centuries before us... Now, he's reduced to a few dusty relics in the corner of a museum. It's ironic, don't you think?"

Polidori nodded. He thought Byron was voicing his own fears about what would become of his poems — if they would be relegated to a museum, too, or worse, be forgotten. He examined an old document in a corner of the display. "Dracula's name means 'son of the dragon' in Romanian. Isn't that intriguing? It sounds quite dark."

"He *was* a dark figure," Byron confirmed, with an odd smile. "He was called 'Vlad the Impaler' for good reason." He gestured to an old German painting showing Turkish soldiers raised up on long poles pushed through their bodies by Vlad's men.

Polidori instinctively drew back from the painting. He noticed, though, that Byron seemed absorbed in the scene, staring at it for the longest time. He seemed deep in thought about it. It was a curious reaction. Was Byron an admirer of the prince?

The next morning, they got off late because Byron overslept. Polidori had a chance to wander the street near the hotel and stopped by a newspaper stand. The vendor, a man named Gunter, dealt with many tourists and spoke very good English. He struck up a conversation about the day's news. "Have you heard about that poor woman?" he began, pointing to the front page of his newspaper.

"No, what's happened?"

"A woman who works at the museum disappeared last night."

"Well, that's a sad coincidence," Polidori said. "A friend and I were visiting there just yesterday."

Gunter warmed up to his topic. "*Ja*. Maybe you met her. She's an assistant. Thirty-two years old, the paper says — an Anna Steinmeyer."

"No, we didn't meet her. We were too engrossed in the exhibits to pay attention to much else."

"*Ja*. She left after work last evening and didn't arrive home, six blocks away. The police think she's been taken. They found her purse unopened on the street near the museum. They're asking for any information people may have."

Gunter then launched into a rant. "What's the world coming to?" he complained. "Somebody can't even walk home safely from work anymore! They don't have enough police on the streets. That's what the problem is. Everybody wants to sit behind a desk these days— too many in charge and too few to do the work, if you ask me. What's next? Am I going to be robbed tomorrow, or my wife? *Ja*, there's no authority on the streets, I tell you!"

At his first chance, Polidori bought a newspaper and made his escape from Gunter and his ravings. His written German was passable, and he read the headline article on the way back to the hotel.

He found Byron awake, looking quite haggard and grumbling he hadn't yet received his morning tea. Polidori held up the newspaper and excitedly told him the news. "I've just heard an assistant at the museum disappeared last night on her way home. Isn't that dreadful?"

Byron looked at him blankly.

91

Hoping for a livelier response, Polidori added, "She works in the Romanian section. Don't you think that's a remarkable coincidence? We might have passed her by yesterday. Then she vanishes overnight!"

But Byron shrugged. Polidori was puzzled at his unconcern but let the matter go. Perhaps it was the wrong time to have brought it up.

Chapter 13

Falding dashed from his coach, through the cold rain, to the entrance of the pub. He opened the heavy wooden door and was greeted by the strong smell of beer and the din of the crowd inside. He went directly to a private room, smiling as he saw his friend enjoying a porter at a table for two. He hung up his wet coat and joined him.

"Miserable day, Edward."

"It is an unseasonably cold spring, Alex. The trees aren't even budding yet... I've gathered from your note that this is more than just pleasure. You're troubled about a friend, it seems."

Falding nodded. He looked over at the well-tailored, middle-aged man across from him. Edward Tanner was a good friend and a fine psychiatrist. Falding needed to confide a few things in him. "You'll recognize the friend in question immediately, Edward. It makes no sense to try to conceal his identity. It's John Polidori."

Tanner did not look surprised. "Naturally, all of this remains in the strictest confidence, Alex."

"As we speak, he's traveling in Europe with Lord Byron, as his personal physician. You've probably already guessed at my concerns. Byron, of course, is a man of such questionable character. I think he's using John for his own ends, some immoral. John is highly principled but young and naïve. I believe he's being drawn in by the poet's fame. And he badly needs the man's approval for his writing, among other things."

"Such as?"

93

"For one, Byron seems to be a kind of symbol of freedom to John."

"What are you most worried about, Alex?"

"I fear he'll be corrupted by his patient. I also fear that John's guilt about being with this fellow will eventually destroy him." Falding was on the verge of tears.

"Are you sure you're not exaggerating the danger here, Alex?" Tanner asked gently.

His friend took a moment to compose himself. "I'm fairly certain, Edward. I mean, it's clear that he's trapped in inner turmoil about the man."

"So, how have you tried to help?"

"I've been patiently listening to his feelings and trying to bring out what keeps on drawing him back to Byron, despite the harm to himself. I've advised him strongly against the holiday to Europe and made clear the possible consequences to him…"

"And?"

"And I've brought out the importance of his not giving the power to define himself as a writer to Byron."

"But obviously, he went with Byron anyway, against your wishes."

"I'm afraid so."

"So, your young friend will have to learn from that experience, whatever it is. Perhaps he'll be a good deal wiser about this relationship when he returns."

"*If* he returns. I'm wondering if he will survive these travels."

"It appears you've done all you can do, as a friend to him. He's made his choices, for good or ill. Let your mind rest on this matter, Alex."

The two drank in silence. Falding listened to the laughter of other patrons enjoying their beer and good company. Revelry was the last thing on his mind right now. But he had forgotten his manners, he thought. "Enough of me," he said. "How are *you* faring, Edward?"

"I've been doing some interesting work with the police lately. Have you heard of the disappearances?"

"The women vanishing from their own homes in London?"

"That's it. Three of them in the last month, mostly upper-crust ladies. Since no bodies have been found, the police think they have been abducted for the purpose of confining them. But they've progressed no further with it."

"And I would imagine they want some insight into the mind of the abductor?"

"Precisely. I have a theory that interests the inspector in charge of the investigation. McLaughlin is his name, James McLaughlin. Have you heard of him?"

"No."

"He's quite a perceptive fellow, most dedicated to his work. He actually cares about justice, a rare quality in Scotland Yard these days, from what I've seen."

"You seem quite taken with the man."

"I am … and you know me. I'm always curious about what shapes people to be as they are. I've made a few discreet inquiries about him."

Falding smiled. "You seem a bit like an investigator yourself, Edward."

"Not quite. It happened that one of my colleague friends knew the McLaughlin family well and was quite willing to tell me about him."

"I trust you weren't disappointed?" Falding replied, still amused.

"No, his story is very moving but also interesting from the psychiatric point of view." He paused to await his friend's reaction.

"I *am* getting curious, Edward."

"I'm told the inspector was quite close to his father," Tanner began. "Fred McLaughlin was an educated man, a barrister. An amateur scientist, he introduced his son to scientific thinking. Even more important, he instilled in the boy a lifelong love of learning. As James grew up, he usually had his nose in a book or two."

"I would imagine like *Moby Dick* or *Treasure Island*."

"You have it. Later on, weightier books on physics and philosophy. Of course, he was a bright student and eventually enrolled at Eton. His dream was to go on to one of the great universities someday…" Tanner's face darkened.

"But?"

"But his world collapsed when he was fifteen. One night, as his father walked home late from work, he was robbed. He resisted and was fatally stabbed."

"How terribly tragic!"

"It was, Alex. The family was now fatherless and young James heart broken."

Falding leaned forward. "And I would think the family soon fell into debt."

96

"Yes. His mother, who was not wealthy herself, did some work outside of the home, but it was not enough. As the oldest boy, James faced hard decisions. He had to give up school and got on as a watchman, patrolling the streets of London after dark."

"An honorable position, but a waste of the boy's fine abilities."

"Indeed. However, his work eventually led him to the doors of Scotland Yard, where he was accepted as a young constable. His talents did not go unnoticed, and he rose steadily to become the youngest inspector to date."

"And how did he ultimately deal with his grief, Edward?"

"Over the years, it appeared that the pain of his father's death faded. In its place was a burning desire to protect others from crime and to give those who committed it their proper due."

"Hence his sense of justice and dedication to his work. I can truly see why you admire him, Edward."

Tanner nodded. "And I think if there's someone who can solve these disappearances, it is McLaughlin … with my help, of course."

Falding grinned. "I'm envious of you, Edward."

His friend laughed. "We *have* been too serious today, Alex. It's Saturday, after all. Let's call for more porter and forget the rest of the world for a while."

The two raised their glasses in salute and drank with gusto.

Chapter 14

Toward the end of May, the poet and his doctor reached the Swiss Alps. The two worked their way down on the fine Swiss roads to the old town of Cologny near fabled Lake Geneva. Byron had rented the Villa Diodati, a stately, elegant home of classic old European style, a short distance from town. The villa was a brief walk from the beach and docks. Around it were lush lawns, vineyards, and beautiful, terraced gardens, gently sloping down to the lake.

The villa also afforded a spectacular view of Lake Geneva. The vast lake had a deep blue hue, turning into shimmering silver as the sun shifted over the day. It was surrounded by rugged, somber mountains against the towering azure skies. As they stood on the balcony looking out one day, Byron remarked eloquently, "If poetry has its inspiration in the beauty of nature, then there is more than enough inspiration here."

Polidori was surprised to discover a small book in the villa's library on the history of the area. "This is quite remarkable," he said to Byron. "The villa has had some very famous visitors. Did you know that John Milton stayed here almost two centuries ago?"

Byron was amused. "Who knows? Perhaps *Paradise Lost* was envisioned right here in the villa. Poetry may live in these very walls."

But the villa had never held any quite like the remarkable cast of writers and poets who would soon come together for a brief summer of creative brilliance.

The rest of the cast made their appearance unexpectedly. Percy Shelley, his fiancée Mary Godwin, and her half-sister, Claire Clairmont, had taken a chateau nearby. This was no coincidence. Claire had apparently had an affair with Byron and became pregnant by him. He had left her after the affair, and she was now on a quest to inform Byron of the pregnancy and rekindle the relationship. Claire had persuaded her two companions to accompany her.

Over the coming summer days, Polidori struck up some friendly conversations with Claire. He had the impression that she felt a bit like an outsider. There was a hint of rivalry with her sister, and he thought she might have invited Shelley and Mary partly to show off Byron. At the same time, Polidori sensed that Byron was less than enthusiastic about his former lover presenting herself again to him in this delicate state.

Polidori was curious about Percy Shelley and learned much about him from Claire. The two sat in the villa's drawing room one morning, waiting to go out on the lake with the others for a day of sailing. He listened intently to the rather plump-faced, curly-haired young woman. "He's already published several works," she said. "His first, at age fourteen, revealed his gift for writing."

"Remarkably young to be published. I regret I haven't read his poems yet," Polidori said.

"Well, he's not yet of Byron's stature in the public eye, but his star is steadily rising."

"I've gathered from the literary society that he can stand his ground with Byron when the two recite. That's no small feat."

"Yes, and to become what he is he had to struggle against tragedy as he grew up. He was severely bullied as a child and withdrew into fantasy. Later his father had tried to declare him mad and place him in an asylum. Fortunately, a sympathetic teacher intervened to save him from this fate. But perhaps the greatest blow came when his marriage failed. Apparently, he suspected his wife and best friend of having had an affair. He withdrew even further into fantasy after that."

"Sometimes," Polidori observed, "the world of fantasy becomes our only solace. But it has also been said that great writing comes first from deep imagination." He paused in thought. Percy Shelley seemed a fascinating fellow he would like to get to know.

Apparently, Byron thought so, too. He became good friends with Percy over the next few months, perhaps seeing himself in the tragedy and brilliance of the young writer. Even Claire was eventually accepted by Byron, perhaps as the lure of sexual pleasures with her became too great to endure.

The good weather only helped their congeniality. The little band spent many carefree, relaxing summer days enjoying Lake Geneva. They swam, sailed until sunset, and rode in the mountains. They were awed by the huge mountain peaks, waterfalls, glaciers, and ancient castles perched on the cliffs overlooking the lake. After coming off the lake in the evenings, they had good intellectual discussions, fine wine, and even liquid opium.

As an added benefit, both Shelley and Byron were capturing their experiences in their writing.

One day, Shelley raised his wine glass to propose a toast to their holiday. "It is a time of great pleasure and great poetry," he said. Polidori, too, found himself happier than he had been in a long time. His doubts about Byron slowly began to fade into the bubbles of his Champagne.

As June progressed, however, dark, violent weather approached from the northwest. A dark undercurrent also began to grow within the group, and Polidori was at the center of it. As he became closer to Shelley, he began to share some of his poems and plays with him. Perhaps he hoped for the recognition that he could never get out of Byron. However, Shelley's reaction was no better, if not worse. Polidori had read to him his poem, "Paradise on the Lake". He was met with a frown. In fact, Shelley seemed irritated.

"I'll be frank with you, my good man," he said. "I'm afraid you're going to need much time under the wing of an experienced poet before striking out on your own."

Shelley's less than flattering remark hardly inspired Polidori's confidence. To aggravate his feelings, one evening he overheard Byron and Shelley talking and laughing in the courtyard about some of his works. "Poor Polidori," mocked Byron. "He actually thinks he's a writer!" Byron's words were seared into the novice poet's memory. He slunk away, never letting on that he heard this conversation, but anger and a desire for revenge were building within him.

His anger grew even more as Byron and Shelley became closer. Claire found him sitting alone one day on the balcony. "Why so glum on such a gorgeous day?" she asked.

He nodded toward the lake. "The two of them have gone off sailing. I should have been invited."

"I've been feeling lonely, too. But they're just going to talk poetry anyway." She sighed. "I confess that can get terribly boring."

"I wouldn't mind talking poetry," he said. "But I'm afraid my company is not good enough for them."

"Well, perhaps two outcasts like ourselves can find good company with one another." She sat down beside him.

He was too polite to decline her offer and stayed with her awhile. However, his thoughts went to the companion he was really looking for, the attractive and thoughtful Mary.

He soon began spending time together with Mary. They would have good conversations over tea, walks along the lovely shoreline, and outings on the lake, sailing. He found himself ever more attracted to her beauty, intellect, and natural compassion.

He'd had much opportunity to study her. Physically, Mary was at that intriguing stage between late adolescence and womanhood. She was full-bosomed but still light and lithe — energetic, yet capable of a calm, mature presence. He noticed her milky white skin could take on an adolescent flush at a moment's notice. Her large eyes sparkled with youthfulness, but their depth reflected the wisdom and confidence of an older soul. Her laughter was never far from the surface, but beneath that was a certain sadness.

Mary was looking for a confidant. "I can't often talk with Percy," she admitted during a morning walk on the beach. Her eyes teared up. "He can't handle deep feelings at all. It's ironic for a Romantic poet, isn't it? The passionate poet can't be a passionate partner."

"That sounds very disappointing, Mary," Polidori said sympathetically.

"I suppose I should have expected it," she said, drying a tear. "He never could voice his feelings to his father without fear of reprimand. So, he wrote them in his books and never got beyond that."

Polidori nodded, understanding completely. He remembered himself as a six-year-old, full of feelings but afraid to tell them to his father. Had he also chosen writing as a safe way to express his feelings?

He listened to Mary attentively for hours as she told the story of the tragedies and triumphs of her life, her hopes and dreams.

"I never knew the love of a mother," she began. "She died shortly after I was born. For years, I felt abandoned by her, as irrational as it sounds."

"I'm sorry to hear that, Mary," he said. He knew what abandonment felt like.

She nodded, her eyes welling again with tears. "The closest I could get to her — the only way I could know her — was through her books. As a girl, I used to go to her graveside to read them."

"That sounds like a wonderful gift she left to you, Mary."

"I could look at it as a gift." She smiled through her tears. "I was very close to my father, as a young girl. I suppose I was trying to make him both mother and father to me. He was also my mentor and taught me how to read and write, as I never had formal education, like most girls. I used to borrow and study books from his fine library. I remember he told me, 'The proper way to study is to read two or three books simultaneously.' He was right."

Mary paused, enjoying her memories. "But in a way, I did have many wonderful teachers. My father was a famous political philosopher who was often visited in his study by noted intellectuals and writers. I used to hide under his couch and eavesdrop upon the many profound conversations and recitations." Mary's face lit up with a smile. "At any rate, I grew to love books and powerful words. I even began to write my own words, creating rhyming children's stories. My stories were later published through my father's bookshop."

Polidori laughed. "That sounds like a delightful beginning as a writer, Mary." He remembered the Tuscan gardens of his childhood. He heard again his mother's voice reading to him. He savored the memories of her patiently listening to his first childish attempts to write poetry. She had had faith in him.

"It *was* wonderful to have my little books on his shelf and so was my life with my father — until he remarried." Her face darkened. "My life turned upside down when my stepmother and her two children invaded our home. She was always resentful of my close relationship with my father. She tried to interfere with it, and I found myself having to vie for affection and time from my father. I was no longer the center of his life."

Mary paused, deep in troubled thought. "Perhaps overwhelmed with all these demands, my father began to withdraw more and more into his study, leaving my parenting to his wife. But she was a poor excuse for a parent. She used me for housework and did not respect my privacy, nor did she encourage my writing. I felt abandoned ... for the second time."

"You must have felt deeply hurt and let down, Mary. Losing two parents must have been more than you could bear."

"It was, and for a long time I did not trust anyone to love me," she lamented. Then her face brightened. "All that changed when Percy came into my life when I was seventeen. He was a tall, elegant, somewhat fragile young man. He was a sensitive writer, and that appealed to me tremendously. He was also well educated through Eton and Oxford and came from a rich family."

Mary went on. "There was something in me that wanted to mother and protect him. He also utterly dazzled me, and we fell in love. But my father did not accept our relationship. You see, Percy was a free spirit who rejected formalities. He began to court me without the permission of my father, who reacted by trying to stop me from seeing him. In rebellion and irresistible love, we ran away to the continent together. A pregnancy soon followed, but the baby was premature and died. I fell into depression after that. I had lost my mother at childbirth; now I could not even be a mother to my own child."

Her confidant listened attentively, trying to understand her times of deep tragedy and joy.

Mary's lips began to tremble. "I had a dream later. It was so vivid, I'll always remember it," she said. "I dreamed that my little baby came to life again — that it had only been cold and that when I rubbed it before the fire, it lived."

"Our dreams do reveal our deepest wishes — not always attainable," Polidori remarked sadly. He wondered why it was that *he* dreamed so rarely, whether dark dreams or dreams of joy.

Mary sat up straighter in her chair. "But I couldn't let all my impossible wishes control my life. I threw myself into my writing, and I wrote through my sadness. Percy encouraged me and became my mentor."

"Good things can come out of dark times," Polidori said. He thought of how he had come from under the shadow of his father to the freedom and friendship of a new country. "Perhaps our tragedies define us, not in their destructiveness, but in how we overcome them, evolve from them."

"Yes, in the deepest moments of my despair, I realized I wanted to be a great writer like my mother. She was one of the first writers about the plight of women, revolutionary even today. I, too, wanted to write about something that mattered, with power and meaning. I knew I wanted to write a great novel, though I was not sure what its theme should be."

And so Polidori began to know the deep person this nineteen-year-old girl really was. As their relationship developed, he revealed his own dreams of becoming a novelist and a playwright. Eventually he got up the nerve to give her some of his works. Mary was much more appreciative of his poems, and his confidence in his writing grew. However, the budding poet began to take her interest and caring as signs of romantic attraction to him. He started to fall in love with her, though he did not declare it

His efforts to woo Mary got off to an uncertain start. One day, an embarrassing incident happened in Mary's presence. There was a rare sprinkle of rain, and Byron was off the lake for the day. He and Polidori had been sitting on the covered lower balcony overlooking the courtyard, when they saw Mary approaching from the beach. Her hair was wet and straggly, and her dress clung to her legs.

Byron suggested, "Why don't you do the chivalrous thing and jump down from the balcony to give Mary your cape."

Foolishly, he took the leap, with the hope of impressing Mary. He had forgotten that his ankle was still healing from twisting it a few weeks before. He turned it again on landing and slid unceremoniously down the wet slope into a mud puddle below, face first.

Mary ran up to him full of concern. "Are you all right?" she asked. "Are you hurt?"

He muttered something, not admitting to the injury. She helped him up as he spluttered to his feet, his face muddied and his pride bruised. He limped back to the villa with an arm over Mary's shoulder. He would not forgive Byron for all this, either.

He could not bring himself to voice his resentments directly to the man but instead became sullen and withdrawn. It did not take long for Byron to notice. He became irritated and short with him, as he was unable to bear any hint of inattention from anyone.

However, Polidori's anger soon broke out in outright arguments with Shelley over what seemed to be trifling matters. What happened next shocked everyone. One day, while the group sat in lawn chairs in the villa's courtyard, Polidori blurted out to Shelley, "I challenge you to a duel, you cur." His words were out before he realized it. The others gaped in his direction.

Shelley tried to laugh off the challenge. "We have been addled by the afternoon wine," he offered.

But Byron was not amused and jumped to Shelley's defense. "I take his place in a duel with the challenger."

Jaws dropped even further, and everyone turned expectantly to look at Polidori. He was so taken back, he could not speak up for his honor and stumbled off in a half daze.

Polidori knew, at some level, that his tensions with Shelley were inflamed by their unspoken rivalry over Mary. He had suspected as much from the cold stares Shelley had been sending his way for some weeks now. The matter came out into the open sooner than he expected. It was a rainy afternoon in mid-June. Shelley and Claire were standing on the covered balcony as the drizzle frothed up the lake. Mary and Polidori sat drinking wine in the drawing room, in a kind of listless daze. Byron was working at his writing table near the main window overlooking the lake.

Suddenly, in charged Percy in a rage. He was followed by Claire, who wore a look of restrained glee.

Percy shouted at Mary, "How dare you have an affair with Polidori! How do I deserve another unfaithful woman in my life?"

Mary stood up, shocked. "What has possessed you? How could you possibly believe that?" She glanced over at her sister, catching her suddenly looking away. She turned to face Shelley like a matador to the bull. "Is this how much you value my love and loyalty, accusing me of being an adulteress?"

"Do you think I am blind?" he fired back. "I see how much time he spends with you. I see how he watches you." He glared at Polidori.

"What?" Mary threw up her hands in disbelief. "I don't know what feelings he may have for me, but there has been no impropriety. He is a friend, even a confidant, but no more. I need someone to whom I can entrust my feelings, since my fiancé cannot cope with either my feelings or his own."

Shelley reddened and took swig of whiskey.

Polidori nervously wondered if he was about to be challenged into a duel. He spoke up in self-defense. "I can assure you, Percy, there has been nothing untoward between us." He didn't know how convincing he sounded.

Shelley sat down and refilled his liquor glass.

Mary turned to her sister, face full of fury. "You little shrew," she shrieked. "How *could* you have spoken these untruths to him?"

Claire blanched. "I thought I could help by —"

"No, you tried to cause trouble with Percy and me." Her voice pitched up another half octave. "You have always been jealous of me. I know you have always envied my writing, even as children."

Claire looked over to Byron with an unspoken demand for him to defend her.

Byron shrugged. "You're a mature woman. You need to fight your own battles."

Her face twisted with rage. "You cad! Is this all I can expect from the father of my child?"

Byron rolled his eyes. "I didn't force you to open your legs."

There was a collective gasp. Claire stood up, smoothed her dress, and stomped out of the room, ramrod straight.

Distracted from their clash for the moment, Percy and Mary left hurriedly for their chateau. Byron seemed unperturbed and resumed his writing.

Polidori was greatly disappointed by Mary's admission that she had no amorous feelings toward him. But at least, he thought, there would be no lead balls flying between Shelley and himself over who was to win her.

Chapter 15

The general dissension turned into sullenness. The companions withdrew into alcohol and opium-induced stupor. Mary and Shelley rarely visited Villa Diodati anymore. A dark cloud had replaced their earlier days of carefree happiness and camaraderie.

The mood was not improved by a tragic incident on the beach, just in front of the villa. The day had begun pleasantly enough for Polidori. After a leisurely breakfast, he stretched his legs on the balcony. The mid-morning sun was a brilliant yellow gold, and the scents of moist garden roses filled the air. But as he looked to the west, he saw the blinding flashes of brass badges and silver buttons. Geneva policemen, in their smart blue uniforms and white belts, stood stiffly on the beach with a crowd of onlookers. They were all gazing down at something on the beach. Overhead, a flock of gulls circled restlessly, their cries harsh and urgent.

Byron had noticed the spectacle too. Overcome by curiosity, he and Polidori walked down to join the crowd. "Back up. Give the doctor some room," an authoritarian voice boomed in French. The crowd retreated a few steps, revealing the town's physician with a leather bag, kneeling over the body of a young woman. The body was lying on its side, pale and water-logged, on the pebbly beach. In the background, little swells rose up in the lake and broke upon the pebbles, relaxing back into the water, contrasting starkly with the tense, grim scene on the shore.

111

Polidori stared at the body, astonished. He knew her. He glanced over at Byron. "Look who it is," he whispered. Byron said nothing, but Polidori noticed a strange look on his face, neither shock nor compassion, but something indefinable.

A loud voice dragged him away from his thoughts. "You there. Over here!" Onlookers were being pulled off to the side for questioning. Soon, the pair was pointed toward the sole constable who spoke English, a man with rather piercing eyes and a look of self-assurance about him. He stood towering over them as they sat, a little like school children, on the stone wall dividing the beach from the lawns above.

The constable took down Polidori's name and began questioning him first. "What is your business here?"

"I'm the physician to this gentleman. We are holidaying here."

"Do you know anything about this woman's death?"

Polidori shook his head. "Nothing," he replied gravely. "It is a complete shock."

Byron agreed, "Most assuredly unnerving." Polidori looked at him, puzzled at his response — *unnerving?*

"Did either of you know her?"

"We both did," Polidori said. "I talked with her a few times. We would see her walk to the beach often, carrying a lunch basket. She always wore a straw hat to ward off the sun and would stay until early evening."

"Anything else you know?"

112

"Yes, she was a schoolteacher in Cologny. This was her first year teaching. She told me she had come from France because teaching posts were hard to obtain after the war. She was unattached and had no friends yet in town. She was spending her summer vacation on the beach reading Romantic poetry."

"You seem to know much about her from a few conversations."

"I take an interest in people, sir."

The constable watched him carefully. "Anything else about her?"

"No," Polidori replied, only vaguely aware of the question. His thoughts had gone back to her body on the beach. He was reminded how fragile life really is. It's like a dove disappearing in a magic act, he thought. Now you see it, now you don't. Only the dove never reappears. He was jolted back to the present by the constable's next question.

"How did you come by the limp in your left leg?"

The question took Polidori by surprise. "Uh, I fell off a balcony," he said — not quite true but convincing enough, he hoped.

The constable finished his notetaking and then fixed Byron with his gaze. "And you? What do you have to say about her?" His voice was as hard as the beach rocks jutting out here and there among the pebbles.

Byron shifted uneasily on the wall. "I had a few chats with her. That's all. I introduced myself to her. I recall she was quite excited that she was meeting her favorite poet and asked me to sign a book of my poetry."

113

"And your name?"

"Lord George Byron."

Byron searched hopefully for a glimmer of recognition in the constable's face but found only suspicion.

His questioner studied him closely. "You appear to be nervous," he observed. "Why is that? Do you have something to hide?"

"No, no, not at all," replied Byron uncomfortably. "But this has hardly been the beginning of a relaxing day at the beach."

The big policeman scowled and was about to chastise him for impertinence but seemed to decide against distraction. "And did either of you speak with her last night?"

Both shook their heads. "It has been some days since I last spoke with her," Polidori said. "Perhaps if I had taken some time with her last evening, this terrible thing might have never happened."

"I've had no time for *tête-à-tête* on the beach lately," added Byron. "Creativity has called, and my readers await me. I've been toiling at my writing table night and day on a new poem."

Their interrogator grunted. "Nevertheless, did either of you see anything suspicious or out of the ordinary on the beach last evening? For that matter, did you see anyone talking with her?" His voice had an edge of frustration.

"No, nothing," Polidori replied. His eyes lowered. "I'm afraid I'm not being terribly helpful to you, Constable."

"I, too, would like to throw some light on this matter, but I have nothing to add, sir," Byron said.

114

The constable concluded by asking where precisely they lived. They pointed up to the villa. He looked toward the villa house and back to the beach, as if tracing the line of sight. Without a further word, he moved off toward another onlooker.

Polidori exhaled slowly, wondering how long he had been holding his breath. "That was excruciating," he said. It reminded him of the feeling he'd had as a child whenever he was scolded by his father for some misdeed.

Byron, too, looked relieved to get out from under the constable's scrutiny but said nothing. Polidori thought he hadn't wanted to admit being ruffled by the questioning.

They were walking back to the villa when they encountered Monsieur Marchand, a lonely widower from a neighboring chateau. He was the local busybody who filled himself with the details of other people's lives, large or small, as they happened on the beach.

"Did you hear that the death was not accidental?" he whispered slyly, like a man revealing a state secret.

"No," Polidori said, "but from the constable's questions, I wondered if they thought the death suspicious."

"Yes, and they weren't too discreet about it, either. I overheard one say it was a drowning, but that she had been a good swimmer and the lake was calm last evening." He looked intently at his neighbors.

"So how did she drown?" Polidori asked.

Monsieur Marchand had all the particulars. "The constables believe somebody drowned her...

115

There were bruises on each shoulder. She may have been pushed or held down in the water."

"The marks of murder," Byron said, almost absentmindedly.

"Yes, indeed," their informant said. "Yet she did seem like such a charming girl, just enjoying her holiday. Why would someone do something so terrible?"

That's always the question, Polidori thought as he looked toward the beach. *And who can reach into the black soul of murder deeply enough to answer it?*

Eventually, the police marched away with the body, after warning the women not to go unescorted in the area until further notice. They returned that evening, half-heartedly patrolling the beach area over the next two days and then disappeared for good. Polidori read a report a few days later in the Geneva newspaper that the police were investigating and had no suspects. That was the last he heard of this sad affair.

Yet his thoughts often returned to the body on the beach. He kept asking himself the unanswerable question: For what reason, mad, evil, or otherwise, would someone take the life of such a young and promising person?

A week after the tragedy, he was no closer to an answer. It was a cloudy day, and there was low thunder in the distance. He was settling into an afternoon nap, not dreaming, exactly, but in the peculiar twilight state between waking and sleep. Suddenly, he saw a vivid image of the teacher from

116

Cologny — not the vibrant person, full of life, that he had met, but her pallid corpse. It was standing on the beach in dim moonlight, its eyes blankly staring. The corpse was handing a book of verse with its blackened fingers to a shadowy figure. Polidori could not see all the details of the dark figure, but he knew suddenly it was Byron.

He sat up with a start, his heart pounding in his chest. Was Byron the murderer? He remembered the stories of the disappearances around the abbey … and then the vanishing of the assistant at the museum. And what of his strange reaction to the painting of the impalements and to the teacher's body on the beach?

His thoughts raced. No! Surely not. Byron was an immoral rascal, all right, but a murderer? He had not shown himself to be violent so far … but he had seemed nervous during the constable's questioning. Out of character for him.

The questions swirled about in Polidori's mind, confusing and disturbing. Was he trying to draw dark connections between things that had no real connection? Perhaps the shock of seeing the poor teacher's body had been too much for him. He poured himself a glass of his liquor. He dearly wished it would quell the churning storm of suspicion within him and his growing anxiety about Byron.

Chapter 16

As June went by, there were signs of reconciliation among the estranged companions. Mary and Percy had made peace and began to visit the villa again. Polidori no longer had to bear the glares from Shelley, and he came to attribute his suspicions of Byron to an overactive imagination. Even Claire seemed to be forgiven for her mischief. Byron and Claire, unable to resist their amorous desires for one another, established a shaky truce.

But nature was to intervene in very unexpected way. Dark, violent weather closed in on the lake in mid-June. No one had ever seen anything like it. For weeks on end, cold, torrential rainstorms assaulted the villa. White-capped breakers crashed on the beaches and flung the docked boats haphazardly onto the shore. Thunderous lightning flashed menacingly. The fury of Tambora had finally come to Lake Geneva.

Inside the villa, boredom and confinement weighed heavily on the occupants. The situation became intolerable, and Byron decided to take charge. He proposed that everyone get together before the cozy fire in the villa's drawing room for some entertainment.

He was met with skeptical looks from the others, who had had enough of rainy day diversions.

"No more cards," Polidori protested.

"No simile games," pleaded Mary.

"If I'm asked to sing along with the piano again, I shall burst," said Shelley.

"No, no, and no!" Byron said. "I've found something more interesting." He pulled out a book

118

of old German ghost stories from a shelf of well-worn titles. He read one about a band of travelers who tell one another supernatural tales and experiences. His eyes brightened. "What if each of us takes on the challenge of writing a frightening ghost story for our mutual entertainment?" He looked around expectantly at the rest. "And we will declare a winner for the best story."

Shelley rubbed his hands together in glee. "What kind of question is this for a writer? Of course, it's on!"

Polidori thought it was intended as a contest between the two literary giants, with not much expected from Mary and him. They were included out of politeness, he suspected. But what was there to lose? "Challenge accepted!" he said.

Mary's smile gave her consent.

Their initial results were abysmal. "I've got nothing notable," Shelley sighed over dinner a few days later. Byron just shrugged, and Mary looked crushed by literary failure. Polidori wrote a poor something, obviously having put little effort into it. He tossed it to the group as bad meat to the literary lions. Needless to say, his work did not impress anyone. Better this, he thought, then having good efforts demolished by geniuses.

Clearly, Byron's plan to improve their spirits was not working, but then some remarkable things happened. One day, around the drawing room fire, they were having an interesting philosophical discussion about whether human beings were governed by free will or the forces of biology. They were asking weighty questions about the principle of life and about science's prospects of ever discovering the power of creating life. What had started off as an intellectual discussion soon grew into a heated debate.

Byron championed the scientific, materialist side of the argument. "Life, including human life, is all a matter of chemical, electrical, and mechanical forces," he asserted. "Understand physics, understand how electricity interacts with matter, and you understand life. Science is discovering more every day and will find, someday, how life itself is created from inanimate materials. There's no need for supernatural notions like soul or spirit." Byron had waved the red cape in the debating arena.

Shelley led the charge. "What proof do you have for that?" he challenged.

"Well, look at Erasmus Darwin's work on galvanism," Byron countered, as if playing a game of verbal chess. "We may have a dead frog's leg, inert and apparently lifeless, but when we apply an electrical current to it, the muscles move once again, as if alive. Electricity must play a part in creating life."

Polidori protested. "The frog's leg moves, but as soon as the current is turned off the leg is still. It was not alive. The frog's leg had already lost the quality that gave it life in the first place. No, there is something else which creates life."

"What is that?" interjected Byron with a skeptical smile.

"It is the presence of life force, which can only be given by God or perhaps nature. Mechanisms and material are necessary for life but not sufficient for it. There is soul in the machine that gives the machine life. The human mind is governed by free will; our thoughts do not come from our chemistry."

Shelley nodded in agreement. "Yes, it's ridiculous to believe the great works of human intellect — our poetry, our science, our art, and music — could come from a machine. They must be the result of a higher form, a soul or great mind, which is a reflection of God."

Polidori, impressed by the eloquent words, added, "Descartes talked about the difference between mind and body. Surely, when Descartes said, 'I think, therefore I am,' he meant that mind and soul are the basis of human consciousness and life. The mind is the essence of human life; the body is the physical vehicle in which the mind and soul operate. The mind, in its free will, directs the body — not the other way around."

Byron sat back, crossing his hands behind his head. "Perhaps," he countered. "But what if Descartes was wrong? What if the human brain is nothing more than matter that produces thought and emotion when stimulated electrically? Perhaps intellect is just a higher order process in the human brain than what goes on instinctually in the brains of animals — higher, but not essentially different, not a product of soul at all. If science understands all the physical connections, it can create or modify life."

Mary looked disturbed and finally spoke up. "But look at all the chaos that man has brought upon this world — wars, disease, poverty, injustice to others. Will not his ignorance and destructiveness necessarily become part of any attempt by science to create life? What disasters, what darkness will befall us on this path?"

Mary's insights seemed to surprise Byron, but not Polidori. He knew her better. He glanced at the others, noticing their tight, serious faces. Mary's comments had been deeply disturbing, and the discussion trailed off into thoughtful, solemn silence.

Mary had taken all this in, like dry ground thirstily soaking up long overdue rain. Later, with a violent electrical storm in the background, she fell into a vivid daydream in her room. She saw the horrific image of a medical student who had violated the laws of nature and God by infusing life into body parts put together to create a hideous creature. The essence of a dark story had come to her.

Two nights later, Mary had honed her story enough to tell it to the others in the drawing room. Polidori knew Byron had expected little from her, but it was clear Mary was, thus far, the most creative of all. He marveled at how she had reached into the nineteenth century human soul and drawn out some of its deepest fears and how she had thrilled and entranced her listeners.

With mock fanfare, Byron pronounced, "Thus far, Mary, you are first in the running for the grand honor."

Mary beamed. "I think I shall call the story *Frankenstein; or, The Modern Prometheus*."

After the group, had broken up for the night, Polidori sat awhile near the waning fire. He thought that Mary's story must have been inspired by her tragic losses. Surely, Frankenstein's monster was brought forth by Mary's unconscious wish to bring her dead mother and child back to life.

He realized that Mary's daydream had fused her dark wishes, the fears of science, and the electrical storm into one horrific image upon which her story turned. He was awestruck. He wondered if he could find within himself the creativeness to write such a powerful and compelling story of his own.

Polidori had encountered the first signposts on the path to becoming a great writer. He now knew that the pain, the hurts, and the nightmares of his life were two-sided. He could be frightened and paralyzed by them, or, like Mary, could draw upon their power to write the terrifying novel he was seeking. From the obscenely grinning clown-like face under his childhood bed might come the malevolent character in his book to be.

Byron was certainly stirred by her tale, for he soon produced and told to his appreciative audience his own eerie story. Polidori would never forget the telling of the tale. A full week later, it still reverberated, like a haunting melody, in his mind.

He remembered how Byron had taken his turn in front of the great fireplace, leaning casually against its broad stones. The drawing room was dark except for the reddish hue of the hot embers. Occasionally, a flash of lightning over the lake would illuminate his features, giving them the look of a grotesque white mask. The others had gathered around him, almost like little children eagerly awaiting the telling of a deliciously frightening tale. They were not disappointed.

The story began with two friends in London in the 1700s, the narrator, who was the much younger of the two, and his friend, Augustus Darvell. It seemed an unlikely relationship. The older man was cold and shadowy about his feelings and needs, but the younger was still attracted to him as a friend.

The two decided to journey together to Turkey, where Augustus's health began to deteriorate alarmingly during their travels. The two visited an old, rundown Turkish graveyard in a remote, desolate area where there was nothing other than some ancient religious ruins. There, Augustus admitted to his friend that he had really come there to die but wouldn't reveal his reason for choosing that particular place or his secretiveness about the matter. He made the friend promise to perform a certain ritual after his death. On the ninth day of any month, he was to throw Augustus's ring into the sea at a particular place. To add to the mystery, he also enjoined the friend to keep his death a secret.

While the older man was dying, there was a remarkable happening. A large bird, a stork with a snake writhing in its beak, landed on a nearby gravestone. It stared at them, refusing to be chased away. To deepen the mystery, Augustus smiled at the bird and said to it, "It's not yet time." He then instructed his young companion to bury him under the gravestone where the bird sat.

The older man died, and to his companion's horror, decomposed immediately, turning black. The story ended with the burial of the older man and his friend's deep grief.

Polidori recalled that, a moment after Byron had finished, a scream pierced the dim room. Startled, everyone arose from their chairs to see Shelley running from the room. He had his hand to his mouth, apparently overcome by fright. Polidori knew Shelley was a sensitive sort but would have never guessed he would be so terrified. The man's reaction was a testament to the horrific impact of Byron's tale. Surely, Byron and Mary were tied for the best story.

Byron did not complete the piece but told Polidori about the frightening path he had intended his story to take. Apparently, the friend was then to return to England, only to discover that the older man he had buried in faraway Turkey was alive in London seducing the narrator's sister.

Polidori was struck by Darvell's mysterious, Lazarus-like return from the dead and his seductiveness afterward. Thinking that Byron would not finish the story, the idea grew within him to develop these strange fantasies into a full-fledged tale. He hoped it would be his great work and began writing feverishly. In his excitement, he couldn't help confiding in Mary about the project. The two met one afternoon over a cup of tea in the villa's kitchen.

She was at first taken aback. "But don't you think Byron will view this as plagiarism?" she asked.

"It's only a story fragment, Mary. I believe he is not going to write it, nor will he care if someone else does."

"But why wouldn't he develop something so original and horrific?"

"Naturally, I can only speculate, Mary. Perhaps he has become bored with it or believes it's beneath him to write it. Perhaps, too, the character of Darvell — cold, manipulative, and seductive — reminds him too much of himself."

Mary still looked uncertain, but her curiosity bested her worry. "Have you a title?"

"*The Vampyre*."

A look of fascination crossed Mary's face. "I remember reading some of the folk tales of old Europe about the dead rising in bodily form... So, what is your vampyre like?"

"It is not a recognizable monster like Frankenstein's creature, but it is horrific in its own way." Polidori saw he had Mary's interest. "The vampyre is a suave, cultured, but malevolent being. It manipulates and destroys the minds of others — a kind of mental vampyre. But at its core, it is a heartless killer."

"So, others may not recognize its evil until too late?"

"Precisely. It's adept and stealthy enough to blend in with London's social circles. It seems no different from anyone else, someone met at a party or passed on the street. Yet it can turn suddenly and violently on its unsuspecting victim."

Mary looked captivated by the idea. "And perhaps *that* is the greatest terror of all: a thing which mimics humanness. We think we can trust it, but underneath it is a foul murderer — the perfect agent of Satan."

"Yes, yes, Mary! You have it! This is the essential nature of the vampyre."

126

Polidori soon learned that he had miscalculated Byron's protectiveness toward the idea. He knew the poet had become aware that he was developing the story fragment. He did not think that Mary had betrayed his confidence. Rather, he suspected that somehow Byron had found his story notes.

Byron became increasingly distant from him and Polidori noticed his stony glances. He felt matters were coming to a head. One day in mid-August, this was confirmed. Byron summoned him to the drawing room. He stood sternly behind his writing table as Polidori sat before him nervously. The aspiring writer felt like an unruly student about to be disciplined by an unmerciful teacher.

"How dare you!" Byron shouted. "You've stolen my ideas!"

"You're talking about the vampyre?"

"Of course, that is what I am talking about!"

Polidori offered justification. "You've written only a skeleton of a story — an unfinished outline."

At this, Byron pounded his fist on the table, sending his papers flying. "No matter. It's mine to finish or not. You've begun your writing career in a most dishonorable manner — as a plagiarist. You have betrayed my trust, Polidori."

Polidori stood up and faced him across the table. "How can I plagiarize what has not been fully written?" he protested.

But Byron was in no mood for fine distinctions. "I dismiss you as my physician," he stated flatly and walked out.

Polidori was shocked by the cold finality of his words. However, he also was relieved at the prospect of escaping the tension of the villa and the corruption of Byron's presence.

He soon packed and said his farewells to the others. He would deeply miss his friend Mary, with her gentle encouragement and wisdom beyond her years. However, as he left Geneva, he knew the story he carried with him would become the most powerful he had ever written.

Chapter 17

Polidori left by coach, travelling down to Italy, where he visited his parents' estate. He was glad to be in the loving presence of his mother. His correspondence with her over the years had not been enough; he had deeply missed her. He was even looking forward to seeing his father again. Time had worn off a layer of his pain about him. However, his father was absent. "Where's Father?" he asked in a disappointed tone.

"He was called suddenly to Rome on business, Giovanni," his mother explained. Seeing her son was saddened, she quickly added, "He'll be home to see you soon. Did you receive my letter of August 3 in Geneva?"

"No. I had left the villa unexpectedly by then."

"Then you don't know that recently he told me he missed you and regrets his falling out with you. Your leaving home seems to have mellowed him, and he knows he made a grave mistake by trying to shape you in his image."

Her son was taken aback. Never would he have thought his father would give up on his ambitions for him, but evidently, he had.

The harshness of the weather from the west had not yet reached the heart of Italy, and they spent much time in the garden together under the warm Tuscan sun. Maria read, while he developed his story further. It felt again like the carefree days of childhood.

He noticed his mother curiously hovering around, trying to steal a glance at what he was writing. Amused, he remarked, "I haven't mentioned it to you, but I've been writing a novel."

"Really!" she said. "What is it about?"

"Well, it's a tale of horror. A suave, outwardly attractive vampyre blends into London high society, terrorizing and seducing it."

His mother laughed. "Terror and seduction at the same time. A delicious combination, I must say! As a little girl, I was frightened by Serbian vampyre tales, but they were always about a rather ghoulish creature who hung about graveyards — never a charming type in high circles. What a creative idea!"

"It's not mine entirely, Mother," he admitted. "I borrowed the idea from Byron, who originated it but didn't develop it fully as a story... You should have been there that night, Mother, in Villa Diodati. In the midst of a thunderstorm, Byron masterfully recited his tale to us, before the fire in the drawing room. We were spellbound, and it was totally frightening. When he didn't work on the story further, I knew I could and must. It will be my most creative work."

Maria smiled radiantly with fond memories only a mother could have. "It was right here, where we sit, that you wrote your first poems and stories as a child. You were inspired by all the children's tales I used to read you. I believe they opened your mind to the wonderful talent within you."

He looked at her, somewhat entranced. His mother's words had touched him deeply. He realized in that moment that all he needed to do was allow his inner writer to flow and express itself. He simply had to get out of his own way — to let go of the notion that only a Byron or a Shelley could show him how to write. He needed to write only from the heart, he knew. He began to write with a gusto and passion he had never experienced before.

Time flew, and his father returned home from his travels. To his son's surprise, he joined them for many long talks in the garden. They embraced for the first time since he was a child. Polidori noticed the white streaks in his father's hair had encroached further. He was older, but was he truly wiser?

"Giovanni, I'm so happy to see you again," he said when he first arrived, full of undisguised joy. "It's been a long time — too long. Are you well?"

"In body, yes. Emotionally, I've been going through some trying times," he ventured, unsure of his father's reaction. "There's been a difficult person in my life."

"Oh? And who is this person?"

"I've been traveling as the personal physician to Lord Byron. You may know of him."

The duke's eyes widened. "Your mother has mentioned his work in passing. But I understand that he has encouraged the Carbonari here in Italy and that he has some notoriety."

"That's putting it lightly."

"How did you ever become involved with such a man?"

Polidori was pleased to hear a concerned tone in his voice instead of criticism. "I was dazzled by his fame as a writer, and I hoped my own writing would gain his approval. But it was a false hope."

His father's response was encouraging. "You're young," he said, "still needing to find yourself."

This observation surprised — no, shocked Polidori. Had his father finally recognized that it was up to his son to define himself, and no one else? *Perhaps people can change and reform, after all,* he thought. *Maybe they are not really prisoners of their pasts...* He admitted, though, that he was puzzled and curious about what had brought about these changes in his father. The duke had always been a man strongly set in his ways. Polidori was still mistrustful and guarded.

As Polidori wrote, he realized he should learn more about the history of vampyrism to bring out the full evil of his character, Lord Ruthven. He had read that Serbia, above all other countries, was the ancient home of vampyre myths. He determined to visit it. His eventual destination would be a tiny, remote village in southeast Serbia called Dubacz. It was said the last vampyre had manifested itself there over fifty years before.

He told his parents his plans, horrifying them both. His mother spoke her fears first. "Serbia is so backward," she said. "It's isolated from the world and steeped in superstition."

The duke nodded. "The age of science has never come to that forgotten part of the world," he observed. "It has been under the rule of the Turkish empire, which has drawn a dark curtain over Serbia for centuries."

"These are the very reasons why I must visit the place," Polidori protested. "I want to look behind the curtain to learn about these superstitions first-hand for my book."

"They mistrust foreigners, Giovanni," his father added. "It could be dangerous, especially for a lone traveler."

132

His parents saw his determination and eventually resigned themselves to his going. They tried to protect their son in their own ways. His mother gave him an old cross that had belonged to an ancient ancestor. His father gave him an old but deadly pistol to carry with him.

After tearful goodbyes, he traveled by coach to the coast and sailed across the Adriatic to the port of Herceg Novi, Montenegro. From there, he took a coach to Dubacz. The journey was long and hard over terrible roads and rough terrain. It was not made any easier by surly border officials, and, as his parents had predicted, people suspicious of strangers.

He arrived, finally, on the tenth day of his journey. His coach pulled into Dubacz in the early evening, where he secured a modest room at the local inn. Shortly after, he went down to the bar and dining room for a meal and to get a sense of the local people.

Chapter 18

It was Saturday night. The bar and dining room of the inn were crowded, mostly with farmers coming to town for their weekend beer. The air was thick with conversation and laughter, not to mention an acrid cloud of tobacco smoke.

Polidori ordered a beer at the bar and asked the bartender if he knew anyone there who spoke English. Seeing his blank look, he tried his luck in Italian. The bartender caught the attention of a big man at the bar, who took a frothy gulp of beer from a huge stein, carrying it Polidori's way.

Polidori gestured him toward the lone unoccupied table in the place. The stranger pulled out a chair and sat down heavily, surveying him with cool, steady eyes.

Polidori introduced himself, extending a hand.

"Drago Dragonovich," the man said without enthusiasm, leaving Polidori's hand in the air. "So, what is an Englishman with an Italian name doing in a little town in Serbia?" he asked his new acquaintance, looking him directly in the eye.

Polidori pulled back his hand and grabbed his mug of beer. "I'm here researching a book."

"You're a writer?"

"I'm a doctor. Writing is a hobby of mine."

"Oh. And what are you writing about, Doctor?"

"I'm here to study the vampyre traditions of Serbia," Polidori replied. The conversation in the background suddenly died, and he felt a dozen pairs of eyes staring at him.

Dragonovich glanced uncomfortably to the side. Leaning in, he said in a hushed tone, "This is only a

134

myth, superstition of course, Doctor. But what you speak of should not be said around here. These are simple people. They are frightened by what you study. The very name is thought to attract evil to the speaker, to the village." Taking another wary look around, he added, "We must not discuss this further." The conversation in the background began to hum again.

"Just one more question," Polidori begged. "Is there anyone I could speak with about the matter?" Dragonovich shrugged indifferently.

Polidori was curious about his rather unfriendly tablemate. "Mr. Dragonovich, if you would forgive my boldness. You speak excellent English. What is it you do here?"

"I'm the chief constable for the area."

"The Serbian police? I didn't know I looked that suspicious."

"You don't. It is my business to know the business of strangers here, if you know what I mean, Doctor."

"I would think you wouldn't have that much crime in a little town like this, Constable."

"We don't anymore. But there are smugglers who run guns through here from Italy to the revolution in Greece. We do not want the Turks on our heads, do we? God knows we have had enough trouble with them. I don't suppose you have an interest in guns, do you, Doctor?"

"No. I have a pistol for personal protection. That is all, sir."

The constable grunted and stood up abruptly. He paused for a moment to look Polidori in the eye, searchingly, before turning away toward the bar.

135

A short while later the barmaid brought a simple meal and some beer. Under the napkin was a small note with three words on it: *See Doctor Radovich.* Polidori looked around, hoping to catch a knowing glance from someone, but the crowd had returned to its revelry.

The next morning, he found the doctor's residence without much difficulty. It was a modest stone-and-timber house on the outskirts of town, which also served as his office. A manservant who could not speak English but understood some Italian greeted him. The servant disappeared into the house to speak with the doctor. Upon his return, it was slowly established that the doctor was busy with a patient and would see him for dinner at six that evening.

He called upon the doctor at the appointed time, introduced himself by title, and was invited into the modest parlor. Polidori thought the place had an air of simplicity and comfort. The only hint of complexity was an old Turkish rug with colorful, intricate patterns woven within it.

The parlor seemed to reflect the character of its owner, a rather affable older man with silver hair and a rather thick, droopy mustache. His mental faculties were not slowed, however, and he was bright and articulate. He spoke good English, gained when he had traveled to England in his youth for some medical training in psychiatry.

Polidori was curious. "How did you come to be a rural doctor, sir?"

"Well, as a young man I started practicing in Belgrade, mostly with the wealthy. But I tired of catering to them and of the crowded city. I felt that the countryside was closer to my soul. Perhaps it would afford a simple life in the midst of natural beauty. I also hoped I could make a real difference as a country doctor with the peasant folk, mostly farmers around Dubacz. The town attracted me in particular because of, shall I say, some special interests of mine."

Doctor Radovich was soon introduced to some of his guest's background. The doctor was curious as to why Polidori had emigrated from Italy. He seemed genuinely interested in his life in England and sympathetic to his work with the poor.

"I loved England when I was there," said Doctor Radovich, "especially the rigor and honesty of its science and its wonderful literature. If I were still a young man, I might well be living there now, but in the beautiful Cotswolds, the land of the Bard."

Polidori smiled in hearty agreement. "I presume you appreciate Shakespeare?"

"I've read all of his plays and seen half as many in the London theaters. I especially enjoyed the supernatural scenes in *Macbeth*."

His young guest laughed. "I practically live in the London playhouses on weekends. I've seen *Macbeth* so often, I could hire myself out to play Banquo and his ghost."

The two continued their lively discussion over a simple but satisfying dinner of traditional Serbian fare. The doctor was grateful to meet another medical man, lamenting that he did not receive many guests who could join him in good intellectual discussion. After the meal, they got down to discussing the young man's reasons for visiting, over some port and a few good cigars. They ignored formalities and called one another by first name.

"So, John, what brings you to our Dubacz and in particular to my door?"

"Well," Polidori explained, "I'm writing a horror story, a novel about a 'refined,' human-like vampyre who comes to London and blends in with London society. I came here to Serbia, where the vampyre legends have been the strongest of all, to do research on the topic. I was anonymously told to see you."

His host laughed behind his cigar smoke. "No doubt anonymously. Your referral was quite appropriate, John. I've taken a special interest in the curious history of vampyrism in Serbia. Something to do with my spare time. The people know of it, of course, and are afraid of my hobby, harmless as it is. But they tolerate me, as I'm the only doctor around." He smiled for a moment. "But tell me, John, why a vampyre for your book?"

"Well, I'm inspired by the horror of the idea that the dead can rise in a malevolent form, and thought it might make entertaining fiction."

Radovich frowned. "Fiction back in England, perhaps, but not fiction here, John. The people actually *believe* these creatures exist. They have been told these stories over and over again as children, from generation to generation, for untold centuries. The terror about this is embedded in their very unconscious. So be careful with your researches, John. Don't be obvious. Play the tourist."

It was Polidori's turn to laugh. "Surely you're joking, Viktor. What are they going to do, hang me because I'm writing a book?"

The doctor regarded him seriously. "That's a distinct possibility. For centuries, people in Serbia and Romania have been accused of being vampyres and were actually executed for it. There have been documented episodes of mass hysteria provoked by the fears of vampyrism. There were searches for suspects and even the unearthing of graves to discover them. The last case of public hysteria was right here in Dubacz about fifty years ago."

"This is what I'm here to learn. Will you tell me about this, Viktor?"

"Of course." Doctor Radovich invited his guest to take pen and paper at his writing table. "A village man called Oleg Jasonovich, a convicted murderer, was hung in the village square and buried. Following his death an unusual number of inexplicable stillbirths and deaths occurred in the area, even among young and apparently healthy people. Fears grew that Jasonovich was responsible and that he was a vampyre who had come back to seek revenge for his execution."

"Pure superstition."

"Yes, but it was real to the villagers. Fears grew even greater when it was discovered that the earth around his grave had collapsed. People believed that he could come and go at will from his own grave. The body was exhumed and found to be in relatively good condition after months of interment. This, of course, frightened the villagers to the point of irrationality. We know now that many natural factors can slow down decomposition. But back

139

then, the people were convinced they were dealing with a vampyre and took traditional measures to prevent it from rising again. They staked it to the ground, decapitated it, and then placed a huge stone slab over the grave, for good measure."

His guest was shocked. "It sounds terribly gruesome to me."

"Yes, and that wasn't the worst of it. Complete panic set in when other graves were found collapsed, and it was suspected that there were more of the 'undead' around. A killing frenzy began. Local people, mostly outcasts such as petty criminals, the insane, and heretics, were accused of vampyrism and executed. This murderous hysteria spread over much of the Balkans until it was finally stopped by a decree from the ruler of Serbia at time, the Austrian Empress herself."

"This seems very similar to reports of the witch hunts and burnings in America, in Salem, I believe. Many innocent people met hideous deaths at the hands of superstition and ignorance."

"I think similar psychological forces were at work, John. At the root of this hysteria were deep fears around death and evil and the need to protect against these threats."

"But why would this take the form of vampyrism in Serbia, rather than demons, apparitions, and the like in other cultures?"

"Actually, most cultures have tales about vampyres. The creatures are called by different names but cause havoc to those around them in similar ways. But as to your question, John, there are reasons why Serbia was an especially potent brewing pot for vampyre legends. These beliefs grew out of ancient Serbian paganism, the old religion, thousands of years before Christianity took hold."

"How so, Viktor?"

"Well, the pagans believed that the soul separated from the body at death. This is common to many religions, but interestingly, they also believed that souls hung about for forty days before passing to the beyond. During this period, the souls, both good and evil, would be involved in the affairs of the living. The good souls would help harvests and do general good. However, the evil souls caused trouble: accidents, illnesses, poltergeist-like nuisances, and so on."

"Sounds frightening in a rather quaint way."

"Yes. However, the really evil souls of past murderers and heretics were believed to be able to reanimate their bodies before decomposing. They were thought to escape their graves, harass and feed upon the living and even violate their former partners and family. These nosferatu were not the suave vampyres of your book. They were ugly, ghoul-like, mindless creatures."

"You've studied psychiatry, Viktor. What were the psychological roots of these primitive beliefs?"

"I believe there were several. Ancient Serbs lived before the age of science, of course, and didn't know the natural causes of things. They could not explain rationally the threats that confronted them, like death, illness, poor harvests, and so on. They could not explain why there were people among them who were different than themselves: the slow and dull, the insane, the eccentric, the heretic, the prostitute, and the criminal."

141

The doctor took a sip of his port. "Without explanation, there could be no power to protect themselves against an unpredictable world. They seized upon superstition to explain the world and to tell them how to deal with it. They personified the cause of many tragedies in the form of the vampyre, which they could then kill. Thereby, they believed they achieved power over the bad things that happened to people."

Polidori nodded. "So, these beliefs helped them understand and control the world about them. But there is a missing link here. Why create something that becomes a problem in itself? The solution comes back to bite you, literally. It doesn't make sense."

Radovich poured the two another drink. "This is your rational mind speaking, John. We can't apply reason to the primitive, instinctual mind that underlies superstition. This is like asking ourselves what a dog is thinking when it behaves in a certain way. Likely it isn't thinking, but it is acting on instinct or habit... So, it is useless to try to make total sense of superstition."

"Do you think there are other reasons for beliefs in vampyrism?"

"Yes, I think that vampyrism represents the unconscious wish for some kind of life after death. In the case of those family members who have lost a close one, grief about the loss creates a desire that the lost person return again. But what creates the frightening belief of the vampyre is the recognition, at some level in the mind, that we are wishing for something unnatural and wrong. With that comes the need for punishment for thinking of such a thing.

142

The result is the mythical return from the dead of someone alien and destructive to us, the vampyre. We are punished for our foolish wishes."

"That's fascinating, Viktor. It reminds me very much of a story read to me by Mary Godwin in Geneva, a young writer who created the tale of Frankenstein."

Radovich clipped the end off a new cigar and lit it. "What's the gist of the story?"

"It's about a scientist infusing life, through galvanism, into dead bodies. Its message is that man should not meddle with the natural forces of creation and death; disaster will come if he does."

"That's an interesting parallel," remarked Radovich, extricating a wayward piece of tobacco from his lips. "I'll have to read her book. What was her name, again?"

"Mary Godwin. Maybe Mary Shelley by the time she publishes... But tell me, Viktor, is there anything else peculiar to the Serb situation that explains the vampyre tradition?"

"Yes, the history of the Serbs and the very nature of their lands are deeply embedded in their psyches. The people truly love this land, and for many centuries, they fought to preserve it against invasions by the Turks of the Ottoman Empire. They have suffered defeat, death, and oppression at the hands of this alien culture — one that has preyed upon them. The Serb's fear of the alien has been unconsciously transformed and personified into the myth of the preying vampyre. The dark mountains and heavily forested, remote areas of Serbia have only served to magnify these fears. What threats will come forth next from these dark forests? It's complicated."

Polidori finished his glass of port. "Yes, I now see why people can become so upset at the mere mention of this topic. It is clear to me now why their fears can be so easily focused on strangers or on those who are different from them in some way."

"I think you are now beginning to understand how important it is that you are covert in your explorations."

"Talking about exploring, Viktor, would you be willing to show me one of the graveyards of suspected vampyres?"

"Of course. There is one about two hours' ride from here in a remote area. We can meet here just before sunrise, if you would like, so we can leave secretly."

And with that, Polidori said goodbye to his gracious host and new-found friend, thanking him for his hospitality and his precious knowledge. He practically ran back to his room at the inn, eager to spice up his story with the vivid images and myths of old Serbia.

Chapter 19

They met just before daylight the next morning. Polidori arrived bleary-eyed, because he had been up late, excitedly garnishing his story with the rich details he'd learned from Dr. Radovich. They set out on horseback for what the doctor called the "unholy place."

"Why exactly is it called that?" Polidori asked.

The doctor gave a wry smile. "The holy men gave it that name centuries ago to frighten people away from the place. They wanted to be certain their precautions to contain the dead were not meddled with or undone."

"How quaint," Polidori remarked.

"Yes, but deadly serious to the old priests … and to the people now," Radovich cautioned. He did not say why that place had been chosen, but Polidori would soon find out.

As they rode on, it was obvious to Polidori why the Serbs were so close to their land. "The countryside is truly breathtaking," he gushed. Lush meadows alternated with forests against a backdrop of grayish blue mountains on the horizon. As they reached the foothills, some of the leaves were turning colour with the first autumn frosts, splashes of rusty reds and yellow golds.

They followed no more than a rough cart trail at best. The pair forded numerous crystal clear streams that flowed down swiftly from the hills to several rivers cutting through the valleys below. Although the day was dull and gloomy, nothing could detract from the sheer, rugged beauty of the place.

145

They traveled for about two hours, stopping periodically for handfuls of soft cheese and a few swigs of wine to fortify them against the slight autumn chill. It reminded Polidori of country picnics as a child in Tuscany.

The ride became more strenuous as they passed through a particularly dense and dark forest, brushing up against the tree branches encroaching on the trail. Polidori was whipped several times in the face by pine branches snapping back from Radovich's horse ahead. "This is quite an isolated place," he remarked, rubbing away the sting on his cheeks.

"Indeed, they did not want the graveyard anywhere near the village."

"More fear of the dead rising?"

"Exactly. The villagers did not fully trust their other precautions to contain the evil ones."

They finally broke into a large clearing with a background of low hills. Polidori was struck by the stark change in scenery. The clearing was completely barren, with no vegetation or grasses, save for a few dead trees still standing. Large, dark rocks jutted up from the black, hardened earth. There was a strange stillness to the place; no sounds of birds or even insects could be heard within it. It was as if nature itself had decided, for some perverse reason, to scour all life from this particular spot. The sullenness of the place could almost be felt.

He looked over at Dr. Radovich. "Is this it, the unholy place?"

The old doctor lowered his head. "I'm afraid so."

"These look like grave markers, but I don't even see any proper epitaphs."

"Superstition at work again, John. The villagers didn't want names on the stones in case someone would read them or say them and attract the evil soul to that person."

Polidori patted his horse on the shoulder. The constable had said something similar in the tavern, he recalled.

They dismounted and walked among the crude markers. There were also massive stone slabs lying flat over each of the graves, partially covered by earth.

"The barrenness of the place is astounding," Polidori remarked. "How is this explainable?"

His guide looked up at the hills. "Well, it's not the work of God or Satan, I can tell you, John. Some years ago, I investigated this place and found natural causes for the barrenness. You see those small creeks flowing down the hills just above us? They flow underground into the cemetery. I examined the geologic deposits on the hills near the creeks and found they contain large amounts of lead and mercury."

"Interesting," his companion remarked, anticipating his line of thought.

"Indeed. The creeks probably carried these poisonous metals down to the ground below for centuries, killing all the plant life in what is now the cemetery. I verified this by sampling the earth in the graveyard, finding it contained the same metals, whereas the lush areas on the cemetery borders are relatively free of the metals. No supernatural forces at work here."

147

"I'm impressed, Viktor. Your methodology seems quite sound. I don't suppose you've told the villagers about your findings."

"No, not wise to let them know I'm poking about in their graveyards and discrediting their superstitions. By the way, I was telling you about Oleg Jasonovich's grave collapsing, causing the vampyre hysteria fifty years ago. Can you guess what caused the collapse?"

Polidori laughed. "I would imagine the creeks have created tunnels under the graveyard into which the earth periodically collapses."

"Good deduction, John. The graveyard is riddled with them. So much for the undead creeping from their graves! By the way, don't step into any hollow in the earth. I'd rather not have to pull you out of one of the tunnels."

Polidori went over to a grave with a particularly large slab. He brushed off a section of the slab and noticed a peculiar marking etched into the stone. "What is this marking?" he asked, tracing its outline with his finger.

"That is a special holy symbol intended to keep the occupant of the grave from rising again. This is Jasonovich's grave; the villagers felt he was the most powerful vampyre, thus warranting special precautions. I'm not sure about the origins of the symbol, but in supernatural lore, closure of the symbol is necessary to contain the evil. Notice how there are no gaps in the engraving — not even minuscule ones — to break the closure. It's pure superstition at work."

They walked solemnly among the graves. Polidori was contemplating, again, how human ignorance begets tragedy. He remembered, for a moment, the misguided medical student in Mary Godwin's story, whose monster had brought about such suffering to others. Many of the people here and their families left behind had paid painfully for their fellow man's ignorance. He said a silent prayer for them and made the sign of the cross. He turned away so that the doctor could not see what he would call his own brand of superstition. Polidori knew that Radovich was a man of pure science and an atheist.

The way home seemed much longer. Polidori found himself tiring, his discomfort worsened by a sudden rain squall that turned into wet snow. He had forgotten the elevation they were at and had not dressed properly. The way back was not made any easier by the streams rising from the rain and their difficulties fording them.

The young author was too tired to write that evening. Taking a few drams of medicinal whisky, he collapsed onto the bed. He fell into a troubled dream. He was hovering over the unholy place. It was night, and he was alone. Suddenly, there was a great rumbling of the earth, as if an earthquake was happening. The great stone slabs were thrown up and out of the ground, canted at all angles.

The scene changed suddenly. He found himself on horseback rushing through the dark forest, whipped by the branches and terrified that the horse would stumble. They were not alone. Something in the blackness, nameless and ominous, followed him. He became caught in the thick brush on the trail. The more he pushed the horse, the more entangled he became. Whatever was behind him was gaining. He panicked, thrashing about wildly, feeling trapped. Polidori took his sword and slashed at the branches holding him. Mercifully, he broke free of the bush, only to have the horse fall trying to get across a swollen creek. He fell into the freezing dark waters. He flailed about but felt himself going down, drowning.

He woke up sweating profusely, wide-eyed with fright. He jumped up and lit the oil lamp, then went to the basin to splash cold water on his face, trying to wash away the terror. He definitely felt unwell. He was fevered and felt a cough coming on. He wondered if he was coming down with consumption. Polidori asked the innkeeper to summon Dr. Radovich. His kindly face, along with his medical bag, soon appeared in the light of the lamp. "What is troubling you, John?" he asked.

Polidori told him of his symptoms, but the doctor didn't seem too concerned. "I doubt it's consumption, John. It's probably just the cold yesterday and the rigors of our ride that have temporarily weakened you. You are not accustomed to the elevation, either, and this will tire people until they are acclimated. In the meantime, I have an excellent tonic to strengthen your body and give it energy to heal."

"Thank you, Viktor, but I've got another problem. I've just had a terrifying dream."

Dr. Radovich listened patiently as Polidori recounted the dream. "Have you ever had a nightmare like this before, John?" he asked when the account was finished.

150

"I'd almost forgotten, Viktor. As a child, I had frightening dreams of being chased by a ghoul or vampyre."

"Some stories you've heard as a child, no doubt."

"Yes, the dreams began after a servant told me the stories of the wandering people, the Roma, coming to Florence. They supposedly brought these creatures with them. Imagine, telling an impressionable young child such frightening things! I often woke up terrified after that. One night, during a summer storm, I thought I saw creatures in the garden, illuminated for a second by a flash of lightning."

Dr. Radovich was thoughtful for a few moments. "That could explain your dream tonight, John," he observed. "Perhaps the old nightmare was brought forth again tonight by the visit to the graveyard and all the talk of vampyres over the past few days. Your weakened condition may have made you more vulnerable to the old dream, as well."

"But, Viktor, there were no vampyres or ghouls, that I know of, in my dream tonight. So it wasn't the same dream."

"It may appear that way, John, but you were pursued by something unknown and menacing in your current dream. This may simply be a mask for the vampyre or ghoul of your childhood dreams. There can be much we don't see going on underneath the surface of a dream; there may be many levels to it."

"Well, if so, is there a purpose to the dreams returning?"

"I cannot say for certain. However, dreams are often attempts to heal emotional wounds, old and new." Doctor Radovich reached into his bag. "I can give you a potion to aid sleep and dreaming. If there is improvement in the dream, then this explanation is probably correct. Not to worry. Come by my office tomorrow, and we'll talk again."

Polidori awoke the next morning startled by the late hour. He had overslept due to the doctor's sleeping potion. His fever was gone, but he was still feeling drained and somewhat tense, he believed from his disturbing dream. Perhaps Dr. Radovich was right. He had overdone it physically and mentally. Nevertheless, he paid the doctor a call, as advised.

Dr. Radovich was sipping his late-morning tea in his parlor. "John! How are you feeling?" he inquired with concern.

"Still fatigued and somewhat anxious. I believe you are right that I overtaxed myself yesterday."

The doctor nodded. "Likely. Some rest and a break from your writings for a few days would probably help a great deal," he suggested. "It'll take a few days for your tonic to work, as well. Then you should be feeling hale and hearty! In the unlikely event your nerves are not better by then, I'll give you a hypnotic herb, if you'd like, and that should do it. Some tea, by the way?"

Polidori waved away the offer. "You're probably right, Viktor," he agreed, feeling better already.

"It might help, though, to tell me more about your dream, John. I have some time."

152

As his new patient elaborated upon the dream, Dr. Radovich listened attentively and did not attempt to interpret or draw meaning from it. Rather, he seemed more interested in hearing the young man's feelings about it. Radovich finally commented, "I see many people with vampyre phobias here, as you might imagine. These patients tell me dreams just like yours. They are terrified by something pursuing them in the dark, unable to see it or escape it... What helps is to have the patient bring his dark fears into the light of the rational mind."

Under the doctor's encouragement, Polidori visualized himself in the dream and talked to himself rationally and reassuringly. It reminded him of how his mother had calmed his night fears when he was a child. He was learning to be his own protective parent in his dream.

Dr. Radovich then asked him to focus on that part of the dream where he used his sword to free himself from the branches of the trees. "This begins your transformation from helplessness to power," he said. "Imagine turning your mount around now. Charge back down the trail, brandishing your sword to confront anything that might be there."

Polidori went on the counterattack in his fantasy dream. To his great relief, all he found was an empty trail in the forest. He had mastered his fear of the pursuer, he felt. He was victorious!

He took Dr. Radovich's advice and rested for the next few days. Thankfully, the dream did not return. He was even relaxed enough to revel in the bar, joining the other patrons teasing the barmaid for a little entertainment. But it was time to leave

153

Serbia, and he stopped by to say goodbye to Dr. Radovich. The doctor was working in his front flower-beds, as was his habit. He stood up and brushed the earth from his hands. "I take it you are leaving, John?"

Polidori smiled. "I've been trying to think of a memorable farewell quote from the Bard. But I've come up empty-handed."

Radovich laughed heartily. "If only we could quote him for every occasion!"

"So, it has to be a message from the heart. I want to thank you, Viktor, for your wisdom, generosity, and all your help — not to forget your general good company."

Dr. Radovich bowed slightly.

Polidori handed him a bottle of fine wine. "A small gift."

"Be sure to send me a copy of your book, John."

"I won't forget."

The two warmly embraced. Polidori walked away, turning once to look back. He saw his friend watching him from his front gate. The two exchanged a parting wave.

He returned the way he had come, crossing the Adriatic back to Italy. From there he took a coach to the French Riviera. He had hoped to soak up some Mediterranean sun before returning to England. But the cold, dark weather had by then come that far south. So, he fortified himself with French wine and a good book next to a roaring fireplace. In a few days, he set out for England in good spirits.

Chapter 20

Polidori arrived in London in late September. He was glad to be home and was heartened by the servants' warm welcome. Even Harris had greeted him with a smile.

It was a relief to have escaped the two temperamental poets he had to deal with over the last several months. He knew this had taken an emotional toll on him and that Falding's warnings had been right. He wondered if the turmoil of his "holiday" in Geneva had been a factor in his collapse in Serbia.

He threw himself back into his work with his patients, feeling again the old sense of purpose and authenticity. Moreover, his confidence in his writing was recovering from the blows he had suffered in Geneva. He started attending the literary society again and mustered the courage to recite to the assembly a poem entitled "A Soul Lost and Regained." The poem, about his experiences in Geneva and his recovery, was well received by the society — even the literati!

He felt uplifted after the meeting and resumed work that night on *The Vampyre*. The next few chapters burst forth from his pen in a torrent of words and images vividly and fully formed. He drew further upon the dark legends of Serbia to add to the power and horror of his vampyre character, Lord Ruthven.

He retired that night feeling jubilant. He believed he had captured the primordial image of horror that matched or outmatched the storytelling of Godwin. Like Godwin's tale, his story played upon the illicit creation of life from the dead, but this was not through misguided science. Even more frightening, creation came from something totally beyond man's control: the supernatural world. The result was the same. Death and tragedy came to those around it, the innocent and guilty.

He fell asleep a happy man, but unwanted images found their way into his dreams. Once again, he was on his horse rushing through the dark Serbian forest, pursued by something unseen and menacing. He struggled against the thick growth, and even the low half-moon seemed entangled in the trees. The scene was made more frightening by the sounds of the wind thrashing the branches. Suddenly, a childhood memory came of the tree shadows, jumping outside his bedroom window in a nighttime storm. His terror now exploded into panic. Even the horse was panicked. Polidori saw the whites of its eyes as it turned to look behind. It, too, was aware of being stalked.

He steadied the animal and tried to steady himself as well. He remembered Dr. Radovich's instructions. He got up enough nerve to turn and face the pursuer with his sword drawn. Something caught up to him, enveloping him even as he slashed at it. He felt himself tumbling down and down into a bottomless pit, screaming and suffocating.

Polidori woke up trembling and bathed in sweat. He lit his lamp to take refuge in its light and warmth. It was mortifying that the Serbian nightmare was back and that his efforts to confront the nameless thing had failed. Quite simply, the shadowy pursuer had overpowered him.

A flood of questions tormented him. What was this dream thing? What did it mean? Why had it come back again, despite Dr. Radovich's treatment? Why did it seem so real and terrifying? His unanswered questions only magnified his feelings of powerlessness and confusion. He took some of Dr. Radovich's sleeping potion, falling into a restless, drug-induced sleep.

He awoke groggy and weak, as if he was coming down with an illness. He felt much the same way as he had that night in Serbia when the dream first happened. He called Harris to inform the infirmary that he wouldn't be coming in that day and told him to send for Dr. Falding.

Alex arrived with his medical bag at the first opportunity. This was the first time he had seen his friend since his return. Alex was shocked by his appearance. The man before him seemed like a small, frightened child, very pale, his eyes dark and sunken, his hands trembling.

"So, John," Alex said. "What's happening?"

Polidori related in a fearful tone the disturbing dreams that had been troubling him and the apparent failure of Dr. Radovich's treatment to get rid of them. He went on at length with an account of his experiences in Serbia.

Alex listened sympathetically, with a measure of fascination. "John, I think you have a very vivid and powerful imagination that was exposed to some very disturbing things in Serbia. All of this, as Dr. Radovich said, has likely brought back your childhood nightmares. Writing your story also keeps the terror going, strengthening it. You need to take a rest from the book."

"But I did for some time, and here it is again! And Viktor's treatment didn't really make a difference... Why do childhood dreams still torment me so? Why can I not just wake up and realize that it was just a dream and there's nothing to be afraid of?"

"The subconscious can work in strange ways, and it can take time to heal itself or to be treated. But it will eventually come along. Not to vex yourself, John. I would suggest some hypnotic herbs for you rather than sleeping potions. These will tranquilize your nerves, and even if you do have the dream, you won't be so upset by it."

Falding took his friend's hand. "In the meantime, have your servants bring you preserved vegetables, fruits, and chicken soup to strengthen you. Hot milk will also bulk you up and is a minor sedative. I'll prescribe a general tonic as well. Send your servant to the apothecaries with the prescriptions as soon as possible. If the dreams don't relent within a few days, we'll do some psychological treatment for them."

But the young author did not heed his friend's advice. Words and images continued to flow profusely from his pen. It was as if the story had taken hold of its author. The tale was telling itself, relentlessly coming to its own conclusion.

The hellish dreams did not diminish, and Falding began treatment the following week. He explained his methods to his patient. "John, I'll have you recite your dream repeatedly, drawing out your feelings, much in the style of Dr. Radovich."

"But it didn't work with Radovich."

158

"Yes, I know. But there was only one session. Besides, we'll go beyond what he did. I'll ask you to recount your dream in different ways."

"How will that help me, exactly, Alex?"

"The only reason the dream is so upsetting is that you believe the dream is absolutely real when you're in it. However, through repetition you will become accustomed to the dream and the feelings it evokes. You'll realize that terror is only a feeling, and a dream is only a dream. There is no danger in either. The dream should lose its disturbing effects on you."

Polidori seemed satisfied, and treatment began. After a few sessions, he had some relief. "The dream is less intense, less frightening," he said. "It's almost as if I'm watching myself in the dream, like an actor in a play. It doesn't seem real."

Falding nodded vigorously. "Good, John. That's exactly what is supposed to happen. You're detaching from the dream."

"But will the dream go away?"

"It may or may not, but if you're not upset over it happening, it shouldn't disturb your sleep. You'll simply dream calmly and even forget you've dreamed."

Unfortunately, despite the initial signs of progress, his dream returned, more powerful and frightening than ever. Falding was puzzled by this unexpected turn. To add to his concerns, his friend was now totally sleepless. Even the powerful sleeping potion failed to help. Falding knew if he did not restore his sleep soon Polidori would weaken

159

rapidly. The situation was becoming desperate for both of them.

Chapter 21

The treatment went on, but Polidori's nightmares stubbornly continued to torment him. Falding decided to do dream analysis to draw out the deeper meaning. He asked his patient to record his dreams for their sessions.

One cold but sunny fall day, the two met again beside the fire in Polidori's library. Polidori presented a most striking and unusual dream and told of the remarkable turn of events that followed.

"I actually had a wonderful dream last night — a welcome relief after all of the nightmares," he began. "I dreamed I was looking from a hilltop at a springtime field covered with millions of wildflowers, colored brilliantly in deep oranges, yellows, and touches of mauve. As I walked down to pick some, an amazing sight presented itself. The multitude of flowers rose into the sky and transformed into beautiful butterflies. Yet there was order in the apparent chaos of color and movement. The butterflies were linked together in little circular chains, wreaths of color against the deep blue sky. Each wreath helped another to rise even further above the fields.

Polidori paused, looking exhilarated. "As they rose, I was drawn into the vortex caused by their mass movement. I found myself flying along with them, and I became a giant butterfly interlaced with all of the others. The feelings of elation and freedom were indescribable. I rode the wind currents, soaring through and above the clouds, gliding, twirling, and whirling to dizzying heights, leaving below all my cares and worries upon the earth. I was king of the sky.

"Yet in the distance there were dark clouds rolling down the mountains. Before they reached me, I awoke. Morning had come, and I rushed downstairs to record the dream in my study. As I wrote out this delightful dream, something truly remarkable happened. I heard a gentle fluttering, a light tapping upon the study window. I turned, and there on the windowpane was a beautiful butterfly with the same brilliant markings as in my dream — a type I had never actually seen before in this part of England."

"That's remarkable, John."

"I was … transfixed. I went to the window to gaze at this wonder, but the joy of the moment was short-lived. The sky suddenly blackened, and a violent thunderstorm rattled the windows; the heavy rain pinned the butterfly to the windowpane. At that moment, a dark mass struck the window with a loud thud. Startled, I jumped back to see a large black crow snap up and devour the butterfly, tearing off its wings. Bits of the butterfly were scattered over the windowsill. The crow perched for a moment on the windowsill, the remains of the butterfly hanging out of its beak. It stared at me with beady red eyes and then flew off with its prey into the storm."

Polidori remained quiet and contemplative. Falding asked, "How did you feel as you described the first part of your dream to me, John?"

"I felt wonderful and free. I knew I had the power to recover from this despair and to throw off these dark dreams."

The psychiatrist was intrigued. "What in the dream gave you that power, John?"

"I think it was linking with the other butterflies that helped me rise high above the earth, and yet I was able to be me, too, to fly free on my own."

"So, your close connection with others gives you strength and the power to heal, yet you are not so close that you cannot be yourself."

Polidori seemed moved. "When you say it that way — yes," he said.

"Is there something else in the dream that gives you power to recover, John?"

"I believe that the side me that loves the beauty and wonder of natural things gives me strength."

"The artistic side of you?"

Polidori smiled broadly. "Yes. I remember being in that beautiful Tuscan garden with my mother, as a child. I was so curious about everything that was happening there, writing stories, drawing the flowers, the birds, and the other inhabitants of the garden. It was all totally wondrous to me."

"How do you feel now, remembering the garden?"

"I feel safe. I feel my roots and being close to my mother. I feel joy again. I feel childlike wonder again."

Falding placed his hand on his friend's shoulder. "Yes, and I believe you have the power to bring these wonderful feelings back into your life again... But there are some obstacles on your path. Your dream ends with some dark clouds rolling down the mountainside. How did you feel about that, John?"

Polidori shifted uncomfortably in his chair. "I was troubled. Something was coming to spoil the joy and freedom I had in that moment. I tried to put it into the background and then woke up. It was like closing the doors and windows to a summer storm that's coming, but it's still rumbling low and flashing faintly in the distance."

"John, we often try to block out the dark times and the pain in our lives to protect ourselves, but if we let them come, we can learn from them. Can we return to the actual coming of the storm and the crow? How did you feel about them?"

Polidori's face darkened. "I was angry that the storm had drenched and pressed the butterfly to the window. I felt my anger turn to rage as the crow devoured the butterfly, at its cruelty toward something so innocent and beautiful." He became tearful.

Falding leaned in. "What are you feeling now, John?"

"I'm sad that bad things happen to spoil the good things in life, the precious moments of joy. I sometimes feel that my life is like a child's sandcastle. My happiness can be swept away in a moment by a stormy tide. What is the point of being happy, if this is only going to be taken away again?"

"So, you hold on to your despair... It's predictable. Better to do that than to be happy and not know when your happiness will be lost?"

Polidori nodded.

The psychiatrist probed more deeply. "Do the crow and the storm evoke other feelings in you?"

Polidori was silent, but Falding could tell he was stirring feelings, though perhaps not yet

164

consciously. "John, have you had deep feelings of anger and sadness toward people in your life who were important to you?"

Polidori's eyes seemed to glaze over, and he continued to be silent for a time. He spoke at last. "I don't know. I cannot recall any feelings like that, right now."

Falding knew Polidori was blocking feelings at some level in his mind, and he tried to draw them out. "Not even about Lord Byron and your father? Have they not been the most important and the most hurtful men in your life?"

More silence and a look of confusion on his patient's face.

Falding decided to cast out further interpretations to see what he could draw in. "John, I wonder if each, in his own way, has thrown a shadow over your life and your happiness? Could it not be that you have feared losing your freedom to be you, losing part of yourself to them, just like the butterfly trapped on the window by the storm and devoured by the crow?"

His patient's persistent silence prompted Falding to interpret it as well. "Do you think, John, that you have had dark feelings toward these two that you have avoided, submerged in your unconscious, beyond easy reach — just like when you woke up to avoid facing the coming storm in your dream?"

Falding really did not expect an answer to these questions and asked no more. He thought there was an irony in his second question. Polidori had confessed that he regarded Byron as a symbol of liberation, but what if it was indeed true that he also

165

feared losing his freedom under the spell of the famous man? That would have been a wrenching dilemma.

He could not point this out now, but his friend had been given something to reflect on. The seeds were planted; it was his choice to tend them or neglect them. What he would do was unclear. However, what remained clear was that his road to recovery would be a long and difficult one.

Chapter 22

Polidori had truly missed Mary since leaving Geneva and had decided to correspond with her. He finished composing a letter to her in his library on a bright Saturday afternoon.

Dearest Mary,

I hope this letter finds you well and that you and Percy are enjoying your holiday.

Is the weather still so atrocious? I am also very curious about how your Frankenstein is developing.

I have gleaned a wealth of knowledge about vampyre lore from a fascinating visit to Serbia, from which I have recently returned. I am making good use of this, and my character Ruthven is rapidly becoming a worthy vampyre!

I regret to say, though, I have been mysteriously afflicted by nightmares since Serbia. You might imagine the effects of insomnia that come from these. My psychiatrist friend Alex Falding and I are working diligently on the matter, and I suspect we will soon attempt to understand the deeper nature of these distressing dreams. So not to worry.

I have missed your thoughtful and encouraging presence, and I hope we will correspond regularly.

I remain yours,
John Polidori

He did not confide in Mary that he had been thinking about other, rather unusual ways of understanding his nightmares. He felt that Falding was about to take the path of drawing out the unconscious causes, as he had done with the "butterfly" dream. The rational part of his mind wanted to believe in such natural, scientific explanations — exactly what he would tell his own patients if they encountered disturbing dreams. Yet somehow these explanations did not sit well with his intuitive side. He had particular reservations about Dr. Radovich's opinion that he had overtaxed his unconscious mind with frightening images in Serbia. Part of him felt treated like a child who had nightmares after listening to a frightening story. But he was not a child, he protested inwardly. He no longer had to look under his bed for the bogey-man.

However, no matter how much he tried, he could think of no alternatives to Dr. Radovich's diagnosis. That left only irrational possibilities. There had to be something stirring within his sleeping brain that could not be understood in rational, scientific terms. He wanted to rebel against such mystical thinking, but he forced himself to continue this train of thought. Could there be some kind of genuinely occult phenomenon, something supernatural that was responsible for his nightmares?

He remembered that as a curious student in Rome, he had acquired a book on the occult. He retrieved the tattered, cloth-bound book in his library. He turned to a yellowed report within it on the subject of dreams, written by an Indian mystic in 1760.

The dream is another level of being — a shadow world within sleep. The dreamer is more open to the spiritual realm than in the awake, conscious state. He may transform into the subtle body, the soul, and travel outside of the physical body, tethered to it only by a thin thread.

But the dreamer must be careful not to be away too long. His absence creates a void in the dream mind, which may be invaded by another traveler. Such a traveller may try to take over the dream mind. The invader can manifest itself in nightmares and may even battle the dreamer for possession of the material body.

Polidori shook his head, reprimanding himself for entertaining such superstitious notions. Surely, they were too incredible to be true. Before the nightmares began, he had dreamed only rarely. This would have left little opportunity for a "dream traveler" to invade him. Besides, he never recalled having a traveling dream at any time in his life. How could the report apply to him? He reached out again to rational reality. Had he really ruled out all the scientific possibilities? How could he know?

He fled from this confusion, throwing himself into his story. He had already begun developing Lord Ruthven's dress and appearance. Ruthven was portrayed as a tall, gaunt figure with a pallid face and cold gray eyes. Otherwise, his features were strikingly handsome. He was totally dressed in black, wearing a large red ruby ring with an elegant silver symbol on it.

Polidori felt the ring should reflect the two sides of Ruthven: suave and civilized but also brutishly malevolent. He thought of overlapping the symbol on the ruby with a mark of evil, but what? He remembered the unholy place in Serbia and the symbol he had traced on Oleg Jasonovich's tombstone. No, it wouldn't do. It was Christian. But what if he changed it to represent evil in some way? He took his pen and drew and redrew the symbol, manipulating it, changing its form, until at last he found the perfect shape for his purposes. Polidori sat back in his chair, appreciating his work. Ruthven now had a ring admirably suited to his dual nature.

Satisfied, he returned to the core problem: the mystery of his nightmares. He remembered they had first occurred the night after he had been writing his story in the Serbian inn. The story had become particularly powerful and intense as he wrote into it the evil, horrifying details from the accounts of vampyrism in Serbia. The dreams had gone away for a long while when, under the advice of Dr. Radovich, he stopped writing the story. They had returned when he had resumed his writing in London. There had to be a connection between his writing and the disturbing dreams.

A vivid scene from the distant past suddenly flashed into his mind. He saw himself as the four-year-old in the Tuscan gardens with his mother, laughing at the hummingbird landing on his finger. It was so real that he could hear the whirring of its wings and feel the tiny claws grasping at his finger. The memory left him as suddenly as it had come. But why had the memory come? What was it telling him? He had no answers.

It was getting late, and all this intense effort had tired him. He took some of Alex's hypnotic herb and slipped into sleep.

Deep in the night, he awoke with a start. He sat upright on the bed, fully awake and vigilant. The hairs on his skin were bristling. It was a moonless night and perfectly dark in the bedroom. He looked over to the left, and there before him, no more than six paces away, were two red eyes glaring at him in the darkness. Whatever they might have belonged to was vague and formless, as if part of the darkness itself. A cold, fearful realization seized him. They were the same eyes as on the crow that had watched him through his study window.

The eyes stared, unblinking. In shock, Polidori could not resist staring back into them, transfixed. They exerted a kind of pressure on his brain, which became a searing pain. He did not know how long this lasted. It was as if this was happening in a strange part of time and space. But, mercifully, the eyes faded at last and vanished altogether, as mysteriously as they had come.

He collapsed exhausted into his chair, with a severe headache. He could not stop trembling, so great was his terror. He took a gulp of whisky to calm his nerves, struggling to place the stopper back into the decanter. But he could not get the image of those piercing, fiery eyes out of his brain. He fled to the safety of the drawing room downstairs. He sat before the fire, awake all night, determined to have Harris fetch Falding at a decent hour.

The psychiatrist was at his side at first light, and Polidori recounted his bizarre experience. Falding listened patiently to the whole story. When it was finished, he took a deep breath and spoke. "John, this was a hallucination, a false perception that didn't exist outside of your mind. It only *seemed* to be real. I believe that the vivid images of your nightmares, combined with the memory of the crow at your window, entered your visual pathways

171

tonight. A hallucination was created. All of this has the same root cause: unconscious feelings are coming to the surface, first in dreams, then in a hallucination."

"But, Alex," Polidori protested, "this was so real, almost palpable. It was just as real as you are, right next to me now." He pushed his friend's shoulder gently with a finger to demonstrate the point. "It was not imaginary."

"John, the mind can be subtly deceptive. It doesn't just passively register what is out there, outside of itself. It tries to construct reality, too. It can project its needs outside of itself, making them into visual images that it regards as real."

His young patient looked perplexed. "What do you mean, exactly?"

"Look at the phenomenon of the mirage, for example," Falding elaborated. "People lost in deserts are known to hallucinate oases in the distance. Their intense thirst creates these images, which seem so real that they walk further into the desert toward them, perhaps dying in the attempt. Similarly, unconscious needs can create false visual images. I believe this is what has happened to you."

"But why the red eyes? Disembodied red eyes?" Polidori asked in agony.

"Well, you mentioned that the red eyes were those of the crow which came to your study window. The crow's eyes must have some kind of unconscious meaning for you. This should become clear as we explore the unconscious mind more deeply."

Falding put a reassuring hand on his friend's shoulder. "In the meantime, if the hallucination reoccurs, know there is nothing real or dangerous about it. The eyes are only a reflection of your mind. As your mind heals, they will vanish for good... Not to worry, John. We'll get together again, soon."

Part Two
The London Terrors

Chapter 23

It was the early morning of October 18, 1816. Constable Johnson was on patrol on a cobblestone street in East London. His lantern could barely penetrate the profound darkness. He turned up his collar against the cold, foggy air.

Occasionally, he would see the shadows of couples against the walls of the tenements or in the alleys between. The constable ignored them. They were the street women and their clients. He had been told long ago that headquarters was interested only in criminals and the gangs.

So far, all had been quiet. The residents of the tenements had long gone to bed. He looked at his pocket watch. It was 2:00 a.m. *Six more hours to first light*, he thought, *and then home*.

Suddenly, high-pitched female screams broke the silence. He blew his whistle and ran toward the sounds. A tearful, near hysterical woman almost ran into him at the entrance of an alleyway. At first, she stared at him, unable to utter a word. Then she screamed, "In there!" pointing to the alley. "Mary, mother of God!"

Johnson rushed into the alley, only to stumble out a few moments later, retching. The whistles and lights of the other constables converged on the alley.

Inspector McLaughlin and Sergeant Higgins of Scotland Yard arrived at the murky scene of the murder at about three in the morning, tired and irritable from being woken up so early. They entered the blind alley carefully along the walls, so as to avoid overly disturbing the scene.

The body lay on the ground in the alley. In all his years of policing, McLaughlin had never encountered anything so unnerving. What was once a person appeared now as a crumpled heap of clothes and gore. The body was horribly mutilated, the eyes gouged out as if they had been spooned out like jelly from a jar. The neck had a jagged wound, which had bled out to a dark pool on the ground. There were five red blotches on her throat.

"There's something on the forehead," observed McLaughlin. He looked closer. "Why, there's a mark carved into her forehead by something sharp, perhaps the tip of a knife blade. It looks like some kind of odd design. It's geometric, for God's sake!"

Higgins looked astonished. "What does it mean? Why would the killer do that?"

"I don't know, but I think it must symbolize something for the murderer. It's bizarre."

The light from the lanterns projected their shadows grotesquely onto the stone walls of the adjacent building. The shadows swayed dizzyingly back and forth as the lanterns swung on their hinges, amplifying the sickening effects of the scene.

The situation became even stranger as the scene was further examined. "Higgins," McLaughlin said, "look at the ground. What do you notice amiss there?"

Higgins looked down and paused. His jaw dropped. "Why, there's only one set of footprints into the alley."

"Yes, and they look like the victim's size. And look how there are drag marks between the prints. There's no blood trail from the entrance of the alley or any sign of violence at the entrance."

"So, she's been dragged from the street and killed in the alley."

"Exactly."

"But how could that be? Where are the murderer's prints, Inspector? The blighter didn't just float in and out of here."

"No, it's inexplicable. Obviously, there's something we aren't appreciating here." He stepped back from the body. "Higgins, the eyes are nowhere to be seen on the body or in the alley."

"You mean ... they've been taken?" asked Higgins, his voice rising in pitch.

"Evidently so."

"But why, sir?" exclaimed Higgins, his eyes widening with horror.

"Well, I'm not sure... I wonder if the murderer took her eyes as a kind of gruesome memento."

"You mean a trophy of some sort? Like those hunters in Africa?"

"I'm wondering... I just hope we don't have here a collector of human trophies," McLaughlin said darkly. He glanced over at Higgins. The sergeant's face looked almost as pallid as the victim's.

Searching for more details, the inspector looked up the wall of the building. "Look, Higgins. About eight feet up. There's blood with blond hair, like the body's, stuck to it. Now, how was the body raised that high and why?"

Higgins shook his head in disbelief.

McLaughlin noticed the constables were confused and bumbling about in shock. He issued a flurry of orders. "Let's get to the bottom of this, men. Johnson, fetch a ladder and look for any evidence that the murderer used the roof — a rope or pulley up there or any footprints. Higgins, have the men fan out in the area. Look for anything unusual. See if there are any witnesses and what friends and family might know about this. Find out if she had any disagreements with anyone, and if anyone had a grudge against her. Look for evidence of prostitution... And Higgins, for God's sake find out what's holding up the doctor."

McLaughlin's official report, October 20, 1816:

Brutal mutilation murder of a thirty-five-year-old flower vendor, one Molly Muggins, in the East End. Body found by a female friend. No signs of robbery, sexual assault, or prostitution. No obvious motives. No murder weapon found or suspects identified. Inexplicable evidence at the scene: lack of murderer's footprints, evidence that the body had been lifted eight feet up the adjoining building's wall. Strange geometric design or symbol etched into the victim's forehead. No signs body was hoisted up from the roof of adjacent building. Old rope found on roof — possibly left by workmen, along with other debris — was not sturdy enough to have lifted body. No footprints or other indications that murderer used roof. Consulted professor at the university regarding symbol. Says design does not resemble any known religious, magical, or secret society symbols. He will do further research on it.

Report from examining physician, Dr. J. Caruthers:

Victim did not die from blood loss but from strangulation. Appears victim was suspended up the side of the wall, over eight feet high. Strangled by one powerful hand. No explanation for these highly unusual findings.

Recommendations:

Double patrols in the area. Continue questioning of local people. Inquire about possible reward for information.

Chapter 24

On the bitter afternoon of October 18, 1816, Dr. Falding heard a rapid, insistent knocking at his residence door. He opened it to find Polidori's butler, Harris, shivering on his doorstep. "Doctor, you must come quickly," he implored. "Master Polidori has taken a turn for the worse."

Falding left a note under the doorknocker cancelling the appointment with his next patient, with apologies. He grabbed his medical bag and hurried after Harris to Polidori's home, which was not far away.

Falding found him in his library curled up in a stuffed chair, pale and disheveled. A newspaper was strewn over the table in front of him.

"John, what is it?"

Polidori just looked at him, apparently unable to speak, and handed him the front page of the morning newspaper. **BRUTAL MURDER IN EAST END OVER NIGHT!** Falding read the rest out loud. "Molly Muggins, aged thirty-five years, was found by a friend, savagely murdered in East London overnight. Police would not reveal details of the scene, but there appears to have been a dreadful mutilation, according to the distraught friend. The friend also remarked that Molly seemed distressed for several days before her murder, but Molly wouldn't reveal what troubled her. Police are investigating, but as yet have no suspects."

"Well, this is very sad, very tragic," Falding said. "As you know, better than most, there's much violence in the East End. What is it that disturbs you so about Miss Muggins, John?"

Polidori closed his eyes, as if mustering all his strength to speak. "Alex, it — it was not a person who killed that woman."

Falding stared for a few moments at his friend. "Well, what did then?"

"The manifestation did it. The red-eyed thing did it!"

The psychiatrist was astonished. "John, we have established that the red eyes are a hallucination, a creation of your unconscious mind for certain purposes. A hallucination cannot kill someone."

"I — I wish I could believe that. I would be more than happy to surrender to your treatment if what you say is true. But it's not true. The red eyes are real, and whatever they belong to killed that poor woman."

"Well, even if we were to assume that there is a malevolent presence — which there isn't — why *must* it have murdered that woman?"

"It is as I feared. For a while, I thought the manifestation only tortured mentally. It tormented my mind with its silent, relentless, glaring presence. But as I stared into its eyes, I sensed the hatred and cruelty deeply within its black heart. It's a ruthless killer without conscience or morality to govern it... Then the most incredible of thoughts came into my head! This was like the character of my book, Lord Ruthven! The red-eyed manifestation *is* the incarnation of Lord Ruthven, the torturer and the murderer!"

"Let me get this clear, John. You're claiming that the red-eyed 'manifestation' is your character, Ruthven, becoming real, and that it murdered that poor woman."

"Yes. Last night the eyes disappeared for a few hours, returning later in the night. I believe it was doing its murderous business then with the victim."

"But John, the hallucination has disappeared for days on end as our treatment took hold. There were no murders on those nights, to our knowledge."

"Yes, but *this* time it stepped out for a brief period to do its killing, Alex. I'm positive of it. I could sense its gloating, its feelings of power and dark satisfaction, when it returned. I believe it savored the killing even more because it had latched on to her, torturing her mind, days before. This was why Miss Muggins was reported by her friend to be distressed prior to her murder."

"I believe you are now developing delusions," said Falding, his voice full of concern for his friend's sanity. "A fictional character cannot kill anyone, any more than a hallucination. Your unconscious has caused you to believe your hallucination and your character are murderers in order to express the anger that you have toward your father and Lord Byron."

"But why would my unconscious take that path?"

"Because by expressing anger in this way, you don't have to take responsibility for it. You make it into something murderous outside of yourself and beyond your control. Don't you see, John, that we need to help you voice that anger directly, in healthy ways, and accept it as a part of you? It is no sin, no crime, to be angry, given what you went through with Lord Byron and your father before him."

"But, Alex, surely the red-eyed crow devouring the butterfly at my study window was an omen that

181

the murderous part of the manifestation was yet to come. The killer crow at my window was real. It foretold that the manifestation would kill soon in the human world, and it did. Here's the proof before our eyes, in the newspaper."

"John, let us apply our God-given reason here. The appearance of the butterfly was a pure coincidence, a chance event and no more. The crow was simply a higher creature in nature's order. Insects, like the butterfly, are its prey. The crow just happened to find the butterfly at its vulnerable moment at your window. There is no deeper significance here."

Polidori crossed his arms over his chest. "I believe this thing is as real as the natural world you describe, Alex. I don't believe that the appearances of the butterfly and the crow were pure chance. It stretches the mind too far to believe that! The butterfly was the incarnation of the butterflies in my dream, the crow the embodiment of the coming storm."

Falding sighed heavily. The psychiatrist in him could not tolerate this foray into the world of the supernatural. "It stretches the mind too far that these creatures were created by your dream!" he said. "A dream is only a dream and not a thing in the real world." And so, the debate went on in its frustratingly circular way.

Chapter 25

Inspector McLaughlin attended the humble funeral of Molly Muggins several days after her murder. Formally, he was there to pay the respects of Scotland Yard; personally, he came out of sympathy for her tragic circumstances. It seemed to him only yesterday that he had lost his father in another brutal murder.

It was cloudy and gloomy — a fitting day for the occasion, McLaughlin thought. The trees stood like bleak, naked clusters of sticks with their dried-up, yellowed leaves strewn on the ground around them.

There were few present besides the inspector. Molly had no family, having somehow made her way as an orphan on the streets of East London since she was eight years old. A couple of her female friends stood around weeping as the vicar offered his prayers. Sadly, though most of her worldly goods were sold, a casket could not be afforded for her. She had to be wrapped and buried in her best blanket.

McLaughlin walked away after the ceremony in a dismal, brooding mood. He mused that here was a human being who had loved and been given love. She'd had the courage and the resourcefulness to survive the world of poverty. Then she found herself in the wrong place at the wrong time, and her young life had been extinguished for no apparent reason. The waste and the tragedy of it all were striking and incomprehensible — even to a veteran copper like himself, who was supposed to be hardened to such things.

He looked upon the hills surrounding the cemetery, hoping for some distraction from his painful thoughts. He caught sight of a high, ornate iron fence beyond which were massive marble and fine stone monuments. It was obviously a cemetery for the wealthy. McLaughlin shook his head slowly. Class disparities carried on even into death.

He knew Molly would not have come to this sad ending had she been born into a wealthy family. Life at times seemed to be a roll of the dice, a series of random events without meaning to connect them. He was not a religious man, but he felt the need to talk to a god, if there was one. And he left that sad place saying a silent prayer for Molly Muggins and for everyone.

Inspector McLaughlin had been most uneasy since the murder and funeral of Molly Muggins. The department had made no progress in its investigation and had no suspects. The grim details of the murder — the ghoulishness of it, the strange symbol cut into the victim's forehead, the lack of apparent motive — suggested to him the work of a mad-man. This was someone who killed for bizarre reasons or perhaps for none at all. At any rate, the murderer would kill again, he believed.

In the early morning of October 25, 1816, his worst fears were confirmed. At 3:00 a.m., he was suddenly roused out of his bed by persistent rapping and someone calling for him at his front door. He fumbled and grumbled his way through the dark in his night-clothes, pausing only to curse when he stubbed his toe on a wayward piece of furniture.

McLaughlin found Higgins at the door, looking grim. "There's been another murder in the East End, Inspector," he announced. "One of the lads on patrol found the body. I don't know the details, but it looks bad, sir — very bad."

The murder scene was in a particularly poor district of East London. The old, rundown brick and stone tenements were coated with the gray grime of centuries of neglect. There were black cavities in the walls where the brick or stone had fallen out. The streets were littered with this debris, making it difficult for horses and people to walk. The air was foul with the pungent smell of refuse and sewage in the streets. There was a choking, smoky haze from the stoves of those able to buy a few morsels of coal to keep away the autumn chill.

McLaughlin and Higgins were not prepared for what they saw. The behavior of the constables was the first clue that something particularly shocking had happened. They were milling around, shaking their heads and talking in low tones. They gaped up at the tenement wall facing the street. McLaughlin followed their gaze. Suspended high up the wall was the body of a man, his limbs splayed in an upside-down position against the wall.

The inspector approached the body. He saw that rusty cast-iron spikes had been driven through the ankles and wrists, deep into the mortar between the bricks. The body reminded McLaughlin of a side of meat stretched out to dry and cure on a pole frame.

"Christ, Higgins, look at this!" McLaughlin exclaimed in disbelief. "Why would someone do this? *How* would someone do this...? The body's big, and he must have been a powerful man who couldn't have been easy to overcome. And to lift all that weight that high, hold it up, and spike it? Unbelievable!"

Higgins shook his head. "There must be a ruddy bunch of 'em to do that …maybe some gang of murderers They had to have rope and pulley to hoist him up that high, Inspector," he ventured. "No way round it, unless we're dealing with a bloody magician!"

"We'll have the doctor look for any rope marks on the body," the inspector replied. "And look, there's no blood loss from the spike wounds. In fact, look at how pale and white the body seems ...he's been exsanguinated, for God's sake!"

"Ex — what?"

"Exsanguinated, Higgins. The blood must have been drained from the body before it was hung up."

"But there's no blood on the ground, Inspector. Where is it?"

"I don't know, but it could have been drained with embalming tools, with needles, tubes, and the like."

"But who would have the nerve to spend all that time taking out blood and hanging the body up, Inspector, when the police are all around? And for what blinking reason?"

McLaughlin reflected on the question for a few moments. "To deliberately frighten and shock, Higgins — to let others know he has the power to do what he wants, when he wants, with impunity. It's a demonstration to us and to Londoners." He paused to chew over his own words. He hoped he was wrong about this, for if not, they were all in for a fearful ride.

Inspector McLaughlin spoke to Sergeant Mulligan. The sergeant had been supervising the questioning of the crowd, which had by then gathered around, gawking and pointing. "Do we know anything, Mulligan?"

"Yes, sir. This is or was Johnny McIver, well known in this area as a coalman. You know, he runs after the coal carts going down the street to snag pieces of coal that fall off. He sells it to those who can afford it."

"Anyone who would want to harm him?"

"No, Inspector. They say he was a gentle, well-liked man with no grudges against him."

"Robbery?"

Mulligan shook his head. "No, sir. He had nothing to rob, really."

"Anyone see anything, Mulligan?"

"Again, no, sir. People were too frightened to come out of their tenements when they heard the screaming."

"Anything else, Sergeant?"

Mulligan had nothing to add.

"Well, keep a sharp eye out, then, and continue your questioning at first light, including family or friends, if he has any. And Higgins, make sure that you get the body down before dawn. We don't want this displayed for the morning traffic, do we?"

McLaughlin wrote up his report a few days later. It was the same pattern: facts not easily explained, the same design carved in the forehead, no useful information gathered, and no suspects identified. The coroner had added to the mystery in that he found no rope marks on the body to indicate hoisting. Not unexpectedly, he determined that the body had indeed been exsanguinated, for whatever reason, through openings in major blood vessels. Embalming tools could have been used.

Obviously, the same murderer or murderers committed the crime, McLaughlin concluded. The weird nature of both crimes tended to confirm he or they had to be quite mad. As the inspector finished his report, he felt a cold stab of fear in his stomach. There would soon be other mutilated bodies on the streets of London, he knew, and he had not the slightest idea how to prevent the impending massacre.

The second murder was not the only matter that occupied the authorities that night in East London. A Mr. Peter Wallington, who lived a few blocks from the crime scene, summoned the police shortly after midnight.

Mr. Wallington was a city clerk who had fallen on hard times after his dismissal. He reported that he and his family had been terrified by a sudden, terrific pounding on his front door. Wallington described to Constable Murdoch the sheer terror of the moment.

"The noise was deafening, and the force of the blows shook our tenement and frightened us out of our beds. I feared the hinges of the door would give way under the powerful pounding and that the door would burst in, letting in whatever violence was out there. There were no words coming from the intruder, just a loud wailing mixed with what sounded like crazy laughter. It was low in pitch, yet it was high. I could not tell if it was a man's or a woman's voice.

"My wife, Betsy, hiding behind me, began to shake uncontrollably, screaming, 'Don't let it in! Don't let it in! It's the devil himself come for us!' A devout Catholic, she called upon the Virgin Mary to save us and thrust a cross in front of us toward the door in her trembling hands.   "The pounding then stopped, just as suddenly and mysteriously as it had begun. Then I noticed a putrid smell coming from under the door. A few hours later, I finally worked up the nerve to crack the door open and peer into the night. I saw only the thick fog rolling and roiling around in the dark, empty streets."

Chapter 26

Falding sat with a cup of tea in his drawing room, reading the newspapers spread over his dining table. The murder over-night had made the front pages. Once more, the details were sparse, and he suspected the police were purposively revealing little. However, rumors abounded on the streets. The newspaper vender had remarked to him that it had been another mutilation murder. He knew Polidori had probably read the reports by then, so he decided to visit him promptly.

Falding found him in his chambers in the early afternoon, still in his evening robe. He sat down beside him.

"I knew it would kill again," Polidori mumbled.

"Why?"

"Because it has the taste of blood and of its own power to spill it."

"But we don't even know if the murders are connected."

"It faded out again last night, to find a new victim, I'm sure. Then it briefly returned again. I sensed its victory and ghoulish glee. It killed that poor man, most definitely. I have no doubt that it mentally tortured him first — we just don't know about it yet — for this is the pattern of Ruthven."

"Your character, again."

"None other. When it is finished manipulating its victims, toying with its prey, it ruthlessly kills them. It is the heart of evil, Alex. It wants to destroy my very soul. It *will* go on killing again and again, until somehow stopped."

"John, I hope you see that all this is simply poetic imagery symbolizing your fears of your unconscious anger. I believe you are afraid that if you actually did voice your anger, it would destroy your world."

"What does that have to do with Ruthven?"

"As we have discussed, Ruthven symbolizes anger toward Byron that you cannot express directly to him. Instead, you have made him the villain in your book... You must admit that Byron and Ruthven have many common qualities: arrogance and cruelty, but also cultivation and attractiveness. Need I go on?"

"Do as you please," Polidori remarked.

"I can add that perhaps you've also expressed your anger indirectly by taking Byron's ideas for the story away from him, making them your own. You can do no greater damage to a writer than by taking his words from him. Our goal is clear. We must help you voice your anger directly and constructively."

Polidori took a deep breath. "I know your analysis makes sense from the psychiatric perspective, Alex. But is it the deepest level of the truth, here? I have given this matter much thought of late. As you know, I've been having recurring dreams about the butterfly and the crow appearing at my window and about the hummingbird in the garden. At first, I was unable to understand why. However, I have now realized that my unconscious has been trying to tell me something I once knew as a child…"

"What is that?"

"That my mind has a special ability to animate my thoughts."

A worried look crossed Falding's face. How deep into delusion was his friend about to go?

"As I grew up, my rational mind began to dismiss this belief as magical thinking. I blocked and forgot about it, even though many other events in my life seemed to reflect my thoughts. I chose to view these happenings as mere coincidences... I know now that the borders between my mind and the outer world are not as tight and rigid as with most people. My thoughts, therefore, influence the world around me, as others use their hands to manipulate the world."

"Like those who claim to move objects with their minds?"

"Yes, Alex, that is a special case of mind and world melding together. The whole matter of my Serbian dreams and the manifestation became clear when I looked at them in this light. My thoughts can make things happen in the world, so why could they not give life beyond my book to my character, Ruthven? I know it sounds incredible."

"That's quite an understatement, John."

"Regardless, Ruthven found his way into my dreams. He had chased me into the forest, trying to destroy me as he had the other characters in my book. Ruthven then managed to manifest himself outside of the dreams. My dark thoughts have become dark incarnations. I am now a victim of my own story's plot!"

"John, no disrespect intended, but listen to yourself! The merging of mind and world! Incarnations of thoughts and dreams! This *is* magical thinking — the stuff of myths, folktales, and children's stories. Before the era of science, people viewed the world in these terms, just as Dr. Radovich said. It is not the rational, adult mind at work here."

"Alex, why must something that doesn't follow conventional reason necessarily be irrational? There are different forms of reasoning and logic about the world. Who is to say if any one necessarily holds the whole truth?"

"Well, tell me, if the manifestation, Ruthven, has been created by your thoughts, why can't you just change your thoughts and annihilate it? Why not finish your book by having Ruthven destroyed? Good over evil?"

"God knows, I've tried, Alex. I've ended my story with Ruthven meeting his end. I've even meditated about destroying him. None of it works. It's still attached to me, like a malevolent leech, sucking the life out of me and using me as a host to give it a foothold in this world."

"Then doesn't that prove your thoughts really don't influence reality or materialize?"

"No, it's not proof, Alex. I know my thoughts originally created Ruthven, but somehow, he has come to have an existence independent from my thoughts. I don't know why, but I feel something has happened which makes him beyond my control."

"But, John, isn't it much more likely that this means that Ruthven only exists in your mind, in your imagination? The hallucination and your beliefs about it are deeply rooted in your mind and are not easy to get rid of. There is probably a part of your mind that wants to keep them, for your manifestation serves certain mental needs within in you, as we have discussed. All of this comes back to helping you meet these needs in healthy and rational ways."

Seeing Polidori was unconvinced, he decided to take another direction. "John, your 'butterfly' dream told us it was your close connection to others that gave you the strength to heal. Have you been in touch with your friends lately?"

"I correspond with Mary, who is still traveling on the Continent. William Lyons comes by to visit me when he can, and this is comforting."

"Good. Have you confided any of this in them?" Falding asked, hoping they had offered some rational perspectives on his problems.

"I told them much about the nightmares and the sleeplessness, but no more. They are dear friends, but I fear they will think me truly mad if I reveal it all to them."

Falding sighed, feeling thwarted at every turn. However, he knew that Polidori was desperate enough not to abandon their work together. His friend's solutions were failing, and there was nowhere else for him to turn.

Chapter 27

Inspector McLaughlin had become increasingly desperate by mid-November, 1816. Four more murders in the same gruesome style had been inflicted on East London since the exsanguination of Johnny McIver. Tragically, Scotland Yard was no further ahead in solving them. The inspector was under immense pressure from the superintendent and the public to find the "East End Murderer," as the newspapers had named him.

East Londoners were by then too frightened to venture out at night, and the old streets were virtually deserted after dusk. The police had quadrupled their presence in the area at night to surround a district quickly if an alarm was sounded.

The men were on high alert, but the dark nights and thick fogs of the season helped neither their work nor their nerves. It took immense courage to patrol the streets alone in these abominable conditions, with a murderer on the loose — even if the men were within whistle distance of their comrades.

On November 20, 1816, a chorus of police whistles suddenly disturbed the early morning silence in East London as constables rushed toward a woman's screams in Whitechapel. A young woman was found sitting on a door-step, crying and distraught. She covered her face with her hands as the police struggled to get a word out of her.

"What's the trouble, miss?" the burly constable kept on asking.

She finally spoke through her fingers. "A — a bloke came at me... out o' the fog."

"What did he look like, miss?"

"Couldn't tell. 'Twas too dark. He was big, though."

"Did he do or say anything?"

"Said nothin'. But kept on t'wards me. Kept starin' at me, he did."

"That's what frightened you?"

"Aye, but there was somethin' about him." She uncovered her face. "Was up t' no good. The devil's work."

"How did you know that?"

"Just felt it. I screamed. Then he was gone in the fog."

One of the junior members, Constable Coxwell, had been on the outskirts of the district, rushing through the fog to join the others, when he had a dramatic encounter. McLaughlin met with young Coxwell the next day to receive his report personally.

It was obvious to McLaughlin that Coxwell was still shaken and deeply disturbed by the incident. Gripping a cup of steaming tea for comfort, the constable began his report in a quivering voice. "At about 1:00 a.m., I heard the whistles and began running toward them. Suddenly, out of the fog came a huge, dark figure. It was possibly cloaked and hooded. I couldn't tell exactly. It sped toward me eerily, without sound, it seemed, and collided with me. It was very heavy and solid. I got knocked to the ground. My spectacles flew off, and my helmet rolled down the street. The lantern fell and smashed apart on the cobblestones. I was completely in the dark."

Coxwell paused, caught up in the terrifying memories of the scene. "I got the wind knocked out of me, but I pushed myself up on my elbows and blew my whistle with what breath I had left. But the figure had vanished into the murk. All that was left was some kind of putrid odor."

McLaughlin looked his constable in the eye. "How is it that the figure approached you silently? Footsteps are quite loud in empty cobblestone streets."

"I don't know, sir. It seemed that way. The whole thing was queer. I've never smelled anything that bad either, not even the street rubbish in the East End. And getting run into that way! I now know what it would be like to be trampled by a runaway horse, but it was no horse."

The inspector stared at the young constable. "It's bizarre, certainly. I'll give you that."

Coxwell looked beseechingly at McLaughlin. "Sir, the lads will think I'm mad if I write this up."

The inspector smiled. "Write your report anyway. We need every piece of information we can get on this matter, inexplicable or not." He put his hand on his constable's shoulder. "Are you all right, Coxwell?"

"I'm plenty sore, sir, and shaken up. But I'll get by."

"If you do need some time off…"

"I'll be all right, sir."

After Coxwell left, McLaughlin poured himself a cup of tea, contemplating his constable's strange account. Here they were, he thought, with another mystery in a plethora of mysteries. He had no reason to doubt the truth of the report. Although inexperienced, Coxwell was nobody's fool. He had more formal education than most constables.

It may have been their first contact, literally, with the murderer, the inspector mused. If so, they now knew some things about him. On the other hand, could it have been simply a perverted individual fleeing after an attempt to molest a solitary young woman? Perhaps time would tell.

Chapter 28

Treatment was going at a glacial pace with Polidori, who never missed an opportunity to argue that some kind of supernatural entity had attached itself to him; his considerable intellect made him an able debater. Falding decided to take an entirely different approach and use hypnosis in his treatment. Through this time-honored method, he hoped to get around Polidori's formidable conscious defenses to work directly with his unconscious mind. After all, the psychiatrist believed this was where the disturbances were coming from in the first place.

The two met over an afternoon cup of tea in Falding's library to discuss using hypnosis. Polidori was skeptical, to say the least. "Alex, I've heard hypnosis is no more than hocus-pocus," he remarked, "a parlor game played by magicians and entertainers duping the well to do."

Falding took this with a grain of salt. "John, hypnosis is probably more misunderstood than any other medical method. We can easily dismiss what we don't understand."

"Well, all right Alex, why don't you enlighten me?" Polidori asked with an edge of sarcasm.

The psychiatrist ignored his tone and went on. "Well, for a parlor game, hypnosis has been around for a very long time. Hypnosis actually goes back to ancient times, when it was used to heal the sick in the temples of Greece and Egypt."

"Antiquity is interesting, but what is old isn't necessarily good. Look at ancient magic and astrology. Haven't we given up on those in medicine?"

"True, but hypnosis has modern roots, too. Look at the work of Mesmer. Have you heard of him?" Falding asked hopefully.

"Vaguely. Wasn't he some kind of medical quack?"

"Some of his jealous rivals wanted people to believe that, but nothing could be further from the truth."

Falding went on to tell his friend the fascinating story. "Anton Mesmer," he said, "was an Austrian physician who used a form of hypnosis with his patients in the late 1700s. He had remarkable success in curing many illnesses of the body and mind, so that he was much sought after as a healer in the high society of Paris and Vienna of the time."

"But hearsay and popularity tell us little about skill," observed Polidori. "I presume you have an example of a patient so helped?" The scientific side of him was surfacing.

"Yes, indeed. That would-be Mesmer's most famous and controversial patient, little Marie. Marie was a child prodigy, a talented Viennese singer and pianist — so talented that she played before the Austrian royal court. Sadly, Marie had been blind since she was three years old. The Austrian Empress was impressed by little Marie and most sympathetic toward her. She granted a pension to the child."

"What had caused the blindness?" asked Polidori, his interest piqued.

"Well, little Marie's doctors had considered her incurable due to damaged optic nerves, but we now think the 'blindness' was hysterical, induced by her mind. Fortunately, she saw Mesmer for hypnotic treatment and miraculously regained her sight."

"That's amazing," commented Polidori. "The mind curing the body!"

"It *was* remarkable, but the jubilation was short-lived. Her parents were persuaded by other physicians — apparently anxious to protect their practices from Mesmer — that Marie's recovery was not real. They portrayed Mesmer as a charlatan. Some physicians even told the parents that if word got out that Marie was no longer blind, they would lose Marie's pension. Treatment with Mesmer was stopped, and the child tragically relapsed back into blindness."

"How dreadful it must have been!" said Polidori. "Can one imagine it? Losing her sight after it was restored, betrayed by her own parents and physicians!"

"It must have been devastating to the child," Alex agreed wholeheartedly. "However, the medical world learned from Marie how powerful the unconscious mind truly is and how potent hypnosis can be in healing the mind and body."

"How did this mysterious 'hysterical blindness' come about? I've never heard of it."

"Well, it appears that little Marie had not wanted to see something painful in her world, perhaps around age three. It is believed that her unconscious protected her by removing her very ability to see. Mesmer, through hypnosis with the unconscious mind, initially freed her sight from the painful memory. He was a true healer after all. He might have saved her from a life of blindness had he been allowed to continue his work and strengthen her healing."

"I've heard, though," remarked Polidori, "that he had some very strange ideas about how hypnosis worked and some peculiar devices that he used with his patients."

"He did, believing that he could transfer a kind of healing energy called animal magnetism to his patients. And he did so in very dramatic ways."

Polidori remarked acidly, "Alex, this is sounding more like sorcery than science. Surely you don't believe in the animal magnetism theory?"

"No," Alex said. "Today, we psychiatrists don't believe in it. We now think that Mesmer, with all his devices, was really inducing a hypnotic trance. He focused and relaxed his patients, suggesting they go into trance and be cured. He was like a Byron of the medical world — flamboyant, dramatic, marvelously skilled — perhaps beyond his time."

Polidori laughed at the comparison to Byron. "So, Mesmer was actually using the power of belief to heal," he ventured.

"Precisely, John. Modern hypnotists believe that hypnosis is a special state of mind that opens the door to the unconscious, which is especially susceptible to suggestion."

His friend looked thoughtful. "It sounds quite powerful, like the power of dreams to heal or destroy," he observed.

"Yes, John. In fact, dreams are created by the unconscious, which strongly influences the whole mind and body. It's much more powerful than the conscious mind. The conscious mind is like the tip of the iceberg, while the unconscious is like the massive part underneath the sea — the part that can sink a ship. So, powerful is it that even hallucinations can be induced and then removed in people through suggestions to the unconscious."

Polidori was gripped by his words. "Alex, I see what you're getting at. Since you believe that the manifestation is only a hallucination, you must think that hypnosis could remove it, and the disturbing dreams too."

"Exactly. I know you don't believe you're having hallucinations. But if hypnosis works and the red eyes disappear, then the problem must have been in your mind and not in the supernatural realm. Correct?" Appealing to the scientist in Polidori, Falding added, "Hypnosis will be a test of whether or not the 'manifestation' actually exists, as you believe,"

Although he had hoped to hook the rational side of Polidori, it was the irrational that replied. "But what if hypnosis opens my mind up too much, and the manifestation gets deeper inside my mind?" he asked anxiously.

"No, John," the psychiatrist said. "You will not lose control or awareness in hypnosis. Hypnosis is a natural state of mind, anyway, much like a daydream. You will have control of it the same way you are able to come in and out of a daydream at will. Not to worry."

Polidori seemed more reassured.

"Oh, by the way," Falding added, "I had mentioned that modern hypnotists do not believe in mysterious invisible energy like animal magnetism. The modern view is that hypnosis works at the deepest level by changing the balance of the four humors in the body and mind."

This seemed to impress Polidori, who of course put much stock in the four humors theory in his own medical work. The psychiatrist was jubilant, for he appeared to have gained a willing subject for the hypnotic method. There was now hope he could remove the stubborn hallucination from his friend's mind.

204

Chapter 29

The scandals in London over Byron had eventually quieted enough for him to return safely to town. The uproar had not hurt his standing in the social circles. In fact, he was even more popular on the soiree circuit as the wayward lord of London.

McLaughlin and Higgins had been following his antics for some time in the newspapers. The accounts provided some entertainment at the office and some badly needed comedic relief from their investigations.

One morning in late November, the two huddled around McLaughlin's stove behind their newspapers. After reading about another of Byron's escapades, Higgins remarked, "The man must be completely insane."

"Well, he's done mad things anyways, Higgins. Did you ever hear the one about the monk's skull at his grand ball, the summer before last?"

"No. I just heard about the buffoonery with the snake. What's the monk's skull about?"

"Apparently, an old monk's skull was found in the garden of the abbey. He used it to propose a toast at the grand banquet. Can you imagine?"

Higgins exploded into laughter. "It's hard to beat that, sir. He must sit about thinking of ways to outdo himself."

The laughter gradually subsided, and the newspapers were tossed into the old stove. McLaughlin grew pensive. "We've always thought that a madman was behind the murders," he remarked quietly, almost to himself.

Higgins looked dumbfounded. "You don't seriously think Byron's a suspect, do you, sir?"

McLaughlin finished lighting his clay pipe. "Well, we have some evidence that he is mad and we also know that he has a strange following. We've thought that it could take a gang to carry out those murders."

"True sir, but he's not shown himself, so far, to be a hot-headed bloke."

"Well, apparently, the uncle who bequeathed him Newstead Abbey was thought to be both mad and violent. Byron's mother reputedly had a violent temper, too. Over the years, we've gotten reports from the constabulary in Nottinghamshire that there have been quite a few disappearances from the villages near the abbey. Some bodies have been found on the border of the Byron estate. The villagers have suspected Byron, but he was never investigated in the matter."

"I don't like the sound of that, sir, but it's all — how do they say it — circumstantial, isn't it?"

McLaughlin nodded. "Well, I've also read lately that in Geneva Byron offered to take a friend's place and duel with his own physician. I'd call that a violent threat."

"Right, but why would any murderer want to bring attention to himself in the papers, like Byron does?"

The inspector puffed thoughtfully on his pipe. "But we could reverse that argument and say that a murderer could cover himself by playing the harmless scoundrel not to be taken seriously. I know it's not much, but I think it deserves a preliminary look anyway, Higgins. We don't exactly have a long list of suspects, do we? For a start, have one of the men ascertain Byron's whereabouts on the nights of the murders."

Chapter 30

As it turned out, the investigation did not have to wait for a report on Byron. Two days later, a breathless Higgins arrived back at McLaughlin's office. He announced jubilantly that a suspect for the murders had been arrested in the early-morning hours,

"What have you got, Higgins?" McLaughlin queried, with a note of skepticism.

"Well, sir, we were called to some trouble in East London. A bloke and a prostitute were arguing over money when it seems he dragged her into an alley and started to choke her. Her friends saw her, and their screams brought the lads quickly. They collared him in the alley before he could do any damage."

"Hm. Our stepped-up patrols appear to be working, then. Go on, Higgins."

The sergeant's excitement grew. "Well, he fits what we know of the murderer. He's a big, strong man in his prime. He wore a black cloak and hood and had a coil of rope hung on his belt. He also carried a walking stick that hid a sword with dried blood on it. The walking stick had a strange symbol on its handle, matched by a symbol on a ring he was wearing."

In the background, they heard sounds of jubilation and congratulations from the hallways and cheering from the streets. "Evidently, word of the arrest has already gotten out," remarked McLaughlin, looking like he wished it hadn't. The inspector returned to the evidence. "What's the symbol like, Higgins?"

Higgins pulled the ring out of the handkerchief in his breast pocket. It was a gold ring with a red gemstone serpent coiled around a tiny, golden cross. "Looks like it could be a symbol of the devil, sir."

"Possibly, but it isn't the symbol on our victims' foreheads... Where's the rope, Higgins?" Higgins pulled out a small coil of thin rope from a wooden box. "Not sturdy or long enough to hoist our victims, either," McLaughlin added.

Higgins frowned. "But why would he carry it, sir? He must have planned to tie somebody up."

"Perhaps, but let's take a look at the sword." McLaughlin reached down for the walking stick, which was wrapped in a cloth and withdrew the sword. He saw that the sword was heavily bloodied. "Look. The blood pattern is in jagged spurts along the blade, suggesting it was from slashing someone rather than stabbing. Obviously highly suspicious... Well, who is this man, Higgins?"

"He's a blinking baron, one of the House of Lords, a Lord Winchester."

"So, we've caught a big fish."

"Humph. And a high and mighty one, at that, sir. He's been going on about our 'insolence' all morning. Says he's an important man who'll have all our jobs if we don't let him go straight away."

"Does he admit to anything?"

"He says he fondled the girl, but says she panicked and thought he was choking her. Says he's hurt no one and was in the area only to dally with the women of the street."

The inspector's face hardened with suspicion. "And what about the rope and sword?"

"He says he likes to truss them up once in a while, but he wouldn't talk about the sword."

"No doubt. The bugger would implicate himself in something."

"He won't talk about the symbol, either."

"Now *that's* interesting. Why so, I wonder? He's holding back quite a lot here for a man who declares he's been unjustly arrested. Anything else, Higgins?"

"Yes, sir. He's got really big and powerful hands and arms for someone who hasn't done a lick of work in his life."

"Yes, you'd think he'd be soft from sitting about in the upper chamber all these years, living off his inheritance. Possibly, he disciplines himself with physical exercise."

"That might do it. We *were* thinking it'd have to be a powerful bloke to strangle the victims the way they were and to hoist them up and all."

The sounds of cheering were building to a crescendo outside the office. They went to the window to take in the scene. People were dancing in the streets, and the church bells were pealing.

Higgins grinned. "It looks like the king's ruddy birthday."

McLaughlin frowned and turned away from the window. "Well, I truly hope there is cause for celebration, Higgins."

As more information came in about the lord over the next few days, it began to look as if McLaughlin's reservations may have been justified. Higgins and McLaughlin met in the latter's office to discuss the latest findings.

Higgins began a rather grim report. "Our men checked out the lord's bloody sword with some of the East End prostitutes he had been with. They say he got into a duel with one of their pimps over money and slashed him up."

"Unsavory and violent," replied McLaughlin, "but apparently, nothing to do with the murders."

"Yes, sir. That's only the start of the bad news. You were right about the rope being too flimsy. The girls said it was to tie them up during the act. They were all right with that."

"I see what you mean by bad news, Higgins."

"That's not the worst of it, Inspector. Winchester's got an alibi for the night of the second murder. He says he was in a hunting party with other lords, well outside of London, the evening of the murder and following morning. The others say that's true."

McLaughlin sighed wearily.

"Any good news from your side, sir?"

"Somewhat. I've looked into the symbol on Winchester's ring and walking stick with a professor at Cambridge, Phineas Sage."

"Never heard of him."

"He's quite well respected in his field. He studies the history and meaning of all manner of symbols and imagery. He's a rather odd fellow, though."

"Odd, sir?"

"Yes. He's said to have a private interest in magic, of all things. It is even rumored that he knows some of its practitioners in England — if he's not one himself. And this, apparently, is a matter of conjecture among his students and colleagues alike."

"Well, we just might need a magician to solve these murders. Did the professor come up with anything, Inspector?"

"Yes, Higgins. He thought the symbol might represent the antichrist, but he didn't recognize it as belonging to any known cult."

"So, it could be that Winchester is a devil worshiper?"

"That remains a distinct possibility."

The lord was questioned again, later in the day, this time by McLaughlin. He met with Higgins shortly afterward. "Winchester steadfastly denied any link to the murders," he told his assistant, "or to Satanists or a secret society, for that matter. I pointed out to him that the East End is a risky place for a man of his position to frequent. I asked him why he would take such a chance."

"What did he say, sir?"

"He said it was his own business and that I should tend to mine."

"Cheeky blighter. Did he say anything about his ring?"

"Yes. He said it had been passed on through the male generations of the Winchesters for centuries. Its meaning was lost long ago, he claims."

"Do you believe him?"

"Not entirely, Higgins. It looks too ominous to be simply a family heirloom."

"Are we going to let him go, sir?"

"Not yet. We'll keep him as our guest awhile, just to make sure something hasn't been overlooked. But we can't hold him too long without stronger evidence. There's pressure from on high to release him. It looks like he has connections after all."

212

"When we do let him go, Inspector, will we have a man keep watch on him?"

"Certainly. There's too much doubt about the fellow."

Another disastrous blow to the investigation of Lord Winchester came on the 24th of November. While he was still cooling his heels in prison, another mutilated body was discovered. Higgins had called at McLaughlin's home around midnight, bringing the bad news. "There's been another murder, Inspector," he announced, looking panicked. "One of our constables!"

"My God! Who, Higgins?"

"Well, we don't exactly know."

"What do you mean, Higgins?"

"I mean, we think it's Constable Johnson, who was patrolling that area, but..." Higgins lowered his head.

"But, what? Spit it out, man!"

"Sir, he — his head — is missing. It's gone."

"Missing? You mean he's been decapitated?"

"That's about it, sir," replied Higgins, looking as if he was about to be sick.

The two arrived, trepidatiously, at the site of the murder at 12:40 a.m. It was the ghastliest scene yet. The headless body of the constable lay spread out on the cobblestones like a heap of rubbish discarded on the street. Once again, a crowd from the local tenements was milling around, being questioned by Sergeant Mulligan and his men.

213

McLaughlin approached him, not sure if he wanted to hear the grisly details Mulligan might know. "Your report, Sergeant?"

"I'm afraid we have very little, sir."

McLaughlin had a sinking feeling of déjà vu.

"There is no evidence at the scene and nothing to show how poor Johnson was beheaded. But the wounds are jagged. It wasn't something sharp, like a knife or sword. There are no witnesses stepping up, so far. People were in bed."

"Any signs of struggle?"

"No, sir. There are no signs that he tried to defend himself. But he'd had time to blow his whistle, for it was heard by nearby patrols who rushed to the scene. It was all over by the time they got there."

McLaughlin looked around at the street and its dark, dilapidated tenements. "Scour the area, Mulligan. Find — find the rest of him. Call in reinforcements, if necessary."

It was a long and anxious night of fruitless searching, but at sunrise the severed remains of Constable Johnson were found, not far away.

Mulligan had come running breathlessly toward McLaughlin and Higgins. He stumbled on a raised cobblestone, his helmet falling onto the street. "S — sir. Over there!" He pointed to a fenced front yard a few hundred yards away.

The trio hurried to the spot, followed by a troop of constables. McLaughlin saw Johnson's head impaled on the sharp tip of an old iron fence. His eyes were wide open, registering the last visual impression he would have of this world.

McLaughlin thought the head looked like a pumpkin skewered by a spear. He gagged and put his hand to his mouth. Higgins covered the lower half of his face with his collar and stepped back. The men stood in wordless shock, trying to fathom what they were seeing.

The inspector pointed to the blood vessels, bone, and tissues hanging out from where the neck had been. "It — his head's been torn off the body."

"Nobody would have the brawn to do that!" said Higgins.

"No, not unaided." McLaughlin searched desperately for some words of logic and reason that might explain the seemingly impossible. "The murderer must have had some diabolical device to apply such force," he said. But he wasn't entirely convinced by his own words. As he stared at the abomination, he wondered anxiously how in the world he could ever tell the man's poor family what had happened to him. He had heard the words "crisis of faith" before. Now he truly knew what they meant. He asked himself why he had joined the force in the first place. What could he have been thinking?

He gathered the courage to inspect the severed head more closely. He took out his handkerchief and wiped the blood splatters off the forehead.

Higgins cursed. "That frigging symbol again."

McLaughlin seemed not to pay attention to the comment. He had noticed the scalp seemed oddly canted. He warily poked at it with the tip of his walking stick. It fell into the skull with a sickeningly wet sound to reveal an empty brain case. The men jumped back.

215

"His brain is gone! It's been taken!" shouted Higgins. Mulligan turned to the side and began to retch.

This was all McLaughlin could bear. He staggered back from the hateful thing. His reason wavered, and he felt the urge to run in panic from the scene. He managed to walk away, only through great force of will, into his waiting coach. He wiped the sweat from his face and spent some minutes collecting himself.

He knew the murderer was getting bolder in his attempts to frighten London. He was now trying to intimidate the police and undermine the people's confidence in Scotland Yard. The timing of the murder was no accident. It was to show that he was still loose in London and to discourage premature celebrations about his capture. The inspector felt another cold stab of fear in the pit of his stomach as the driver mercifully took him home.

Chapter 31

As McLaughlin had foreseen, the brutal murder of Constable Johnson had its intended effects. Shock, horror, and grief shook the foundations of Scotland Yard. A great gloom hung over the department, which seemed virtually paralyzed by the tragedy.

McLaughlin was only too aware that the police looked terribly inept and helpless in the wake of the worst murder to date. A newspaper had asked acidly, "How can the police protect the public when they can't even protect one of their own?" It was the worst kind of indictment. East Londoners' fears grew to panic proportions, matched by loud, widespread demands for an arrest.

To add to McLaughlin's worries, the superintendent was beside himself with rage over the constable's murder and the lack of a suspect. McLaughlin and Higgins were called in for a thorough dressing down on the matter. McLaughlin feared they would get dismissed if no one was collared soon.

Scotland Yard's preliminary investigation revealed that Byron was in London at his quarters on the nights of the murders. The police did not have any idea about his itinerary in London on the nights in question and couldn't find out without revealing their suspicions. Either his servants or Byron himself would have to be directly questioned. Scotland Yard wasn't prepared to do that yet, as it didn't have grounds to approach a person of Byron's influence and status. Accordingly, McLaughlin decided to have Constable Dickson follow Byron while he was in London.

It took a few weeks for Dickson to report back. Dickson was the punctual type, and he arrived at McLaughlin's office at exactly 10:00 a.m. as agreed. The inspector glanced approvingly at the clock and gestured his constable toward a rather hard-looking oak chair in front of his desk. "So what do you have on Byron, Dickson?" he asked expectantly.

"Well, sir, his main interests appear to be attending soirees in town and fine dining, but he has unsavory habits, too."

"I've no doubt about that."

"Right, sir. He makes the rounds to the gambling establishments — cards, horses, and the like. He stays till all hours and then usually stumbles out drunkenly to his coach."

"I'm not surprised. His expensive tastes are matched only by his exorbitant debts. We're quite sure his publishing royalties and House of Lords stipend don't cover his expenses. Ergo, he becomes a betting man."

"A chancy way of paying down his debts. Usually his coachman takes him directly to his quarters after his outings, but sometimes he travels to East London for the services of the women there."

"That certainly fits with what we know about the man's sexual appetites."

"Yes, I've spoken to the prostitutes afterward to see what kind of man he is with them and if they have any complaints. Knowing I was a copper, most of them told me what I could do with my middle finger, but a few talked."

218

"That's a miracle."

"Indeed, sir. Byron apparently has some particular preferences, mainly tying up and whipping, but nothing really injurious. There were some red blotches on them, but no bruises or cuts. They don't seem to be afraid of him, either. All said they'd take him back as a customer and that he was well paying. But one said he's probably not a good man to cross."

"Oh?" asked McLaughlin, perking up. "What's that about?"

"She said that one night her pimp tried to overcharge Byron, who then reached into his waistband for the handle of a pistol. Needless to say, the pimp backed off in a hurry."

"No doubt. That's the sort of information we're looking for, Dickson — his disposition toward violence. Try to cheat him and it's revealed."

Dickson nodded. "Another thing, too. It was rumored that one of the women had been afraid of a stranger, a man who had approached her in a dark cape and hood."

McLaughlin picked up his pipe and scraped out its cold contents into an ash tray on his desk. "It's interesting that Byron has worn similar clothing at night when he visits London. This was also the garb of the dark figure who ran down Coxwell."

"Perhaps it's not all coincidence, Inspector."

McLaughlin frowned. "That's the question…"

Dickson shifted in the uncomfortable chair, apparently emptied of information. "Shall I keep an eye on him further, sir?"

"By all means. Stay on him. And good work, Dickson."

Dickson smiled appreciatively and left the inspector to his thoughts. McLaughlin stood up and walked to the window. Londoners were flitting by in the chilly autumn air. They were busy with their lives, oblivious to the desperation behind the walls of Scotland Yard. He asked himself how long it would take the murderous stalker to tire of the East End and bring his mayhem to the rest of London. Perhaps some of the passersby outside would be next.

A few days later, their man watching Lord Winchester, Constable Murdock, reported he had followed him into a downtown tavern. Winchester had sat down with another gentleman — none other than Lord Byron. The two appeared to converse intensely, but Murdock was unable to get close enough to hear them. After a few minutes, the two stood up and shook hands. The observant constable noticed that they had identical rings, gold bands with a red gemstone serpent coiled around a cross.

Higgins and McLaughlin discussed Murdock's report at length over a cup of tea in the inspector's office. "Well, his interest in harlots puts him in the area of the murders, and often enough too," remarked Higgins.

"Yes, but we still don't know if he was there on the nights of the murders."

"Yeah, but he puts them through some pretty rough play, sir."

"Indeed, although nothing violent. They weren't afraid of him."

"What about the twin rings?" queried Higgins. "That's no fluke. It could be a cult, and from the looks of the snake they're not good blokes."

McLaughlin put down his tea-cup. "We *were* talking about how the murders may have required more than one person to carry them out. And Winchester lied about his ring being solely a family heirloom. That's highly suspicious, obviously. But we shouldn't assume it's necessarily a cult ring. It may signify something else that Winchester wants to keep quiet. We need to look further into the origin of the rings. Both went to Cambridge. We may find out more about the relationship between these two there. Let's get on with it, Higgins."

Chapter 32

Higgins soon reported to McLaughlin what he had learned about the Cambridge connection. "We questioned some of their old school-mates and professors from Cambridge. They said Byron and Winchester were trouble-makers in school, always breaking one rule or another. But they were slippery blokes and never got caught. A bunch of them would be seen in the library reading books on witches and magic and such."

"On the occult?"

"Yeah, that's the word. It was even said that they did animal killings. What's it called?"

"Ritual sacrifice."

"Yeah, that's it. But nobody could prove it. A minister at Trinity College got the closest to it. He had noticed them with the devil books and had asked them about it. They laughed it off. Said it was just curiosity. But the minister said he got a package in the post a few days after. In it were the bloodied talons of a hawk. 'Course he took this as a warning and was too scared to bring up the books again with the students. He's still scared. He asked us not to tell anyone about what he'd said."

McLaughlin stoked his stove with a few more pieces of coal. "That's practically proof they were killing animals. This sacrifice business may also fit in with Byron's whipping the women in the East End. He may have a partiality for pain."

"Well, we've got nothing more, Inspector. The school mates or the professors don't recall the names of the others, nor any odd rings, either."

"Hmm. Nevertheless, I don't like what I'm hearing. Let's keep up our watch on these two for now. If there is a cult out there, they will do it again."

McLaughlin couldn't shake off his uneasy feelings about Byron. He knew he had little upon which to base his suspicions, but the clamor for an arrest was growing louder. He had to be seen to be doing something.

Out of desperation, McLaughlin decided to take the risk of approaching the superintendent about the matter. One gray day in mid-December, he arrived nervously at the latter's spacious, rather coldly furnished office on the second floor. He had never gotten used to his superior's stern, formal demeanor, but at least, he thought, the man applied the whip equally to everyone.

After listening closely to the story, the head of Scotland Yard said what McLaughlin already knew. "You don't have much against Byron, or Winchester for that matter."

"I realize it's not substantial, sir," McLaughlin remarked defensively.

"Not substantial? It's almost invisible, McLaughlin! Unsavory behavior with the women and similar tastes in jewelry make neither a murderer. A student prank is hardly convincing, either. I fear we're at risk of overreacting to Byron's eccentricity."

The superintendent stared stonily at McLaughlin. "Byron is a man of great influence, with powerful connections. We have to have evidence to approach him. I've already had my wrists slapped over the Winchester affair."

"Yes, sir, I realize that," McLaughlin said uncomfortably.

The superintendent sighed and sat back pensively. "Nevertheless, I'm hearing, almost daily, that the fears of East Londoners about these unsolved murders are building. We're being seen as doing nothing about them by the newspapers and some senior government officials. Moreover, Byron's scandals may have weakened his position with some of the powerful... I'll have to think about it, McLaughlin. I'll let you know of my decision."

Shortly after, McLaughlin and Higgins met again to discuss the investigation. McLaughlin complained, "The world's too complicated these days for an old policeman. Politics, newspapers, public opinion. Sometimes, I wish for the good old days."

"The good ol' days, sir?"

"Indeed. Things were much more straightforward then... Did I ever tell you about McGregor?"

"Bruce McGregor, the Glasgow inspector?"

"Yes. But he wasn't an inspector when I knew him. We were London watchmen together before we joined the department and became good friends." McLaughlin laughed. "He was quite eccentric. He had a passion for all things French. He devoured the French newspapers, traveled in France at every opportunity, and took a French wife. There was a standing joke in the department that he was really a reincarnated Frenchman."

"Sounds like quite the character, sir."

"Yes, he was, but he also had a good head for investigation. Together we solved many a crime, not a few of them over a pint at the Pig's Head. I sorely missed him when he took the position in Glasgow."

"Too bad he's gone, sir. We could use a hand right about now."

"There's not much chance of that, Higgins. We're on our own, I'm afraid." *That about sums it up*, he thought. *On our own against a murderous enemy we can't begin to comprehend.*

McLaughlin did not have to wait long to be summoned back to the superintendent's office. It was late in the day, and the last rays of the sun faded behind the darkening buildings to the west.

The inspector found himself once again under the unflinching scrutiny of the head of Scotland Yard. The man across the desk looked even sterner than usual, if that was possible. "Well, McLaughlin, I've approached some senior officials on the Byron matter. They've given the department permission simply to interview Byron and his servants, *without* any allegations."

"Thank you, sir."

"Well, I truly hope you're right about him. I've had to collect on some favors owed me in order to pursue this matter."

As McLaughlin turned to leave, he wondered why the superintendent had taken such a risk. His superior wasn't known to do personal favors for his staff. Evidently, he was more afraid of being perceived as doing nothing than he was of offending Byron's powerful friends.

Higgins and McLaughlin soon paid a visit to Byron's apartment in wealthy Piccadilly. They were met and escorted into the luxurious, spacious drawing room by his manservant. They found Byron in a silk robe sitting at a writing table, with papers and a glass of wine in front of him.

"Sir, these are the gentlemen from Scotland Yard," announced the servant, taking his leave.

"Lord Byron?"

"Yes."

"I'm Inspector McLaughlin, and this is my assistant, Sergeant Higgins." Higgins nodded and kept to the background, notebook in hand.

"Would you gentlemen care for a glass of wine?"

"No, thank you, sir. We're on official business."

"Well, Inspector and Assistant Higgins, what official business brings you to my door today?"

"We would like some information relevant to an investigation we're conducting."

"Oh, and am I a suspect in this investigation, Inspector?"

"No, but your information may prove helpful."

"Well, always glad to be of service. Ask away, Inspector," replied Byron with a flippant twirl of his hand.

McLaughlin ignored his gesture. "Where were you, Lord Byron, on the nights of October 18th and 25th?"

"Direct and to the point, Inspector. I'll have to get my social calendar for that period." He rose and went to the door, asking his servant for his calendar. He flipped to the relevant dates. "Ah, yes. I was at

226

Mrs. Twillingdale's soiree from 9:00 p.m. to 1:00 a.m. on the 18th, and at Mr. Chesterton's home on the 25th for some port and cards, all evening."

"When did you say you left Mr. Chesterton's?"

"I didn't. But I'd say I left about two that morning."

"On the 18th, where did you go after the soiree?"

"My coachman picked me up, and we went straight home, where I remained all night."

The inspector persevered. "And on the 25th, what happened after 2:00 a.m.?"

"I came straight home, like a good boy."

"Would you mind if we confirmed your information with your hosts and servants?"

Byron smiled. "Not at all."

McLaughlin probed further. "Did you visit East London at any time on these dates?"

"No. As I said, it was directly home for me. Am I being investigated, Inspector? It certainly feels that way."

"We're just after some basic information, that's all."

"Hmm," said Lord Byron. "If memory serves, those dates fall in the week of the East End murders, don't they?"

"How do you know that?"

"I read the newspapers, Inspector. Dreadful happenings, and I hope you catch the culprits. But in case you think I'm a violent man, let me say that as a poet I express my feelings in words, not in malevolent deeds."

"That's not what I've heard."

"What *have* you heard, Inspector?"

"I heard that when in Geneva last summer, you offered to take a friend's place in a duel and would have carried it out, excepting that the challenger withdrew."

"Pure speculation, Inspector. My offer was simply a prank intended to defuse the situation. I had no intention of dueling anyone, I can assure you. Those were only words, Inspector, not actions. Let's not confuse the two."

McLaughlin disregarded the condescending tone. "How about the night of November 24th? Where were you then?"

"Hmm. Was that the night of the last murder, Inspector? Let me see…" He consulted his calendar again. "I was right here at home, writing a poem."

"No diversions to the East End?"

"No. When I write, I have no time for distractions. I owe my readers that much."

"Can anyone verify your whereabouts that night?"

"Yes, my servants."

"And that would be an independent observation, I suppose," McLaughlin commented sarcastically. He maneuvered further. "We also hear you have dealings with certain women in Whitechapel."

"Impressive. You've done your studies, Inspector."

"You admit that?"

Byron produced a thin smile. "I acknowledge that. I don't believe it's a crime."

"Have you ever caused injury or fright to these women?"

"As I say, I write about my feelings, not blindly or brutally act them out. The answer is no, Inspector."

"We hear you restrain and whip the women. Are they harmed in that practice, Lord Byron?"

"You *have* studied the life of Byron, sir. Congratulations. Yes, I have my titillating practices, which I think the women enjoy as much as I. Again, the answer is 'no' to injury."

"But you do cause pain?"

"Pain and pleasure are closely related feelings for me and my partners."

"Does the giving of pain extend beyond the bordello, Lord Byron?"

Byron sighed impatiently. "No. I may be risqué and eccentric, but I'm neither a fool nor malevolent, sir."

McLaughlin changed direction again. "I notice you're not wearing a ring today, Lord Byron."

"No. I am not usually adorned around my home. Is that illegal?"

"No, but if you would indulge my curiosity, do you own a ring with an ornamental serpent on it?"

"Why, yes. It's my favorite ring."

"Will you enlighten me on what the serpent symbolizes?"

"Yes, it symbolizes nothing. I simply like snakes. I keep one as a pet at Newstead Abbey, you know."

McLaughlin kept the questions coming. "Were you aware that someone else in London has an exact twin of this ring?"

"Well, no. And if you are going to ask me to explain this, all I can say is that either it's a happy

229

coincidence, or the person has good taste and bought one just like mine."

"Is this a specially made ring, signifying your membership in a society, secret or otherwise?"

"In answer to the first part of your question, I've had this ring for so long, I honestly don't recall how I came by it. To the last part, since when does a decent Romantic poet go around keeping secrets about his life? That is antithetic to our art."

"I take that as 'no' to the society?"

"That's correct, Inspector," replied Byron, an edge coming into his voice.

The verbal jousting between the two went on like this for some time, but McLaughlin failed to fluster Byron. There was little to show for the interrogation except for Higgins' notebook full of inconclusive detail.

Subsequent interviews with the servants and hosts proved no more revealing. The servants reported that they could not remember his whereabouts during the evenings in question. Whether they were truthful or simply protecting their master, McLaughlin did not know. His hosts were no more definitive in their memories about the elusive Byron.

The Inspector was not to be daunted, however. Something damning would turn up on Byron, he thought, and Constable Dickson was just the man to find it.

Chapter 33

McLaughlin and his wife Lisbeth had enjoyed twenty good years of marriage together. She was a few years younger than him and generally a good match. They were not able to conceive children and had accepted that fact long ago. They contented themselves in their relationship, which was very close; she was the first person he had allowed himself to love since the death of his father. Jiggs, their dog, brought them even closer together. Jiggs was not only a wonderful companion but perhaps a kind of substitute child.

Lisbeth was the traditional middle-class wife of the time. The home was her domain, and she was an excellent domestic manager. She would keep the hired tradesmen on their toes, and they knew better than to try to dupe her.

Lisbeth was a down-to-earth, cheerful person. Moderately religious, she attended the local Catholic Church conscientiously. She had no superstitious inclinations that McLaughlin was aware of. That was fine by him, for superstition and the supernatural in general had no place in the hard reality of his world as a police inspector.

Lisbeth, like her husband, had experienced a generally happy childhood. The only dark cloud happened upon her when she was just four years old. She had kept it a childhood secret until she told McLaughlin about it many years later. The two were sitting on the settee in the drawing room, looking out the window at the late fall scene in the garden. He had just gotten up to throw a log in the fireplace.

"This reminds me of another fall day," she said with a distant look in her eyes. "I've never told you about it."

Her husband turned and looked over at her curiously.

She took a deep breath and exhaled slowly. "I was in the park with my mother, playing with the autumn leaves. I remember piling them up, imagining they were all sorts of things of interest to a four-year-old. My mother left me briefly unattended. I can't imagine why, but she did. A strange man, a tall man in black garb, with dirty teeth, approached and tried to entice me away with some sweets. I don't know why, but I ran away from the man — call it the wisdom of childhood. The man chased after me, still offering the sweets, but I ran into my mother's arms. She glared at the man, who retreated into the woods."

McLaughlin shook his head. "We arrest depraved people like that in the parks all the time. It's fortunate you ran."

"Yes, but I didn't escape him entirely."

"Oh?" her husband asked, puzzled.

"After that, I began to have frightening dreams." Lisbeth began to cry.

Her husband sat down beside her and put a comforting arm around her shoulders. "The long distant past," he said, taking one of her hands in his.

"Yes, mostly. The nightmares faded as I got older, perhaps displaced by the cares and concerns of growing up…"

"But?"

"They may still happen in times of turmoil and trouble."

"Well, be sure to confide them to me if they do," he advised gently. "Besides, do I not do a good enough job at keeping the big, bad world from our door?"

She smiled. "My *great* protector!" she said, with much exaggeration.

Indeed, up to now McLaughlin had done very well in his role of protector. There were many pressures as a police inspector, but he rarely talked to Lisbeth about them. He accepted the common belief among men at the time that women were fragile, hysterical creatures, easily prone to fainting spells if over excited.

However, the murders had gotten badly out of hand. Disturbing memories of the crimes began to torment him. The image of the lifeless head of Constable Johnson could and would intrude into his mind upon the slightest reminder. Sometimes he even imagined the eyes of the severed head following him. He knew he could not afford to be distracted. The investigations needed a clear head and a steady hand.

But he also knew he could no longer control the memories with sheer power of will. He felt he could not reveal his feelings about the murders to his colleagues and certainly not to the superintendent. In desperation, he broke his cardinal rule and turned to Lisbeth. It was a mutually satisfying arrangement at first. Liz greatly appreciated being his confidant and excelled at it. Her husband felt relieved to be able to voice his feelings. All seemed well.

Unfortunately, as fall barely turned to winter, Liz's nightmares returned. She would jump up from her sleep, trembling, bathed in sweat, wide-eyed with terror. He could not distract or console her for hours afterward.

At first, she refused to talk about the dreams, but one night she relented. "It's always the same," she began. "I see myself alone on a narrow city street at night, illuminated only by the faint, flickering light of the lamps. The street and buildings are mostly in shadows, obscured by mist. I become aware of something stalking me silently in the murk. I begin to run in panic, chased by whatever it is. All the doors in the buildings are locked, and no one is answering my calls for help. I am terrified and alone; no matter how fast I run, the pursuer is getting closer and closer to me. Then the dream vanishes, and I am next to you in bed."

"What do you think is going on, Lisbeth?" her husband asked.

"I am tempted to say it is like my childhood nightmare, yet it isn't. I am not being chased by a man, but by something black, formless, and absolutely silent."

"Do you suppose this is an adult nightmare, caused by something happening in your life now?"

"I don't know, for I also feel like the little girl — helpless and deserted."

"A vague, black figure is how people have described the London murderer. Do you think that my telling you about the murders is giving you these dreams?"

"It could be," she said, perplexed, searching for an answer. "Yet, I feel somehow there are many layers to the dream. I can peel one layer away, and there is another."

234

"What are these layers, Lisbeth?"

"I'm not sure. The man in the park is perhaps one; the horror of these murders may be another. It is all these things, but I feel the deepest layer is yet unseen, yet unknown."

"Lisbeth, this doesn't sound like you. This seems mystical, like the words of tea-leaf readers or the diviners of tarot cards."

She pulled away from him. "It is the only way I can describe what's going on right now. You ask me a question, and then you invalidate my way of answering it," she shot back angrily.

"I'm sorry, Lisbeth. I guess I'm just worried and frustrated, wanting a rational answer to this too quickly. I want to fix the problem for you."

"You can't fix it, James. I simply need you to listen to me right now and to try to understand as much as you can."

He decided to stop talking with her about the investigation. He knew he was trying to fix her again but thought this might help her get rid of one layer of her dreams. Unfortunately, it didn't. The nightmares only worsened, and she began to suffer from sleeplessness. To worsen matters, Lisbeth was resentful over losing her role as confidant.

At his wit's end, he summoned old Dr. Larson. McLaughlin didn't have full confidence in him. Then again, he didn't trust the doctor's profession in general. Their medical bags were filled with too many ancient Greek remedies and too little science, he thought. But where else could he turn?

Dr. Larson examined her and gave his considered opinion. "The nightmares have to do with hysteria," he pronounced.

"Hysteria? What is that?" McLaughlin asked, bewildered.

"Hysteria means 'wandering of the womb,' in Greek," the doctor said.

"What does that have to do with anything?"

"She tells me the nightmares are worse during her menses, so they must be influenced by her female humors."

McLaughlin looked even more baffled. "So, what do you recommend?"

"I'll give her some potions for nerves and to rebalance her humors. Be sure to consult Mr. Jordan, the chemist. He's got the purest ingredients."

Unfortunately, even the purest of potions did nothing to improve her symptoms but seemed only to make her drowsy and ill-tempered. The situation became even more alarming when she began to interpret her dreams in a most disturbing way. One evening, she asked her husband to sit down with her in the drawing room. "James, I know what that deep layer is," she announced.

"Oh?" he said, a little uneasy about what he was about to hear.

"Yes, I think I'm being visited in my sleep by some kind of force that has found me, an intruder."

"What?" he exclaimed in disbelief. "This is most unlike you, Lisbeth! What in the world would give you this idea?"

"If the dreams came only from childhood fears and the murders, I know I could manage them and make them go away. No, there is something much more powerful than that, something evil in the dreams. I sense its malevolence toward me *and* you. It wants to harm me, and through me, you."

"You say the dream figure is using you to get at me? Whatever for?"

"I feel that for some reason it does not want you to solve these murders. I don't know why."

"You mean it's trying to interfere with the investigation? Do you hear what you are saying?"

"I know it sounds mad, but my last dream was different. Before I woke up, I saw a red serpent coiling around me and squeezing the life out of me. It spoke to me. It said it was going to kill me and that you were next."

For a fearful moment, McLaughlin's rationality wavered again. His mind rushed into suspicions about the red gemstone ring and a cult manipulating Lisbeth's dreams. He imagined spells and chants being transmitted through witchcraft to his wife. But he remembered that the professor had said that images of snakes, particularly red or black ones, symbolize unconscious fears and are not uncommon in dreams. It wasn't anything more than that.

"Lisbeth," he said, "this is totally irrational. Dreams are private creations of the mind. They cannot be invaded by anything."

"They are too real to just be ordinary dreams," she protested.

"Lisbeth, your mind is simply grasping for an explanation, and it has found the easiest one: superstition. I believe your dreams are coming from worry, worsened by your exhaustion. You're afraid that the murders will not be solved, and the

237

happiness we had before them will not be regained. You fear that I will be personally destroyed and ruined if we fail to capture the murderer."

But Lisbeth would have none of this. "I'll find my own solution to the dreams."

"And that might be?"

"You'll find out in good time, James."

Upon returning from work the next day, he caught sight of Father Callahan's carriage leaving the courtyard. He greeted his wife in the vestibule. "I see Father has had occasion to visit us," he remarked.

"Yes, I asked him to come."

McLaughlin thought that her face looked brighter and calmer. "About your dreams?"

"Yes. I told him about the signs of malevolence in my dreams. He said he didn't have much experience in such matters. But just in case, he would perform a ritual that might be helpful. He sprinkled holy water in the house and garden, giving them a blessing in the name of Christ."

"Oh, I see," her husband said neutrally. He was not particularly impressed by the priest's ministrations, but Lisbeth was looking better. He was not about to take away hope from her.

As it turned out, there was a huge difference in her afterward. To his great relief, she settled down and slept better, and her dreams went away. She seemed to be rapidly returning to her normally happy self. If this was a case of divine intervention, he was all in favor of it.

Chapter 34

All went well in the McLaughlin home for some time. Despite the problems with the investigation, McLaughlin kept the details away from Lisbeth. He was even able to find ways of better managing his intrusive memories of Constable Johnson.

But the happy times were not to last. One day in early December he came home from work after dark. He found Lisbeth in the drawing room, anxious and distracted once more. After he had asked her several times what was going on, she finally blurted out, "It's the strangest thing. All afternoon, I felt I was being watched through the window from the bushes in the garden. I could not shake off this feeling, even when I closed the curtains."

"What makes you think this, Lisbeth?" he asked.

"I don't know. It's a feeling. How do you explain a feeling?"

"Well, Lisbeth, just because we feel something to be true, that doesn't mean it's true," he observed. "I'm sure this is your imagination getting out of hand. You haven't heard about the investigation from me, and perhaps you're deeply worried about how it's going, and your mind has taken an irrational turn."

"Well, that's just it, James, I haven't been troubled about the investigation or thinking about it all," she corrected. "This has come out of nowhere."

He took the lamp and searched around in the garden, hoping to reassure her. He returned in a few minutes, rubbing his hands to warm them. "I found

239

no signs of an intruder," he said. "The garden, including the bushes, did not appear to be disturbed. There were no footprints on the frosty ground."

"I know what I felt."

"Lisbeth, the lock and chain were still on the garden gate. An intruder would have had to vault over a six-foot iron-spiked fence — a foolish, if not impossible endeavor."

"Yet we sometimes simply know things," she said. "Haven't you ever felt someone out of line of sight was looking at you, and you turned and found out it was true? How do you account for that rationally? There was someone or something out there, James."

Lisbeth's suspicions of an intruder were worsened by a very disturbing event a few days later. It was so upsetting that she had taken the unusual step of sending a message to her husband to come home from work. McLaughlin soon arrived, hurrying apprehensively into the house.

Lisbeth, looking flushed, put her hand on his arm. "Jiggs is gone!" she cried. "I let him out in the garden and called him back shortly, but he didn't come. I looked everywhere in the yard and in the neighborhood, calling his name."

The couple searched the garden again. McLaughlin peered behind a bush near the fence. He beckoned to Liz. "Over here," he said. They looked at a small opening where the fence had fallen into disrepair.

"I suppose it's possible he wiggled his way out of that, but it would be very tight," said McLaughlin.

Lisbeth looked skeptical. "He's never tried to escape before, though he's had other opportunities."

Sadly, Jiggs never did return. Over the days that followed, a dark cloud of grief fell over the family. After all, Jiggs was more than a dog; he was a family member. To exacerbate the grim mood, Lisbeth began to view the matter through the lens of the supernatural. "This proves what I've been saying. Jiggs has been taken."

"By whom?"

"By the same thing that's been watching me from the garden." She glared at him. "Why didn't you listen to me?"

McLaughlin met her anger with silence. It was pointless to argue with her about it, he knew.

Soon after the disappearance of Jiggs, Liz's bad dreams returned to torment them both.

"The intruder is back in my dreams," she announced.

McLaughlin gravely needed a fresh approach to the problem. He decided to hire a man servant, a sturdy fellow in his thirties. Hopefully, he would be a protective, reassuring presence for Lisbeth. For good measure, he would even train him in the use of a pistol, which he kept, along with another, in the upstairs hallway cabinet.

As it turned out, McLaughlin found a fine servant. Lisbeth responded well to him, and thankfully, her bad dreams seemed to subside again. Her healing was also helped by their taking another dog, a great white Pyrenees, into the family.

241

All seemed to be going much better until that fateful night in late December. It was a particularly windy night. The air was cold and heavy, with the possibility of snow. A pale moon hung in the sky, with streams of dark clouds hurrying across its face.

McLaughlin had not yet come home from work. Lisbeth sat before her mirror in her upstairs bedroom getting ready for bed, the dog at her side. The man-servant had also retired to his quarters.

At about 8:00 p.m., Lisbeth noticed that the dog was restless, sniffing and whining at the closed bedroom door. The dog refused to settle and became agitated, barking and growling ferociously. Then Lisbeth was startled by a huge crash, apparently coming from the darkened first floor. The whole house seemed to shudder.

Lisbeth was stunned for a moment and then flung open the bedroom door. She peered around the door frame into the hall but saw nothing out of the ordinary. Suddenly, the servant rushed by her and grabbed a flintlock pistol from the gun cabinet. Warning her to stay in her room, he cocked the gun and headed downstairs, trailed by the fiercely barking dog.

In a few moments, Lisbeth heard the ferocious sounds of the dog going on the attack, followed by the servant shouting out something — an order, she thought. The blast of a pistol thundered up the stairs, followed by a terrible scream and then total silence.

She retreated further into her bedroom, fumbling for her crucifix. She began a desperate prayer, a whispered plea. "The Lord is my shepherd; I shall not want. He maketh me to lie down in green pastures—"

She heard a thumping from downstairs. *What was it?* The crucifix shook in her hands. She knew she must get to the gun, but this was only a distant call in her mind, muffled by fear. A cool, sobering breeze blew in from the hallway, crossing her face. Her prayerful whispers began again. "He leadeth me beside still waters. He restores my soul. He leads me in the right path for his name's sake—"

She stepped unsteadily into the hallway, afraid to look around, and bumped into the gun cabinet. The door was ajar, and she picked up the double-barreled pistol, heavy and foreign to her. She stumbled down the hallway, making it to the top of the stairs. With sweaty hands, Lisbeth struggled to cock the triggers — *one, two ... there*. But it wasn't enough to comfort her. She peered apprehensively down the darkened staircase, straining to catch every bit of light from the faintly moonlit rooms below. "For you are with me, your rod and staff they comfort me—"

She tightened her grip on the gun and for the first time felt its solidness and a hint of the power bound up within it. For a moment, she thought this thing of metal and fiery powder might protect her. *God helps those who help themselves...* Then Lisbeth heard a dragging sound and the jarring crash of splintering glass and wood. *Oh, God,* she thought in anguish, *there's something down there. I can't see it... Steady. Steady. Focus, dammit!*

An acrid cloud of gun smoke rose up to meet her. Suddenly faint, she teetered on the stairs. *Run! Run! Get out!* came the silent words of panic starting from somewhere deep in her body and flooding up into her brain. She stopped and forced herself to

243

breathe, gripping her crucifix so hard it bent in her hand. "You prepare a table for me in the presence of mine enemies—"

She pushed back her panic. Her feet found the landing. At first, she could see nothing in the gloom and smoke. The hairs on her neck stood up straight. "You anoint my head with oil. My cup—"

Her eyes suddenly saw the thick oak front door lying shockingly on the floor. One corner of it dangled from the bottom hinge. The dog lay motionless and bloodied on the floor near the door. The cold night wind whistled through the gaping doorway, rushing past her toward the drawing room on her right. With her heart pounding in her chest, she turned to see the curtains billowing out the drawing room windows. The windows had been completely shattered, their frames broken up like kindling. It looked like the windows had exploded from the inside into the garden beyond. "My cup runneth over. Surely goodness and mercy shall follow me all the days of my life and I will dwell in the house of the Lord forever—"

Biting her lip, she edged toward the huge hole that had been the window. Lisbeth held the gun even tighter, afraid of what she would see. Her fear was justified. There in the garden, eerily lit by the moon, was the servant, hanging from a thick limb of the old oak tree. A chain from the garden fence was coiled around his neck. His head was canted to the side, his neck apparently broken. His lifeless eyes were frozen wide with fear. His entrails appeared to be protruding from a large gash in his abdomen. He reminded her of a big, wide-eyed rag doll, carelessly hung up on a hook, with its stuffing coming out.

She caught a sudden movement in the shadows of the garden. Reflexively, she raised and fired both barrels of the pistol in quick succession toward the movement. The deafening blasts flung her backward into the settee, draping her over it, her nightgown blown up over her face. She struggled to get her breath, choking and tearful from the gun smoke. Wiping the tears from her eyes, she managed to crawl out of the settee to the window. Lisbeth began to panic again. Had she shot the intruder … or was she going to be next?

Chapter 35

McLaughlin returned home that night around 9:00 p.m., unaware of the scene of chaos and death that awaited him. His first warning that something was very wrong was the presence of a constable at the open front door to the house. His heart beating hard, he hurried up to the constable. "My wife?" he asked.

"She's unharmed, Inspector. But I am sorry to say the servant is dead."

McLaughlin whispered, "My God," and rushed past the constable into the hallway. He almost stumbled over the family dog, lying still in a pool of blood, its neck apparently broken. His eyes frantically darted about, searching for Lisbeth. He found her in the drawing room. She sat near the upturned settee, her face blank and blackened by gun smoke.

He sat down beside her and took her hand, finding it cold and limp. She gave no sign of recognizing him. "Liz. Liz?" he asked desperately. He rubbed her hand frantically, hoping to instill some life in it.

"She's received a bad shock," said a male voice behind him. McLaughlin turned to find Dr. Nelson, who had been summoned to examine the body and attend to Lisbeth. The doctor drew him off to the side. "It will take some time for her mind to come back, Inspector. She's fortunate to have survived. She appears to have kept her wits about her and fought back." He gestured toward the pistol on the floor next to her. "That's a good sign she's got the strength to recover from this."

246

McLaughlin nodded and returned to his attempts to revive his wife. He vaguely heard in the background a sergeant asking the doctor if he had finished examining the body. Lisbeth just sat there, her eyes empty, unresponsive to his efforts.

Lisbeth was mute for several long days afterward. Her husband patiently tended to her and gave her calming medication prescribed by the doctor. However, McLaughlin knew this was much more than a matter of medication: it was a battle for her mind. He told her stories about other hard times — when both of them had been put to the test. He reminded her of how, in the end, they had come back from adversity and had won the day.

Slowly, Lisbeth showed signs of returning. At first, he could tell she was listening to him; then flickers of life came back into her eyes. At last, she took a deep breath and uttered a great cry of fright and rage, followed by a cascade of tears. She began to speak after that.

She voiced her anger first. "You didn't listen, James," she berated. "You didn't listen to the dreams, to the warnings that *it* would come."

He was tempted to be the chastising parent again, but thought better of it. He heard her out.

"It *did* come. It smashed its way in here, killed the dog, and murdered the servant." She lowered her head in silence then looked back up at him. "It would have killed me, too, had I not shot at it twice in the garden."

McLaughlin looked at his wife in awe. He'd always known she could stand her ground, but this! She had acted beyond human endurance.

247

Eventually, he became the policeman again in their talks. "Did you see him at all, Liz?"

"You mean did I see *it*? No, not a sliver. I only heard some of the terrible things it did to the poor servant. He had gone downstairs first — yes, brave soul — followed by the dog, our faithful dog. All they wanted to do was protect me." She sobbed in anguish and guilt.

"Then you came down."

"Yes."

He shook his head in disbelief. "The fear must have been unbearable. Surely, many would have simply frozen at the top of the stairs and been stalked and killed by the murderer. How did you do it, Lisbeth?"

"With this," she said, clutching the bent crucifix still around her neck.

McLaughlin nodded. "And with your strength of will, Lisbeth ... and the pistol." He did not want to tell her what he believed had happened. He had been careless, he thought. The murderer had followed him home, probably from one of the murder scenes. It wouldn't have been difficult in the miserable fogs and dark nights of the past autumn. At any rate, the culprit had known where they lived and waited for the right moment to strike. He had done so savagely, not only through hanging the servant, but according to Doctor Nelson, almost completely disemboweling him. Most of the entrails were missing. The dreadful, unmistakable mark was on the man's forehead.

McLaughlin thought that if Liz hadn't made her surprising stand, there was no doubt the murderer

248

would have been waiting for him, too, when he arrived home. He would have killed them all.

This fellow was clever. What better way to show just how powerless and bumbling Scotland Yard was than by murdering its senior inspector and his family in their own home? It was a vicious ploy, but that was all — no supernatural claptrap here. The murderer would yet make his first big mistake, McLaughlin believed. He'd come close to doing just that by misjudging the bravery of his wife.

In the days that followed, the inspector placed some of his men on twenty-four-hour watch on the house. He also discussed with Lisbeth moving to another residence for added safety. He had hoped such measures and the voice of reason would help her, but he soon realized these had made no impression on her fear for their lives. She was still convinced something supernatural had forced its way into their home and would come again. McLaughlin was seriously considering having her see a good psychiatrist. He thought Lisbeth was beyond what help he or others had been able to give her.

Chapter 36

News of the horrific invasion and murder at the McLaughlin home spread quickly through the department. Higgins and the men expressed their heartfelt sympathies to McLaughlin. Even the superintendent stepped out from behind his stony face to offer measured support.

The incident, added to the death of Constable Johnson, brought Scotland Yard to a new level of shock and gloom. To make matters worse, the newspapers reported the attack, so the department seemed even more weak and inept in the face of the East End murders.

The police were deeply pessimistic that they would ever get their hands on the perpetrator or perpetrators of the crimes. Depressingly, Byron and Winchester had convincing alibis for the night of the murder at McLaughlin's home.

The mood of Scotland Yard suddenly changed one day in mid-January, when Dickson and Murdoch arrived excitedly at McLaughlin's office to report some startling news.

Dickson took the lead. "Sir, we were separately following the coaches of Byron and Winchester late last evening. They knew they were being followed and were being evasive. They were running at high speed, making sudden turns down side streets, trying to lose us. It was completely reckless; they could have run over somebody in the dark. Obviously, they were up to something."

Dickson paused for a breath. "We kept on them. They didn't lose us, but I believe they thought they had given us the slip. We followed them to an isolated mansion on the outskirts of northeast London. They parked their coaches among a dozen others in the courtyard, their drivers loitering around, chatting."

Murdoch took his turn. "Both of us tied up our mounts in nearby woods. Neither of us knew about the other. We crept up to the windows of the mansion's drawing room, practically bumping into one another. The curtains were closed, but there were some openings in them, giving us a view inside. It was a strange sight."

McLaughlin gave Higgins a knowing glance. He had his suspicions about the general nature of what had been happening in the drawing room.

Murdoch went on. "There were a dozen individuals in red cloaks with hoods over their heads. They were standing around a thirteenth, who seemed to go about some sort of ceremony at a heavy stone or marble table. On the table was a gold cross, about a foot high, with a ruby-red ornament in the shape of a snake curled around it. There were silver cups and a silver dish, which appeared to be full of animal innards. Two candles lit up the table-top. The silver candle holders had the same red snake coiled around them and—"

Dickson broke in. "The leader was reading from a very thick, old-looking book on the table. He gestured from time to time to the group, which chanted something that we couldn't make out. Now and then, the leader would pause and turn to throw what appeared to be a powder into the blazing fireplace behind him. An eerie green flame would

251

shoot out. The others around the table then took turns throwing something into the dish of entrails."

"After all this," added Murdoch, "they washed in some bowls. They sat in a row at a very long, narrow table, breaking bread and drinking what seemed to be wine from a glass pitcher. It looked for all the world like — you know — the painting *'The Last Supper.'* For the whole ceremony, their faces were hidden in the deep hoods, so we couldn't make out Byron or Winchester."

"Following the meal, the group disbanded," said Dickson. "We rushed back to our mounts, preparing to follow Byron and Winchester again. The coaches began to leave with their hooded owners, but to our surprise, two of them — we could not see whom — got into Byron's coach. The coach took off suddenly at a breakneck pace. We almost didn't catch them, but we finally got on them and followed the coach, unobserved, to the brothel district of East London."

The inspector and Higgins listened with rapt attention. They sensed something even more bizarre was imminent.

Dickson's excitement mounted. "The coach dropped off the pair at a rundown tenement and drove on. We watched as the two went into the tenement; we drew up to the door, listening. In a few moments, all hell broke loose. We heard a high-pitched scream from a woman's voice inside. Naturally, we started pounding on the door, shouting to be let in, but there was no response. We had to shoulder the door in. We rushed inside the shabby quarters, only to see the tail end of one jumping through the window. The other had disappeared, apparently out the window, too."

Murdoch was ashen as he described the scene. "A woman in her thirties lay on the bed, badly bleeding from her wounds. A fancy knife with the same snake around its handle was on the floor. The woman was alive, and Dickson stayed to tend her. I gave chase to the pair, who were running down the street. I could hardly see them in the low light."

Murdoch dramatically described what happened next. "I ran after them for about a block. They didn't listen to my orders to stop. I knew I was about to lose them in the dark and pulled my pistol and fired a shot at one of them. He seemed to stop for a second, and I thought I'd hit him, but he ran on and disappeared. They got away — both of the buggers. Excuse the language, Inspector."

McLaughlin took a few moments to absorb what he had heard. "Higgins, take two men and bring Byron in for questioning, without delay. Keep in mind he may be carrying a pistol. Arm yourselves accordingly. Gather any evidence at his apartment, too, such as the ring and any bloody clothes. Inspect the coach for any evidence and talk to the driver."

After his men had left, McLaughlin became thoughtful. Was a satanic cult at work here? This would make sense of some key details of the murders: the missing body parts of the victims and evidence that it would take more than one man to carry out the brutal crimes. What if it had been his poor servant's entrails there in the pan as part of some demented ritual? Byron and Winchester's alibis for the night of his murder may not have meant they were innocent. They may have had their fellow members carry out the murder in their stead. In fact, that would handily divert suspicion away

253

from Byron and Winchester in the general matter of the murders. If that were so, it was most clever!

A few hours later, Byron was unceremoniously brought to police headquarters and held in a room while McLaughlin and the rest reviewed the evidence gathered.

"What have you got?" McLaughlin asked Higgins.

"Well, we couldn't locate the ring, and Byron claimed to have no idea where it was."

"Convenient," remarked McLaughlin sarcastically.

"We also checked all of his wardrobe we could find, but there were no blood stains or signs of street dirt... We *did* find a red stain on the seat of the coach, maybe dried blood."

"Did you talk to the coachman?"

"No. He was apparently off duty, and we didn't know his whereabouts, but we'll track him down soon enough. We asked the chemist to have a look at the stain."

McLaughlin sighed. "Well, let's see Byron." He braced himself for the encounter.

Byron was brought roughly into McLaughlin's office and told to sit down. McLaughlin and Byron glared at one another for a few seconds in silence, their animosity almost palpable.

The inspector made the first move. "Well, Lord Byron, our paths seem destined to cross."

"Is it destiny or simply your habit of harassing me, Inspector?"

"Be careful, Byron. We do have evidence of your wrong-doing this time. You can't hide behind your glib comments anymore."

"What am I supposed to have done *this* time? Plotted to blow up parliament on Guy Fawkes Day?"

"Not quite, but something serious enough. A woman in the East End, a prostitute, was cut up very badly early this morning. She would have died but for the intervention of a constable. Your coach was observed to have dropped off two hooded individuals at the woman's door. These two were in there with her while the crime was in progress. How do you account for that, Lord Byron?" His question held a hint of triumph.

"So, are you implying I was one of the perpetrators, Inspector?"

McLaughlin gave him a steely look. "Well, it was *your* coach."

"Most certainly I was not there. I was at a meeting with friends in North London. While at the meeting, my coach was stolen and the driver commandeered by two men. Verify that with my driver, if you want. I was nowhere near East London early this morning."

"We tried to talk to your coachman, but he's conveniently unavailable," retorted McLaughlin.

"Well, I'm not my coachman's keeper," Byron shot back.

"Higgins, show Lord Byron what we have." Higgins laid a piece of heavy, folded cloth on the desk, unfurling it to reveal the dagger inside. "Anything about this that's familiar to you, Lord Byron?"

"No, should there be?" he asked, as a line of beady sweat formed on his brow.

"The serpent on the handle is identical to the one on your ring and to Lord Winchester's."

"I hadn't made the comparison."

"Well, we have." McLaughlin stepped toward him. "We've seen Winchester's ring and know it's identical to yours and to the dagger's serpent. Why wouldn't we believe that you were one of the two at the scene of the attack?"

Byron shrugged. "Flimsy evidence, Inspector. No court would convict me on that."

The inspector ignored his brazenness. "And would any of your 'friends' be able to confirm your whereabouts last night, after the meeting?"

"Why, yes. The host would be able to."

"And who might that be?"

"That would-be Lord Warrington. He has an estate just on the outskirts of North London."

"And what is the nature of your relationship with Lord Warrington?"

"He is a friend. A group of us friends get together at one another's homes for cards and port once in a while. Is that illegal, Inspector?"

"No. Unless your meetings are more sinister than that."

"What are you implying, sir?"

"I'm saying you and the twelve others were observed conducting bizarre rituals at Warrington's mansion last night. No more of your pretenses. Do you deny this, Lord Byron?"

Byron looked nervous. "Well, I don't think there's anything wrong with belonging to a religious group, which it is. Would you call prayers and faith

256

'sinister,' Inspector? Would you arrest your minister or priest for the offense of practicing his faith?"

McLaughlin resisted the temptation to roll his eyes. "So now it goes from port and cards with friends to a religious meeting," he said acidly. "What are we to believe, Byron?"

"You're avoiding my question, sir. Are prayers and faith sinister?"

"It depends on what you are praying to," McLaughlin shot back. "What might that be?"

"Well, if you must know, we believe in mystical forces that exist through all nature, including humankind, that create life and order in the universe. It is the old religion of nature worship, going back thousands of years, at least to the time of the Druids. Now, is that so dreadful? Has freedom of religion in England ceased to exist?"

McLaughlin ignored his questions. "We know there were sinister elements in your ceremony, Byron. The evidence was on a stone table at the center of your rituals: a silver dish, which appeared to be full of entrails, and a large gold cross with an ornamental red serpent coiled around it. The serpent was identical to that on your ring and Winchester's, too, just like the serpent on the dagger."

A flash of panic came and went in Byron's eyes. "More assumptions, Inspector," he countered. "Your men mistook the situation. There were no more entrails there than on your breakfast plate this morning. It was merely a pan of weeds from the marshes, in their natural habitat of water. It's all part of nature worship, and that includes the snake symbol. Nothing malevolent about that!" he said, looking victorious.

"We have an opinion otherwise, from a learned person."

"Oh? And who might that be?"

"A professor at Cambridge, who studies symbolism, tells us the serpent coiled around the cross embodies the victory of evil over good."

Byron snorted. "I went to Cambridge. I know the professor you speak of and that he spouts off to his students far more fiction than he does facts."

"Nevertheless, Byron, we are led to suspect you and your associates are part of a satanic cult, which exists for malevolent purposes. We believe that after your ceremony two of you left to commit a black deed — to remove organs from a living human being for your rituals."

Byron threw back his head and laughed derisively. "I compliment you on your creative imagination, Inspector. But, unfortunately for you, it will not persuade a magistrate. If this dagger was indeed the weapon at the scene, then it was stolen by the same rogues who stole my coach. They used both to commit a crime for their own purposes. These acts would never be condoned by our members."

"Well, tell me, Lord Byron, if this religious group of yours is so innocent, why do you keep it such a secret? In fact, you have lied to me about its existence on three occasions — once tonight and twice in our first meeting. You also lied when you denied there was no symbolic meaning to the serpent on your ring — which, by the way, has conveniently disappeared."

"Touché, Inspector. I freely admit I was not entirely forthcoming. But what would *you* do if you belonged to a religious group that people would view as quite strange, at the very least, and misunderstand or perhaps even fear? Would you reveal your religious beliefs, especially if you were a member of the House of Lords, a part of government? I would say you'd be as secretive as I have been... As for my ring, I'm sure I simply misplaced it. I've been quite distracted lately by all the unwarranted attention from the police.

McLaughlin had had enough of Byron's maneuvering. "Higgins!" he roared. "Throw this man in a cell where he belongs!"

And that was the end of the encounter, with McLaughlin apparently, the loser for the time being.

Chapter 37

The police wasted no time getting out to Warrington's estate, all four taking the fastest coach available. On the way, they discussed Byron's interrogation.

Higgins spoke first. "He's a slippery one, all right. Hard to pin down."

"I thought I had him checkmated several times, but he always had another move," observed McLaughlin.

"I think you were close to cracking him, though, sir. He looked mighty nervous as you tied him to the ceremony at Warrington's — too nervous for it to be a nice little religious get-together." Dickson and Murdoch nodded in agreement.

McLaughlin then remembered what Byron had said to them back at headquarters: "Your *men* mistook the situation." McLaughlin wondered aloud how Byron had known there was more than one agent at the scene at Warrington's.

"Unless he was at the prostitute's in East London and knew that he had been followed from Warrington's by at least a couple of men who were yelling and pounding on the front door," replied Higgins.

"It could be, Higgins."

"But also, sir, it's likely Byron knew both him and Winchester were being followed for some weeks. Maybe he guessed that both of our men had followed them to Warrington's last night. So we had to have at least a couple of men spying on the ceremony."

The inspector shook his head. "It's just the kind of guessing game we get into whenever Byron turns up in the investigation," he lamented. "But I must say, the story of his coach being commandeered is too convenient to believe. These people, I think, have probably sworn loyalty to one another. It's difficult to believe that two of their own would betray the rest in such a dramatic and risky fashion. This had to have been planned by the group. But the thing is, we can't prove all this — not yet. We'll see what we can get out of Warrington and company."

"Let's keep our fingers crossed," remarked Higgins, "that Byron hasn't gotten to him first, through a messenger, so that they could get their stories right."

McLaughlin sighed. "We just don't know, Higgins. We'll shake it out of Warrington, if we have to. By the way, Higgins, what was Byron's reaction when you collared him this morning?"

"He didn't seem shocked or surprised. In fact, it seemed he didn't give a fig about it."

"That's interesting. Did he expect us, then? And if so, was he at the crime scene and knew we were coming for him?" The two fell into thoughtful silence.

The police coach pulled up in Lord Warrington's courtyard within the hour. His mansion was impressive. It looked as if it had been the front of an ancient castle, which had been rebuilt into a stately country residence. It was surrounded by acres of forest and meadows, eventually turning into murky bogs and marshes in the distance.

Dickson and Murdoch brought the others to the windows of the drawing room, showing them the viewpoint from which they had seen the ceremony. The curtains were now open. McLaughlin looked inside, but everything appeared to belong to an ordinary upper-crust drawing room.

The master of the estate was at home. The group showed their badges and asked to speak with him. They were led into the massive drawing room.

"Sir, I'm Inspector McLaughlin and these are my assistants, Sergeant Higgins, and our constables, Murdoch and Dickson."

"Well, this is all quite unexpected," remarked Warrington, who looked rather overwhelmed at the sight of four burly policemen standing in his drawing room. "What — what can I do for you gentlemen?"

"We're carrying out an investigation and would like some information from you."

"Of course, Inspector," he said. His voice sounded welcoming, but his eyes looked wary and apprehensive.

This was not lost on McLaughlin. "Was Lord Byron part of a gathering here last night?" he asked, observing Warrington closely.

"Why, yes. Why do you ask?"

McLaughlin ignored the question. "What time did he leave?"

"He left about six thirty in the morning. He had some trouble. Some rogues stole his coach, and he had no way of getting home immediately."

McLaughlin probed further. "After Lord Byron left, did you at any time receive a message from him or from anyone else?" And he quickly added,

262

"Before you answer that question, keep in mind we had the place under observation last night, and that any attempt to mislead a police investigation is a serious offence."

Warrington looked aghast. "I would never dream of such a thing. I'm shocked you'd imply that... No. I never received a message from Byron or anyone after he left. Why in the world would I have?"

McLaughlin ignored this question, too. "What was the purpose of your gathering, Lord Warrington? Again, keep in mind it was under observation by our constables here." He gestured to Murdoch and Dickson.

"Uh, periodically we have a religious meeting here and at other homes of the faithful."

"And what are your beliefs?

"We're nature worshipers, Inspector. We are against the misuse of science in the world and wish to return to earlier, natural values."

"Does your ceremony include animal entrails?"

"Good God, no! We are respectful of our fellow creatures."

The inspector was relentless. "Our men tell us there was a dish of entrails here. Where is it now? In fact, I see none of the paraphernalia used in your ceremony."

"We put it away," replied Warrington. "My family does use the drawing room for our usual activities."

"Let's see the paraphernalia," demanded McLaughlin. They were brought to an adjoining room and shown the ceremonial objects. "I presume this is the ceremonial dish? I notice it has been washed out."

"Well, it was filled with weeds from the marshes as part of our ceremony. They're put back, afterward, into the earth from which they came. No entrails here, Inspector."

McLaughlin looked unconvinced. "Is this all your apparatus?"

"Yes."

"Where's the cross with the red ornamental serpent upon it, Lord Warrington? Have you misplaced it?"

"Of course not. I forgot it's usually placed in the drawer, here." He pulled it out.

"What's the meaning of this piece?

"It symbolizes our worship of nature, Inspector. The good of the natural world."

"Serpents generally don't signify good, especially red ones. In fact, they often refer to evil. Is this a satanic symbol?"

The lord seemed shocked again. "Absolutely not. The serpent represents a creature connected with the earth and the goodness of the earth. That's all."

"So, you do not have a satanic cult here?"

"Good lord, no. We're nature worshipers, as I said."

"Is there something else missing from the ceremonial gear?" McLaughlin asked sharply.

"No, I don't think so."

"How about this?" McLaughlin gestured to Higgins, who produced the ceremonial dagger out of one of his coat pockets.

"Oh! I thought I'd misplaced that. I forgot."

"You do seem distracted today, Lord Warrington."

"Where did you get that, Inspector?"

"It was found at the scene of a near-murder."

"What?"

"Yes. How would you account for it being there, sir?"

"I — I haven't the faintest idea," stammered Warrington.

"Let me illuminate you. Two individuals from your group, dressed in red cloaks, emerged from Byron's coach in East London and cut up a prostitute before escaping. They left this dagger behind after they were interrupted. Now, what would two of your 'worshippers' be doing in East London with your ceremonial dagger and Lord Byron's coach?"

"I can't imagine. Our group has sworn allegiance to one another. If these are the facts, they violated our sacred trust."

"We believe that these two were out to remove organs from the victim, to use later in a satanic ritual. What do you think of that?"

"That would be unthinkable!" cried Warrington. "It would be a violation of our basic principle of nonviolence to all creatures."

"Yes. Yet here is your ceremonial knife, fresh from such a violation."

Warrington looked panicky. "These two, whoever they are, must have somehow stolen it. It's — it's unbelievable!" he cried.

"We need to know the names of the others who attended the meeting."

The aristocrat folded his arms across his chest. "I'm sorry, Inspector," he said. "I can't give you those names. They are people of note, people with influence, who cannot be revealed."

"You *will* reveal them, sir," McLaughlin threatened, "or I will haul you down to headquarters."

The onslaught was too much for Warrington. "Very well then." He sighed, sitting down at his writing table and scribbling the names down on a sheet of paper.

Before they left, the lord was asked to show them the grounds, so they could look for further evidence. They were particularly interested in any signs of recently disturbed earth and whether any bodies or body parts had been buried on the vast acreage — although it would have been easier to submerge anything incriminating in the swamplands beyond. Nothing unusual presented itself to the police.

However, there was an unexpected turn of events as they approached the edge of the forest near the bogs. McLaughlin was talking to Warrington when he was interrupted by Higgins. "Sir! Inspector!" McLaughlin didn't pay any attention. "Sir! Sir!" insisted Higgins.

"What is it, Higgins?" said McLaughlin irritably.

"Look over to your right, toward the swamp, behind that tree," said Higgins, pointing in the direction.

McLaughlin turned and saw someone observing them from behind a tree. "Stay where you are! Scotland Yard," he yelled.

The person bolted toward the swamp. Murdoch, the most athletic of them all, took off after him but lost him in the tall reeds of the swamp. He returned somewhat winded and disheveled.

"Do you know who that was?" McLaughlin asked Warrington.

"No, I've never seen him before. I have no idea what he was doing there."

"Are trespassers common here?"

"No, Inspector, it's too remote, and there's little big game for poachers. The alkaline nature of the ponds also makes for bad-tasting fish."

"Well, another mystery. There's much of that going around today, it would seem. I — what in the world is that smell?"

Everyone looked at Murdoch. "I took a tumble in the bog, sir," he confessed. "I must have brushed up against something."

"Are you all right, Murdoch?"

"It's nothing, sir."

"Well, for God's sake then, stand downwind, man!"

Murdoch shuffled away sheepishly.

The four left in their coach with poor Murdoch in the corner, still reeking of something. The rest sat as far away from him as the cramped quarters would allow.

"Warrington's hiding something," commented Higgins. "He looked scared enough."

"I'll wager he and the others have agreed on a common version of events for last night," McLaughlin added. "The cock and bull story of the coach being commandeered, for one."

"And the dagger being stolen is the other," said Higgins.

"My bet is that Byron was at the prostitute's last night," ventured Murdoch. "Along with Winchester."

"I can tell you it was not a pan of weeds we saw in there either," remarked Dickson. "It was animal or human. No question."

Murdoch's unwanted odor wafted through the coach. "That's absolutely putrid!" objected Dickson.

"Putrid?" repeated McLaughlin. "Why, that's what Coxwell said when he was knocked down the night of the second murder. There was a putrid smell in the aftermath."

Higgins added, "That poor bloke Wallington said the same thing the night the pounding happened on his front door."

The men looked at one another in puzzled silence.

The police interrogated the other members of the suspected cult and came away with nothing to show for it. Moreover, Byron's driver, who was eventually found and questioned, confirmed the story of his coach being commandeered at Warrington's. Indeed, thought McLaughlin, their suspects were doing remarkably well at concealing their malevolent activities and purposes, whatever they were. The police were frustrated further by the chemist's report that he was unable to identify the reddish substance found in Byron's coach.

Byron had to be released, after three days, for lack of evidence and through political pressure upon the superintendent. McLaughlin and Higgins were furious. Higgins spat out his ire about the superintendent. "We know which side his bread is buttered on... And guess who he'll come complaining to when Byron and his blokes kill somebody else."

McLaughlin was more cautious with his words. "There's not much we can do about it, right now. We'll keep close watch on Byron and his fellow 'worshippers.' They will blunder again, and this time we'll have them, political pressure or not."

Chapter 38

It was a bright winter's morning in late January. Falding had visited Polidori in his dining room to share breakfast and inquire about his mental state. Uncharacteristically, his young friend was quite cheerful that morning. All seemed well among steaming tea and crumpets — until Polidori made a sudden announcement.

"I have just recently sent a note to Scotland Yard," he said.

"About what?" Falding asked, nearly choking on his crumpet.

"I sent a note confirming my guilt in the recent London murders."

"You did what? You know you had no part in the murders! What did you hope to gain from such folly, John?"

"But I *am* responsible for these deaths," he protested. "I created the perpetrator of these horrible crimes, so I am no less guilty than it. It might as well have been my own hand that killed them. Perhaps if I am arrested and punished for these deeds, I will atone for my sins in the eyes of God. Perhaps then He will see fit to remove this hateful manifestation from the world."

As Falding began to reply, there was a heavy knock at the door. "Scotland Yard!" came a muffled, rather authoritarian voice through the thick oak door. As Harris unlocked the door, two burly men in heavy woolen greatcoats invited themselves in and pushed by him. The older man was bespectacled and graying, slightly stooped below his six feet.

"I am Inspector McLaughlin," he announced, brushing a dusting of snow from his greatcoat. "This is Sergeant Higgins. We are looking for Dr. Polidori."

"That would be me," said Polidori.

"And you are, sir?"

"I am Dr. Alex Falding, his friend and psychiatrist." Falding studied the inspector for a few moments. *So, this is Tanner's champion*, he thought.

"Very well then," said the inspector impatiently. "We have much to talk about."

Polidori gestured everyone toward the stuffed chairs in the drawing room, while Higgins stood watchfully in the background. As they seated themselves, the inspector pulled out a rather foul-smelling pipe from somewhere in his coat, lighting it adeptly. He wasted no more time getting down to business.

"Well, Dr. Polidori," he began gruffly, "what do you have to say about your note?"

Falding slowly shook his head, knowing full well what his friend was about to say and that it wouldn't go over well with their two visitors.

Polidori began to relate his supernatural tale. A derisive snort came from the background, and the inspector shot a quick disapproving look in Higgins' direction. The inspector resumed listening to the incredible account of the murders.

When Polidori was finished, there was dead silence. The inspector spoke first. "As police, we deal with facts and reality, not supernatural fantasies and dreams, Dr. Polidori. We can assure you we are looking for a human suspect in these murders, so if you are unable to provide us with anything more, we will be going." He paused ominously and then said, "Furthermore, if you didn't have such an obvious mental condition, I would charge you with mischief and attempting to mislead the police in an investigation." Once again there was a snort in the background.

Falding interjected. "Inspector and Mr. Higgins, I must truly apologize for the behavior of my friend and his taking up your valued time. Dr. Polidori is, of course, suffering from delusions and under my care."

"Well, I think perhaps he requires further care from you, Doctor," remarked the inspector acidly as he began to rise to his feet.

Polidori suddenly stood up, protesting that he had an explanation for the crimes, as incredible as it may have seemed. He begged for a chance to prove it.

The inspector sighed and sat down again. "This is against my better judgment, but I'll give you five minutes. Let's see what you know... In the case of the last murder, what was the position of the body?"

Polidori looked bewildered.

"All right then," continued McLaughlin, "how was the person murdered?" Seeing that Polidori was again at a loss, he stood up once again.

But then Polidori cried out, "I know something — it — it came to me in a dream. I had some images of the murder in my dream."

"We don't have time for this nonsense," snapped McLaughlin. "Higgins, we will be leaving."

Polidori cried out, in horror, "Disemboweled! Disemboweled! I saw a disemboweled body in my dream, as clearly as I see you now."

The inspector said nothing, but his face seemed to show focused interest in what Polidori was saying. "Why couldn't you answer my first question?" he challenged.

"I just get snippets of the murders. I don't know why," replied Polidori, bewildered. Once in a while, I am able to see what Ruthven sees and think what it thinks."

"Surely you don't think he's a suspect, Inspector?" Falding interrupted. "As his psychiatrist, I can vouch for the innocence of Dr. Polidori. On the night of the last murder, I spent a sleepless night ministering to him, and I can assure you that he did not step outside the door that night. He could *not* have committed or known anything about that murder."

The inspector, Falding thought, appeared suspicious and puzzled at the same time. He looked both of them closely in the eye. "We'll be watching you carefully, Dr. Polidori," he threatened. "As for you, Dr. Falding, your alibi for your friend had better be true. We'll be looking into it." With that, he and Higgins left abruptly.

Falding set out for home deeply troubled. He assumed that the inspector would find better suspects than his friend, but he was left with disturbing questions. Did Polidori really know something about the last murder? Had McLaughlin's reaction confirmed that Polidori did indeed have some facts? If so, how could he have acquired this information? How could any rational man believe his incredible account?

He searched for likely reasons for the possibility that Polidori would know some restricted information. Perhaps an examination at the morgue had become known to him, considering that he was still part of the medical establishment. Yet so was Falding, and he did not hear of it — strange.

Furthermore, word of such a gruesome crime might also have spread quickly through the streets, despite the best police efforts to contain the details. Polidori might have heard it from the postman or the maid, for all Falding knew. He was, after all, friendly with the common people.

The psychiatrist was left in confusion about what had just happened and that night fell into restless, dream-filled sleep.

Chapter 39

It was the beginning of February. Despite Falding's initial optimism, his friend was not progressing in his hypnotic treatment, to say the least. He continued to claim Ruthven haunted him relentlessly, disappearing at will to carry out more diabolical murders.

Falding decided to consult with his colleague, Edward Tanner, about the matter. The two met over a glass of sherry in Tanner's library, surrounded by thick books on every conceivable subject. Several were authored by Tanner himself. Falding thought proudly that he was a true man of knowledge.

Falding was also proud of Polidori, whose book, *The Vampyre*, had recently been accepted for publication. He had heard the publishers were enthralled by it. But what should have been a moment of great joy for him and Polidori was clouded by the latter's inconceivable beliefs about his character, Ruthven.

Falding spoke for some time about his difficulties treating the young doctor. "He's resisting hypnosis, Edward. He will not go even into light trance and has trouble giving over to the free flow of imagination. I believe he's unwilling to let hypnosis work, since this would disprove the existence of his 'manifestation.' He would then have to face deeply painful underlying feelings in his unconscious."

Tanner listened carefully and finally spoke. "So, he is both a friend *and* a patient of yours, Alex? Don't you think your boundaries with him are unclear? So, that you are neither entirely his friend nor entirely his psychiatrist?"

"I know it seems professionally unsound, Edward. But I believe I know him so well from our friendship, I'm able to grasp his mind more deeply in treatment."

"Nevertheless, Alex, it can work both ways. Perhaps your friendship can also blind you when he becomes your patient. Is it not possible that some of the difficulties treating him have to do with this confusion?"

Falding sat back thoughtfully, not entirely surprised by the question. "I could not rule that out," he admitted. He found himself admiring his friend's wisdom even more. "What do you think I should do? It's gone too far. I can't just abandon him."

Tanner did not hesitate. "I think you should refer him to someone else for the deeper aspects of treatment."

"To whom?"

"There's little question. Eddington's your man, Alex."

"Charles Eddington?"

"Yes. You must have some familiarity with his work."

"Enough to know he has a remarkable reputation as a hypnotist."

Tanner nodded. "And well deserved, every bit of it. I worked with him a decade ago. I think he's done more than any man to advance the use of hypnosis in medicine, well, since Mesmer. By the way, not many know it, but he was actually the student of one of Mesmer's disciples."

"I do know, thankfully, that he doesn't believe in animal magnetism."

"No and he doesn't need the theory, either. I've watched him work powerfully with the unconscious and succeed with many difficult mental conditions. If anyone can get through to John, it is Eddington."

A few days later, Polidori agreed to see the hypnotist, especially after hearing about his considerable reputation. Falding took this as a hopeful sign. Was his friend, for whatever reason, becoming more open to the psychiatric approach to his problems?

Falding accompanied him for his first visit to Dr. Eddington. They met him in his office at Cambridge University. The place looked like an explosion of papers, open books and scattered pens.

In some ways, Eddington matched his office. His silvery, unkempt hair fell to his shoulders, and a bushy white mustache grew wildly in the general area under his nose. He was carelessly attired, as if the matter of dress was a mere afterthought to him. Overall, he fit the popular image of an eccentric academic. However, he made up for this with his warm, sympathetic smile and bright, twinkling eyes, which reflected a still-sharp intellect.

Dr. Eddington immediately engaged Polidori. "John," he began informally, "Alex has told me about your difficulties. You believe the character of your book appears to you and mentally tortures and murders others. Is that right?"

"Basically, yes."

"So, you do think your character, Lord Ruthven, is real, then?"

"Yes, I do."

Eddington's eyes fixed upon him. "But you must not completely believe it. If you did, you wouldn't have come to see me, would you? True?"

Polidori nodded.

"How much doubt do you have that it is real, John? Ten percent? Twenty percent? More?"

Polidori shrugged. "I don't know."

"Take a guess, John."

"Maybe ten percent."

"All right, we can work with that," reassured Eddington.

"Yes. For God's sake, sir, I need relief from all of this."

"I can understand that, John," Eddington said sympathetically, "but we need to have a picture of what is going on first. It's tempting to use psychiatric jargon and call your symptoms hallucinations or delusions. However, change does not come from the names we give to problems."

Eddington waited for reaction from Polidori. Receiving none, he added, "We *can* say that your book's character likely represents a part of your personality that is battling with other parts for dominance of the mind. Hypnosis can be used to resolve this conflict. Makes sense so far?"

"Yes, let's get on with it, Doctor."

Surprisingly, Polidori went into trance easily under Eddington's guidance. He appeared to trust Eddington's ability to help him, Falding thought. Perhaps he was finally willing to face his emotional pain and give hypnosis a good attempt. Falding did not know what had brought this about, but he suspected that his friend's desperation to get better was at the root of it.

278

Eddington then introduced a remarkable technique that Falding had never seen before. "John," he said, "I would like you to visualize your book's character, Ruthven... Do you have it?"

"Yes."

"Good. Have you ever spoken with your character before, in your imagination, I mean?"

"No."

"All right, John, I'd like you to imagine having a conversation with your character now, as two actors would dialogue in a play. How does it begin?"

Polidori paused for a moment and then spoke directly to his character. "Ruthven, who are you? What are you? Are you Satan or one of his followers?"

"Does your character say anything, John?" Eddington prodded.

Polidori gave a voice to Ruthven. "Satan! Hell! These are but convenient fictions. All of them!"

"Whose fictions are they, Ruthven?"

"Your own church's, you gullible fool!"

"But why would the church be untruthful, deceitful?"

"It's simple, Polidori. To have power over its believers by manipulating their fears of sin and hell."

"Sacrilege, Ruthven. How dare you demean the church!"

"Polidori, when you have no other defense, you climb up on your high horse of righteous indignation!"

"No! I defend the church, heretic!"

279

"You abandon your Christ's teaching of humility, Polidori. You are guilty of the sin of pride. You are a hypocrite! A sinner!"

"You have avoided my question, Ruthven. Who are you? You hide behind those red eyes. Too cowardly to show yourself?"

"Polidori, you can thank your God I do not reveal myself. It would be the last thing you would ever see!"

"All you can do is threaten. You are brutal and hideous, Ruthven."

"Tsk-tsk. So, you abandon your principle of love for others, too! You *are* a hypocrite."

"How could one love an abomination, a beast like you? God help me!"

"Do you really think your God hears you, Polidori — that he will help you, or even cares about the affairs of men?"

"Yes. The loving Father eventually answers our prayers."

The character snorted. "What kind of loving father brings man into the world of suffering? What kind of god brings man into life and then gives him the knowledge of his own mortality, of his own death? Doesn't that sound cruel and corrupt? What sort of love is that?"

"The mark of a man is what he has done with that life before death."

"How noble, Polidori! What do you or any other man have to show for your puny, miserable lives, devoid of any meaning? What difference do *you* make in the great scheme of things?"

"Small acts of kindness and love multiply to strengthen the whole of humanity; that strength is eternal."

"Only a Romantic poet, an idealist, could believe that sentimental nonsense. There is no such thing as altruism. All acts — no matter how generous they seem — ultimately serve self-interest. The root of man is selfishness. Didn't you know that, Polidori?"

"Only someone without a soul could believe that! I pity you."

"Do not pity me, Polidori. Fear me!"

"Ruthven, God is watching you. It is you who should fear."

With that, the confrontation ended. Eddington guided Polidori out of trance. He paused, gathering his thoughts, making sure that his patient was back to normal consciousness.

He smiled kindly and observed, "Clearly, there is a struggle of opposites within your mind, John. Powerful disagreement, even hatred, exists between them on some important questions about life. This is how healing begins: with the expression of the conflict. Later, confrontation turns to true dialogue, and reconciliation can begin. Come to see me again, John."

His new patient looked uplifted, and it was obvious from his smile that he would visit Dr. Eddington again. Falding, too, was pleased with the session. Eddington, he thought, had lived up to his reputation. He had drawn out elements deep within Polidori's psyche, some quite surprising. Irreligious sentiments, cruelty, and selfishness had arisen, embodied in the words of Ruthven. These qualities

281

were the total opposites of what Falding knew of John's personality. The duke had evidently made much more of a mark on his son than Falding had thought. This had lain deep in his friend's unconscious until revealed now through Eddington. Perhaps, he mused, the old doctor's unusual methods held the key to eliminating Polidori's hallucination of Ruthven, once and for all.

The day after Eddington's session, Falding went to visit his friend to gauge his reactions and unfortunately to bring very disturbing news. Polidori seemed unusually cheerful, but noticing his visitor's glum expression, he became somber. "Alex, usually it's me who's dispirited, not you. What's happening?" he asked.

Falding hesitated. "I've got some bad news, John. I heard Charles Eddington died last night."

Polidori stared at him. "It was Ruthven, again. I know it," he gasped.

"John, Eddington was getting on. He had a heart condition, and sadly, it was his time."

"You don't think it's strange he died the very evening after he saw me?"

"No, it had nothing to do with that."

"But it did, Alex. I felt stronger and more confident after seeing Eddington. Ruthven feared that he would be too effective with me. Ruthven couldn't let that happen and couldn't let him live."

"So why hasn't your book's character dispatched me, if he is the murderer?"

"Because I think Ruthven sees your treatment as ineffective. To him, your work continues the fiction that he is simply a figment of my imagination.

282

Ruthven is able to hide behind this notion. He does not have to reveal his presence and his true nature to you. He is amused watching us debate, feeding upon our frustration and pain. He's toying with us."

"So, you're saying our treatment is actually helping this imaginary entity by providing it concealment and some entertainment? That's quite a twist!" Falding shook his head wearily. He did not have the energy or the will at that moment to debate his deluded friend once again.

Chapter 40

McLaughlin had been looking forward to a quiet Saturday evening with Lisbeth before the drawing room fire. They were settling down on the sofa when he heard loud knocking at the front door. He opened the door to encounter a junior constable who had come to urgently summon him down to the river.

McLaughlin and Higgins arrived at the riverside two hours past sunset to see a group of constables holding their lanterns over what seemed an old well. A band of men who appeared to be vagabonds cowered around a low fire nearby.

The inspector stood silently for a few moments taking in the curious scene and then approached his man in charge. "Your report, Sergeant Mulligan?"

"Sir, one of our constables, patrolling about twenty minutes from here, was approached on the street by these men." Mulligan pointed toward the shabby group around the fire. "They rushed up to the constable, frightened out of their wits…"

"Go on, Sergeant."

"They said they had been drinking around the fire here, making merry, at about dusk. Then one of them apparently threw an empty liquor jug into the well. Suddenly, these blokes heard a loud screeching coming from the well and thought they saw a large, dark shadow whirling over it."

"What did they think it was?" McLaughlin queried.

Mulligan smiled. "They said it was the devil laughing and he was coming for them from the mouth of Hell."

McLaughlin remembered Peter Wallington's story of the intruder at his door. "The devil does seem to be getting about these days," he remarked sarcastically.

"Yes, sir. They said that after the commotion at the well, they bolted from the place. All except an old man who refused to leave the fire, saying, 'I'm too old and drunk to run off. I'm staying, be damned the devil.' Within a few minutes, though, his mates thought better of leaving him behind and returned for him, but he was gone. All that was left was his hat and his prized possession, a half-empty bottle of rum. Terrified, they ran for the constable."

"Any evidence of violence, Mulligan?"

"No, sir. No blood or body parts or weapons left behind. Nor any tracks to the well, except for the bloke who threw in the jug."

"Any to the river, Sergeant?"

"Lots of smudged prints there." He nodded toward the vagabonds. "They've gone back and forth to the river."

"This is a dry well. Let's get a man down there," McLaughlin said. "Any volunteers?"

The constables looked uneasily at one another.

"All right," McLaughlin said impatiently. "Carter, let's get a rope on you."

Carter was soon lowered into the well, his lantern dimming as he descended into the dark depths. The rope went slack. "I've reached the bottom, sir," he yelled up. "There's a large cave here. The smell is awful."

McLaughlin leaned further over the well. "Do you see anything in there, Carter?"

"Yes, sir. I — get me out of here!" he shouted.

His comrades frantically pulled him up from the well. Suddenly, a huge black mass roared out of the well, scattering the policemen.

McLaughlin scowled. "Well, here's our devil." He and the constables swatted at the air, trying to get rid of the torrent of frightened bats around them.

Hoping the bats had departed for a while, the police explored what seemed to be a huge cave beneath the well. "This is not a cave. It's a tunnel," observed McLaughlin. He pointed at the distant shadows. "It's a stonework tunnel leading to others."

Mulligan, who had been exploring ahead, called to the others. "There's remains here!"

McLaughlin and Higgins hurried up to Mulligan, examining his discovery. "These are human skeletal remains, all right, but they look very old," McLaughlin noted.

"Sir, there are some arrowheads and axe blades, even some coins, mixed with the bones," said Higgins.

"An old battle scene?" queried McLaughlin. "Let's search as far as we can tonight. We'll get the historian from the university to look at these bones."

Chapter 41

There had been a lull in the East End murders since the intrusion at the inspector's home several weeks before, but McLaughlin suspected the murderer would try again to shock the city and show the police were powerless to stop him. He expected any day to hear Higgins rapping at his front door in the middle of the night with news of another victim.

He thought the murderer would go after someone high in authority next, perhaps himself or the superintendent. The inspector had been very careful since the horrific incident at his home. He had insisted that the superintendent be accompanied by a guard. McLaughlin himself now regularly carried a pistol in his waistband and one of smaller caliber lashed to his calf, for good measure. He continued to be vigilant when returning home from headquarters, making sure he was not followed. He had learned his lesson at great cost.

On February 5, 1817, the investigation took an exciting turn. McLaughlin and Higgins received an unexpected visitor in the inspector's office.

"Well, Inspector Bruce McGregor." McLaughlin beamed. "What brings you so far from the hallowed halls of Glasgow?"

"Good to see you, James." McGregor warmly shook hands with his old friend. "I'm here about the London murders. We've been following the investigation, of course. We know you lads have been having a rough go of it."

"That's putting it mildly, Bruce. It's been hell on earth, I can tell you."

McGregor nodded sympathetically. "Any progress so far?" he asked hopefully.

"Not a whit, I'm afraid. The murderer is elusive. He strikes at night and leaves little to go on. There could be more than one. A strange cult may be involved."

"Sorry to hear about the murder of your servant, James."

"Not to mention my wife being frightened half to death," added McLaughlin, giving McGregor a grateful look for his kind words.

"So, he definitely wants on the front pages, frightening everyone with his power to kill at will, does he?"

"We think that's part of it," agreed McLaughlin. "But there's also pleasure in the act of killing involved with it and possibly cult-like rituals. Body parts from victims have been removed, perhaps for some kind of deranged religious ceremony."

McGregor shook his head in disgust and looked intently at McLaughlin. "Well, I have some news you may find intriguing," he said. "You recall my interest in the French newspapers?"

His friend nodded with a smile.

"With all the trouble with Napoleon, my newspapers from France had stopped, but began to trickle across the channel at war's end. I've just now fully received the back copies of my favorite newspaper." He handed his colleague the front page of *La Gazette,* dated October 7, 1816. "It refers to the escape from a French prison of one Jean-Marc Malvois. He was a murderer over at least a ten-year period in France during the war. In fact, it's speculated that he may have used the war as a kind of cover for his murders. People weren't paying much attention to the crimes with all the news of the war filling the newspapers."

McLaughlin looked skeptical. "It's extremely unusual for a string of murders to go on for that long. Usually, the murders mysteriously stop or the killer is caught. It's one or the other."

"The murders were highly unusual in general," observed McGregor. "The suspect was a huge man, a kind of giant, who apparently could literally tear apart his victims, if you can believe it. Some part or parts of the bodies would be missing from the murder scenes. To this day, apparently, no one knows the reason. Another peculiar thing was that the murderer had a particularly offensive body odor, which the prison doctor said was due to a rare medical condition. I personally have never heard of it before."

McLaughlin and Higgins exchanged a look, thinking the same thing. The inspector put words to it first. "There are some marked similarities with our murderer."

Higgins added, "And from the date of the newspaper, he escaped just before the East End murders started. This could be our bloke, Inspector!"

"It does sound interesting," remarked McLaughlin, "but let's not jump to conclusions."

"Right," agreed McGregor. "You've got to admit it's tantalizing, though... Now, if only the French police had any idea of where he is."

"If he did make it across the channel," ventured McLaughlin, "it would be a perfect way of evading the Paris police. It would be a fresh start, a new country, where his identity and criminal deeds would be unknown to the authorities."

Higgins jumped in excitedly. "We can check the shipping lines for somebody who looked like him, sir. A huge bloke like him with a bad smell. Hard to miss. We'll get more about his looks from the French police."

"Very good, Higgins, you can see to it." said McLaughlin. He indulged in some cautious optimism. *Maybe Higgins is right and this is our man*, he thought. *It explains some puzzling evidence at the murder scenes... But first we have to prove he was here in England during the period of the murders, and that isn't necessarily going to be easy.*

Higgins interrupted his reflections. "Is that all, Inspector?"

"No, there's another matter, Higgins. What of the old fellow who disappeared at the river? Any sign of him yet?"

"No, sir. Nothing found in the far tunnels, or in the river, either."

"He was apparently drunk and could have fallen in the river and gone down."

"His mates didn't believe that, though, sir. Said they'd left him for only a couple of minutes. They believed he wouldn't have gone anywhere without his bottle of rum, let alone without his hat. They're keeping to their devil story. Said it was no bats they saw at the well. Swore their mate had been snatched by old Beelzebub himself... Anything from the history teacher, Inspector?"

"Yes, his findings are very interesting. He said the tunnels are apparently old aqueducts from the Roman town of Londinium. He examined the bones and the objects found with them and believes they were from much later, the ninth century. He thinks that Londoners may have tried to hide from Norse raiders in the aqueducts but were found, and a battle ensued. Hence the weapons with the bones."

Higgins was unimpressed. "So, we've found out a lot about history but not much about the old man. It's an odd disappearance, though. You've got to admit that, sir."

"Indeed, it is. Perhaps the river will reveal something to us yet."

Chapter 42

As it turned out, McLaughlin soon became so intrigued by the prospect of Malvois being the London killer that he decided not to wait for word from Higgins. With the superintendent's blessing, he booked passage on a ship to France to visit the Prefecture of Police in Paris.

He walked into the French police headquarters on February 9th. The building was a huge mansion in French classical style, made of white stone gone gray over the decades. The interior was much more colorful and ornate. Grand old paintings lined the walls of the lofty hallways, and marble pillars ascended to the roof. It had probably been confiscated from a wealthy aristocrat during the revolution, McLaughlin guessed.

He learned the grim details of the Paris murders from Chief Inspector François LeClerc, who had investigated the killings from the beginning. "Jean-Marc Malvois," said LeClerc, "was molded into a brutal killer by the poverty, violence, and crime on the old Paris streets. He began with petty crime but then joined the street gangs, robbing and murdering well-to-do Parisians. Eventually he satisfied his murderous instincts when he became a paid assassin for the gangs. He protected their territories from rivals and kept their own members in line."

"A professional criminal — the worst kind," remarked McLaughlin.

"Indeed. We also think he killed for his own dark and demented reasons, possibly for the enjoyment of killing. We began to find many bodies that had been torn apart, likely while the victims were still alive."

McLaughlin winced at the gruesome details. "How did you finally collar him, Chief Inspector?"

"I would like to say as a result of our thorough deductions and investigation. But it was only through sheer luck. An observant witness called the gendarmes, who caught Malvois dismembering a body. We thought we finally had him."

"But he got away. I can only imagine how galling it must have been for you and the Prefecture. How could it possibly have happened?"

LeClerc's brow furrowed. "Malvois was awaiting trial when he managed to escape. His success was perplexing, even unbelievable. There had been only one escape in fifty years from the central Paris prison where he was kept. Yet Malvois managed to overpower no fewer than four guards. He took their keys, walked out of the prison, and disappeared without a trace."

"It sounds impossible without help," McLaughlin observed.

"I believe so, too. An aristocratic-looking gentleman, speaking French with an accent, had visited Malvois just before the escape. It is suspected this man bribed a prison guard to aid Malvois. Shortly after, the guard came into a windfall. But we were never able to prove it was a bribe."

"So now he's out there, doing God knows what."

LeClerc sighed with resignation. "Unfortunately, we have a very good idea what he is doing. Malvois is caught in an endless cycle of rage and violence. He will keep on murdering. He will be stopped only by his arrest or his own death."

These were chilling words to McLaughlin. He knew that if Malvois had made it to England and really was the London murderer, they were facing a formidable opponent. Would they be able to stop him?

After a day of conversation with LeClerc, McLaughlin returned to London headquarters gloomy and apprehensive. He was filled with far more questions than answers about Malvois.

He thought that by then Higgins would have searched the passenger lists of the channel ships for some sign of the killer. McLaughlin almost hoped that the fugitive hadn't crossed to England; that way he would remain a French problem. He realized that it was a fool's wish, for it would not solve the London murders.

As it turned out, his wish was not to be granted. He had barely set foot in his office when an excited Higgins rushed in with a report that McLaughlin was not sure he wanted to hear.

"Sir, good news!" gushed Higgins. "We found that a passenger looking like Malvois crossed the channel from France last October 9, just before the London murders started. He was wily about it. Tried to cover up his tracks, we think, by boarding a small French freighter, *Le Champlain*, from a tiny port in France. It sailed to Bridgewater, a port not much bigger, in Somerset."

"Clever, indeed."

"Yes, sir. The crew said they were uneasy around the bloke 'cause of his size, but he was none too friendly either. Kept to himself and said nothing the whole trip. The clincher was that the crew remarked about his bad smell."

McLaughlin swallowed hard. He remembered LeClerc's warning about Malvois.

Higgins noticed his superior's worried look. "What is it, sir?"

McLaughlin exhaled slowly and sank into his chair. "This man, Malvois, is a particularly violent criminal: cruel, without conscience, clever at his gruesome work and adept as an assassin for the street gangs. It took the Paris police ten years to catch him, and even then, they were lucky."

McLaughlin wiped his brow with a handkerchief. "He may or may not be our killer, but if he's here, we're going to have to deal with him, one way or the other. Maybe in addition to whoever is doing the East End murders. If we don't get him ... well, we'll have a lot more bodies in the London streets."

Higgins, to his credit, didn't get caught up in the inspector's dark mood. "If the blighter's here, we'll get him, sir. But tell me, from your talks with LeClerc, does Malvois match up enough with our murderer?"

"In many ways, he's like the East End murderer," replied McLaughlin, "but in some ways not. We know already that both are huge, powerful men who are capable of ripping up their victims and making off with body parts."

"Not to mention having a god-awful smell," added Higgins.

"So, it appears. Both killers are also cruel, but in different ways. LeClerc said the Paris killer ripped up his victims while they were still alive. We have no evidence of that with our killer, but he's mentally cruel. He appeared to stalk and torment Molly Muggins before he murdered her. Perhaps he stalked my wife, as well, in the garden, before the night of the murder at my home."

McLaughlin went on. "Both of the murderers have been clever and elusive in their crimes, leaving little to trace them with. Both committed their crimes in ways that are difficult to explain. LeClerc said that Malvois mystified them with how he could spirit away and then murder his victims without being seen. Even in busy streets in the light of day or when the victims were with friends. Until the last, he was able to remain undetected, although gendarmes were swarming in the area shortly after the murders occurred."

"I wonder how the bloke came to be so slippery?" asked Higgins.

"LeClerc told me that Malvois, as a young man, apparently did a stint as an assistant in a Paris magic show. The French police surmised that this experience and his high intelligence helped him learn the art of deception."

"Yes," agreed Higgins, "to this day we haven't been able to figure out how our man did some of the killings; they often didn't make sense... And then to get through our patrols like he was invisible... A magician's helper, you say. Well, that's as good as anything we've come up with, sir."

The inspector frowned. "But there are a couple of important pieces of evidence that don't fit in with our London murderer at all. One is that a characteristic sign of our murderer is missing in the French murders. According to LeClerc, there have been no symbols engraved in the foreheads of the Paris victims or in other body parts. If the murderers are one and the same man, how do we explain this?"

"That's a head-scratcher, Inspector."

"It's puzzling... Also, Malvois' crimes were usually gang-related. We have no evidence that the London crimes had anything to do with the street gangs or the criminal underworld. None of the victims could have been of any interest to criminal elements."

"So, if Malvois is our man, he could have killed—"

"For personal reasons," interjected McLaughlin. "LeClerc did mention that Malvois *could* kill for his own dark reasons. He was apparently abandoned as an infant on the steps of a church orphanage. As he grew up, he was tormented and bullied by other children because of his size and peculiar odor."

"He got off to a bad start."

"It gets worse. Ironically, he became a bully himself and was severely punished, to the point of abuse, by the nuns at the orphanage. LeClerc believed that from this terrible childhood came Malvois' feelings of rage toward the world and his ruthlessness and violence."

"He sounds like a one-man army."

"Yes, and the simile is hardly reassuring. But Malvois' cleverness may also explain some of the mismatch between the London and Paris murders. If he is the East End murderer, what if he introduced an entirely new element into his murders in England — a very conspicuous one, at that — the symbol on his victims?"

"Why would he do that?"

"That way, neither we nor the French police would be as likely to connect the London murders to his crimes in France; the symbol may be another cover for him, a diversion."

Higgins looked thoroughly baffled.

"I know, Higgins, it's a lot of conjecture. At best our theories might be no more than fantasy. We need to start gathering some facts, like if he really is here in London, obviously. LeClerc said that he tends to live cheaply in abandoned buildings, especially old factories. Let's have the men begin a district by district search of disused buildings, in case he has decided to call one of them home. Question the local people about any large strangers or foreigners who have recently appeared in their neighborhoods."

"I'll get the lads right on it."

"Also, we know he is from the criminal underworld. Let's find out what our informants have to say about any newcomers to the London street gangs. This is your area, Higgins, but I'm curious. Who's our most experienced informant?"

"That would-be Jimmy. Jimmy MacAvoy. He's worked the East End markets with a gang of pickpockets since he was an urchin and moved up to full-time snitch for us about six years ago."

"It appears he'd know the criminal comings and goings on the street."

"Right, sir. The bloke knows more than most. But there's always a snag with Jimmy."

"Oh?"

"Yes, sir. He plays a double game. He's a snitch for the street gangs too. We got word of this years ago, and use Jimmy to feed what we want to the

298

gangs and hoodwink them. But if we can get the truth out of him, we'll soon find out about Malvois."

"I take it Jimmy can be persuaded in that vein."

Higgins nodded.

"Very well then, Higgins. Let's find out what we need to know."

Chapter 43

Falding often found himself thinking of Eddington's death. He mused that his passing had been tragic in more than one way. His friend had lost a doctor who might have been able to treat him in a most powerful manner. A suitable replacement for Eddington could not be found, either. For the time being, he was forced to continue deep treatment with Polidori, despite Tanner's warnings. This concerned him greatly.

Eddington's death had been tragic in Polidori's eyes, too. He felt he had lost his best hope for getting rid of Ruthven, and he was getting no better from treatment. Science was failing him, he thought. His mind returned to the occult as a possible solution to his problems. Out of desperation, he decided to do something quite out of character. He would seek the services of a practitioner of the occult, in hope of getting rid of the damnable dreams and his thought incarnation. Polidori turned secretly to Madame Carissma Carmelle.

Madame Carmelle practiced the spiritual and divining arts. Her services were popular among some of the wealthy ladies of London, who usually wanted to know if their husbands were dallying with younger women or what the future held for them in the London social circles.

She was also in demand as a medium, claiming she could contact the spirits of those who had passed on. Her clients swore that she was often in possession of details no one else could possibly know but themselves and the dearly departed.

A female assistant admitted Polidori to her parlor. It was quite dark inside, the windows and the rest of the room totally covered by purple drapes from ceiling to floor. The room was sparsely furnished. There was a lit candelabra on a small cabinet in one corner next to a small red couch. An old oak table with two chairs facing one another stood in the center of the room. An oil lamp sat on the table and an astrological chart was pinned to the curtains. The glass globe of the flaming lamp was tinted, creating a circle of pinkish red light around the table.

He was seated at the table on a comfortable French provincial chair with a leather seat. The assistant gathered some information for Madame Carmelle: his birthday for astrological purposes, his birth order (only child), and the sum of the birthdates in his family.

Shortly thereafter, in came Madame Carmelle through a doorway behind one of the drapes. She sat down, folding her hands together on the table. She was a rather plump, pear-shaped, middle-aged lady wearing a large, wide-brimmed hat. It was festooned with a colorful plume of feathers.

Madame Carmelle scanned him with her unusually large, moist eyes, which seemed capable of taking in all possible visual information about him. Overall, she gave the impression of a large, exotic bird staring at him from the other side of the table.

"Welcome, Doctor," she said in a surprisingly deep, resonant voice. "What can I do for you, sir?"

"I would think, given your profession, that you would already know that," Polidori challenged.

She frowned. "I am a diviner and spiritualist, not a mind-reader," she retorted.

Polidori realized he had not begun well with Madame Carmelle and decided to resist further jousting. He told her at length about his being tormented by nightmares and the malevolent, red-eyed manifestation that he was certain had latched onto him. He went on to tell her that this being was an incarnation of his vampyre character and that it was responsible for the killings in London. Polidori added that his psychiatrist did not believe him and was treating him for a disorder of the mind.

Madame Carmelle listened intently, never taking her huge eyes off him or even taking the time to blink. She appeared to take his story in stride.

"I have encountered spirits that have latched onto people before," she stated, looking quite serious. "Nefarious ones, too, but mostly poltergeists that are nuisances — never any murderers. However, let us see what your dreams reveal." She took out a heavy-looking clear crystal ball and pressed it with two hands to his forehead. "It will draw out your dream," she declared.

It felt very cool against his forehead but pleasantly so. Madame Carmelle held it there for a few moments. Then she withdrew the ball and shook it vigorously. A creamy white mist or vapor suddenly formed within, which she said was the physical manifestation of the dream.

Her new client thought the mist looked like a chemical reaction of some sort, begun by her agitating the ball. This did not increase his confidence in her powers. However, given her considerable reputation in high places and his desperation to get better, he decided to give her the benefit of the doubt.

Madame Carmelle peered intently into the ball, turning it gently. She squinted a little. "It's resisting," she said. She set her jaws and placed both palms on the ball, closing her eyes and concentrating on it. After about a minute, she opened her eyes and frowned. "It does not reveal," she lamented. "Its message is too cloudy."

No doubt, Polidori thought. *It is quite foggy in there.*

The spiritualist did not give up, however. She took both his hands in hers, squeezing them firmly, her eyes closing again in concentration. Suddenly, she began to vibrate. Her eyes rolled back, and her teeth chattered. Then she screamed as if in pain and put her hands to the sides of her head. She shrieked, "Don't come near me!"

Thinking she was talking to him, he blurted out, "Really, madam, I have no intention—" Before he could finish, she stood up abruptly, knocking her chair over backward. She started running about the room in circles, trembling violently and frothing at the mouth.

It was all quite alarming. Polidori thought she was having grand mal, but people in seizures usually fall down unconscious, not run about in circles, he reminded himself. He stood up to try to restrain her, but she escaped from his grasp and hurtled right into the wall. She bounced off the wall and fell to the floor, her head bloodied, continuing to convulse.

By this time, her assistant had come in. She fetched a spoon with which Polidori depressed Madame Carmelle's tongue. He made an effort to stop the bleeding and put a cold compress on her head. Her feet were raised to get blood to her brain.

Polidori told the assistant he was a physician and asked if Madame Carmelle had any history of seizures. "Not to my knowledge," she said. "Although her sister did."

"What kind?"

"The large kind," she replied.

"Grand mal?"

"Yes, I believe."

"I recommend you summon her physician," he said. "I'll remain with her in the meantime." He wrote a brief note suggesting that the physician bring a hypnotic herb to sedate her. He noticed that she had stopped her tremors and regained partial consciousness, appearing disoriented.

"Where — where am I?" she mumbled, wincing as she brought her hand to her head.

"You're in your parlor, madam. You've had a seizure, I believe, and struck your head. It's all right. You're recovering now."

"I don't remember hitting my head. I recall getting a pain in my head when I took your hand. My sight faded and then nothing." She tried to prop herself up on one elbow.

Polidori laid her arm flat and gently lowered her back to the floor. "Unconsciousness is part of having a seizure. Your head pain may have been a forewarning of it. It will take a few minutes for you to fully regain consciousness. I've sent for your physician."

Her physician soon arrived. Satisfied treatment had been properly given so far, he gave her a hypnotic potion. They lifted her up onto the couch to rest.

"It looked to me like a seizure," Polidori said. "Grand mal, but a strange one in that she ran about the room. Does she have any history of seizures?"

"None," the doctor said, puzzled. "She has been troubled by her marriage of late. Evidently, her husband has been involved with other women for some time, and she recently discovered it."

This piece of news did not improve Polidori's confidence in the spiritualist's powers. He left the matter in her doctor's hands. He doubted he would see her again — not that she would give him an appointment anyway, he imagined. As he left, the glass globe on the table caught his attention. Instead of its creamy mist, it seemed to have a reddish tinge to it, but perhaps this was simply the reflection of light in the room.

Chapter 44

Since matters had been relatively quiet regarding Byron and the suspected cult, Higgins sent out Murdoch and Dickson to find Scotland Yard's chief informant, Jimmy MacAvoy.

Murdoch came upon him in the back room of a dilapidated drinking house on an East London side street. He was sitting at a rickety old table with a bottle of rum. The constable sent for Higgins and took it upon himself to rough Jimmy up a bit in the meantime.

"What's that for?" whined Jimmy, getting up from the floor and dusting himself off.

"Just to keep you honest with the sergeant when he gets here, Jimmy. You have a bad habit of talking out of both sides of your mouth."

As Jimmy was about to reply, Higgins walked into the dingy back room. "Jimmy," he began with false concern, "you're looking a bit worse for wear these days. Better start taking care of yourself, man."

Jimmy felt his jaw and scowled at the two policemen, reserving the worst of it for Murdoch.

"Come on, Jimmy, you know you need a shove once in a while to get the truth out of you."

"Part with a few more quid and you might get better service," Jimmy shot back.

Higgins ignored his cheekiness, but Murdoch took a threatening step in Jimmy's direction.

"All right Jimmy," continued Higgins. "We want to know some facts here, and they'd better *be* facts."

"Like what?"

"Like have any fresh faces turned up in the London gangs lately, since the fall, especially?"

Jimmy hesitated, his eyes darting back and forth between the two policemen.

"Just answer the question, Jimmy," ordered Higgins impatiently.

"Yeah," said Jimmy, at last. "A big Frenchman was asking around if anybody needed a tough bloke."

"A tough bloke?" asked Murdoch, puzzled.

"Yeah, you know, to push people around for the gangs or to get rid of them, if that's what it takes." Jimmy looked at Higgins, amused. "Your man here's not been on the street long, has he?"

Murdoch took another step toward Jimmy.

"Get back to it, Jimmy. So was the big man hired?"

"Don't think so, guv. Nobody heard of him. Some took him to be a copper. Some were just plain scared of him."

"About what?"

"Heard he was a cranky sort of bloke, touchy. Wouldn't take much to rile him. And with his size and all, that could be right bad."

"So, what became of him?"

"Went from gang to gang, like I say, looking to be hired, but none would have him. Then nothing was seen of him." Jimmy snapped his fingers. "Gone like that."

"Jimmy, we want to find this sod. Ask around on the streets about him. If you come across something, we could make it worth your while."

"Why do you want him so bad? What's he done?"

307

Knowing the less Jimmy knew the better, Higgins avoided his question. "Just find out where he is, Jimmy, or find something that might help us track him down."

"It's to do with the killings, ain't it?" Jimmy guessed correctly.

Higgins evaded him again. "Now that you mention it, Jimmy, have you heard any more about the murders since our last chat?"

"Nothing. Not a peep," said Jimmy.

"Do the gangs know anything? Are they involved?"

"Listen, the gangs don't want this on the streets. Bad for business. People are scared to go out after dark. If the gangs knew something, they'd let you know. They got nothing to do with none of it."

"All right, Jimmy, we'll be looking into your story about the Frenchman. If it doesn't hold up, you'll get another visit from this gentleman." The sergeant nodded toward Murdoch.

Higgins and Murdoch discussed their meeting with Jimmy on the return trip by coach to police headquarters.

"Do you think he's lying?" asked Murdoch. "Could he be covering for the gangs? We know they feed us nonsense through Jimmy. They're paying him, too."

"Well, you never know about Jimmy, but I think he's telling the truth on this as far as the murders go. Why would the gangs want to do in people who could never hurt them, like the flower girl and the coalman, for instance?"

"You've got a point there, Sergeant."

308

"Yeah. And why would they make the murders so bloody that the papers would get a hold of it for sure? It doesn't make sense. The last thing the gangs want is to be in the front pages. That could bring us down on their heads. They know we've been asking questions already in the East End... No, they just want any blokes who are in their way, dead — quiet like. Anything else, like Jimmy says, is bad for business."

"What about what he says of the Frenchman, Sergeant?"

"I think he's honest there too. What Jimmy says fits what we know of Malvois, but keep an eye on him on him, Murdoch. If there's nothing from Jimmy in a week or so, let's have another chat with him. Call in our other snitches, if need be. Somebody out there has got to know something about Malvois."

Higgins was soon knocking on McLaughlin's office door, eager to inform the inspector of the news from Jimmy. McLaughlin listened intently. "It appears to be Malvois," he finally remarked, his tone betraying both anxiety and excitement at the news. He thought how ominous it was that the French murderer had actually come to London. Yet here was a convincing suspect in the murders, and his arrest in the matter might be imminent.

McLaughlin's thoughts rushed forward. "If Malvois is still here in London, and he's not working for the gangs, how is he supporting himself?"

"No idea, sir."

"It would be difficult. Unless he has other connections here in England."

"Like who, Inspector?"

"Well," said McLaughlin, measuring his words, "recall that LeClerc had suspected that an aristocratic gentleman helped Malvois escape from prison. And that he spoke French with an accent. Then Malvois came to England soon afterward."

Higgins shook his head, puzzled. "What are you getting at, Inspector?"

"I'm wondering if this was an *English* aristocrat who arranged the escape to England."

"One of ours? But who and why?"

"Let's think about it, Higgins. Now, who in English high society might have need of a murderer who dismembers his victims?"

Higgins' face brightened. "You think Byron and his lot brought him across as their killer?"

McLaughlin nodded. "It could have been the cult. Their bringing him across would be — how shall I say it — mutually advantageous. *He* makes a living, safe from the French police, and gets to kill again. *They* get a murderer who provides them with gruesome body parts for their ceremonies."

"And maybe one who can't easily be tied to them," added Higgins.

"Precisely. A convenient little arrangement."

Higgins grew thoughtful. "But then again, sir, if he was brought across the channel by Byron and his bunch, why would he have gone to the gangs for work?"

"Why indeed. Remember, Malvois comes from the criminal underworld. He needs them as one would need a family. He belongs with them. He would try to join them, even if he was working for the cult, too. And maybe he wasn't getting his fill of

310

killing with the cult. Eight victims, as far as we know — not enough for a killer as bloodthirsty as him."

"But there's something else that doesn't fit, Inspector. A couple of cult members tried to kill the prostitute that night in East London. Why do that if they had Malvois to do the job? Why take the chance?"

"Well, how do we know that Malvois wasn't one of the two, dressed up like the cult? Maybe, in that case, Malvois couldn't do the job alone."

"Why not, sir?"

"I don't know. Perhaps they needed some specific organs in good condition, and Malvois' crude methods or his knowledge of anatomy wouldn't suffice. It's pure guess-work at this point, but we'll get to the bottom of it."

Higgins hadn't run out of questions. "Well, if Malvois works for the cult, why would they want that bloody mark to be left at the murders? What's the symbol to *them*? What's the tie-in?"

"That's just it, Higgins. The symbol can't readily be linked to them. It's not the symbol on their rings or ritual instruments, or anything to do with Satanism that we know of. The symbol may divert suspicion from the cult, just as it does for Malvois, as we discussed."

A memory flashed in Higgins' mind. "I recall, sir, the day we were at Warrington's, and Murdoch chased a bloke into the swamp. He lost him, coming back with that smell... Could that have been Malvois that day?"

The two looked at each other, mulling over the matter. Eventually, McLaughlin broke the silence.

311

"Again, we're in need of some facts. Find out if a member of the cult or perhaps an assistant crossed the channel just before Malvois' escape. Determine what hotel he may have stayed at and when he returned. Of course, he might have used a false name, but perhaps he was careless about that. Also, ask our informants if there's any word, any rumor, that someone outside of the gangs may have hired Malvois, particularly someone in the upper class."

Chapter 45

The winter was deepening. Polidori had still not progressed in his treatment, despite Falding trying every healing method he knew. The psychiatrist had consulted his colleagues in London about Polidori's care and read extensively in the psychiatric literature regarding treatment of his peculiar problems. However, nothing useful came of it all.

Polidori had eventually confessed to Falding about his ill-fated visit to Madame Carmelle. The psychiatrist was only too aware of the young man's frustration with his treatment. He sensed his patient was turning again toward the occult to free himself from the "manifestation."

One day, the pair was sharing a pot of tea and biscuits in front of the large corner windows of Falding's drawing room. They sat amidst lush plants placed to take advantage of the bright afternoon sun. The warmth and greenery contrasted sharply with the chilly, barren February scene outside.

Polidori brought up the topic of the occult. "Why don't we put all of this to the test?" he suddenly said.

"What do you mean?" Falding asked, perplexed.

"I heard there's someone in London who has quite a reputation for her ability to contact the after world, a Miss Penelope Clairvoy."

"A medium? You're not going to say what I think you're going to say!"

"Probably. If there's truth to what she claims, why not use her services to contact Charles Eddington? Perhaps we'll hear directly from him what caused his death and if there's anything I can do to rid myself of this abomination."

"I was afraid you were going to say that. John, you're a scientist! This is not a test — it's mystical nonsense, and mediums are outright charlatans. They have all sorts of ways of finding out information about their clients and telling them what they want to hear. The mediums exploit the grief and loneliness of their clients. I recall you were attracted by Madame Carmelle's reputation, as well. In the end, you were convinced she was a fraud."

"In looking back on it, I'm not so sure, Alex. I've wondered if the seizure she seemed to have was not a seizure at all but perhaps a genuine possession of her by the manifestation. What if it had felt threatened that she would help me to understand its true nature and purpose and interrupted her efforts by inducing seizure-like behaviors? After all, didn't she scream 'keep away from me!' I thought at the time that she was talking to me, but now I think she was trying to confront an invasive presence in her mind."

"So, you're saying Madame Carmelle was attacked by your character to protect itself? John, you've said to me that it looked like a seizure and that she had some family history of epilepsy."

"Yes, but I also said it did not appear to be a normal seizure at all. When epileptics go into seizure, they lapse into unconsciousness — not run around the room."

"John, as a doctor, you know as well as I that symptoms don't always fit exactly and that there are always exceptions to the rule… You know, I believe you're now trying to draw me into your delusional system, and I won't permit it! I cannot help you if I'm delusional, too."

"Still, perhaps Madame Carmelle had some genuine powers that attracted the manifestation — and I'm not trying to draw you into what you call a delusion. I'm saying that if the medium really can contact Eddington, we can know the truth of his death. He'll tell us whether or not he was killed by the manifestation. The medium cannot deceive us about this. She has no way of knowing that I suspect there was supernatural foul play in Eddington's death if I don't tell her."

Falding knew how strong-willed Polidori was and that he was fighting a losing battle against his friend's latest plan to prove he was right about the manifestation. Falding eventually relented. "Look, John," he said, "it's against my better judgment, but I'll still go with you to the medium. Not because I give her any credibility. Rather, I feel it's my duty protect you from being taken in and from the further damage that will cause you."

The following week, he reluctantly went off with Polidori to see Miss Clairvoy. He thought she must have a prosperous business as she lived and practiced in a mansion in Mayfair, a well-to-do area of London. Polidori had told him that she had plied her trade for the past twenty years and had many clients who regularly consulted with her on matters of the after-world. Apparently, they were ardent believers that she could put them in touch with those who had passed on.

The room her assistant led them into was unexpectedly sparse. There was a small, round table,

315

with simple straight-backed wooden chairs around it. Sitting on the table, at its center, was a large, lustrous globe made of a golden metal. It was about twelve inches in diameter, perched on four ornate silver legs. The globe, the two were told by the assistant, served to focus energy and to connect all of them present with one another and with the "beyond."

The scene was made more dramatic by the fact that the only light was afforded by a single candle on the table. Beyond its small circle, little could be discerned in the darkened room.

Miss Clairvoy appeared from the darkness rather abruptly, giving them a bit of a start. She introduced herself and invited them to sit down. She was a pleasant, slender, older woman. She appeared quite kindly and sympathetic, qualities Falding imagined would serve her well with her clients. He also noticed she was dressed entirely in black, which tended to blend in most of her with the dark background. This gave the strange effect of accentuating her pale face and hands in the candlelight, making them appear slightly disembodied. It was quite disorienting, he thought. But perhaps that was what she was trying to achieve.

"What can I do for you gentlemen today?" she asked with a broad smile.

Polidori spoke up. "I'm the one requesting your services, Miss Clairvoy. I'm John Polidori, and this is my friend, Alex Falding."

The medium nodded. "Tell me, what is it you are seeking, Mr. Polidori?"

"Well, some time ago, an acquaintance of mine, a Charles Eddington, died quite suddenly and unexpectedly. I understand you can contact the dead. I would like to get in touch with him about the circumstances of his death and to ask if he has anything he would like to say to me."

"Very well, Mr. Polidori. Let us see if we can open a link to this person. Let us all place our hands on the golden globe in front of us and close our eyes. Feel the cool, soothing surface of the globe. Simply relax and let your minds just drift for a while, breathing easy, so that each breath is a relaxation breath... Now, go ahead and allow the memory of Mr. Eddington's face to come to you, as it was in life. Allow it to form ever more clearly and vividly in your mind."

As they absorbed these words, a clear, strong image of Dr. Eddington's face filled their minds. The globe seemed cooler to the touch.

The medium drew the two in further. "Focus upon the face more intensely, without forcing. If other thoughts come, do not attach to them. Simply pay attention to the space between the thoughts."

Miss Clairvoy's voice became deeper and more forceful. "Now, let us all concentrate on opening a tunnel to this person. Imagine the tunnel forms in the space between spaces, in the moments between the moments of time, connecting you to Mr. Eddington and to all of us."

"Now, I will ask Mr. Eddington if he is available to us. If he speaks, it will be through me, through my connection to him and through the globe to you. As he speaks, allow the image of his face to brighten, to intensify. Mr. Eddington, are you available to us?" Complete silence. She repeated, a little louder, "Mr. Eddington, are you available to us?"

"I am," came a rather hollow, low voice through Miss Clairvoy.

"Mr. Polidori very much needs to know something from you. Will you tell him?"

"I will, if I can," came the monotone reply.

Polidori hesitated but got up the nerve to ask his question. "Dr. Eddington, will you tell me how is it that you came to die the night after I saw you, so suddenly it seemed, so unexpectedly?"

"It was a strange death," came the reply. "I died in a memory... You must know first of something that happened a long time ago. I visited my cousins at their country home when I was five years old. The children ran off to play. We had been warned not to visit the old, unused part of the great building, as it was unsafe. We disobeyed, and I was led by my cousins down into a vast cellar with many rooms in it. We opened the door to a musty old room, its stone walls dripping water."

There was long silence. "Will you tell me more, Dr. Eddington?" Polidori pleaded.

"My cousins played a prank on me. They locked me in the room, running off, laughing. It was completely, dark except for the light from a single candle that I carried. I thought I heard rats scurrying in the shadows. I screamed to be let out, but there was no answer."

After another long pause, Polidori asked, "Can you tell us what happened then?"

The unearthly voice continued its account. "I searched for a way out but found only cold, wet walls. Panicking, I lost my balance and fell into a

318

deep, old well in the floor. I struck a ledge and lay there above the dark, still waters below, for the longest time. My head was bleeding, and I went in and out of unconsciousness… Suddenly, a blinding light filled the well, and my father swept me up into his arms. The next I knew, I was safe in my own bed at home."

Polidori stared at Miss Clairvoy, astonished. He pressed his palms more firmly on the globe.

The voice went on. "The memory of the well came back to me the night of my death, as I sat near the drawing-room fire. It was so vivid that it seemed to be happening in the moment. I was on the well's ledge again, injured. But this time, as I lay there, I heard strange whispers in the darkness. They seemed to arise from the black water beneath me."

"'Your father will not come for you in time,' the whispers said gleefully. 'This well is your grave.'

"And then I saw my child self-die on that ledge. In shock, my old heart gave way. I collapsed and died in reality, before the fire."

The pitch of the voice climbed. "Whatever was in that well is here with us now — in this time and place. It — it is a great danger to you and to the others. Be vigilant, be —"

"Dr. Eddington?"

"It does not want me to talk to you further. It puts a heavy weight upon me — it — chokes off my words — I —"

The voice stopped. They opened their eyes and took their hands from the globe. Falding looked over at Polidori, who looked deeply affected by the experience, entranced even. The psychiatrist had had

319

enough. It was a cleverly staged act, he thought, which would only strengthen his friend's delusions.

"Look," he said to Clairvoy, "I know what you're playing at. You had to have some way of knowing John's fears that something supernatural was harming him and murdering others. You play acted all this by faking a 'spirit' Eddington who claims supernatural forces gave him a heart attack by altering a memory... Do you know Carissma Carmelle? Did you become aware that John had seen her and of the details of his problems? Do you mediums collaborate about one another's clients?"

She gave him no reply, which only served to heighten his suspicions. "I'll wager you also read the obituaries all the time to find out any details you can retell to relatives, disguised as information from the dead. And I know very well that Eddington's obituary said he had passed away suddenly at his home from suspected heart failure. Did you read that obituary?"

Clairvoy replied calmly. "I did not create this reality today, Mr. Falding. The only problem here is that it's not *your* reality."

Falding stood up angrily. "Let's get out of here, John. She continues with her trickery. I should inform the authorities!" They left abruptly, with no payment rendered.

The two were barely out of the door when the debate began. "It was too real for it to have been trickery, Alex. It was entirely believable."

"It was believable only because you wanted to believe it, John. You were looking for confirmation that Eddington was killed in a bizarre manner."

"But how could anyone have possibly staged something so convincing and elaborate?"

"John, I wasn't going to mention it, but I took the liberty of looking into Miss Clairvoy's background. Thirty years ago, she was on the London stage. She was an actress! She's evidently still plying her old trade."

"But, Alex, there's something more. The little boy in the well was abandoned at the last by his father. I, too, felt abandoned by my father. How strange. Was it just coincidence?"

"I doubt it. Perhaps she's found out about that from Carmelle, as well. It's all part of drawing you into her fantasy, today."

"But I did not tell Madame Carmelle about my father at all. How could she have possibly known?"

"Let's remember that these mediums make use of common human fears to enhance their trickery. Children have inherent fears of abandonment by their parents — part of their survival instincts. The fear of falling is another. Clairvoy was clever enough to weave such fears into convincing messages from beyond. That's how she makes her living."

Polidori gave him a skeptical look. He was about to reply when the two reached their coach. They boarded, stalemated once again.

Chapter 46

McLaughlin stood warming his hands over his office stove, deep in thought. The East End had been strangely quiet. No more mutilation murders had been reported for some time. He was most uneasy. What was the murderer doing or planning in the shadows? When would they discover the next scene of carnage? Neither Byron nor Winchester had been in the area recently. Did that account for the lull? He heard Higgins at the door and invited him in.

Higgins rushed into the office. "We've got what we're looking for!" he blurted out. "We looked at the passenger lists to and from France, and an English gentleman traveled to France on the *Star of England* a week before Malvois' escape. He returned to England the day after Malvois bolted."

Higgins went on breathlessly. "The purser of the ship remembers him because the man traveled alone, which is rare for the gentry. They travel with servants. The clincher is that he fits the description of Malvois' visitor in prison."

"Very interesting, Higgins. Did he stay at a Paris hotel?"

"A gentleman with the same name and description, speaking French with an English accent, registered at the Hotel Lafayette in Paris. The concierge remembers him because the man paid not in Francs but in British pounds and kept a tidy sum of gold in the hotel safe, which he took out a few days later. The concierge also noticed that the man wore a fancy ring, red ruby and gold, but couldn't remember any more about it."

McLaughlin nodded thoughtfully. "So it seems likely that Malvois was visited by this English gentleman and perhaps aided in his escape by him, as well."

"But there's a fly in the ointment, sir, because his name was not one we know to be connected with the cult, or whatever it is. We've checked the birth records. People with that name were not from the upper crust. They didn't fit the description of the gentleman and had an alibi for the week or so of the travels to France. None wore unusual rings, either."

"It could well have been an assumed name," countered McLaughlin.

"Right, sir... There's another big piece of news, Inspector. Jimmy's got back to us. He's found out — if he's to be believed — that the big Frenchman is still in London, living alone. Jimmy repeated his story that the gangs would have nothing to do with him. But he says nobody knows where he's hiding out, exactly."

"Do you think we should believe Jimmy's story?" asked McLaughlin. "Perhaps he had his hand out for telling us something that he thought we wanted to hear."

"Normally, I wouldn't trust what the blighter says," replied Higgins, "but he knew what was good for him if he lied this time. His story is also backed up by one of the lads on patrol near the Thames' docks. Street people told the constable that they had spotted a big man, a stranger, in the area but didn't know where he was living. Then the constable saw signs of someone living in an old, run - down water mill by the river. There was light from a few chinks in a blacked out window and some wisps of stove

323

smoke coming from the building … and hear this. Big footprints in the snow were seen coming and going from the mill."

"That fits where he likes to live, according to LeClerc. It could be him, Higgins," McLaughlin said with uncharacteristic optimism. "Perhaps we finally have him."

"And that could lead us straight to Byron and his slippery mates."

"Yes, if only that might be," replied McLaughlin, saying it almost like a prayer. "It's been a long, hard road," he sighed, "but maybe, just maybe, we're coming to the end of it."

The police moved on the mill at dawn the following day. The sky was overcast and the air cold and heavy, threatening snow. The mill was little more than a hulking wreck, shadowed against the faintly lit sky to the east. Stones had fallen out of its walls and lay scattered on the frozen ground, capped with snow. Some of the heavy timbers of the roof had crumpled in on one end of the building. The old, rusted water wheel lay motionless in the sluggish waters of the river, having stopped its turning long ago.

It was the perfect haunt for Malvois, thought McLaughlin as they approached the mill. As the constable had said, faint light shone from a crack in the window.

Higgins and McLaughlin made their way cautiously to the front door. Murdoch positioned himself out back in the event the suspect attempted to escape that way. The two listened carefully at the door. McLaughlin took a deep breath. "Ready?" he whispered to Higgins. They burst in on a large man who looked like Malvois. He was sitting alone at a table illuminated by a single oil lamp.

"Scotland Yard! Stay where you are!" yelled McLaughlin.

The big man stood up suddenly, snarling something uncomplimentary in French, his face contorted with anger. He rushed at them with surprising speed, knocking over the table on his way. The oil lamp burst into flames on the floor.

McLaughlin pointed his cocked pistol and fired. He couldn't believe that he had missed at that short range, but he had. The big man was on him before he could reach for his leg gun. McLaughlin found himself picked up like a sack of flour over the man's head and flung backward a good ten feet. He landed heavily on his back on the cold stone floor.

He lay stunned for a few moments, expecting to hear the report of Higgins' pistol at any second. Instead, there was a loud click. Higgins' gun had misfired! The next thing McLaughlin saw was Higgins hurtling over him through the air, landing somewhere behind him with a loud thump.

McLaughlin sat up, expecting to be manhandled at any moment, but the giant man had turned away, running toward the back door. McLaughlin took hold of his leg gun and fired. This time he didn't miss; the ball caught the man in the upper right back or shoulder. He yelped with the impact but kept on going. He disappeared out the door, leaving a trail of blood behind him.

Higgins emerged, swearing mightily, from a thick cloud of dust in a bin of old burlap bags where he had landed.

"Grab him!" McLaughlin shouted as he scrambled to his feet. The two rushed in pursuit out the back door. They almost stumbled over Murdoch, who was spread out on the ground, apparently unconscious; whether he had been pummeled or simply run over by the big man was unclear.

The trail of blood led to the bank of the river near the mill, but their target was nowhere to be seen. McLaughlin tended to Murdoch as Higgins searched downstream for their suspect. He even found an old bateau and crossed the river to search on the other bank. But the man had disappeared; whether he had escaped or had gone down in the river was anyone's guess.

The aftermath of the struggle was chaotic. Murdoch had partially revived, and held up by his colleagues, stumbled in a daze to the waiting coach. In the distance were shouts and yells as people ran toward the mill with water buckets. The bells of the old fire wagon could be heard approaching.

McLaughlin looked back and saw that the roof of the mill was on fire. It was an odd time to be philosophical, but the thought struck him that the old mill had died many years before; its cremation was long overdue. Now, if only its latest inhabitant had also met his end, he mused darkly. They might never really know.

Chapter 47

In the days following the séance, Polidori was mysteriously silent. Falding guessed that his friend had decided to ignore his arguments that the medium was a fraud. He feared the séance had only served to strengthen Polidori's belief in the "manifestation" and that it had killed Eddington.

Polidori's desperate and restless mind began to think further about religion as a way of liberating himself from the thing he believed had latched onto him. He had already been praying to be released, but thus far his prayers had apparently gone unanswered. Frustrated, he eventually decided to visit his parish priest, Father O'Kenny, for confession and guidance. He was hoping against hope to find healing in the church, not to mention an ally in Father O'Kenny in the matter of the manifestation.

Father O'Kenny was an older priest, having served in several parishes in London for over thirty years. He had emigrated as a young priest from Southern Ireland and had faithfully served the church ever since. In many ways, he was quite traditional, but he had an unorthodox side, too — strongly rooted supernatural beliefs beyond the Christian Trinity. He didn't openly talk about the subject, nor did he go so far as the rites of exorcism. However, he quietly referred parishioners he felt were victims of possession or hauntings to the specialized services of others.

One February afternoon, Polidori called upon Father O'Kenny for confession at Saint Anthony's Church, a few streets from his home. He could see the shadow of the priest behind the black latticed screen in the confessional. The confessor began in the usual way. "Bless me, Father, for I have sinned. It has been many months since my last confession."

"What is the nature of your sin, my son?" the priest asked.

"I have harbored deep hatred in my heart toward a man who is the greatest poet in the world but the greatest scoundrel in it as well."

"My son, hatred hardens the heart and harms its owner most. Your sin is ultimately against yourself. Say three Hail Marys and reflect upon forgiving this man."

"I have a more serious sin to confess, Father," Polidori added hesitantly. "My acts have led to the murders of others."

"What acts are these, my son?"

"I have created an evil entity, which has become beyond my control and committed the murders."

"What entity is that?"

"I am a writer who wrote a book about an evil character, a vampyre named Lord Ruthven. Ruthven somehow became animated, first in my dreams but then in reality. Out of his innate cruelty and lust for power, he psychologically tortures me and other victims and brutally kills others, too. He carries out the dark plot of my book in the real world."

There was a long pause before Father O'Kenny replied. "As a priest, I have heard of many strange happenings beyond the understanding of the church or science. But the mind can also deceive. Have you the opinion of a psychiatrist on the matter?"

"I have, and he believes Ruthven is a creation of my imagination. But his treatment has failed so far, and this tells me the manifestation is something that exists beyond my mind. It is real."

"But if this is so, how can God forgive you for a crime that you did not commit?"

"I created the murderer, so I am as guilty as it."

"But even if, as you say, you created the murderer, surely it makes the choice to carry out the plot to commit the murders — not you. To hold yourself responsible is like saying the parents of a child who commits murder are responsible for the murder. No. You are not responsible in the eyes of God. Therefore, I cannot offer you penance."

Noticing Polidori's look of disappointment, he hastened to add, "But do not despair, my son. I can send you to someone who may be able to help." Father O'Kenny wrote a letter of introduction and handed it to Polidori as he left.

Chapter 48

It was a cold, snowy day at Cambridge University. Professor Phineas Sage opened his door to receive a visitor. "Thank you for seeing me so quickly, Professor," said Polidori.

The professor motioned him toward a chair. "Some tea, perhaps, to take off the chill? These old offices are often cold and drafty in the winter. Bad for the bones, I think."

He poured some steaming tea as he read the brief note from Father O'Kenny. "Ah, yes. Father periodically sends me those with unusual, unexplained experiences. Usually, by the time they arrive at my door, these people have left behind them a long trail of frustrated and perplexed physicians and clergymen. But what can you tell me about your situation?" he asked with a kindly smile.

Polidori went on to give him an account of his strange experiences and fears. He was becoming weary of futilely going over the same ground again and again.

"And I suppose your psychiatrist thinks you're delusional and that feelings from your unconscious are surfacing and transforming into hallucinations."

"That's about it."

"There can be some truth in this viewpoint. There are often dark, submerged feelings in the person. However, I believe that in some, the feelings don't cause hallucinations, like the psychiatrists think. Rather, sometimes the dark emotions attract rather nasty, unnatural visitors — evil entities that will attach to the person. They feed upon these emotions, voraciously. They are nourished and strengthened by them."

Polidori was relieved that he was being taken seriously. "But what are these manifestations?"

"No one actually knows. It's all speculation, really. Each expert has his own theory about them. What *is* known is that there have been reports of such things throughout recorded history and that they are notoriously difficult to expel once they have latched on. Even the rites of exorcism through the Catholic Church have a dubious record of getting rid of them once they have invaded the person."

"But how could it be possible to get rid of them if their nature is not understood? In medicine, we need to know the cause of a disease to treat it."

The professor looked thoughtfully at him for a few moments. "There are ways," he said, "that most people don't want to know about — are afraid to know about."

"That would be magic, I assume."

"Magic indeed," replied Sage with a serious look. "I know many are skeptical about it. They have seen the entertainment magicians. These charlatans know how to deceive and manipulate the senses through their tricks and pick the pockets of their audience. They give true magic a bad name."

"So, you believe true magic exists, then?"

"I certainly do. I've witnessed it. We come to know magic exists when we realize the universe consists of infinite possibilities. History is full of examples of how what was thought to be impossible came to be possible, even in the sciences — *especially* in the sciences."

"What exactly is magic, Professor Sage?"

The professor took a deep breath. "Well, it's based on the belief there is a natural, primordial energy that flows through and permeates the world, including human beings and all life. This energy is thought to transform itself into the forces we know in science: gravity, electricity, magnetism, and all physical forces. It is said that this energy is undetectable and unmeasurable in its primordial state, but as it transforms itself or differentiates into the forces with which we are familiar, we can observe and quantify it. Science uses some of these forces to do work. The water mill uses the flowing stream, water flowing downhill to the pull of gravity, to turn the millstone."

He paused to allow his visitor to absorb his message. "What we call 'magic' is a way of utilizing the primordial energy for purposes of healing and protection *or* for selfish, destructive purposes. I study and concern myself with the constructive use of this energy — what some would call 'white magic.' So you see, there's really nothing supernatural about magic. We call what we don't understand 'supernatural.' Magic is simply a part of the natural world which we have not yet discovered scientifically."

"So how can all of this help me?"

Professor Sage took a sip of his tea. "I can bring you to people who practice magic, who utilize this energy for healing and growth."

"You mean witches, I gather?"

"You could call them that, and also 'warlocks,' if you will. But they prefer to call themselves the Lucans, meaning, in the old Anglo-Saxon language, 'the enlightened ones.' They have the old

332

knowledge. They know how to control the primordial energy."

"But how do I know I can trust them?" Polidori asked anxiously.

"Because most of those that I have referred to the Lucans have been healed, and none have been any worse for the experience. Also, Father O'Kenny has placed his trust in me and the others, or he would not have sent you to me. Besides, I'll accompany you and be with you at all times during the ceremony. Do not vex yourself over this, John."

Professor Sage went on. "In fact, an important part of your healing through magic is fully trusting in the magical process and those magicians who carry it out. Permit me to give you an example. You are a physician and are aware of the great plague that struck Europe in the 1600s, including London. It was deadly to most who contracted it, and physicians of the time were helpless to deal with it."

"Sad facts, I'm afraid."

"Yes. But what you may not know is that out of desperation some went to the magical healers of the day. Some of these survived at a much higher rate than those treated by traditional medicine or left untreated. But others didn't survive. There are reports that those who survived had truly believed that the magicians would help them; the non-believers died. The power of the mind helped to strengthen the healing benefits of magic."

Polidori was relieved that there was another learned person besides Father O'Kenny who believed him about the manifestation. He felt understood and no longer completely alone in dealing with it. However, even after all Professor

Sage's explanations and reassurances, he remained uncertain about the Lucans. This was much more than speaking with a spirit through a medium. It evidently involved their manipulating a fundamental energy within himself and the universe. He was not about to throw himself rashly into their arms. So, he thanked the old professor and said he would consider the matter further.

Chapter 49

Two weeks had passed since the failed attempt to capture the infamous Jean-Marc Malvois. Despite exhaustive searches along the river, no trace of the French murderer had yet been found. To add to the mystery, no more mutilated bodies had been discovered for some months, in the East End or elsewhere.

McLaughlin and Higgins met again in the inspector's office. Their faces showed no signs of relief, only tension and apprehension. They had recently become aware of another disturbing problem — a puzzling surge in reports of people disappearing in East London.

"What are the latest figures this week?" asked McLaughlin.

"Sir, there's been a half dozen more disappearances in London this week alone, for a total of thirty since December."

"That means a fifty percent increase in reported disappearances over the past two months."

"I'm afraid so, Inspector."

"So, what is going on?" asked McLaughlin, more to himself than to Higgins. "All right, let's review what we know. The disappearances have involved both men and women, almost equally, from the poor districts. Few bodies have been found so far, and no witnesses have come forward. No definite crime scenes have been established, but we suspect that the victims were in remote areas of the East End or the river on the nights of their disappearances."

"Where our patrols are thin, sir."

"Yes. And in most cases, no reasons have been discovered for the victims to disappear of their own accord, such as suicide or escape from brutal spouses or families. We must assume that they have been snatched, but how … and why?"

"A lot of people are gone without a trace, sir. It's like they dropped off the face of the earth." Higgins looked expectantly at McLaughlin.

"Are you thinking, Higgins, that the East End murderer is at work in these disappearances?"

"I'm wondering, Inspector. We haven't heard from him in a while."

"It seems unlikely, Higgins. The two bodies discovered so far showed no signs of mutilation. As far as we know, the last mutilated body was in my garden two months ago in December. And we don't know if Malvois is even alive."

The inspector bolstered his argument. "If it's the East End murderer, he has unquestionably changed his pattern. He's been very public about it in the past. He's had no qualms about leaving mutilated bodies behind for all to see. Nor did Malvois in France. If our murderer is behind many these disappearances, he's being very secretive, concealing the bodies. Why would he do that?"

"What if he learned his lesson after breaking into your home, sir? After all, he almost met his maker that night. Got three shots fired at him at close range and got attacked by a big dog, to boot… And, before that, he must have known we were getting better at closing in on him in the streets. We nearly caught him the night he scared the girl in the fog. Seems he even ran into Coxwell that same night."

The inspector listened with a skeptical expression.

Higgins went on. "I mean, sir, could be he felt he was pressing his luck by murdering in well patrolled areas. So now he kills them quick in out-of-the-way places and hides the bodies. All *we* see are people disappearing. He's clever about it. Has his way with little chance of getting collared, maybe laughing at us all the while."

McLaughlin gave his assistant an exasperated look. "It seems more plausible that the murders have actually stopped. It was only shortly after the murder of my servant that we discovered what could well be a cult at Warrington's and began to watch Byron and Winchester, interrogating all of them. Under all this scrutiny, it may be that none of them dared involve themselves in further murders, perhaps not even using Malvois... And in the unlikely event you *are* right, Higgins, what can we do about it? There's nothing to go on, and our patrols are stretched. We can't be in all places at once."

Higgins was unpersuaded. "Inspector, what if we put out some warnings to the East End not to go out after dark because of the disappearances?"

"And panic the public again, when we really have no evidence the killer is still out there? The superintendent would never allow it. He would say that there have always been unsolved disappearances in London and that we can't link the recent increase with the East End murderer. And he would be absolutely right."

"But to do nothing —" Higgins slowly shook his head.

The sergeant's disappointment was not lost on McLaughlin. "Very well, Higgins. We'll ask our informants about the disappearances. We can also do another search of the ships' passenger lists to find out if anyone resembling Malvois has left the country."

Higgins' face brightened. "Very good, sir."

"And we'll search the cult members' properties once more, in the event Malvois is still alive and has been taken in and hidden by one of them."

Chapter 50

For some weeks after meeting Phineas Sage, Polidori reflected deeply on the matter of magic and read a few books on the subject suggested by the professor. He came across many references to how believing in magic was crucial to obtaining results, just as the professor had said. After long meditation and soul-searching, he finally felt prepared to take the leap of faith and meet the mysterious Lucans.

Polidori's first encounter with the Lucans came on a chilly late February morning, just before dawn. He accompanied Professor Sage to a remote, frosty meadow on the outskirts of London. It was still dark, and the stars and full moon shone brilliantly.

The two encountered a large number of carriages parked on the road. The Lucans had gathered around a low fire in the center of the nearby meadow. Polidori took them to be mostly professional or businesspeople.

He soon met the group's leader, Lucinda, a tall woman in her forties. She was dressed unpretentiously but fashionably. Lucinda noticed his surprise. "We are not what you expected." She smiled. "Old hags in rags, stirring a caldron full of unmentionable things, perhaps? Well, fortunately, this is not Shakespeare, Dr. Polidori. We have no need of props or bad tailors in our craft. Ours is the work of the mind."

Lucinda looked deeply into his eyes. "The professor has explained your dilemma. With your permission, we will perform a ceremony of purification and protection. Its purpose is to rid you of the manifestation and keep it from returning by placing a barrier between it and you. Do you freely give us your consent to do this, Dr. Polidori?"

"I do," he said.

"Would you give us your trust and faith for the next hour?"

"I will."

"Do you swear to it?"

"I give you my word."

"Very well, then. I will sense you," she announced. She approached him and faced her palms toward him, about six inches from his body. She then moved her hands along his outline from head to toe and back up again. It was like she was using her hands as a divining rod.

She frowned and closed her eyes to focus more intensely. She made another pass over him and said, "I feel its presence. It is here with us now." Raising her voice, she announced to the gathering, "Let it be declared that this man, John Polidori, has come to us to be purified and protected. He is surrendering to our collective power, our will, to bring this about."

Lucinda continued with the ceremony. "Let us all look up to the heavens. Raise up your arms; reach out to the skies. Open yourself to the stars and to the moon. See and sense the order in the skies. Sense the gravitation that keeps all things in their orbits. Feel the pull of these celestial objects upon the Earth, upon the sea and tides, upon us, upon Dr. Polidori. Let us stay with this pull... Be aware of it with all your mind, all your senses..."

Lucinda paused, watching her flock. "Now sense the gravitational force very deeply. Sense within it. Feel the underlying presence of primordial energy. Open your total being to it. Feel it stream into and through you. Stay with that experience. Let it build up and strengthen within..."

She guided her followers into action. "Now, keeping your focus, gather around Dr. Polidori in a close circle, bringing your palms to six inches from his body. Feel yourself transferring the primordial energy to him. Feel it flow through your arms and fingers outward, releasing the healing energy into his physical body. Stay with this experience..."

Polidori was startled to feel something shifting in his feet and calves. Then he became aware of a chill or vibration, which began in his knees, intensifying as it flowed upward. He could feel the blood pumping in the veins of his neck.

"Let the energy now flow into his emotional body," Lucinda directed her followers.

Polidori began to feel a vague upward surge of feeling within his stomach and chest, which transformed into flickerings of joy and elation. These began to merge with the vibrations in his body.

As Polidori felt these transformations, the sun began to rise in the east, at first faintly and coldly. As it cleared the horizon, it cast light and warmth on the proceedings.

The ceremony was repeated for the rays of the rising sun. The group reached out as a flower would orient to the sun, under instructions to draw in and release its underlying energy to Polidori. The Lucan leader then deepened the flow of energy into his mental body and beyond. "Transfer the energy to the unconscious and upward through the conscious mind to the higher mind," she directed. "Then sense the energy flowing outward, connecting with all things."

341

Polidori felt another powerful shift. His body and emotions were connecting with his mind and beyond, blending in with the others and the world. He had always known that he was more open to the world than others, but now he actually felt his skin was no longer his boundary. He was only a drop of water in the great sea of the universe.

A half hour after sunrise, the ceremony was complete. Lucinda stood silently for a few moments, head bowed. Without looking back, she and her followers drifted silently away to their waiting carriages.

Polidori and Professor Sage were alone in the field. Sage saw clearly that a remarkable change had come over his acquaintance. Polidori didn't appear to be the same man who had begun the rituals. He stood noticeably straighter, like a man with a great weight taken off his shoulders. He appeared younger and more vibrant. The weariness and anguish had cleared from his face and the frown from his forehead. The professor walked silently with him to his coach. No words needed to be said between them.

As he walked on, Polidori admired the beautiful winter sunrise — not as an object to be seen, but as a felt part of him. It was the dawn of a new day. Was it also the dawn of new possibilities in his life, of new ways of being?

Chapter 51

The day after the Lucans' ceremony, Polidori could not contain his excitement. He visited Falding to recount in detail the events of the past few weeks: the visits to the parish priest and the professor and, of course, the encounter with the Lucans. He declined to talk about the results, believing this would be premature. However, by early in March, he was prepared to confide in Falding.

It was a beautiful Sunday afternoon. The sun was unusually strong, and the icicles and snow were melting in the welcome warmth. Polidori and Falding were enjoying one of their rare walks together. They watched as children frolicked in the fading snow, accompanied by indulgent parents.

Falding raised the topic of his friend's progress. "So, how have you been feeling lately, John?"

Polidori's broad grin said it all. He replied jubilantly, "The red eyes have gone. They have totally vanished! I am actually able to sleep again."

Falding stared at him in surprise.

"And my dreams are even pleasant, for once. No more nightmares!"

Falding put a celebratory hand on his friend's shoulder. "Why, that's wonderful, John!" he said. He felt a wave of relief. The hateful vision that had tormented Polidori for so long had apparently disappeared. "The old John I know is returning!" he said exuberantly.

Polidori's reply was unexpected. "I sometimes feel, Alex, that I will not miss my old self. I feel that I am beyond it."

"Beyond it?"

"Yes, I feel that I have been transformed. I experience myself in the world in new and wonderful ways."

"You rouse my curiosity, John."

"It's difficult to explain … but I feel very rooted in the present moment. I am not as attached to the past … or to the future."

Falding nodded, listening intently.

"I am less attached to myself, as well. I feel a strange oneness with the world — and such deep feelings of peace and joy!"

Falding's face brightened with a smile. "That's quite remarkable. I am reminded very much of the transcendental experiences reported by the Eastern meditators and mystics… So, I gather you attribute these changes to the Lucans' ceremony."

"Of that there is no doubt. I began to feel this way as the Lucans worked in the meadow that night to link me with what they call the primordial energy."

Falding looked over at some children squealing in delight as they slid down a small hill in the park. They were totally lost in the joy of the moment, he thought. It was almost as if his friend had been restored to the blissful innocence of childhood — a state of grace, some might call it.

But the psychiatrist in him was not entirely convinced. He was deeply concerned that the changes might be due to Polidori's strong belief that the Lucans' ceremony would work — bolstered by the confidence that Father O'Kenny and Phineas Sage had shown in the Lucans. He couldn't bear to tell his friend that he doubted the power of belief alone would prevent the hallucination from returning

344

or maintain his "transformation." Unfortunately — tragically — he turned out to be right.

A few nights later, Polidori summoned him in panic. Falding found him sitting in his night clothes on the edge of his bed, hunched over disconsolately. Polidori turned his pale, horrified face toward him. "It's back!" he cried. "Ruthven has returned. It's right there."

Falding looked over at what he saw as an empty chair.

Polidori put his head between his hands. "The pain in my head is far worse. He is punishing me for trying to get rid of him …the Lucans have failed. Despite their confidence, all they could do was temporarily restrain Ruthven. It has overcome their shield around me! Can nothing stop it?" he wailed. "Even God has forsaken me."

Falding could think of little to say that might console his friend. He thought it was no wonder that the Lucans had emphasized belief in their methods as essential to healing through magic. The power of belief was the only hope they could really offer, and sadly, in Polidori's case it was not enough. He reached into his medical bag for a vial of opium to sedate him.

Polidori's condition continued to deteriorate over the next few weeks, and he fell into deep despondency. "Nothing will destroy it," he said one day to Falding. "It has undermined the spiritualists and killed Eddington… And now it has defeated the Lucans. There is no hope for me!"

Falding listened in sympathetic silence.

"I don't even read the newspapers anymore," Polidori lamented. "I can't bear to read about these terrible murders, and I cannot face the pain of my guilt over them any longer."

"But John," observed Falding, "there have been no reports of murders for some months now."

"No matter. A creature like Ruthven cannot stop itself from killing. He is clever, perhaps hiding their remains. They would simply be missing persons, and no one would even think of connecting them with the murders."

"Why would the murderer suddenly become so secretive in his killings?"

Polidori had a ready answer. "As I have told you, I do catch glimmers of its thoughts. I sense Ruthven feels he is taking a risk murdering so openly. Although he is powerful, he is not invincible. I believe he needs to incarnate fully to do these murders. In this state, he may be vulnerable to the police or others, for a time."

Falding's treatment continued to be of no use. Polidori's condition was worsened again by sleeplessness. He was but a shadow of the man Falding used to know. He claimed he was being drained of his very life force by what he called this leech upon his body and soul.

On the nineteenth of March, Falding became particularly alarmed when Polidori began to talk of suicide. "Ruthven is commanding me to suicide," he announced unexpectedly.

"Your character now speaks to you?"

"No, it inserts its thoughts in my mind," he murmured hollowly.

346

Falding's brow wrinkled with worry. "What was your response?"

"I vowed I would never act on suicide, and I accused it of coercing me to commit what is a mortal sin in the eyes of God. I warned that it should fear for its soul, if it had one, for counseling me to commit such an act."

"Have you been thinking of suicide since, John?"

"No, but I fear that my mind is breaking down and that I'll no longer be able to resist its attacks upon me. Ruthven wants to get rid of me, to punish me finally for trying to dislodge him. He wants the ultimate revenge — to betray my own beliefs by taking my own life. I sense he has somehow acquired the power to exist fully without me. Perhaps he has found a host in another's mind."

Falding listened, astonished. He knew he had reached his limits with Polidori. "John," he said, "I can no longer be responsible for your safety and for the integrity of your mind. I have no choice but to commit you to the Bethlam Asylum."

"The asylum? So, you finally think I am mad and beyond help?" Polidori asked, wounded.

"No, John," Falding reassured him. "But I fear your mind could collapse. They will keep an eye on you at the asylum until you recover."

"But Alex, I've sent patients there. It's little more than a jail, medieval in its methods. At the very least commit me to a private institution."

"But you've dealt with the older, less enlightened psychiatrists at Bethlam. Things are changing. I know some of the progressive psychiatrists there. They are using some new

347

treatments that look promising, that are not yet in use at the private asylums."

"Like what?"

"Well, there's a new approach which changes the mental faculties by manipulating the brain," Falding offered hopefully. "It's called phrenology. I've only recently learned of it, but I hear it's revolutionary."

"But nothing has worked for me so far," countered Polidori despondently. "They'll eventually give up on me and lock me up for good."

Falding placed both hands on his friend's shoulders. "I won't allow that to happen, John. I won't give up on you, either. I'll be following your progress regularly. Do you remember how hopeful you were about Eddington's hypnosis treatment when you saw him? How do you know you won't feel the same way about phrenology?"

After some hours of arguing, his friend eventually relented, very reluctantly. The two set off by coach to the asylum, just south of the River Thames. As Bethlam came into view, Falding thought the attempt a few years before to give the building a benign, neoclassical look had failed miserably; it still resembled a fortress.

Falding did not have to be reminded that "Bedlam," as it was popularly called, had a long history of inhumane conditions and neglect. He had seen the locks and chains as well as the ice-cold baths and purges passing for treatment. He also knew that, sadly, it had been a dumping ground for those society wanted to rid itself of, from criminals

348

and the mentally disturbed to unwanted wives and the political rivals of the powerful.

But times were changing, and humane treatment was being practiced by some of the psychiatrists at the asylum. Falding had confidence in one of the reformists and phrenologists there, Dr. Pomeroy, whom he had known well at medical school. Polidori would be placed in the special phrenology section. Falding believed it would take nothing less than a revolutionary approach to finally free his friend from his disturbances.

Dr. Pomeroy met them at the great entrance. He was a tall, kindly, gray-haired man, impeccably dressed. He greeted Polidori warmly and had the attendants escort him to his room.

"So I gather he is a physician, Alex," Pomeroy remarked.

"Yes, although he has not practiced in quite a while now, with his condition."

"Understandable. I hear that he has worked extensively with the poor. Very laudable. Far too many of our patients here are from the poorer classes, and I suspect that poverty has much to do with illness of the body and mind. Don't you think?"

In no mood for an intellectual discussion, Falding brought the topic back to his friend. "Before he became ill, John had been trying to bring public attention to the problem of poverty. It means much to him."

"He seems to have a well-developed conscience and sense of compassion."

Falding frowned. "Perhaps too much. His conscience prevents him from being able to fully express his feelings toward others. I believe he has a severe conflict within his personality — so severe that he handles it by transforming part of it into a hallucination. He sees a vision of the malevolent character in a book he has written. He believes the character is the East End murderer."

"Yes, so many of our patients here mistake the contents of their mind for outer reality. The key to healing is to realize that the mind is situated in the brain. If the brain can be changed, so can the patient's beliefs and perceptions, including delusions and hallucinations."

"How will this influence your treatment of John?"

"In phrenology, we believe we have found ways of manipulating the brain through putting pressure on points of the skull. We will stimulate that part of Polidori's brain that distinguishes between self and non-self, between internal and external reality. This could help him rid himself of his hallucination. To dispel the delusion of the murderer, we stimulate the rational parts of the brain."

"I think John would say that his brain is sensing something real out there, an actual evil presence."

Pomeroy leaned toward his colleague. "So why not challenge him to test out his idea? If our work makes it disappear, it was not real after all. Let's make use of Polidori's belief in the methods of science as part of his treatment — make our treatment an experiment of sorts, for him."

"I tried to do that in John's treatment, but it didn't work. But perhaps your approach manipulating the brain might be more appealing to John, given his medical background. He and I would only be too relieved — no, eternally grateful — if

350

your experiment works. Godspeed with it. Please keep me closely informed of your progress."

"Very well, then. In the mean-time, try not to worry about your friend, Alex. He is in good hands, and we will keep a very close watch on him."

Before Falding left, he visited Polidori in his "room," which was little more than a tiny cell with a simple bed. The ceilings were quite high and the barred window also at a great height. It was not possible to view the grounds through it. He brought some books he thought might interest him. One was a volume by a noted Scottish scholar in phrenology.

Falding encouraged him to be hopeful about his recovery and promised to visit him and consult with his psychiatrist regularly. As he walked from the room, he was profoundly sad and guilty about leaving Polidori — even though his friend needed to be protected against himself.

Falding went home and fell into a restless sleep. At about three o'clock that morning, he was summoned back to the asylum by Dr. Pomeroy. He knew from his ashen face that the news was grim.

"Alex, I — have some terrible, tragic news," Pomeroy began hesitantly. He took a deep breath. "About an hour ago, Dr. Polidori was ... found hanging in his room. He was dead from suffocation and could not be revived."

Falding stared at Pomeroy in shock and anger. "I brought him here," he shouted, "to protect him from himself. How could this have happened?"

Pomeroy looked down and replied almost inaudibly, "The attendants were instructed to watch him closely. They informed me that emergencies

351

briefly took them away from their watch. I am afraid there was an opportunity for him to commit suicide. He took advantage of it by knotting the bedclothes together and hanging himself from the bars of the window."

"I thought suicidal patients weren't supposed to have bedclothes," Falding retorted, stabbing an accusing finger at Pomeroy.

"Yes, these are standing orders, Alex. Still, they left bedclothes in the room when, uh, they were called away for an emergency," he said defensively. "I — I know, Alex, it is utterly inexcusable."

"Inexcusable? You might as well have given him a pistol to put to his head! How do you find the words to describe that?"

"It's unspeakable. There will be a full accounting for this."

"Accounting? I demand a full police investigation! Someone should be clapped in irons for this!"

"Alex, I know he was your friend and that you entrusted him to our care," Pomeroy placated. "What can I say? I feel terrible about what has happened. I can't believe that it has happened... Does he have a family? Do you want me to write them?"

"No, I'll do it. I'll write to his parents in Italy. He's their only child, and they're going to be absolutely heartbroken," Falding said, wiping the tears from his cheek in a defiant sweep of his hand.

Pomeroy bowed his head. As Falding turned to leave, he remarked, "I honestly don't know how he did it, Alex. It seems much too high for him to hang himself from those bars. No one has ever hanged himself from that height ... it's unbelievable!" He shook his head.

Falding was too exhausted to ponder his words and too filled with guilt and grief that he had brought his friend to the place of his death.

Chapter 52

John's funeral was held at St. Anthony's Church and led by Father O'Kenny. The old priest gave the eulogy.

"As his parish priest, it falls upon me today to send off the soul of John Polidori, who has died so unexpectedly, so tragically. I cannot say that I knew him well, but I suspect that is the circumstance for many of us, in time. How deeply do we know those around us before they have passed on to God? How many of us have regretted this omission, too late?

But I know, looking out on all those present, that there are many here who cared deeply about him, and I think felt equally cared for by him. In the end, touching the hearts of others and, in turn, being touched by them, are some of the deepest experiences in this life. This was all the more remarkable for this young man as he came alone as an immigrant from a distant, foreign land and built a life here in which he included many others that I see here today — his friends, his colleagues, his loyal staff, his patients and the poor of London in general that he labored so tirelessly to help.

I know personally what it is to emigrate to another country. I came here as a young parish priest from Ireland, thirty years ago, and know what a struggle it is merely to feel one belongs. John, through his compassion and service to others, rose far beyond that basic struggle.

John's deepest struggle was with something else. He was struggling with his inner torments, for his very soul. Whether he won this struggle, I cannot say, for death is not always a sign of defeat; victory or defeat are defined by how we carry on that struggle in our lives.

John came to me in a moment of great need. Helping him was beyond my powers, so I sent him to those I felt could help him. But sadly, it was not enough despite their best efforts, which I know they truly gave.

We may ask ourselves why this wonderful young man was taken from us so early and so tragically. Those who knew him the best must be tormenting themselves the most with this question... I can only humbly say that we cannot know the mind of God or his purposes, which are far beyond our frail understanding. But there are greater purposes at work, which give our lives and our deaths meaning; this much I can assure you. And with this message, I commend to God the soul of John Polidori... In the name of the Father, the Son, and the Holy Ghost. Amen."

After the ceremony, the funereal coach, followed by a procession of mourners and their carriages and coaches, moved solemnly to the mortuary. All came but his parents, who had likely not yet even received word. Falding noticed Polidori's close friends, William Lyons and Mary Shelley, with whom he exchanged sad condolences.

The crowd mostly stood around despondently, helpless in the face of death. Most were shivering slightly. It was not only from the coldness of the place, Falding thought, but from their cold fear as they thought hard about their own mortality. He noticed Polidori's servants seemed particularly distraught, huddling against the mortuary wall as if to ward off the cold and their despair. He was coping no better with the death, he realized. He had been unable to bring himself to view the body at any time.

Dr. Pomeroy was also there, staying mostly in the background. But after the brief ceremony was over, he placed a hand on Falding's arm and gestured him to a private corner.

"Alex, once again, my sincere apologies and condolences for Dr. Polidori's death," he said in a low voice.

Falding nodded neutrally.

"I don't know if this is an appropriate time or not, so I'm just going to say it, Alex. We conducted a full investigation into the circumstances surrounding the suicide, and we accept full responsibility for it. Some of the attendants were found to be negligent and were dismissed. We've also made some important procedural changes in the case of suicidal patients and —"

Falding interjected, "Is that what John Polidori *was* — a subject of *procedures*?"

Pomeroy was taken aback. "No, no, Alex, nothing like that. I meant that we've taken really important steps to prevent this from happening again."

"Pomeroy, my resentment and grief are still strong, no more so than on this day. So if you are expecting congratulations —"

"No, Alex, of course not. I'm simply trying to tell you we've done a lot of soul-searching over this. His suicide has strengthened the position of the reformists at the asylum, and we're ridding the place of inhumane treatments and conditions. There's

356

even a plan to involve the attendants in treatment so that healing becomes part of everyday life at the asylum, not merely during doctors' visits. Much has been learned since the death of your friend."

Falding nodded. "I'm glad to hear of it and that John's death had some meaning. It is something I can tell his parents when they arrive, and I can offer them some small consolation."

"Good, I'm glad," said Pomeroy, looking relieved. But his reprieve was brief.

"And what of the police?" Falding asked sharply. "Did they investigate?"

"They did. They will not act. They found the conduct of the staff to be neglectful but not criminal. I know this seems cold and matter-of-fact, Alex, but there it is. I know you don't agree with this."

"You're damn right I don't agree with it. The police make fine points of law and sit on their arses if they can. I'm going to raise a stink about it! I know one of them ... McLaughlin, I believe his name was."

With that, Falding stormed out of the graveyard, Dr. Pomeroy trailing behind unhappily. As he reached the street, a wave of guilt and sadness arose within him. Looking back at the cold mortuary, he felt that he was leaving his friend alone yet again.

After the funeral, he set about putting Polidori's affairs in order as the executor of the will. Polidori had left most of his worldly possessions to the Whitechapel Infirmary, including the royalties from his book, if any. Of course, he left his servants ample funds for their retirement. But he left Falding the most precious gift of all: his diary. His will stated that he hoped it would finally help his friend understand him.

When Falding began to read the diary, he discovered another matter that needed to be put in order. Polidori had noted that he told Dr. Radovich he would send him a copy of his book. There was no further mention of it, so Falding sought to fulfill his friend's promise. He sent a letter, along with the book, to Dr. Radovich in Serbia:

Dear Dr. Radovich,

It is with a heavy heart that I tell you John Polidori has died, almost a month ago, tragically by his own hand. I understand John had promised to send you a copy of his book, and in his name, I discharge that promise. John spoke highly of you, of your commitment to science and of your good work with your patients. He was especially grateful for your help in understanding the vampyre traditions of Serbia, which greatly helped him complete his book.

I hope you find it interesting reading. I know John would have hoped you would enjoy it.

Sincerely,
Dr. Alex Falding, London
April 16, 1817

More than two months later, Falding received a letter from Dr. Radovich:

Dear Dr. Falding,

I am heartily sorry and shocked to hear of John's death. He was such a brilliant and compassionate young man with so much to offer to the world. His death came far too early.

I enjoyed spending our brief time together, immersed in the old myths of Serbia. I am gratified I was able to help him with his book, which I am anxious to read. I hope his book will be his legacy to the world. His concept of the sophisticated vampyre is such a frightening and malevolent idea that I think it will capture the imagination of his readers.

There was a happening here in Dubacz, last fall, that would have greatly interested John. On October 15, an earthquake struck the area. It was only a minor trembling in Dubacz, but it appeared much worse to the east, in the foothills.

Later, a few hunters passed through this remote area and happened on the "unholy place," the old cemetery for those suspected of having been vampyres. The graveyard had been severely disturbed by the earthquake. Headstones were knocked over, and the great stone lids on the tombs were thrown up every which way. The stone cover of the most notorious of the "vampyres," Oleg Jasonovich, was completely split, right through the sacred symbol in its top.

Word of this alarmed the villagers, who were afraid Jasonovich had been freed and was stalking the land again. The people here deeply believe in these myths, and any sign of disturbance in these graveyards arouses hysteria. Let us hope this does not provoke a wave of accusations and persecutions, as it did in the old days.

But I go on too long.

Yours sincerely,

Dr. Viktor Radovich, Dubacz

June 19, 1817

Chapter 53

Summer had fully come to London. Colorful flowers were in full bloom in the leafy green gardens. The warm sun comforted its citizens.

To the relief of the police, the disappearances had greatly abated to normal levels for that time of year. Despite Higgins' suspicions, no links to the East End murderer had yet been found. Frustratingly, the London informants could provide no insight into the entire matter.

Six months had now passed since the last mutilated body was found hanging in McLaughlin's garden. The inspector was convinced they had intimidated Byron and the apparent cult into giving up their murderous practices, at least for now. He crossed his fingers that the heinous murders were finally at an end. East Londoners, he knew, were breathing easier and had been venturing out onto the old streets in the evenings.

The police were not idle, however, and continued their close watch on Byron, Winchester, and company. Scotland Yard was ever alert for any signs that Malvois may have survived the attempt to arrest him in the old mill. Moreover, the investigation of the disappearances continued despite the lack of results. Higgins was convinced that the East End murders had never really stopped and that mutilated bodies of the missing would yet turn up with the hated symbol upon them.

One beautiful June morning, Higgins came into McLaughlin's office with his latest report on the murder investigation. The inspector was looking forward to some new information, but he knew he would enjoy theorizing and bantering with Higgins, anyway. The two had become much closer while working together on the murders.

"Well, Higgins, what do you have for me today?" he asked cheerfully.

"Well, sir, our men report that Byron and Winchester seem to have behaved themselves. They haven't been seen together, either. Neither have the others."

"They know we're still watching them, I'm sure."

"Byron won't have to worry about us too much longer, Inspector. He's leaving the country again."

"Oh, to where?"

Higgins grinned. "We hear to Greece. Word is that he's going to help the Greeks in their revolt against the Turks. We hear he's even going to head up a Greek force."

McLaughlin shook his head in disbelief. "I doubt he has any formal military experience, let alone officer's training. The Turks know the business of war and *mean* business. He's going to get himself killed over there, not to mention a lot of people under his command."

"If some Greek general don't get rid of him first for dallying with his daughter," Higgins quipped.

"Talking about debauchery, I hear he's recently seduced someone quite close to our royals. He's probably fleeing the scandal."

"Not a good idea to cross the royals."

"Yes, and perhaps he's distracting attention from the matter by playing the soldier hero. Clever."

"Maybe he's scared of us, too, sir."

"I can only hope... How about Malvois? Any trace of him?"

"No, sir. Nothing on the river-banks and no sightings of him in the districts. Even Jimmy's heard nothing about him, he says."

"What about the search of the cult members' estates?"

"We searched all thirteen properties. Twelve were clear. On one there was an old gamekeeper's cottage we had been to before. It was empty before, but this time it showed signs of someone living in it. It's off the beaten track and falling apart, but we noticed heavy coach tracks going in and out of the place. The owner, Lord Haltonbury, says he has no idea what that's about and denies hiding Malvois."

"Hmm," said McLaughlin warily. "These culprits seem to regard the truth as something to play with when it suits them. Keep an eye on the place in the event that whoever was living there returns. We can't afford to be complacent about Malvois."

"If he's about, sir, we'll get him."

"Any luck with the ships' passenger lists?

"There's no sign Malvois left the country by ship, Inspector. Seems he's still here, alive or dead."

"I suppose, though, he could have paid for a private vessel, perhaps a fisherman or weekend sailor, to take him across. Anything in the French newspapers?

"No mention of any sightings of Malvois or his kind of murders there, sir."

"Right. He always was an elusive bugger, anyway."

362

McLaughlin rose to pour them both a cup of tea. "Oh, by the way, Higgins, there's something I forgot to tell you. A few months back, I had a very angry visitor here, a Dr. Falding. Remember? Polidori's psychiatrist?"

"Polidori? Oh, the writer bloke who thought his character was the East End murderer."

"That's him, Higgins. The psychiatrist had said he came to a bad end — a suicide at the asylum."

"Sad, and him a doctor and all, too."

"Yes, he had somehow been left alone with some bedsheets at Bedlam. Falding said it was the attendants' fault and loudly demanded charges be laid. I referred him to Ashton, who handled the investigation. However, I tried to explain that neglect is not necessarily a crime, but he accused us of splitting hairs and not really giving a damn about the matter. It was frustrating. There was nothing I could do to change his mind. You know how it goes."

"Yes, and we are blamed for doing nothing."

"Yes, that's for certain, and I don't think Falding will stop there. He says he knows people higher up and will see justice done."

"Uh-oh. Ashton's in for it."

"And perhaps the department too," remarked McLaughlin.

"Talking about Dr. Falding, though, remember he gave Polidori an alibi for the night of the murder at your home, and we were going to look into it? How did that turn out, sir?"

"I sent Murdoch to determine the whereabouts of Falding that night with both Polidori's servants and Falding's. But no one appeared to recall

363

anything about that. Whether it was protecting Falding and Polidori, or for some other reason, I don't know. So, we're still left with the question of how Polidori knew that one detail of the last murder, the disembowelment."

"I take it you don't believe a dream told him." Higgins grinned.

"Right," said McLaughlin wryly. "I'll wager that he somehow learned of the detail through rumor, or perhaps his connections with the doctor at the morgue."

"So, we really don't know, sir."

"That's about it, Higgins," sighed McLaughlin. "Isn't that the lot of the policeman — in the dark more often than not?"

Higgins nodded. "I meant to ask how Mrs. McLaughlin is doing."

"She was completely unnerved by the horror of that night, but she has been faring much better lately. Thankfully, her nightmares have stopped and she seems to be more cheerful by the day."

"Glad to hear it, sir!"

"I think that the cessation of the murders in East London and our move to a new residence have greatly helped her. She knows, too, that I'm very careful to avoid being followed on my way back at night. Our coachman takes a roundabout route and doesn't stop directly in front of the house.

"You can't be too careful, especially if the big Frenchman is still kicking."

"Yes. My relationship with her will take more time, though. She still feels that I didn't listen to her dream premonitions and almost got us killed. But I think as long as there are no further murders like these, she'll eventually find her old self."

Higgins looked unconvinced. "I hope for her sake and everybody else's that more bodies don't start turning up, Inspector."

"Well, Higgins, how do you account for the fact that the disappearances are reduced to their usual summer levels for London? Has the killer stopped snatching people, too?"

"Maybe the figures are higher than we think, Inspector."

"What do you mean?"

"It's struck me, sir. What if he's been after people nobody would miss or report as missing, like street beggars or people who keep to themselves? I talked to a few of the lads who patrol Whitechapel. They said that, now that I mentioned it, they've noticed some of the street people aren't in their usual spots. It does seem odd."

"But these people come and go, Higgins. Besides, the killer must be incredibly skilled to conceal his victims so thoroughly. Surely, some would have been discovered by now. Many have gone missing, we think, near the river. If he's been using it to dispose of the bodies... Well, the Thames almost always gives up its dead."

"He's clever, though, Inspector. Clever enough to murder people in ways we still can't figure out. He'd find ways to hide the bodies for good. If he weighted them, they'd never come up."

With that, the discussion trailed off into doubt and further conjecture, as usual.

Part Three
A Glimpse of the Truth

Chapter 54

Decades passed. Cities and institutions have a habit of getting through times of terror and darkness, though it may take many years. London and Scotland Yard were no different.

December 28, 1836, was bitterly cold. A tall man hurried through the flurries, across a large courtyard. He stepped into the vestibule of Scotland Yard's headquarters and unfurled the scarf from his face. Time had not passed James McLaughlin by. His hair was now shot through with white streaks. His face was heavily lined with the years, but his blue eyes were still clear and alert.

He made his way down the familiar hallway to his old office. He paused to smile at the name on the door, *Inspector J. Higgins*, and knocked twice.

"Superintendent McLaughlin!" cried Higgins as he opened the door to his visitor. "Or should I say, retired Superintendent McLaughlin."

"How are you, Higgins?" McLaughlin asked, warmly shaking his hand.

Higgins smiled and invited him to sit by the old stove, hot from the bright red coals. "I'll put on a pot of tea," he said. "So, what brings you this way? Retirement not agreeing with you?"

"No, no. Don't you recognize the date, Higgins?"

"The date?"

"Yes. It's twenty years ago today that the last murder happened in my garden."

Higgins looked at the calendar in surprise. "Why, so it is. God, those were dark days, sir. I recall how everybody held their breath, day after day, in case another body would turn up or there'd be another bloody headline in the papers."

"And I remember, Higgins, there was many a night I expected to hear you at my door, at some ungodly hour, with news of another murder. Terror like that takes a long time to pass."

Higgins sat back in his chair. "But the main thing is that the murders did stop."

"I remember it took quite a while for you to admit that, Higgins. You were convinced the East End murderer was behind the disappearances."

Higgins looked a little embarrassed. "But when they settled down to normal and stayed that way, it was hard to blame the murderer."

"Especially, Higgins, when we found out the street people weren't being snatched with any greater frequency. But I grant you, we never did get to the bottom of why the disappearances had been so high for those months after the East End murders stopped."

"The same old arguments are going on around here about the murders, sir. Some still think it was Malvois who was the killer all along —"

McLaughlin interjected, "Yes, and since he never did reappear anywhere, we'll never know about his guilt."

"Then, of course, there's those who blame Byron and the other aristocrats."

"I still believe they had blood on their hands in the matter. But I confess that at some point I knew we'd never prove it or even that they were actually members of a cult."

Higgins poured them each a cup of steaming tea. "Well, sir, if it was Byron, he'll never be brought to a magistrate now."

"Yes, and his death was quite an irony," McLaughlin observed. "One would expect a heroic end for him, dying in battle in Greece or the like. But to leave this world in such a mundane way — during treatment by an incompetent Greek doctor, of all things!"

"An odd way for him to go. Rumor has it that after his body was returned to England, his mates tossed his journal into the fire. Refused to have it published, like he wanted. I guess so no one would find out how bad a bloke he really was. Who knows, we might have even found out something about the murders from it."

"Too late now," remarked McLaughlin. "The world will never know of the true depths of his depravity... By the way, did you know that another noted poet— one that Byron befriended — also met an untimely death?"

"Hadn't heard."

"Well, Percy Shelley, the Romantic poet, drowned while sailing in the Mediterranean, some years back. Apparently, he used to race his boat against Byron and had it modified to gain advantage over his competitor. Unfortunately, this could cause the boat to become unstable, and it sank in sudden storm, taking him and a friend with it. His poor wife was extremely distraught." McLaughlin sighed.

"Everything comes to its end." He took a sip of his tea and gestured toward the old wooden cabinet, still in its place in the corner. "Have you finally closed the file?"

"I did. Marked it 'Unsolved,' of course."

McLaughlin raised his cup to Higgins. "And with that, the East End murders became history."

"I guess it's official, sir. It all ended with the bang of a stamp."

Chapter 55

Falding met Polidori's old friends at a fine dining house in central London. It was the evening of the twentieth anniversary of Polidori's death, March 20, 1837. The party gathered around a table off to the side with a good view of the surrounding square, brightly lit by the gas lamps on ornate iron poles.

They smiled a little uncomfortably at one another, not quite knowing how to begin. Time had made its mark on those present in different ways.

William Lyons had grown grayer and even more corpulent since the days of the literary society. However, he had never lost his earthy wisdom and winning sense of humor.

Mary Shelley was now an elegant, mature woman, though looking worn from her struggles against the rigid morality of English society. She had never been forgiven for living unmarried with Shelley in her younger years. She was a sort of outcast, ironically like the nameless creature of her book. She had made a point of breaking the rules by attending the dinner unescorted. She doubled her rebellion by giving permission to the men present to call her by her first name.

Alex Falding had become stooped with the burden of his long professional practice and his anguish over the years about his friend's fate. But his face still shone with intelligence and compassion.

"Well, here we are," Falding began. "Three of us united in memory of the good man we once knew. Thank you for coming with so little notice."

"It was a wonderful idea to meet on this occasion," Mary said.

"I wholeheartedly share that sentiment," Lyons added.

"It seems only yesterday that I met John at Lake Geneva," Mary continued. "But it is really a long time ago, now. Time has not dimmed my appreciation for him."

Falding leaned toward her. "John told me much about that summer at Lake Geneva and the night you told the story of Frankenstein to your companions at the villa."

Mary smiled, her mind suddenly dancing with fond memories.

"I've read your book, you know."

Mary's smile grew broader. "*And* did you like it?"

"I did — immensely... Is it doing well?"

"I seem to have struck a chord with it," Mary said cheerily. "The bookshops can't keep it on their shelves. My only regret is that more women aren't able to read it." The two men nodded sympathetically.

"Perhaps you don't know this, Mary," Falding remarked, "but you also deserve credit, in some measure, for John's vampyre story."

"How is it so?" Mary asked in flattered surprise.

"Well, John told me he had been inspired by your story. He had learned from you that to write *The Vampyre,* he had to embrace the tragedies in his life and the dark, unconscious forces in his mind."

Mary looked astonished. "As a young woman, I wrote the story for reasons outside of myself — at first on a dare and then to give serious warning to

371

mankind of the dangers of science. I recognized, only much later in my life, that there were reasons deeply *within* me that also stirred the writing of *Frankenstein*."

She paused, visibly moved. "I know now John understood those reasons. He had looked into my soul, long ago at Lake Geneva." She brushed away a tear and took a drink of her wine.

There was a long, thoughtful silence at the table. Falding turned to Lyons. "And how about you, William? I'd heard many years ago from John that you were writing a book about Byron. Have you finished it?"

"I have, just in the last year. I am now the biographer of Lord Byron, unofficially, you understand."

"How has it fared?" Mary asked.

"It has been well received at the literary society, I'm pleased to say. It's popular with the public too — shocking to some but entertaining to many."

Mary laughed. "That sounds a good deal like Byron, all right."

"I had hoped that the book would be deeper," Lyons lamented. "But that was difficult with all the hearsay and gossip about the man. The final blow came when his friends burned his journal to prevent its publication."

Mary did not look surprised. "A book on Byron would test any writer. I doubt he truly confided in anyone."

Lyons sighed and brought the conversation back to Polidori. "I remember when John and I first met at the literary society. He was so determined to become a Romantic poet. I find it ironic that he became famous for writing a book about a vampyre! Life can take such strange twists and turns!"

Falding poured himself another glass of wine. "I seem to be the only one here who hasn't published a book. But you know, I'm working on one."

"Oh, please tell us about it," Mary said, intrigued.

"Well, it's about John." The others looked at him in surprise. "Yes. I've anguished in silence about him long enough. The mystery surrounding his life must be told to the world."

"Mystery?" Lyons asked. "We have obviously missed something about our old friend."

"Undoubtedly, you have. It is known only to a very few, mostly to myself as his former psychiatrist. If I told it to you, you would find it quite unbelievable."

The curiosity of the others was obvious. Falding seized the moment. He cleared his throat and began the strange account of their friend's short, troubled life, the "manifestation," and the London murders. He included the findings and reports of Scotland yard, gained from his consultations with Inspector McLaughlin as part of writing his book.

By the story's end, the candle on the table had burned down to its stump, and the empty wine bottles had multiplied. His table mates stared at him in wordless astonishment. Both were intelligent people, versed in the ways of the world, but it was clear even they could not fathom what they had heard over the past few hours. Falding had watched as a train of feelings crossed their faces during his narration: amazement, skepticism, puzzlement. But at the end, they voiced heartfelt sadness over the depth of their friend's suffering, which had not been entirely known to them until now.

Eventually, the dinner group broke up at the late hour. They promised to meet again to discuss the matter. Understandably, Mary and William desired some time to absorb and consider the curious account.

Falding returned home from the dinner feeling strangely dissatisfied. Finally telling the story had not given him the relief he had thought it would. He was exhausted and once again found himself troubled by the familiar doubts and regrets over his friend. He went to bed with a heavy heart.

He fell into a restless sleep and deep in the night had a vivid dream. He dreamed that he had a strong urge to go to his study on some important matter, though he didn't know what. In his dream, he descended the stairs by candlelight to the darkened first floor. Sensing he was not alone, he peered into his study. A shadowy figure sat next to the study window at the fringe of the candlelight. Falding held the candle high to throw more light on it. There before him sat Polidori, as a young man not a day older than when Falding knew him.

Polidori was no more than a few paces away yet seemed strangely distant. The candlelight illuminated him, yet did not. The light seemed to flow around him, faintly blurring his outline like a fine, translucent mist on the edges of a waterfall. He was there in the moment but also seemed outside of time and duration, as if he existed in between the ticks of the old clock on the mantle. Despite the figure's eerie appearance, Falding remained unafraid, more curious than anything else.

The dream visitor stared directly at him, unblinking, his face waxen and expressionless. His lips were working as if speaking, but no words could be heard. Straining to hear him, Falding asked over and over again, "What are you trying to tell me?" The silent lips just kept on moving persistently, incomprehensibly. Falding searched for some signs of meaning, some hints of feeling in that frozen face, but there were none to be found.

He heard a distant pounding echoing in the background, drawing him toward it. He woke up in his bed aware of the doorknocker rapping insistently. He descended the stairs and opened the door to find a rather nervous-looking attendant from the asylum pacing on the front steps.

"Sorry to disturb you, Doctor," he said, "but there's been an attempted suicide at the asylum." He added breathlessly, "It's Dr. Jacobson's patient, but he's away, and I understand you are on call, sir."

"How's the patient doing now?" Falding asked.

"He seems all right now, Doctor, but we'd still like you to look in on him. It's been quite a night, I can tell you, sir. The patients have been restless all night and would not be settled down... And then, this attempted suicide!" He shook his head.

The two left by coach for the asylum. As they traveled through the morning gloom, Falding recalled his dream. So strange, he thought. What could it possibly mean? The dream figure was obviously trying to give him a message of some kind but could not make it intelligible. What was the message?

Suddenly, fear welled up within him, a nameless dread he could not attach to anything in particular. With great force of will, Falding managed to push down the panic. The effort exhausted him, and he lapsed into a stupor.

After a few minutes, his mind cleared enough to look for explanations. Having spent most of the evening reciting the story of Polidori, he decided it was no wonder he'd had a dream about him. Perhaps the dream figure's inability to make itself understood reflected his own lingering doubts that he had really understood his friend or truly known him. The psychiatrist wondered if he had been overconfident, even arrogant, in his diagnosis of Polidori's condition. Had he done enough for him? Should he have referred him for more opinions from his colleagues or searched further abroad for studies on his condition? Would he still be alive today if he had been in a private institution? A dozen things he might have done and didn't do rushed through his mind.

But why the fear? It seemed an extreme overreaction to the dream. Unless he really *did* know, in some dark corner of his unconscious, what the dream figure was trying to say. Perhaps he was deeply afraid of that message. Was it some kind of warning? He did know that he could not allow himself to become preoccupied with such thoughts. There was work to do at the asylum, and he had to get a hold of himself.

They arrived at the gates of Bethlam. The massive building loomed up darkly, illuminated only by scattered pinpoints of light from the attendants' stations and the yellowish gaslight at the main entrance. They de-coached and stood impatiently before the main doors, waiting to be admitted. Falding heard the double locks click open and the thud as the main bolt was drawn back. The heavy doors ponderously swung open, and they made their way down the empty, darkened corridors to the patient's ward, where they found Mr. Fitzgerald, the chief attendant. Fitzgerald was a veteran who had risen through the ranks at the asylum over the past thirty years. He had seen it all: the many years of neglect and misery in the great institution, the coming of the reforms, the struggles between the old and the new.

He informed Falding of the situation with the clear brevity that comes only from long experience. "Sir, this young man was admitted earlier in the day by his physician, suffering from hallucinations and anxiety. He seemed to settle, but around 2:00 a.m. he was found hanging in his cell from bed sheets knotted together. He was kicking out, flailing his arms and turning blue in the last stages of suffocation. We got him down in the nick of time. Miraculously, he seems to have escaped serious injury, and he's resting comfortably now under sedation — right behind you, sir."

This was definitely déjà vu, Falding thought. "Fitzgerald, you know there are standing orders never to allow new patients bed sheets," he chided.

"Yes, Doctor, I know, but he did not seem suicidal in the least, and we were quite surprised by this attempt. We were also puzzled by how he managed to do it."

377

"Hmm. Did he say anything before he was sedated, Fitzgerald?"

"Yes, sir. He was raving something about being frightened by a book he had been reading prior to his admission. I know it well, sir."

"Oh?"

"Yes. The book has been the rage since it came out twenty years ago. In fact, it was written by a patient we had about that time, a fellow named John Polidori."

Falding stared at Fitzgerald in stunned silence, struggling to absorb what he had just told him.

"Sir," Fitzgerald added, "the patient also complained about a severe pain in his forehead, just before we sedated him."

Falding walked unsteadily over to the young man and saw the ugly red swelling on his forehead... He did not need to examine him to know what it was.

Epilogue

I have been asked by the publisher to write this epilogue to the book my father, Dr. Alex Falding, wrote about John Polidori. The occasion is the twenty-fifth anniversary of its publication. Since it was first published, the book has gone through a dozen printings to keep up with its popularity. It was time, the publisher suggested, to honor it with an epilogue.

The publisher has asked me important questions: "What are the legacies of Dr. Falding's book and of Polidori's life? How did your father finally account for the strange happenings he describes in his book?"

I could begin in detail about Polidori the writer and how he expanded upon a brief outline of a tale that a master writer couldn't or wouldn't finish. Indeed, it was no small feat transforming this fragment into a story of horror and seduction that has captured the public's imagination for almost two generations.

I could also elaborate upon his efforts to bring attention to the tragedy of poverty in our society and how he was a dedicated defender of the poor and powerless.

These are important matters, but I think there is even greater significance to Polidori's life and the remarkable book about him. This is the lesson that, as thinking beings, we need to look more deeply into our beliefs about what is true and what is real about ourselves and the world. The bizarre events described in the book tell us that there are truths and realities beyond the precise scrutiny of science or what we perceive with our five senses. These truths may not fit into an equation, show up under a microscope or be seen with the naked eye, but they exist, nonetheless.

And here I come to the notion that each truth has its edge. The edge is not a well-defined wall but a border where another truth begins. The world could be said to contain an infinite number of truths, layer by layer, where there is no ultimate truth, no bottom. Peel off one layer and another is revealed. The only ultimate thing we can say about the truth is that it is an enigma.

In the end, my father concluded that something supernatural had indeed materialized and carried out the horrid murders in London. It had reappeared in the attempt to kill the young patient at the asylum. He also suspected that it was behind the spate of disappearances, as well.

Polidori had intuitively recognized this manifestation as the purely evil force it was and tried to confront it, ultimately dying in the attempt. His psychiatrist and Inspector McLaughlin had denied the very existence of the manifestation and tried to transform it into something rationally explainable — to turn it back into their own truths.

My father came to accept the existence of the malevolent entity only when it was so shockingly put to him that he had no other choice. I can only imagine that terrible moment of realization when he saw the symbol on the young patient's forehead in the asylum. He knew then that he had been completely wrong about Polidori's experiences and had not taken off his blinders in time to help his friend or the other victims. He was at the truth's edge.

What seem to be dark and catastrophic times in our lives can stir profound growth within us. Recognizing his tragic mistakes, my father began to explore and research other realities, gradually coming to a deeper understanding of what had happened. This helped him heal, too. He was finally able to let go of the guilt that had weighed down on him for so many years. No psychiatric treatment could have touched something that had existed outside of his patient's mind.

He thought that even Polidori had not fully grasped the nature of the manifestation. He contended that the young author had not actually incarnated Ruthven. Rather, he believed that Polidori's thoughts about his character and his horrific book had actually attracted to him something buried in the unholy place, something that had stalked and killed in Serbia for untold centuries.

My father believed that the unique connection of Polidori's mind to the world and his redrawing of Jasonovich's symbol to form Ruthven's ring had inadvertently allowed the entity to escape from its earthy Serbian prison and incarnate in London. Although unknown to any at the time of the murders, it was the pattern on Ruthven's ring that the entity had carved into the foreheads of his unfortunate victims. This was a dark and mocking symbol of the entity's liberation and of its power to kill.

However, my father did not pretend to have all the answers. He was left with many questions about the nature of the manifestation and its purposes. The manifestation remained largely shrouded in mystery.

I am convinced that Polidori's struggle with the evil presence and his eventual death were not without meaning. He had fought its relentless attempts to destroy his values as a man, never giving in. It could only resort to destroying him physically under the guise of suicide in the asylum. It destroyed his body but could not vanquish his soul. I believe Polidori's ultimate legacy to the world is his example of immense personal courage in the face of terrible adversity.

There is a poem called "Horatius," by Lord Thomas Babington MacCaulay. Here is an excerpt that I believe would be a fitting epitaph for John Polidori.

Then out spake brave Horatius, The Captain of the Gate:
"To every man upon this earth, death cometh soon or late,
And how can a man die better
Than facing fearful odds,
For the ashes of his fathers and
The temples of his God."

Jonathon Falding, London, 1865

382